THE ONLY THING BETTER THAN CHOCOLATE

Janet Dailey
Sandra Steffen
Kylie Adams

ZEBRA BOOKS
KENSINGTON PUBLISHING CORP.

http://www.kensingtonbooks.com

ZEBRA BOOKS are published by

Kensington Publishing Corp.
850 Third Avenue
New York, NY 10022

All Kensington titles, imprints and distributed lines are available
at special quantity discounts for bulk purchases for sales promotion,
premiums, fund-raising, educational or institutional use.

Special book excerpts or customized printings can also be created
to fit specific needs. For details, write or phone the office of the
Kensington Special Sales Manager: Kensington Publishing Corp.,
850 Third Avenue, New York, NY 10022. Attn. Special Sales
Department. Phone: 1-800-221-2647.

Zebra and the Z logo Reg. U.S. Pat. & TM Off.

First Printing: January 2002
10 9 8 7 6 5 4 3 2 1

Printed in the United States of America

Praise for Janet Dailey

"Janet Dailey's name is synonymous with romance."

—*Tulsa World*

"Janet Dailey's mastery of sweeping romance, divided by loyalties and searing passion has made her one of the best-selling authors of all time."

—*Lanier County News* (Georgia)

"A master storyteller of romantic tales, Dailey weaves all the 'musts' together to create the perfect love story."

—*Leisure Magazine*

Praise for Sandra Steffen

"The charm of this tale lies in its lovely portrayal of complex family relationships."

—*Publishers Weekly* on *The Cottage*

"A charming, intense story. High drama and gentle reflection—the perfect mix."

—Stella Cameron, *New York Times'*
best-selling author on *The Cottage*

"A compelling, heartwarming tale. Sandra Steffen is a talented new author to watch."

—Kat Martin, *New York Times'*
best-selling author on *The Cottage*

Praise for Kylie Adams

"A talented and creative new voice has just joined the romance genre. This debut novel by Kylie Adams is a funny, sexy and slightly off-the-wall treat. Keep your eyes on Ms. Adams!"

—*Romantic Times* on *Fly Me to the Moon*

"This side-splitting tale is so unique that it leaves you drained, the characters so droll that they leave you speechless. Her book cover should be flame-retardant. You'll love every moment."

—*Rendezvous* on *Fly Me to the Moon*

"An original, witty, sexy love story."

—*The Romance Journal* on *Fly Me to the Moon*

BOOK YOUR PLACE ON OUR WEBSITE AND MAKE THE READING CONNECTION!

We've created a customized website just for our very special readers, where you can get the inside scoop on everything that's going on with Zebra, Pinnacle and Kensington books.

When you come online, you'll have the exciting opportunity to:

- View covers of upcoming books
- Read sample chapters
- Learn about our future publishing schedule (listed by publication month *and author*)
- Find out when your favorite authors will be visiting a city near you
- Search for and order backlist books from our online catalog
- Check out author bios and background information
- Send e-mail to your favorite authors
- Meet the Kensington staff online
- Join us in weekly chats with authors, readers and other guests
- Get writing guidelines
- AND MUCH MORE!

**Visit our website at
http://www.kensingtonbooks.com**

CONTENTS

The Devil and Mr. Chocolate   7
     by Janet Dailey

I Know I Love Chocolate   121
     by Sandra Steffen

Sex and the Single Chocoholic   253
     by Kylie Adams

THE DEVIL AND MR. CHOCOLATE

Janet Dailey

Chapter One

Kitty Hamilton, owner of Santa Fe's renowned Hamilton Art Gallery, lolled in the expansive tub, surrounded by mounds of scented bubbles. Her long chestnut hair was pinned atop her head, no longer contained in its customary severe bun.

Scattered about the spacious bathroom were pillar candles. Their wavering yellow flames created a certain ambience to accompany the first movement of Mozart's Serenade No. 13 playing softly in the background.

A bottle of champagne poked its neck out from the bucket of ice sitting on the tub's ledge. On the opposite side sat a plate of chocolate-dipped strawberries. Kitty selected one, took a bite, and moaned in her throat at the delicious combination of juicy sweet berry and decadently rich chocolate. A sip of champagne provided the perfect complement to the treat. She dipped the partially eaten strawberry into the champagne and took another bite.

"Perfect," she murmured with her mouth full.

Beyond the bathroom's long window, with its view of the high desert mountains, a crimson sun hung on the lip of the western horizon. The sky was a wash of magenta, rose madder, and fuchsia bleeding together. Its flattering pink light spilled into the bathroom, but Kitty took little notice of it.

Having lived in Santa Fe most of her life, she had grown used to the spectacular sunsets and sharp clear air for which the city was known and with which artists were so enamored. At the moment she was much too busy luxuriating in her sensuous bath to admire the view. It was too rare that she had the time to indulge herself this way. But tonight was a special night. Very special.

Remembering, Kitty smiled in secret delight and sank a little lower in the tubful of bubbles, convinced she had never been this happy in her life. Perhaps the world always seemed this glorious when one was in love; Kitty honestly couldn't say. But she knew she wanted to revel in this giddy contentment she felt. It was a thing to celebrate— and an evening to celebrate. Hence the strawberries and champagne, the music and candlelight. She wanted everything about this evening to be special, from beginning to end, with nothing to spoil it.

On that note, she splashed more champagne into her glass and plucked another chocolate-dipped strawberry from the plate, then alternately sipped and nibbled. She silently vowed again that, for once, she was not going to be hurried. She wanted the evening to begin with sensuous pleasures and end with sensual ones.

Suddenly the bathroom door swung open, startling Kitty. Surprise quickly gave way to annoyance when Sebastian Cole walked in, all six feet two inches of him. He was dressed in his usual T-shirt, jeans, and huaraches, but for a change he didn't reek of turpentine and oils. Judging from the wet gleam that darkened the toasted gold color of his hair, Kitty suspected he had come straight from the shower.

"Sorry. I didn't realize you were in here." He threw her an offhand smile and walked straight to the vanity table.

"Now that you do, you can leave." Irritated by the sudden sour note in her evening, Kitty set her champagne glass down and reached for the loofah sponge. Having known Sebastian for nearly twenty years she was well aware that even if he had known she was in there, he would have walked in anyway.

"First I need to borrow your razor." He began rummaging through the contents of the top drawer. "Don't you usually keep your spare ones in here?"

"It's the drawer on the other side." She rubbed the soap and sponge together and wished she was rubbing the lathered bar over his face. "With the fortune your paintings are bringing, I should think you could buy your own razors."

"But with the commission you make from selling them, you can afford to supply me with a razor now and then. Besides, I ran out." He opened the other drawer and took out a disposable razor. "Why should I go all the way to the store for one, when you live right here in my own backyard? Correction, my front yard."

"You really need to find a larger studio, Sebastian. That one is much too small."

"It suits me." Razor in hand, he turned to face the tub and sat down on the vanity, stretching out his long legs and giving every indication that he intended to stay awhile.

Stifling the urge to order him out, Kitty struggled to ignore him. But Sebastian Cole was much too compelling to ignore. She had never quite identified the exact cause of it. At forty, he still possessed the kind of leanly muscled physique guaranteed to draw a woman's eye. His rugged features stopped just short of Hollywood handsome. And there was something striking about the contrast of golden blond hair and dark, dark eyes. Or maybe it was all in his eyes, and that devilishly lazy way he had of looking and absorbing every minute detail of his subject, not with an artist's typical dispassion but with a caress.

And he was doing it to her now. Kitty could feel his gaze gliding along her outstretched arm, the slope of her shoulder, and the arched curve of her neck. Her nerve ends tingled with the sensation of it.

She flicked him a glance, feigning indifference, although, of all the feelings Sebastian had ever aroused in her, indifference had never been one of them. "Was there something else you wanted?"

"Thanks. Don't mind if I do," he said in response, and pushed away from the vanity table, crossed to the tub, reached across its width to lift the champagne bottle from its icy nest. Taking the water glass by the sink, he filled it with the bubbly wine, then returned the bottle to its bucket. "And strawberries drenched in chocolate, too. Perfect."

He popped one into his mouth while somehow managing to extricate the cap from it, and chewed with relish. "Mmm, good," he pronounced, and washed it down with a big swallow of wine. "The chocolate is obviously from La Maison du Chocolate. Had another batch flown in from Paris, did you?"

"Wrong," Kitty replied with some pleasure. "The chocolate is Boulanger's."

"Boulanger's?" Sebastian frowned in surprise. "That's a new one."

"It's Belgian."

"Ahh." There was a wealth of understanding in his nod. "In that case, I'll have another."

Kitty watched in disgust as he consumed another chocolate-covered strawberry in one bite. "How can you devour it like that? It's a treat that should be savored."

"My mistake. Let me try again." He picked up a third and nipped off the end, the gleam in his eyes mocking her.

"Oh, eat it and be done with it," Kitty declared with a flash of impatience. "That's what you want to do anyway."

A blond-brown eyebrow shot up. "My, but you are in a bad mood tonight."

"I was in a glorious mood until you showed up," she retorted, and switched from lathering her arms to soaping her legs.

"Of course you were," he replied dryly. "That's why you're here lazing in bubbles, surrounded by candlelight and music, sipping champagne and eating strawberries dipped in chocolate. Consolation, I imagine, for spending another lonely evening all alone. If I had known, I would have asked you to join me for dinner."

She hated that smug look he wore. "For your information, I already have a date."

"Johnny Desmond's back in town, is he?"

"I wouldn't know."

"Not Johnny, huh. Then it must be—"

Kitty broke in, "It's no one you know."

"Really?" The curve of his mouth deepened slightly. "Something tells me you've been keeping secrets from me."

"I wouldn't call it a secret," Kitty replied smoothly. "My private life is simply none of your business."

"Then, this isn't a business dinner," Sebastian concluded.

"Not at all." This time it was her smile that widened. "It's strictly pleasure. Wonderfully glorious pleasure."

He released an exaggerated sigh of despair. "Don't tell me you've fallen hopelessly in love again."

She paused, staring off into space with a dreamy look. "Not again. For the first time."

"That's what you said about Roger Montgomery and Mark Rutledge," Sebastian reminded her, naming two of her former husbands.

Doubt flickered for a fleeting second. Then Kitty mentally shook it off. "This time it's different." Lifting a leg above the mound of bubbles, she reached forward to run the loofah over it.

"You have beautiful legs," Sebastian remarked unexpectedly, studying her with an artist's eye. "It's a pity I don't have my sketch pad with me. You would make a marvelous study with the soft froth of the bubbles, the porcelain-white gleam of the tub and tiles, and the cream color of your skin. The darkness of your hair, all tumbled atop your head, and the flaming sunset behind you adds the right shock of color." His eyes narrowed slightly. "But I would need to move a couple of the candles closer."

She could see the painting in his mind and knew exactly where he wanted the candles placed. It was something she took for granted, dismissing it as the result of the two of them working so long and so closely together over the years.

"Stick to landscapes. They sell," was her response.

"So speaks Kitty Hamilton, art dealer," Sebastian replied with a bow of mock subservience.

"Well, it's true. The painting you described might be appropriate for the cover of a romance novel, but for something more artistic, it needs to be midnight-black beyond the window, creating a reflection in the glass, with a vague scattering of stars and a pale crescent moon. Now, *that* would be a great study in blacks and whites."

"Probably." Sebastian was clearly indifferent to the suggestion. "But any artist can do a black-and-white. I'm talking red-and-white."

Kitty was momentarily intrigued by the thought. "You would need a redhead for that."

"The glow of the sunset has given your hair a red cast."

"Really?" She looked up in surprise, then curiosity. "How does it look? I've been toying with the idea of having Carlos add some red highlights. It's so in right now."

"Don't." He drank down the last of the champagne in his glass, set it aside, and reached for the loofah sponge in her hand. "Here. I'll wash your back for you."

Distracted by the shortness of his answer, Kitty automatically handed it to him. "Why?"

"Why what?" He soaped the sponge into a thick lather and rubbed it over her back in slow, massaging strokes.

"Why wouldn't I look good with a few red highlights streaked through my hair?"

"I know you too well. You wouldn't be content with a few. Before it was finished, you'd be a flaming carrottop."

"Not necessarily."

"Everything is always whole-hog or die with you." His voice had a smile in it. "It can be love or business; it's always both feet. Speaking of which, who is the new love of your life?"

The hint of ridicule in his voice made Kitty loath to answer. Which was childish. After tonight, it would be public knowledge.

"Marcel Boulanger."

"Sounds French."

"Belgian."

"My mistake." The drollness of his voice was irritating, but the kneading pressure along the taut shoulder muscles near the base of her neck made it slightly easier to overlook. "Boulanger," he repeated thoughtfully. "It seems as though I've heard that name before. What does he do?"

"His family makes chocolate. In fact, many consider it to be the finest in the world."

"Ah," he murmured in a dawning voice. "The strawberries."

"Dipped in Boulanger chocolate," Kitty confirmed, and sighed at the remembered taste of it. "Even you must admit, it's absolutely exquisite chocolate. And it's no wonder, either. Marcel regularly travels to Central and South America to select only the best cocoa beans."

"I'm surprised he hasn't been kidnapped and held for ransom."

Kitty stiffened in instant alarm. "Don't say that. Don't even think it!"

"Sorry. So, when did you meet Mr. Chocolate?"

"Almost three weeks ago. He came by the gallery with the Ridgedales. He's staying with them," she added in explanation. "So of course, I saw him again that evening at the Ridgedales' preopera cocktail party."

"And you were smitten?" Sebastian guessed.

"Instantly." She almost purred the word as that deliciously exciting feeling welled up inside her again.

"Love at first bite, you might say."

"Very funny, Sebastian," she replied without humor.

"I thought it was. Obviously you're in love, since you seem to have lost your sense of humor."

"I'm very much in love," she declared with feeling.

"And how serious is Mr. Chocolate?"

"Very. He's asked me to marry him."

"And you said yes, of course."

"Naturally."

"A man who makes chocolate—how could any woman refuse?" Sebastian murmured.

But Kitty was too wrapped up in her memory of Marcel's proposal to pay any attention to Sebastian's sardonic rejoinder. Besides, she was too used to them.

"It was such a romantic setting. Dinner in the courtyard, just the two of us, crystal gleaming in the candlelight, the air scented with gardenias in bloom. There at my chair was a single red rose and a small gift. I opened it, and—do you know what I found inside?"

"An engagement ring. Not really very original."

"Oh, but it was," Kitty insisted smugly. "Maybe the ring part of it wasn't original, but the box it came in definitely was. It was made out of chocolate. Perfect in every detail, too, right down to the slot to hold the ring."

"Milk chocolate or dark?"

"Dark. It even had the Boulanger family crest embossed on top of it."

"On top of the ring?" Sebastian feigned shock.

"No, on top of the box."

"I hope the ring wasn't made of chocolate, too."

"It's one hundred percent diamond." She held up her hand, wagging her fingers, letting the stone's facets catch and reflect the light. "All three carats of it."

"That's as bright as a spotlight. Be careful. The glare from it can blind you."

"It is eye-catching, isn't it?" she murmured, admiring its fiery sparkle.

"That's one word for it," he responded dryly, and dipped the loofah in and out of the water. "Hand me the soap, will you?" She slipped the scented bar off its ridged ledge and passed it to him. "I'm not surprised you fell madly in love with him. Chocolate's a turn-on all by itself. Who needs foreplay when you have chocolate, right?"

She threw him a look of disgust. "You can be so crude sometimes, Sebastian."

"That's not crude. It's the truth. It has something to do with endorphins. Oops, I dropped the soap." He groped underwater for it, his hand sliding along the curve of her hip to her thigh.

A second later, Kitty felt the bar squirt under her leg, and his hand immediately came over the top of her thigh to search for it between her legs. He quickly became dangerously close to areas she didn't want touched by him.

She pushed at his arm. "Stop it. I'll get it myself."

"Wait. It's right here. I can feel it."

"Don't! That's not it!" As she squirmed to elude his playful fingers, she slipped in the tub. She yelped in alarm as she started to slide under the bubbles. "Stop! I don't want to get my hair wet!"

"I've got you." His muscled arm was a band across her breasts, hauling her back upright.

Suddenly everything about this scene seemed much too intimate. There she was naked in the tub with his hands all over her. And Kitty realized that at some point she had lost control of things. Worst of all, Sebastian knew it.

"You bastard. Let me go!" She tugged to free herself of his hold, but between her wet hands and his wet arm, she was hardly successful.

"I'm only trying to help," he protested.

"Help, my foot. You're copping a feel, and you know it." Abandoning the useless struggle, she located the loofah sponge and slapped at him with it.

"Hey!" He jerked back to elude contact with it, but he couldn't elude the splattering of water droplets and bits of foamy bubbles. As he reached up to wipe at his face, he accidentally bumped the plate of strawberries, knocking them into the tub.

"My strawberries," Kitty wailed.

"Let me get that plate out of there before it gets broken." He plunged both hands into the water.

"Just leave it alone," she exploded in anger, and pummeled him with her fists. "Get out of here! Out! Out! Out!"

"Will you stop it?" he yelled above her shrieks of outrage, hunching his shoulders against the raining blows.

The bathroom door burst open. Kitty squealed in dismay at the sight of the thunderous look on the face of a tall, dark man with distinctively Gaelic features—the man who was her fiancé.

"You! Get away from her," Marcel Boulanger ordered in that gorgeous accent of his.

Sebastian started to rise, then lost his footing on the wet floor and slipped halfway into the tub.

"It's all right, Marcel," Kitty rushed. "It's not what you think."

"Who is this man?" he demanded, his accent thickening noticeably.

Half in and half out of the tub, Sebastian replied. "I'm her husband. Who the hell are you?"

"Your husband?" Marcel scowled blackly at Kitty. "What is this he is saying?"

"He's my *ex*-husband." She hurried the explanation and pushed Sebastian the rest of the way out of the bathtub, while trying to hide her own self among the bubbles. "We've been divorced for years."

Whatever comfort Marcel found in that, it was small. "What is he doing here now?"

"I live here," Sebastian answered, rising to his feet.

Kitty hastened to correct that impression. "Not here, precisely. At least, not in the house. He has a studio out back. He lives there."

"A studio? This man is an artist?" He eyed Sebastian with considerable skepticism.

In all honesty, Kitty had to admit that Sebastian didn't fit the popular image of an artist. He certainly didn't possess the temperament of one. He was much too easygoing.

"This is Sebastian Cole. The Ridgedales have two of his landscapes hanging in their Santa Fe home." Conscious of the rapidly dissipating bubbles, Kitty reached for the oversize bath towel lying on the tub's tiled ledge.

The doubtful look vanished as Marcel smiled in recognition of the name. "Ah, yes, you are—"

"Please don't say the great Sebastian," Sebastian interrupted, his mouth slanting in a wry smile. "It makes me feel like a trapeze artist in a circus. Plain Sebastian will do. You must be Mr. Chocolate."

Confusion furrowed his brow. "*Mais non*, my name is Marcel Boulanger."

"He knows that . . ." Kitty gave Sebastian a dirty look as she maneuvered closer to the side of the tub. "It's just a nickname he gave you. It's his idea of a joke."

"I sampled some of your family's wares earlier," Sebastian remarked. "Kitty had a plate of strawberries dipped in your chocolate. Unfortunately I knocked it into the tub."

"That's what he was doing when you came in—looking for the plate." With one arm holding the towel high above her breasts and the other hand trying to hold the ends together behind her back, Kitty attempted to stand.

"Let me give you a hand." Sebastian moved to help her out of the tub.

"I can manage just fine." As she drew away from his outstretched hand, she stepped on a strawberry, slipped, and pitched forward with a yelp.

Sebastian caught her, swept her out of the tub and into the cradle of his arms, towel and all. Kitty was stunned to find herself in such a familiar position, and not altogether sure how she had gotten there. But the memories were much too strong of all the times their arguments had ended like this, with Sebastian sweeping her off her feet and carting her off to the nearest soft or flat surface and there making love to her. Most satisfactorily, she recalled as color flooded her cheeks.

"Put me down," she snapped.

"Whatever you say, kitten." He released her legs with an abruptness that took her by surprise.

She managed to retain her grip on the towel as she hissed an irritated, "Don't call me that. You know I hate it."

Sebastian simply smiled with infuriating ease and turned his attention to Marcel. "Since I understand congratulations are in order, you might as well know she has a temper."

"I do not!" She stamped her foot on the plush bathroom rug. The muffled sound didn't add much emphasis to her denial.

Sebastian ignored her. "I wouldn't worry about her temper, though. I'm sure you already know about her secret passion for chocolate. It doesn't matter how mad she gets, just pop a piece in her mouth and she'll melt in your arms."

"That is not true." Kitty pushed the angry words through her teeth and hurriedly wrapped the towel around her. "You're making me seem like some foolish female, or worse."

"Well, you're definitely female." His twinkling glance dipped to her cleavage.

Kitty wiggled the towel higher. "You came in here to borrow a razor. Take it and leave."

"She's a little upset about the loss of the strawberries," he explained to Marcel. "She hates to waste good chocolate."

"Go." She pointed a rigid arm at the door.

He cocked an eyebrow. "Now, you know you don't want me dripping water all through your house." He pulled at the side of his T-shirt, reminding her that half of his clothes were soaked. She hesitated fractionally, visualizing the trail of water through her beautiful home. "You still have that spare terry-cloth robe hanging in the closet, don't you?"

She hated the way Sebastian made it sound as though he knew where everything was. Of course, the truth was he did. She shot an anxious look at Marcel, worried that he might put the wrong construction on that.

"Yes, it's hanging—"

"I'll find it," Sebastian assured her, and he headed for the bedroom, a faint squelch to his woven-leather sandals.

Kitty didn't draw an easy breath until he was out of the room. Even then, she was a little surprised that he hadn't lingered to make a further nuisance of himself. Fixing the warmest smile on her face that she could muster, she crossed to her fiancé.

"I am so sorry about this. It must have looked

awful when you came in—a strange man in the tub with me. Thank God, he was fully clothed, or—'' She broke off the rush of words and allowed chagrin to tinge her smile. ''It's absolutely impossible to explain any of this. You would have to know Sebastian to understand.'' Then it hit her that she hadn't expected Marcel to arrive until much later. ''What are you doing here anyway?''

He seemed a bit taken aback by her question. ''Your maid let me into the house as she was leaving. I heard your cries and thought you were being accosted by some thief.''

''No.'' She shook her head. ''I mean—I thought you weren't going to be here until eight o'clock.''

From the bedroom closet came Sebastian's muffled shout, ''I found it!''

Deciding it was best to simply ignore him, Kitty bit back the impulse to shout back at him to put on the robe and get out. ''Pay no attention to him.'' She laid a hand on Marcel's arm, drawing his attention back to her when he half turned in the direction of Sebastian's voice.

''Yes, that is best,'' he agreed, then explained, ''I came early to your house because I received a phone call from home this afternoon. My *maman* has taken ill. Nothing too serious,'' he inserted when Kitty drew a quick breath of concern. ''But I must fly home to Brussels tomorrow. It is my desire that you come with me. I wish to have my family meet with you.''

''You mean . . . leave tomorrow?'' she said in shock, her mind exploding with hundreds of problems that would create.

''But of course. We would leave in the morning.''

''Marcel, it simply isn't possible for me to fly off

at the drop of a hat. Not with everything that's going on at the gallery. This is one of our busiest times of the year. I—"

"Surely your assistant is able to take charge while you are gone."

"Harve is very competent," she agreed. "But I have a special exhibit scheduled in two weeks— actually less than that. The shipment should be here in two or three days. And there are so many other things that must be coordinated. Honestly, it just isn't possible. I'm sorry, Marcel, but—"

A bare-shouldered Sebastian stuck his head around the bathroom door. "Sorry to interrupt, but I need a towel to wrap my wet clothes in."

Teeth gritted, Kitty snatched a towel off the bar and shoved it into his hands. "There."

"Thanks." With a smile and a nod, Sebastian was gone.

Struggling to regain her calm, she faced Marcel once again. "All things considered, I think it would truly be best if I met your family another time, especially since your mother isn't well."

"Perhaps it would be," he conceded, then reached out to grip her upper arms, his gaze burrowing into her with intensity, his eyes darkened with a passion that so thrilled her. "But it pains me to leave you even for a day."

"Me, too." The agreement came easily.

With a groan of desire, he pulled her against him and his mouth came down to claim her lips. But Kitty found it difficult to enjoy the devouring wetness of his kiss when any second they could be interrupted by Sebastian again. After a decent interval, she drew back from his kiss.

"We still have tonight, don't we?" she murmured, one hand on the lapel of his suit jacket and the other pressed against the front of the towel to keep it in place. "After all, we do have an engagement to celebrate."

"Indeed, we have much to celebrate. It may require all night."

"I certainly hope so," Kitty replied, then stepped away when he would have kissed her again. "Why don't you go fix yourself a drink while I finish up here? I promise I won't be long."

As Marcel released a sigh of regret, Sebastian rapped lightly on the door, then looked around it, this time bundled in a white terry robe. "I don't mean to keep busting in on your little tête-à-tête, but I thought I should let you know I'm leaving."

"Promise?" Kitty retorted with a touch of sarcasm.

"Cross my heart."

She didn't believe him for one minute. "Marcel, why don't you go with him and make sure he actually does leave?"

"With pleasure," Marcel declared, clearly as eager to be rid of him as Kitty was.

"Something tells me Kitty doesn't trust me." Sebastian's grin was wide with mischief.

"I wonder why," she murmured, and followed both men into the bedroom, then ushered them out the bedroom door and closed it behind them.

Alone in the bedroom, she stood there a moment and struggled to regain that gloriously happy feeling she'd felt earlier. At the moment, she was much too annoyed with Sebastian. The man had an absolute talent for getting under her skin.

Determined not to let him spoil any more of her evening, Kitty stalked to the huge walk-in closet.

The plush throw rug was damp beneath her feet, a reminder that Sebastian had been there before her. As if she needed one.

"Put him out of your mind, Kitty," she muttered to herself, needing to hear the words.

Chapter Two

Sighing, Kitty scanned the clothes in her closet. Now that Marcel had arrived early, she no longer had the luxury of dressing at her leisure. She told herself that she truly didn't mind. It was better to look on the positive side of things; this much-anticipated evening would simply begin earlier than she had expected. Now that she had finally gotten rid of Sebastian, everything was going to be as wonderful as she'd thought.

In the closet, she loosened the towel and used the drier portions of it to wipe the remaining moisture on her skin, all the while surveying her vast wardrobe, regretting that she hadn't already decided on something to wear. Until now, it was a decision that hadn't needed to be hurried.

"Too bad Picasso isn't around to do an abstract of this—Woman's Derriere Amidst a Swirl of Clothes."

At the first sound of Sebastian's familiar voice,

Kitty wheeled in fury, snatching the towel back around her. "Don't you ever knock?" she hurled angrily.

He stood in the closet doorway, clad as before in the white terry robe, a portion of his wet jeans sticking out of the rolled-up towel under his arm. "It's a bad habit I've got, I'm afraid," he replied without a smidgeon of remorse.

"It's one bad habit you need to concentrate on breaking," she retorted, then demanded, "What are you doing here again? I thought you'd left."

"I forgot the razor." His expression was much too benignly innocent to be believed.

"On purpose, I'll bet," Kitty guessed, eyes narrowing on him. Careful to keep her bottom covered, she turned back to face the racks of clothes. "Get your razor and leave. Better yet, forget the razor and grow a beard. It would fit the public image of an artist."

"You wouldn't like it," Sebastian replied easily. "I tried growing one before, and you didn't care for the way it scratched, remember?"

"That won't be a problem anymore."

He snapped his fingers as if only recalling their divorce at that moment. "That's right. You're engaged to someone else now, aren't you?"

"As if you didn't remember." She let the sarcasm through.

"Have you decided what you're wearing for the big dinner tonight?"

"That's what I'm doing now."

"I recommend the cranberry silk number."

"Good. That's one I definitely won't choose," Kitty retorted.

"You should. I have to swallow a groan every time I see you in it."

There was a part of her that was secretly pleased she could still turn him on. But only a small part.

She cast a challenging look over her shoulder. "The razor?"

"Right. That's why I came back, isn't it? I'll just get it and leave."

"That would be an original idea," Kitty muttered as he turned to leave.

Sebastian swung back. "Did you say something?"

"Not to you. Go." She waved him out of the closet.

This time when he left, Kitty wasn't convinced he was gone for good. And she was determined that he wouldn't catch her again without a stitch of clothing on. Hurriedly, she discarded the towel and donned a set of nude lingerie from the drawer. After quickly riffling through the rack of dresses, she selected a simple but elegant sheath of white lace with a plunging keyhole back. She removed it from its padded hanger and wiggled into it.

Still there was no sign of Sebastian, no sound at all to indicate he was anywhere in the vicinity. Kitty wasn't sure whether that was a good thing or a bad thing. But she couldn't help being suspicious of the silence.

Crossing to the built-in shoe caddy, Kitty considered the possibility that he might have actually left. A second later, she stiffened, panicked by the sudden thought that he was out there talking to Marcel. Heaven only knew the sort of things Sebastian might be telling him. Sometimes the man was a devil in disguise with an absolute knack for making the simplest thing sound outrageous.

She bolted out of the closet and stopped abruptly as Sebastian came out of the bathroom. "You're still here." It was almost a relief.

"As usual, you forgot to let the water out of the tub. While I was at it, I went ahead and retriéved the platter and the strawberries." He showed her the plate of sodden strawberries and partially melted chocolate.

Recovering some of her former annoyance, Kitty retorted, "When did you appoint yourself to be my maid?"

"I could have left it, I suppose. But I don't think it would have been a very pretty sight come morning. You need to tell Mr. Chocolate that the flavor combination of bathwater and his chocolate is a poor one."

"Will you stop calling him that? His name is Marcel."

"Whatever." Sebastian shrugged off the correction. "Actually the strawberries didn't fare too well in the bath either. Their flavor got pretty watered down. Here. Try one." He picked up a limp berry that dripped a mixture of brown and pink juice.

Kitty was stunned he would offer her one, even as a joke. Well, the joke was about to be on him, she vowed, and took the berry from him and squished it against his mouth.

Laughter danced in his eyes as he scraped the remains of it off his face and onto the plate. "I'll bet that felt good," he observed.

"Actually I got a great deal of satisfaction out of it."

"I thought you looked like you wanted to hit something," he observed.

"I wouldn't if you would just leave."

"Is that what you're wearing tonight?" he asked, ignoring her broad hint.

"Please tell me you don't like it. Then I'll know I have chosen the right dress."

"You look fabulous in it."

She heard the hesitation in his voice. "But what?" She was furious with herself for seeking his opinion. She blamed it on her respect for his artistic eye.

"I was just thinking—don't you think virginal white is a bit of a stretch?"

Glaring at him, Kitty demanded, "Give me that plate of strawberries so I can shove the whole thing in your face."

When she made a grab for it, Sebastian held it out of reach. "I don't think so," he said. "Something tells me you'd break it over my head. What do you say we call a truce, and I'll stop teasing you."

"I have a better idea. Why don't you go home?" Kitty suggested, then remembered, "You did get the razor."

He set the plate on a dresser top and patted the pocket of his robe. "Right here."

"Then leave, so I can get dressed in peace."

"Let me fasten that hook in back first. You know you'll never be able to reach it yourself."

To her irritation, Sebastian was right. Against her better judgment, Kitty turned her back to him, giving him access to the hook.

"I could have had Marcel fasten it for me." She could feel the light pressure of his blunt fingers against her skin as he drew the two ends together.

"I have no doubt he would have been delighted to do it."

"As long as you understand that."

"You need to wear your silver shawl with this, and those silver, strappy heels you have."

"That's probably a good choice. Silver is in this season," she recalled thoughtfully. "And I will need something later this evening to ward off the chill. What about jewelry? How about the necklace of turquoise nuggets?

"Everybody will be wearing turquoise. And it would be too chunky with the lace. Try that slender silver choker with the cabochon pendant of pink coral."

Kitty didn't need to try it. She could already visualize it in her mind and knew it would be perfect.

"Have you set a wedding date yet?"

"No. We planned to talk about it tonight." But with Marcel's mother being ill, she wasn't sure it would be an appropriate subject. "It will be sometime soon, though. It's what we both want."

"I guess that means I'll have to start looking for a new art dealer. It won't be easy. You've spoiled me."

"What are you talking about?" She twisted around, trying to see his face.

"Hold still. I almost have it fastened."

"Then explain what you meant by that." She squared around again. "Just because I'm getting married doesn't mean I can't still represent your paintings."

"True, but it might be a little difficult trying to do that from Brussels."

"Brussels?" She turned in shock, not caring that he had yet to fasten the top.

"That's right. According to Mr. Chocolate, that's

where you'll be living after you're married. I suppose you could keep the gallery here in Santa Fe and find someone to manage it for you. Although it would probably be simpler just to sell it."

"Sell the gallery? After I've worked so hard to build it to this point?"

Tilting his head, he scanned the bedroom's ceiling, exposed beams spanning its breadth. "I don't remember this room having an echo."

"Will you be serious?" Kitty demanded impatiently.

"I am serious." He brought his gaze back to her upturned face, a new gentleness darkening his eyes. "I take it you hadn't thought about where you would be living?"

Truthfully, she hadn't given any thought to it at all. The realization made her feel utterly foolish.

Once again, she turned her back to him, aware that those sharp eyes of his saw too much. "I more or less assumed we would be dividing our time between Brussels and Santa Fe. That's what is usually done when two people have separate careers."

"I suppose that could work."

Reassured, Kitty relaxed a little. "Of course it could."

"I guess that means you'll be keeping the house, too."

"Naturally. I'll need somewhere to live when I am here."

"Mr. Chocolate thought you would prefer to sell it and avoid the financial drain of maintaining two households. I told him that you didn't have to look for a buyer. I'll be happy to take it off your hands. We could even work out some sort of arrangement where you could stay here whenever you do come back.''

"That's very generous of you, but I'll keep it, thank you," she stated firmly.

"It was just a thought." The tone of his voice had an indifferent shrug to it, but Kitty wasn't fooled.

"You've had a number of thoughts. It almost makes me think that you're trying to put doubts in my mind about my engagement to Marcel."

"Would I do that?"

"In a heartbeat," she retorted.

"Honestly, I'm not trying to create doubts—"

"And just what would you call it?"

Sebastian finished fastening the hook and turned her around to face him, both hands resting lightly on the rounded curves of her shoulders. "I'm only trying to make sure that you've thought things through a little before committing yourself to this engagement. You tend to be a bit impulsive where your heart's concerned. It certainly wouldn't be the first time. You have to admit that."

"Oh, I do. And the first time was when I married you." Standing this close to him, Kitty found it difficult not to remember how madly in love with him she had been.

"As your first husband, I think I have the right to vet any future replacement."

Kitty bristled. "That is the most arrogant statement I have ever heard you make. And you have made quite a few."

"Why is that arrogant?" Sebastian countered in a perfectly reasonable tone. "You have to know that I still care about you a lot, even if we aren't married anymore. I don't want to see you get hurt again. Believe it or not, I hope Mr. Chocolate makes you very happy."

"Well, I don't," she stated flatly.

A frown of disbelief swept across his expression. "You don't want him to make you happy?"

"Of course I do," Kitty replied in exasperation. "But I don't believe that you do. And his name is Marcel."

"My mistake." He dipped his head in mild apology, a smile tugging at the corners of his mouth.

"You've made a lot of them." Kitty needed to get a dig in to negate the effects of that near smile.

"I have, but you were never one of them, kitten."

"Don't call me that. You know I hate it."

"You used to like it."

"Don't remind me, please. That was long ago. And I was very young and very foolish."

"And very beautiful. You still are." With his fingertip, he traced the curve of her jaw.

The featherlight caress made her skin tingle. "Don't start with the flattery, Sebastian. It doesn't work anymore." She did her best to ignore the rapid skittering of her pulse.

"It's not flattery. It's the truth."

"Then keep it to yourself."

"I will, on one condition."

"What's that?" she asked, instantly wary.

"You see, something tells me that I won't be invited to the wedding—"

"It's a wise little bird that's whispering in your ear."

Sebastian pretended not to hear that. "—So, this may be my only chance to kiss the bride."

"Not on your life." Kitty took an immediate step back.

"Why not?" He looked genuinely surprised.

"Because it's just another one of your tricks. You know there's a physical attraction that still exists between us. You want to use that to confuse me."

"Do you think I could do that with just one little kiss?"

"I am not going to find out," she stated.

"Don't tell me you're afraid? You, Kitty Hamilton?" His look was one of mocking skepticism.

She shook her head. "That's not going to work either. You aren't going to dare me into it, so you might as well give up."

"Now you've hurt my feelings." But his smile mocked his words.

"You'll get over it." Determined to bring this meeting to an end, Kitty stated calmly, "Thank you for hooking my dress. Now, if you don't mind, I would like to finish getting ready. And you, as I recall, were on your way back to the studio to shave—with my razor."

He started to sing, " 'You go your way. I'll go mine.' "

"Don't." Kitty covered her ears. "Singing is not one of your talents. Stick to oils."

"Kiss me and I'll go."

"Not a chance. With my luck, Marcel would walk in to see what's taking me so long. It was awkward enough when he found you in the bathroom with me."

"All right, I'll go. But it's under protest."

"Under, over, I don't care. Just go."

The minute the door closed behind him, Kitty rushed over and locked it. The sense of relief didn't last though. She had the uneasy feeling that Sebastian had given up a little too easily. She wouldn't feel safe until she and Marcel were out of the house.

As much as she would have liked to tarry, Kitty put on her makeup and fixed her hair in nearly record time for her. Taking Sebastian's advice, she wore the coral pendant and matching earrings, slipped on the strappy heels, and draped the silver crocheted shawl around her shoulders. After a satisfactory check of her reflection in the tall cheval mirror, she unlocked the door to the hall and walked swiftly to the living room.

But Marcel wasn't there.

The feeling of alarm was instant. It only intensified when Kitty heard Sebastian's voice coming from the kitchen. The high heels were the only thing that stopped her from sprinting there.

As she entered the kitchen, she saw Marcel comfortably seated at the table. Her glance ricocheted off him straight to Sebastian, leaning negligently against the tiled countertop, his hands wrapped around a toweled wine bottle, his thumbs gently easing out the cork. Marcel rose when she entered.

Her patience exhausted, Kitty snapped, "Haven't you left yet?"

"Really, Kitty," Sebastian said with a mocking *tsk-tsk*. "I credited you with having better powers of observation. Here I am, freshly shaved, wearing dry clothes, and you didn't even notice."

As he took one hand away from the wine bottle to gesture to his change in attire, the cork shot into the air with an explosive pop, caromed off a ceiling vega, sailed past Kitty's head, and bounced onto the floor. Foam bubbled out of the bottle and spilled down its side. Hurriedly Sebastian swung around to pour the effervescent wine into the tulip-shaped champagne glasses on the counter.

"Don't you know you are supposed to ease the cork out of the bottle?" Bending, Kitty retrieved the wayward cork, certain she would step on it if she didn't pick it up.

"That's what I was in the process of doing when I was so rudely interrupted," Sebastian countered smoothly.

"What are you doing back here anyway?" Kitty demanded, unable to rein in her irritation with him.

"I was just telling"—he paused, his eyes twinkling devilishly when she shot him a warning look—"your fiancé that I thought the occasion of your engagement deserved a celebratory toast. So I brought over a bottle of champagne."

Kitty's suspicion warred with her curiosity, but curiosity won. "Why do you have champagne on hand? I thought you didn't like it."

"Ever since your last divorce, I've always kept a bottle in the fridge. That way, the next time you show up at my door in the wee hours of the morning, wanting to drown your troubles in some bubbly, I won't have to go all over God's creation trying to beg, borrow, or steal one." After filling the last glass, Sebastian set down the bottle, then turned with a sudden look of regret. "Sorry. That was bad taste to mention your last divorce, wasn't it?"

Marcel turned to her in confusion. "Your last divorce? What does he mean by this?"

"Don't pay any attention to him. He's just being Sebastian." She directed a careless smile at Marcel and glared at Sebastian when she walked over to pick up two of the champagne glasses. "A name that sounds distinctly like another one," she murmured for Sebastian's ears only.

He merely smiled and picked up the remaining glass. "A toast," he began, and waited until Marcel had a drink in his hand, "to the woman who can still take my breath away, and to her future husband. Happiness always." His gaze was warm on her as he raised his glass to his lips.

Kitty did the same, a little of her own breath stolen by the unexpectedly sincere compliment. But she was careful to direct her tremulous smile at Marcel.

"I must agree with you, Mr. Cole." Marcel flicked him a glance, then smiled lovingly at her. "She is quite beautiful. And never more so than tonight."

Marcel lifted her hand and kissed the back of her fingers, a gesture that came very naturally to him. She didn't have to glance at Sebastian to know that he was observing it all with a droll little smirk.

There was no sign of it, however, when he asked, "Have you already made dinner reservations for this evening?"

"Of course." Truthfully it was an assumption on Kitty's part.

"Somewhere special, I hope." Sebastian took another sip of his champagne.

"Very special," Marcel assured him. "I have arranged for us to dine at Antoine's."

Sebastian cocked a blond eyebrow at Kitty. "Is that wise? First me, then Roger, then Mark. With a track record like that, are you sure you want to go there with him?"

If looks could kill, Kitty would have been staring at Sebastian's gravestone instead of him. "Of course I'm sure," she stated, and fervently hoped that Marcel hadn't followed any of that.

"Antoine's, it is your favorite place, is it not?" Marcel darted confused glances to first one, then the other.

"It's very definitely her favorite," Sebastian replied before she could answer.

"And why shouldn't it be?" She slipped an arm around the crook of Marcel's and snuggled a little closer to him. "The food there is superb."

"You have dined there before with these other men he has mentioned?" Marcel was clearly troubled by that. "They were special to you?"

"I think it's safe to say that," Sebastian inserted. "She married all of us. Not at the same time of course," he added for clarification, then feigned surprise. "Didn't Kitty mention that she's been married three times before?"

"She tells me she is divorced, but I did not know it was from three different men," Marcel replied stiffly, a coolness in the look he gave her.

Kitty struggled to defend the omission. "I thought you knew. It's common knowledge to nearly everyone in Santa Fe."

"That's hardly surprising," Sebastian said, coming to her rescue. "From the sounds of it, you two have had such a whirlwind courtship you haven't had a lot of time to exchange stories about any skeletons in the closet, or—in Kitty's case—ex-husbands. I guess that's the purpose of engagements. Kitty and I never had one. Two days after I proposed, we were married. With the logistics of each of you having careers in different countries, I imagine you're planning a long engagement. Have you decided where the wedding will be? Here or in Brussels?"

"In Brussels, of course," Marcel stated with a certainty that irked Kitty, considering it was something they hadn't gotten around to discussing. And it was, after all, a decision the bride was supposed to make, not the groom.

"Brussels, you say," Sebastian said and sighed. "That's a shame."

"Why do you say this?" Marcel wondered, a puzzled knit to his brow.

"I do all my traveling on the ground. I don't fly, certainly not across an ocean—not even for Kitty," Sebastian added with a smiling glance in her direction. "As much as I would like to be there to see her walk down the aisle, I won't be coming to the wedding."

"You're assuming you would even receive an invitation." Her own smile was on the saccharine side.

"You know you'd invite me, kitten," Sebastian chided. "For business reasons, if nothing else," he added, then chuckled. "I can see the wheels turning already, trying to figure out a way to arrange an exhibit of my works on the Continent. Go ahead, but don't expect me to attend."

"But you wouldn't have to fly. You could go by sea, rent a first-class cabin on some luxury liner and travel that way." Recognizing the value of having the artist in attendance, Kitty chose to work on that hurdle first.

"What if I get seasick?" he countered out of sheer perversity.

"They have a patch you can wear now to take care of that. It won't be a problem."

"And go around feeling all doped up, no thank you."

"Don't be difficult, Sebastian."

He just smiled. "You know you love a challenge. Think how dull your life will be when I'm not around."

"Where are you going?" Marcel struggled to follow their conversation.

"Me? I'm not going anywhere. It's Kitty who will be moving to the other side of the world when you two get married."

She was quick to correct him. "I'll only be there part of the time."

"Why do you say this?" Marcel drew back, again eyeing her with faint criticism. "We will be living in Brussels. It is the place of my business. It is where our home will be."

"Of course, but I do have my gallery here—"

"We will make arrangements for that." He dismissed that as a concern. "Art is better pursued in Europe. Although, after we are married, you will discover that you are much too busy to run some little shop of your own."

For an instant, his attitude made Kitty see red. But she was much too aware of Sebastian and the delighted interest he was showing in their conversation to unleash her temper. She was also aware that the blame for all of this belonged directly at his feet. Sebastian had deliberately brought up this subject to cause trouble between her and Marcel. Therefore she wasn't about to give him the satisfaction of succeeding.

Instead of objecting, Kitty smiled serenely. "It's quite possible you are right, Marcel."

"Spoken like a dutifully submissive wife," Sebastian murmured tauntingly.

Angered that he knew her much too well, Kitty resisted the urge to empty her champagne glass in his face. With an effort, she replied, "You should know."

"Believe me, I do know."

"What is this you know?" Marcel frowned. "I hear the words, but it is as if you are speaking in another language."

"I can guarantee Kitty will explain it all to you later." A smile deepened the grooves on either side of Sebastian's mouth. "I imagine there are a lot of details you two need to thrash out—without a third party listening in. So I'll be going and let you have some privacy."

"That's the nicest thing you've said today," Kitty declared. "The only thing better would be if you actually left."

"Oh, I'm going." He slid his champagne glass onto the tiled countertop, then squared back around. "But before I do—"

She sighed in annoyance. "Somehow I knew you'd come up with something."

"Since I won't be coming to the wedding, with your permission"—he inclined his head toward Marcel—"I'd like to kiss the bride-to-be. I don't know when I'll get another chance. And it's only kosher that I do it in your presence so you don't get the idea there's any hanky-panky between Kitty and me."

"I know not this hanky-panky of which you speak," Marcel admitted, then gestured to Kitty with a flourish of his hand. "*Mais oui*, you may kiss the bride."

Left without an objection to make, Kitty fumed inwardly as Sebastian stepped toward her, eyes twinkling. When his hands settled on the rounded points of her shoulders, she obligingly tilted her head up. His head bent slowly toward her as if he was deliberately prolonging the moment of contact.

At last his mouth moved onto hers with persuasive warmth. Her pulse raced, but she reasoned that it was strictly out of anger and the awkwardness of having Marcel standing so close, observing it all. She held herself rigid, refusing to kiss him back. And that was harder than she had expected it to be. Sebastian was in that familiar, slow lovemaking mode. It had been her undoing countless times in the past.

His lips clung to hers for a moistly sweet second longer, then they were gone. She immediately missed their seductive warmth. It was a vague ache inside, one that prevented her from being glad that he had kept the kiss so brief.

"I honestly want you to be happy, kitten," he murmured.

Determined to break the spell of his kiss, Kitty reached for Marcel's hand. "We will be very happy together."

There was something mocking in the smile Sebastian directed her way before he turned to shake hands with Marcel. "Congratulations."

"*Merci.*" Marcel made a slight bow in response.

"I'll be going now. Enjoy your dinner." With a farewell wave, Sebastian moved toward the back door.

"I'll show you out." Kitty moved after him. "I need to lock the door anyway after you leave."

When he opened the door, she was right behind him. The instant he stepped outside, she muttered a warning, "So help me, Sebastian, if you show up at Antoine's tonight, I swear I will take a knife to every one of your paintings."

He grinned. "Actually I plan on spending the entire evening at home. Alone, I might add. Does that make you feel better?"

"Good night," she said in answer, and closed the door, turning the lock with great satisfaction. Turning back to Marcel, she smiled with genuine pleasure. "I'm ready if you are."

Chapter Three

The Sangre de Cristo Mountains were a black silhouette that jutted into the night sky's star-crusted backdrop. But Kitty took little notice of it as the taxicab moved in and out of the glow from the streetlights that lined the road. She sat silently in the rear seat, her face devoid of all expression.

The driver slowed the vehicle as they approached the tall adobe wall that enclosed her property. Recognizing it, Kitty opened her slender evening bag and took out the fare. When he pulled up to the gated entry, she passed him the money and climbed out.

Using the key from her purse, she unlocked the wrought-iron pass-through door, stepped through, and locked it behind her. Soft landscape lighting lit the flagstone walk that led to the low adobe house. But Kitty didn't take it. Instead, she struck out on the side path that swept around the house to the studio located in the rear courtyard.

Light flooded from its windows in wide pools. She wasn't surprised. Sebastian had always been late to bed and late to rise. She paused outside his door long enough to slip off a silver shoe. With great relish, Kitty proceeded to pound the shoe against the door as hard as she could. The heel snapped off, but she kept pounding until the door was jerked open by Sebastian.

"Kitty," he began.

But she didn't give him a chance to say more. "Don't pretend to be surprised to see me. It won't work."

He glanced at the broken shoe in her hand, then reached down and picked up its missing heel. "Why didn't you simply ring the doorbell?"

"You don't get the same satisfaction out of pushing a button."

"But I liked those shoes." He examined the heel as if checking to see if it could be repaired.

"Here. Have the rest of it." She threw the rest of the shoe at him.

He ducked quickly, and it sailed over his shoulder and clattered across the floor. When he went after it, Kitty stalked into the studio a bit unelegantly wearing only one shoe. She stopped on the Saltillo tile and slipped off the other shoe.

"You like them so much, take both of them." She tossed the second shoe at him, but without the force of the first.

"I didn't expect you home so early. It's barely eleven o'clock." He retrieved the second shoe as well and set them on a side table. "Where did you leave Mr. Chocolate?"

"We had an argument, as if you didn't know." She hurled the accusation.

"Don't tell me the engagement's off? Nope, it must not be," Sebastian said, answering the question himself and gesturing to her left hand. "I see you're still wearing the headlight."

"No, it isn't off. Yet."

"I hope you don't want a glass of champagne. I opened the only bottle I had, to toast your engagement."

"I wouldn't drink any of your champagne if you had it. This is all your fault."

"My fault?" He feigned innocence. "What did I do now?"

"Don't pull that act with me," she warned. "You know exactly what you did. You set out to deliberately undermine my relationship with Marcel."

"How could I do that? I met him for the first time tonight," he reminded her in an infuriatingly reasonable voice.

"Maybe you did," Kitty conceded, then gathered back up her anger. "But you're smart and quick. You can think faster on your feet than anyone I know. And you're an absolute master of sabotage."

"You give me much more credit than I deserve. I want you to be happy. If Mr. Chocolate can do that, then great."

"But you don't think he can. That's the point," she retorted.

"It isn't important what I think. Do you think he can?"

The instant he turned the question back on her, all her high anger crumbled, making room for the doubts and questions to resurface. "I don't know, Sebastian. I honestly don't know," she replied in a hopeless murmur.

"I'll tell you what—why don't we sit on the sofa

and you can tell me all about it." His hand curved itself along her arm and steered her toward the sofa with light pressure.

Without objection, Kitty allowed him to guide her to the sofa, upholstered in a geometric fabric that echoed Zuni design. Flames curled over the logs in the corner fireplace, called a kiva. Before she sat down on the plush cushions, Sebastian slipped off her shawl and draped it over a corner of the sofa back. She sank onto the cushion and curled her stockinged legs under her.

Sebastian crossed to the kiva and added another chunk of wood to the fire, then reached for the iron poker to lever the split log atop the fire.

"Where do you want to start?" he asked, his back turned to her. "The beginning would probably be a good place."

"It began in the bathroom," she retorted with a ghost of her former anger, "when Marcel walked in and found you there. That was difficult enough to explain. Then you had to go and bring up my trio of failed marriages."

"You *are* a three-time loser." He strolled over to the sofa and sat down on the opposite end.

"I'm well aware of that. The trouble is" —she paused and sighed in discouragement—"Marcel wasn't."

"I thought you handled it rather well. It really is common knowledge here in Santa Fe. It wasn't as though you were deliberately keeping it a secret from him."

"I honestly wasn't. But . . . I think it seemed that way to him."

"Grilled you about them, did he?" Sebastian guessed.

"Naturally he asked," Kitty began, then threw up her hands in annoyance. "Why am I trying to make him sound good? Yes, he grilled me about them. And I really got the third degree over you. Quite honestly, I could understand why he did ask. I didn't like it, but I understood. If the situation was reversed, I'd probably do the same thing."

"I hear a 'but.' " Sebastian cocked his head at an inquiring angle.

She flashed him an irritated glance. "Something tells me you already know what it is. You certainly made a point of raising the issue after you so gallantly toasted us."

"What point is that?"

"About the gallery."

His head moved in a sagely nod. "I thought so."

"Marcel didn't say it in so many words, but he wants me to sell it."

"And you don't want to."

"Of course I don't. Why should I? I don't expect him to give up his work when we're married. Why should I give up mine?"

"You could always open up a gallery in Brussels," Sebastian suggested.

"According to Marcel, I'll be much too busy entertaining his friends and family, being a wife, and accompanying him on his business trips. And he believes it's definitely wrong for the mother of his children to work at anything, period. We aren't even married yet and he's already talking about children."

"I always thought you wanted a passel of little ones."

"I do, but I don't plan on becoming a baby

factory right away. I'd like to be married awhile first."

"What about that biological clock ticking away?"

"That sound you hear is a time bomb about to explode." Reacting to her own inner confusion and agitation over it, Kitty rose to her feet and walked to the corner fireplace. "I was so happy until tonight. Suddenly everything is a mess, thanks to you."

"I didn't make the mess. If I'm guilty of anything, it's of opening your eyes to it."

"As I recall, you were never to blame for anything. It was always my fault," she said with a hint of bitterness in her voice.

"I believe the official term was 'irreconcilable differences.' It covers a host of sins on both sides." His mouth twisted in a wry smile of remembrance.

Turning from the flames, Kitty frowned curiously. "Why did we break up? What went wrong?"

"We did."

"Which tells me absolutely nothing." She shook her head in disgust. "I probably got fed up with your enigmatic answers that sound so profound and say nothing."

"No, I'm serious." With unhurried ease, Sebastian stood up and wandered over to the fireplace. "I think you and I stopped trying. It's hard enough for two individuals to live together in harmony, but we also worked together. Maybe we expected too much."

"Maybe we did." She felt a sadness at the thought, and a kind of emptiness, too.

"So, how did you leave things with Mr. Chocolate?"

"Up in the air, I guess." She lifted her shoulders

in a vague shrug, then admitted, "I walked out on him."

"That was a bit on the childish side, don't you think?" His smile was lightly teasing, but his eyes were warm with gentleness.

"Probably. But it was either walk out and cool off, or throw his ring in his face."

"That bad, huh?"

"That bad." Kitty nodded in confirmation. "He never seemed to hear anything I said. If he just would have listened," Kitty murmured, her shoulders sagging in defeat. "Maybe it is inevitable that I have to sell the gallery. I realize that it will be extremely difficult to run it from a distance, and I can't count on finding someone to manage it who will care about it as much as I do. Maybe I will find married life to be as busy and fulfilling as my work. I don't know. But Marcel talks as though this all needs to be set in motion now, before we're married. Why can't it be something I ease into gradually?"

"Have you told him that?" Sebastian dipped his head to get a better look at her downturned face.

"More or less."

"Which means it was less rather than more."

"It was hard to get a word in," she said in her own defense. "He was too busy planning my life."

"Something tells me he doesn't know you very well," Sebastian murmured wryly. "So, what's the next move?"

She moved her head from side to side in a gesture of uncertainty. "I don't know. I probably should call him—to apologize for walking out like that, if nothing else. But he's staying at the Ridgedales'. You know how nosy Mavis is. I hate the thought of her listening in on even one side of our conversation."

"There's always tomorrow morning."

"Marcel's flying back to Brussels in the morning. His mother is ill."

"Oops."

"I know. My timing is lousy," Kitty admitted. "Even worse, he wanted me to go with him. That's why he came early to pick me up."

"And you refused to go, of course."

"How could I? In the first place, I can't take off at the drop of a hat. Who would open the gallery in the morning? And there's the exhibit coming up. There are a thousand things that have to be done in the next two weeks. Besides, even though he said his mother isn't seriously ill, I think it's a poor time to meet my future in-laws."

"It sort of makes you wonder if his mother took sick before or after she found out he was engaged."

Her gaze narrowed on him. "What are you saying?"

Sebastian asked instead, "How old is Mr. Chocolate?"

"Thirty-eight. Why?"

"Is this his first marriage?"

"As a matter of fact, it is. But that's not so unusual. European males tend to marry later in life. That doesn't mean he's a mama's boy."

Stepping back, Sebastian raised his hands. "I never said he was."

"No, you just hinted at it. Broadly."

"It is a possibility, though."

"You're doing it again." Kitty pressed her lips together in a grim and angry line.

"Doing what?"

"Putting doubts in my mind, making me suspicious of my mother-in-law before I've even met her. Why don't you come right out and admit you don't want me to marry Marcel?"

"All right, I don't."

Her mouth dropped open. She hadn't actually expected him to admit it, and certainly not with such aplomb. "I thought you wanted me to be happy."

"I do. Just not with Mr. Chocolate."

"Will you stop calling him that?"

"Maybe you can become a taster for the family business. Sample all the new products, or work on the quality control end."

"It is impossible to talk to you," Kitty declared angrily.

"But you love chocolate."

"As a treat, yes. But I certainly have no desire to make it my life's work." In disgust, she turned back toward the fire. "Why am I even talking to you?"

"Because you know I'll listen."

Kitty was forced to concede that was true. Sebastian didn't necessarily agree with her all the time, but he always listened. Which made it easy for her to return to the heart of the problem.

"I really do love Marcel." Yet saying the words only made her situation seem more confusing.

"As Tina would say, 'What's love got to do with it?'" Sebastian countered.

"It should have everything to do with it," Kitty stated forcefully.

"Maybe." But he was clearly unconvinced.

In some disconnected way, his reply raised another question. "Tell me something," she began, eyeing him intently. "A minute ago, you admitted you didn't want me to marry Marcel, but you never said why."

"Are you sure you want to know?"

"I wouldn't have asked otherwise."

"Okay." He nodded in acceptance. "It's very simple, really. I don't want to go through the trouble of finding another dealer to represent my paintings."

"That is the most selfish thing I have ever heard," Kitty huffed. "And you claim you want me to be happy."

"I do," Sebastian replied easily, giving no indication that he considered it to be contradictory.

"You want me to be happy so long as it isn't at your expense," she retorted in annoyance. "You certainly wouldn't have any trouble finding someone reputable to represent you. As successful as you've become, they'll be standing in line to take my place."

"But I don't want the hassle of all the meetings that go along with deciding which one to pick, not to mention the strangeness of working with someone new. We've been together too long, and I don't have any desire to change horses. Besides, you know me—I'd be just as happy selling my paintings on a street corner. That's how we met, in case you've forgotten."

"I hadn't."

The memory of that day was as vivid as if had happened yesterday. As an art major and ardent fan of works by Georgia O'Keeffe, she had come to Santa Fe during spring break to view the O'Keeffe paintings on display at a local museum. She had also planned to make a side trip to O'Keeffe's former home and studio about an hour northwest of Santa Fe.

Late one sunny morning as she walked along a street, she had spotted a half-dozen paintings propped against the side of an adobe wall, with more standing in a plastic crate. Idly curious, she had stopped to look. Mixed in with some still-life works that showed good technique but trite subject matter were a series of New Mexican landscapes and Santa Fe streetscapes that completely captivated her.

There had been, however, no sign of the artist. Each painting had a price tag attached to it, with none selling for above fifty dollars.

A hand-lettered sign with a directional arrow had instructed buyers to deposit their money in a metal cash box with a slit in its lid that was chained and padlocked to a lamppost. To her utter astonishment, Kitty had realized that this fool of an artist was selling his paintings on the honor system.

At that moment, a middle-aged couple had strolled by, paused to look at the paintings, assumed Kitty was the artist, and begun asking her questions. To this day she still couldn't say why she hadn't disabused them from that notion, but she hadn't.

Before they left, she had managed to sell them one of the Santa Fe street scenes. Buoyed by that success, Kitty had lingered. By late afternoon, she had sold a total of eight paintings, including one of the dull still lifes to a woman who bought it because the colors in it matched her living room.

Concerned that the cash box contained over four hundred dollars and curious about the artist who had signed the paintings as S. Cole, Kitty had waited, certain that S. Cole would show up sooner or later.

But she certainly hadn't expected him to be the tall, blond hunk of man who had ultimately shown up. By then she had already fallen in love with his paintings. It had been an easy step from there to fall in love with him.

"Why?"

Lost in her memory of that day, Kitty didn't follow his question. "Why what?"

"Why did you want to know my reasons for not wanting you to marry Mr. Chocolate?"

"Just curious." She shrugged, finding it hard to return to the present. "I thought it might be something personal. I should have known it would be business."

"Would it have made any difference?"

"What?"

"If my reason were personal."

"Of course not. I'll do what I want to do regardless," Kitty asserted.

"You always do."

Something in his tone made her bristle. "And what's wrong with that?"

Sebastian took a step back in mock retreat, an eyebrow shooting up. "My, we are testy. I thought you might have cooled down a little."

"I have," Kitty snapped, then caught herself. "Almost, anyway." A kind of despair swept over her again. "How do I make such a mess of things?"

"You simply have a natural talent for it, I guess." His smile took any sting from his words. "I have an idea."

"What?" Kitty was leery of any idea coming from him.

"Since I don't have any champagne to offer you, how about some hot cocoa?"

Kitty smiled in bemusement. "Hot chocolate, the ultimate comfort drink. Why not?"

She trailed along behind him as Sebastian headed for the small galley kitchen tucked in a corner of the studio. "Which kind do you want?" Sebastian asked over his shoulder. "The instant kind that comes in a packet or the real McCoy?"

"I should ask for the real thing, but I'll settle for the instant," she replied, not really caring.

"That's not like you." He opened a cupboard door and took a tin of cocoa off the shelf.

"What isn't?" She wandered over to the French doors that opened off the kitchen onto the rear courtyard.

"Settling for second best. Your motto has always been 'first class or forget it.' "

"I suppose." Beyond the door's glass panes, Kitty could see her spacious adobe home, its earth-colored walls subtly lit by strategically placed landscape lights around the courtyard. "I really should go home, just in case Marcel calls." She released a heavy and troubled sigh. "But what would I say to him?"

"I suppose it would be too much to hope that you might say 'Get lost, Mr. Chocolate,' " he said amid the rattle of the utensil drawer opening and the clank of a metal pan on the stove top.

"You'd like that, wouldn't you?" Kitty grumbled.

"More than you know," Sebastian replied. "Would you get me the jug of milk from the fridge? I need to keep stirring this."

As she stepped to the refrigerator, she noticed him standing at the stove, stirring something in a pan with a wooden spoon. "What are you doing?" She frowned curiously.

"Making cocoa—from scratch."

She stood there with the refrigerator door open, staring at him in amazement. "I didn't know you knew how."

"It can't be that hard. The directions are right on the can." He nodded to it, then glanced her way. "The milk," he said in a prompting voice.

Reminded of her task, Kitty took the plastic container of milk from the refrigerator and carried it to the small counter space next to the stove. "Bachelorhood has clearly made you domestic."

"Think so, hmm?" he murmured idly.

"I've certainly never known you to cook before."

"Making hot chocolate doesn't count as cooking. Which reminds me, did you know that chocolate was strictly a drink when it was first introduced?"

"Quite honestly, I didn't. I'm not sure I even care." Kitty watched as he stirred the bubbling syruplike mixture in the pan.

"As a connoisseur of chocolate, you should," Sebastian informed her. "Columbus was actually the first to bring it back from the New World. Nobody liked his version of it, though."

"Really," she murmured, intrigued that he should know that.

"Yes, really. It seems the Aztec were the first to grind cocoa beans and use the powder to make a drink. They mixed it with chilies, cinnamon, and cloves, and cornmeal—the four Cs, I call it."

"It doesn't sound very appetizing."

"I don't think it was. The word 'chocolate' is derived from the Aztec word *'xocolatl,'* which literally translates to 'bitter water.' "

"It sounds worse than bitter." The mere thought of the combination was enough for Kitty to make a face.

"It was drunk by the Aztec, supposedly out of golden goblets, and only by men. They considered it to be an aphrodisiac." He poured out some milk and added it to the dark syrupy mixture. "Naturally cocoa beans became highly prized and were eventually used as currency. In fact, ten beans could buy the company of a lady for the evening." Sebastian wagged his eyebrows in mock lechery.

"How do you know all this?" Kitty marveled.

"I've been boning up."

"Why?"

"To impress you, of course. You're the chocolate maven."

"Hardly." Kitty scoffed at the notion. "I simply like it."

"A lot," he added, while continuing to stir the mixture, waiting for it to heat. "For your information, Cortez was the one who added sugar and vanilla to the brew, finally making it palatable. But it was years, not until the mid-eighteen hundreds, that a solid form of chocolate was marketed—by the Cadbury company, if I'm not mistaken."

"You are an absolute mine of knowledge," Kitty teased half seriously.

"Impressed?"

"Very."

"Wait until you taste my hot cocoa." Using a wooden spoon, Sebastian let a few drops fall on the inside of his wrist, then gasped. "Ouch, that's hot."

"I think it might be ready," Kitty suggested dryly, then shouldered him out of the way. "You'd better let me pour before you accidentally burn your fingers and can't paint."

"See what I mean?" he said. "Who else would worry about me like that?"

"I'm sure you'll find someone." After transferring the two mugs to the sink, Kitty filled them with steaming chocolate from the pan. She passed one to Sebastian, then took a tentative sip from the other.

Sebastian watched her. "What do you think?"

"It's delicious, but much too hot to drink."

"While it's cooling, do you want to take a look at my latest? I finished it about an hour ago."

Kitty was quick to take him up on his offer. "I'd love to."

Sebastian was notorious for not allowing anyone to see a painting while it was in progress. It had nearly driven her crazy while they were married. Over the years, she had learned never to venture into his work space without a specific invitation, or risk his wrath. In that way, and that way only, he fit the description of a temperamental artist, complete with tantrums.

Moving into the heart of the studio, Sebastian crossed directly to an easel and turned it to show her the painting propped on it. She breathed in sharply at this first glimpse of a streetscape. At the same time she inhaled the familiar smells of oil paints and thinner.

The painting was an intriguing depiction of all that was Santa Fe: A stretch of adobe wall with its strange blend of pink and ochre tones set the scene. Placed slightly off center was an old wooden door painted a Southwestern teal green. A niche by the door was done in Spanish-influenced tiles.

Next to the front stoop was a geranium in full flower growing out of a large pot, decorated with Pueblo Indian designs. Propped against the stoop was an old skull from a cow. Most striking of all was the dappled shade on the wall.

"It's stunning," she murmured. "The sense of depth you managed to convey is amazing, simply by showing a few paloverde leaves in the upper corner and letting the intricate shadow pattern on the adobe show the rest of the tree. It's almost eerie, the three-dimensional effect you've achieved. How on earth did you do it?"

"It wasn't that difficult. I simply kept the leaves in the foreground in sharp focus and fuzzed the edges of everything else to create the illusion of depth."

"However you achieved it, it worked," Kitty declared. "But the painting itself addresses so completely the blending of cultures in Santa Fe. You have the influence of Spain in the tiles, the Mexican adobe, and the Pueblo pottery. And the cow skull is a personification of the Old West. As for the geranium, you couldn't have chosen a better flower to denote all things American—and even Old World. And I don't think there's a color more closely associated with the new Southwest than that sun-faded shade of teal green. But I like best your reference to the desert with the depiction of the paloverde tree. It's so much more original than the usual prickly pear or saguaro cactus."

"Most people won't recognize it. It'll be just another leafy tree to them." Sebastian's voice held a faint trace of irritation.

"That's their loss. There will be plenty of others who will appreciate it." If necessary, it would be a detail she would point out to them. "Have you titled it yet?"

"I've been mulling over a couple different ones—either 'A Place in the Shade', or 'In the Shade of Santa Fe.' What do you think?"

Kitty considered the choices. "Both would work, but I like the last one best, because everything in the painting shows shades of Santa Fe."

"I don't know. It almost sounds too commercial to me," Sebastian replied.

Kitty shook her head. "I don't think so. After all, it is Santa Fe you've painted. And wonderfully, too."

"I guess that means you like it." His sideways glance was warmly teasing.

"Like it?" The verb choice was much too tame for her. "I absolutely love it."

It was completely natural to slide an arm around his waist, a gesture that fell somewhere between a congratulatory hug and a shared joy in his accomplishment. His own reaction seemed equally natural when he hooked an arm around to her to rest his hand on her waist.

"Thanks." He dipped his head toward hers.

A split second later, his mouth moved onto hers with tunneling warmth. Kitty was surprised by how right it felt and how easy it was to kiss him back.

The kiss itself lasted a little longer than the span of a heartbeat before he lifted his head an inch, his moist breath mingling with hers.

"You taste of chocolate," he murmured.

"So do you," she whispered back, her pulse unexpectedly racing a little.

She wanted to blame it on her delight with the new painting. But something told her the cause was something a bit more intimate, rooted somewhere in the physical attraction that still existed between them.

Chapter Four

"I have an idea." His half-lidded gaze traveled over her face in a visual caress.

"What's that?" Kitty knew she should pull away, create some space between them, but she was strangely reluctant to end this moment.

"Let's go sit on the sofa and see how the painting looks from there."

It was an old routine they had once shared that Kitty found as easy to slip into as an old shoe, one that offered comfort and a perfect fit.

"All right."

With arms linking each other at the waist, they moved together toward the sofa. Then Sebastian pulled away with an ambiguous, "Go ahead. I'll be right there."

"Where are you going?" She frowned curiously when he circled around the sofa and headed toward the front door.

"To set the mood. There are too many lights

on." He flipped off all the switches in the main area except one to a directional lamp aimed directly at the completed canvas.

"Perfect," Kitty announced in approval, then lowered herself onto the sofa's plush cushions, careful not to spill her cocoa.

"It is, isn't it?"

Before joining her, Sebastian crossed to the kiva and added another chunk of wood to the dying fire. With the poker, he stirred it to life until the golden glow from the new flames reached the sofa.

He retrieved his mug of cocoa from the side table, took a quick drink from it, then made his way to the sofa and folded his long frame to sit down next to her, draping one arm along the sofa back behind her head.

"Better drink your cocoa," he advised. "It's just the right temperature now."

Obediently, Kitty took a sip. "Mmm, it does taste good."

"Not bad at all, even if I do say so myself," he agreed after sipping his own.

"You know, if anything, the painting actually looks better from a distance," she remarked after studying it for a minute. "It seems to increase the illusion of depth."

"It does, doesn't it?"

Some wayward impulse prompted Kitty to lift her cup in a toasting fashion. "To another stunning work by S. Cole." She clunked her mug against his and drank down a full swallow. "Good job."

"Thank you."

She settled deeper against the cushions, conscious of the brush of his thigh against hers, but oddly comfortable with the contact. "I'm glad you didn't have any champagne. Hot chocolate is much better." She idly swirled the last half inch of it in her cup. "The taste is somehow soothing."

"That's due to a chemical called theobromine that occurs naturally in cocoa. It's an antidepressant that lifts the spirits."

"More research," Kitty guessed.

"Yup. And, in addition to theobromine, chocolate also contains potassium, magnesium, and vitamin A."

"Stop," she protested with amusement. "I don't need an analysis. It's enough that I feel more content."

"Content" was the word that perfectly described her mood at the moment. And the quiet setting promoted the feeling with the lights turned down, a fire softly crackling in the corner fireplace, and a beautiful piece of art bathed in light. Background music was the only thing lacking.

"Just a minute." Sebastian leaned forward and set his empty mug on the mission-style coffee table.

"Where are you going?" For an instant, Kitty thought he had read her mind and intended to put on some music.

"Nowhere." Sebastian sat back and instructed, "Tilt your head forward a sec."

"Why?" she asked, but did as he said. She felt his fingers on her hair and the sudden loosening of its smooth French twist as he removed a securing pin.

"What are you doing?" She reached back to stop him.

"Taking your hair down. It can't be comfortable leaning against the knot it's in."

"It isn't a knot. It's a twist." Try as she might,

Kitty couldn't repair the damage as quickly as he could pluck out another pin.

"Look at it this way," Sebastian reasoned. "You'll be taking your hair down before the night's over anyway. Now you won't have to."

He didn't stop until her hair tumbled about her shoulders. "But I didn't want it down yet." It made her feel oddly vulnerable to have it falling loose.

"Too bad," he replied, and ran his fingers through her hair, combing it into a semblance of order. "You have beautiful hair." He lifted a few strands and let them slide off his fingers. "Sleek and soft, like satin against the skin."

"Thank you." But the words came out as stiff and self-conscious as she felt.

"You hardly ever wear your hair down. How come?"

"I prefer it up. It's much easier to manage that way." Kitty refused to pull away from his toying fingers. It seemed too much of an admission that she was somehow affected by his touch.

"And you like being in control."

"As a matter of fact, I do," Kitty admitted easily. "I couldn't successfully run my own business otherwise."

"You know what?"

"What?" She darted him a wary glance as he bent closer to her.

"Your hair smells like strawberries."

"It's the shampoo I use."

"Strawberries and chocolate, now there's a delicious combination."

Only inches separated them. Without warning, he closed the distance and claimed her lips in a drugging kiss. The potency of it scrambled her wits and her pulse. She couldn't think, only feel the persuasive power of it.

Her own response came much too naturally and much too eagerly. Frightened by it, she pressed a hand to his chest, intending to push him away. But the instant she felt the hard muscled wall and the hypnotic beat of his heart beneath her hand, any sense of urgency to break off the kiss faded.

He rolled his mouth around her lips, teasing them apart, then murmured against them, "A kiss like that can become addictive."

Kitty managed to pull together enough of her scattered wits to turn her face away. "That's enough, Sebastian." But her voice was all breathy and shaky, without conviction.

"Why?" Deprived of her lips, he simply began nuzzling her highly sensitive ear, igniting a storm of exquisite shudders.

"Because." She knew there was a reason; she simply couldn't think of it, not with Sebastian nibbling at her earlobe like that. It had always been her weakest point, and the surest way to turn her on.

"That's no reason," Sebastian replied, and licked at the shell of her ear with the tip of his tongue.

Swallowing back a moan of pure desire, Kitty hunched a shoulder against her neck, trying to block his sensuous invasion. "I'll . . . I'll spill my cocoa."

"That's easily handled." Seemingly all in one motion, he planted a firm kiss on her lips, took the cup from her hand, and set on the low table.

Kitty barely had time to draw a breath before he was back, once more giving her his undivided attention. Too much of it and too thoroughly. Worse, she was enjoying it.

Gathering together the scattered threads of resistance, Kitty managed to push him back and twist her head to the side, creating a small space between them.

"Will you stop trying to seduce me?" she said in quick protest.

"And here I thought I was being so subtle." He automatically switched his attention to the curve of her throat.

Kitty slid her fingers into his hair, then forgot why. "Sebastian, I'm engaged to Marcel." She managed to remember that much.

"Maybe you are and maybe you aren't. It sounded to me like it was all up in the air."

"I haven't decided that," she insisted a bit breathlessly.

"I think you have." His mouth moved around the edges of her lips, tantalizing them with the promise of his kiss.

"Well, I haven't." As if of their own volition, her lips sought contact with his.

As his mouth locked onto them, Kitty recognized the contradiction between her words and action, but she couldn't seem to do anything about it. It was difficult to care when the heat of his kiss satisfied so many of her building needs.

"Funny you should say that," he murmured, lifting his head fractionally. "That's not the message I'm getting."

"I know, but . . ."

"Sh." A second after he made the soothing sound, he began a tactile exploration along the bare ridge of her shoulder, nibbling and licking her there.

It was a full second before it hit Kitty that her shoulder shouldn't be bare. The lace dress should be covering it. Simultaneously with that thought, she felt the looseness of the material along her back and the tight constriction of the sleeves binding her arms against her sides.

"You unfastened my dress," she accused in shock.

"You didn't plan on sleeping in it, did you?" When he raised his head to look at her, the firelight's dim glow kept most of his face in shadow. But there was sufficient light for her to see that his eyes were three-quarter lidded and dark with desire.

It was a sight that took her breath away because Kitty knew her own reflected the same thing.

"Of course I wasn't going to sleep in it."

"Then I'm saving you some time." His fingers inched the sleeves lower on her arms, making it impossible for Kitty to lift her hands high enough to push it back in place.

While she could still muster both the strength and the will, Kitty ducked away from him and scrambled off the sofa. Dangerously weak-kneed, she hurriedly tugged the lacy material higher with fingers that trembled.

"Kitty," his voice coaxed while his hand slid onto the flat of her stomach, evoking new flutters of desire.

"Stop it, Sebastian. You're not playing fair." Kitty weakly pushed at his hand.

"When has love ever been fair?" He rolled to

his feet directly beside her, his hands already moving to gather her back into his embrace.

She wedged her arms between them, needing to avoid contact with his hard male length for her own sake.

"This isn't about love. It's about sex," she insisted, half in anger. "You've always known which buttons to push."

"You pushed mine a long time ago," Sebastian murmured as he nuzzled her neck, "and ruined me for any other woman."

"Do you honestly expect me to believe that?" Kitty sputtered at the outrageous lie. "I've seen the parade of shapely bimbos that have filed past my house to this studio. What about that blonde who was draped all over you at the last showing?"

"Cecilia." He nipped at her earlobe while the pressure of his hands arched her hips closer to him.

"Yes, sexy Cecilia, that's one," Kitty recalled even as her pulse skittered in reaction to his evocative nibblings. "What about her?"

"I never said I didn't try to find someone." He lazily dragged his mouth across her cheek to the corner of her lips. "But no one did to me what you do."

"You're just saying that," she insisted, needing desperately to convince herself of that.

"Am I?" He tugged his shirt open and flattened her hand against his chest. She felt the furnacelike heat of his skin and the hard thudding of his heart somewhere beneath it, beating in the same rapid rhythm as her own. "What about the men I've watched go through your life? All those husbands of yours."

"Two. There were only two." Somehow or other, any thought of Marcel had slipped completely from her mind.

"Be honest. Did any of them make you ache like this?" His hands glided over her back and hips, their roaming caress creating more havoc with her senses.

It was becoming more and more difficult to hold on to any rational thought. "You ... You were always good in bed," Kitty said in defense of her own weakening resistance to him.

"Good sex requires two participants. What we shared was special. Unique."

"But it's over." She needed to remind herself of that, but saying the words didn't seem to help.

"Not for me. And not for you either, or you wouldn't still be standing here."

"No." She tried to deny it, but she also knew it was true. "This is wrong, Sebastian."

"Then why does it feel so right?"

She had no answer for that as he claimed her lips in a hard and all-too-quick kiss. "Do you remember the first time we made love?" He took another moist bite of them.

"Yes." The word came out on a trembling breath.

"I'd brought you back to my apartment to look at more of my paintings." His hands, like his mouth, were never still, always moving to provoke and evoke. "It was cold that spring night. I added another log to the fire to take some of the chill off. Remember?"

Unable to find her voice, Kitty simply nodded, her memory of that night and what came next as sharp as his own.

"As I walked back to you, I took off my shirt, wadded it up, and threw it in a corner."

He stepped back from her long enough to peel off his shirt and give it a toss. But in those few seconds, when she was deprived of the warmth of his body heat and the stimulating touch of his hands, she felt horribly lost.

Then he was close again, his hand cupping the underside of her jaw, tilting her head up, his thumb stroking the high curve of her cheek.

"Do you remember what I said to you?" Sebastian asked.

The words were branded in her memory. Kitty whispered them, "I want to make love with you."

" 'Yes,' you said," he recalled, "and the word trembled from you like the aspens in a breeze." His voice was low and husky with desire, just as it had been that long-ago night. "I took you by the hand." His fingers closed around hers, their grip warm and firm but without command. "And I led you over by the fire."

He backed away from the sofa, drawing her with him as he skirted the coffee table and continued to the gray-and-black Navajo rug in front of the kiva. There he halted and kissed her with seductive languor.

When his mouth rolled off hers, his breathing was rough and uneven. "You wore a dress that night, too."

He took her lips again, devouring them with tonguing insistency. At the same time, his hands went low on her hips and glided upward, pushing the lace of her dress ahead of them until the hem was nearly to her waist.

The past and present merged into one as Kitty

automatically raised her arms, allowing him to pull the dress over her head. It flew in a white arc to the floor near a stack of blank canvases propped against the wall. Then the darkening heat of his gaze claimed her as it swept down her body.

"You're beautiful." His voice shook, thrilling her anew.

Kitty spread her hands over his naked chest, the golden glow of the firelight revealing each ripple of muscle. "So are you," she murmured.

In a mirror of the past, her hands moved to unfasten his pants while his fingers deftly unhooked her bra. Both items ended up in a pile on the floor, forgotten as his hands moved onto her breasts, feeling them swell to fill them. Then his hands slid lower to the elastic waist of her pantyhose, leaving his lips to make a more intimate exploration of the peaky nipples he had aroused.

With almost agonizing slowness, he worked her pantyhose down her stomach and hips to her thighs, then lower still to her knees and calves. His mouth followed every inch of the way until Kitty was a quivering mass of need.

First one foot slipped free from the sheer hose, then the other. Without invitation, Kitty sank to the floor, her arms reaching to gather him against her and assuage this physical ache.

They twisted together in a tangle of arms and legs and hot, greedy kisses. She cried with exquisite relief when he finally filled her. After that it was all glorious pleasure as they made love to each other, for each other, and with each other.

All loose and liquid limbed, she lay in his arms, tiny aftershocks still trembling through her, her breathing slowly returning to normal. This feeling of utter completeness was one she had forgotten somehow.

"You are still incredibly beautiful." Sebastian gently tucked a wayward strand of hair behind her ear.

She made a small sound of acknowledgment, then admitted, "I know I feel beautifully exhausted. I don't think I could move if I had to."

"And you don't have to." He folded her deeper into the circle of his arms and rubbed his cheek against the side of her head. "As far as I'm concerned, you're right where you belong."

"That's good to know, because I don't think I can move." She closed her eyes in sublime contentment, without the energy to think past this moment. For now, it was enough.

It was her last conscious thought until a harsh light probed at her closed eyelids. Kitty turned her head away from it and buried her face deeper in a dark, warm corner.

"Sorry, kitten," Sebastian's familiar voice vibrated beside her, thick with sleep. "I don't think that will work. I forgot to pull the shade down when I carried you into bed. That's the problem with this room. The window faces the east. Every morning the sun plows through it and hits you right between the eyes."

"Sun?" Groggily, Kitty lifted her head and peered through slitted eyelids toward the offending light. "You mean—it's morning?" The sun's in-reaching rays struck the stone in her engagement ring and bounced off it in a shower of sparkling colors.

Two separate things hit Kitty at the same time. She was wearing Marcel's ring and she was in bed with Sebastian.

How could she have done such a thing?

As much as she wanted to plead ignorance, Kitty remembered much too clearly that little trip down memory lane she'd taken last night—all except the being-carried-to-bed part. A little voice in her head told her that Sebastian had known all along just where that little stroll would lead.

"You dirty rotten sneak." Kitty scrambled away from him, grabbing at the top sheet to bunch it around her. "You did it an purpose, didn't you?"

"What are you talking about?" Frowning in confusion, Sebastian threw up a hand to block the glare of the sunlight. "I wouldn't have left the shade up on purpose. You know I don't like to get up early. What time is it anyway?"

"Who cares what time it is?" she declared angrily and gave the sheet a hard tug to pull it free from the foot of the bed. "I should never have come here last night," she muttered, mostly to herself. "I should have known you would pull some cheap, rotten stunt like this."

"What the hell are you talking about?"

"Don't give me that innocent look. It may have worked last night, but it won't work now." Kitty fought to wrap the loose folds of the sheet around her.

"Talk about getting up on the wrong side of the bed," Sebastian muttered, eying her with a hopeless shake of his head.

"I shouldn't even be in this bed and you know it. I'm engaged to Marcel. Remember." When she tapped her engagement ring, the sheet slipped.

"I didn't forget." His frown cleared away, its place taken by the beginnings of a smile and a knowing twinkle in his eyes.

"You knew I had argued with him. You knew it and you deliberately took advantage of it," Kitty accused.

"I don't recall hearing any objections." Sebastian's smile widened, as if he found the entire conversation amusing.

"I made plenty of objections. You simply ignored them." Kitty impatiently pushed the hair out of her eyes and looked about the room. "What did you do with my clothes?"

"They're probably still scattered around the studio."

"You loved saying that, didn't you?" The little smirk on his face was almost enough to make her want to walk over there and slap it off him. But Kitty wasn't about to get within ten feet of him again.

Intent on retrieving her clothes and getting out of there, Kitty set off toward the studio's main section.

Within two strides, she stepped on a trailing corner of the sheet and had to grab hold of the foot post to keep from falling face first on the floor.

"That robe I borrowed from you is hanging in the closet. It might be safer to put that on to get your clothes," Sebastian suggested dryly. "Otherwise you're going to break your nose, and it's much too pretty."

"Never you mind about my nose." Just the same, Kitty wadded up the length of sheet and stalked over to the closet.

After a first glance failed to locate the robe among his other clothes, Sebastian called from across the room, "It's on the hook behind the door."

Sure enough, that's where it was. Kitty snatched it off the hook, slipped her arms through the sleeves, and let the sheet fall to the floor, then stepped free of its surrounding pile. Hastily tying the ends of the terry-cloth sash around her waist, she turned back toward the door. To her irritation, Sebastian was out of bed and zipping up a pair of paint-spattered work chinos.

"I don't suppose I can talk you into putting on some coffee," he said with that infuriating smile still in place.

"Good guess," Kitty snapped, and crossed to the door with quick, angry strides.

Sebastian trailed after her at a much less hurried pace, then split away to head to the galley kitchen while Kitty began to search for her clothes. Ignoring the sounds coming from the kitchen, she retrieved her dress from the rack of blank canvases. She found her hose draped over the handle of the fireplace poker. Her shawl was still lying across the back of the sofa. After locating the obvious articles, the search began in earnest.

Sebastian wandered over to watch. "Want some juice?"

"No." Finding nothing more on top of the room's few pieces of furniture, Kitty got down on her hands and knees to look under them.

"The coffee should be done in a couple of minutes. Want me to pour you a cup?"

"No." She wanted to find her clothes and leave, but she wasn't about to ask for Sebastian's help in the search.

"Are you sure? It might improve your disposition."

"If you fell off the face of the earth, that would

improve my disposition." Spying something under the sofa, Kitty reached a hand beneath it and pulled out her nude silk panties. She tucked them in with the wadded-up dress and hose bundled in her arm.

"My, we are in a foul mood this morning."

"I wonder whose fault that is," Kitty grumbled.

"Considering that you and I are the only ones here, it must be one of us."

"I'll give you another clue," Kitty retorted. "It isn't me."

"That narrows the field considerably, doesn't it?" Sebastian replied with a smile as the aroma of freshly brewed coffee drifted from the kitchen.

"Considerably." It was awkward crawling around on the floor while holding her clothes, but Kitty wasn't about to put them down anywhere. Knowing Sebastian, she was convinced he'd probably steal them and hold them hostage. "Where is my bra?" she demanded in frustration. "I can't find it."

"It's bound to be lying around here somewhere."

"That's a lot of help." She clambered to her feet to scan the area again.

"Smells like the coffee's done. Are you sure you wouldn't like a cup?"

"Positive." Kitty circled the area again, checking behind canvases and under sofa pillows.

"Would you like some hot chocolate instead? I'll be happy to fix you a cup," Sebastian offered.

"Not on your life," she flashed. "If it wasn't for you and your hot chocolate, I wouldn't still be here this morning!"

"At least it's not my fault anymore."

"It's all your fault." Kitty looked around his work

area, first high, then low. "I should have known I couldn't trust you."

"Of course you can."

Incensed that he had the gall to make such a claim, Kitty spun around to glare at him, the missing brassiere temporarily forgotten. "No, I can't. I came to you last night as a friend. You knew I was upset over my argument with Marcel. You took advantage of me."

"If there's one person in this world least likely to be taken advantage of, it's you," Sebastian observed dryly and raised his coffee cup to take a sip from it.

"That isn't true." Pushed by the need to confront him, she crossed to the small kitchen area. "You caught me at a weak moment, when I was upset and confused. Did you try to comfort me? No, you fed me hot chocolate, spun tales about it being an aphrodisiac, kissed my neck, and lured me down memory lane."

"Sins, every one of them." He lowered his head in mock contrition, giving it a shake. "I should be ashamed of myself."

"Would you stop making a joke out of everything?" Kitty protested, furious with him. "I am trying to be serious."

"That's ninety percent of your problem, kitten. You're too serious."

"And you treat everything lightly."

"Not everything."

"Ha!" Kitty scoffed. "You don't even take your work seriously. If I hadn't come along, you'd still be selling your paintings on a street corner. You said so yourself."

"True. But that doesn't mean I'm not serious

about my painting, because I am. It's just a question of ambition. And, heaven knows, you have enough of that for both of us."

"Is there anything wrong with that?" she challenged.

"Only when it gets in the way of life and living."

"And my work doesn't," Kitty asserted. "For your information, I have a life. The proof of that is right here on my finger." She shifted the bundle of clothes to her opposite arm and displayed her engagement ring. "If I were all work and no play the way you try to make me sound, I wouldn't have had any free time to date Marcel, let alone become engaged to him."

"We're back to Mr. Chocolate, are we?"

"We've never left him."

"I beg to differ," Sebastian said. "As I recall, you did last night before you showed up at my door."

"I didn't leave him. We were arguing, and I simply walked out before I lost my temper and said something that I would regret."

"So you came here and unleashed it on me." His lazy smile revealed just how little he had been affected by it.

"You deserved it after the trouble you caused," Kitty muttered, controlling her temper with the greatest of difficulty.

"I caused it?" Sebastian drew his head back in mock innocence. "Why are you blaming me? You're the one who argued with him."

"We went over all that last night," she reminded him. "You're not going to bait me into going over it again."

"Too bad." His mouth twisted in a smile of

feigned regret. "Considering the way our conversation last night ended, it could have been a wonderful way to start the day."

Furious beyond words, Kitty growled a sound of absolute exasperation and spun away to resume her search for the missing brassiere. Before she could take a step, the doorbell chimed.

Its ring was like an alarm bell going off. Gripped by a sudden sense of panic, Kitty froze in her tracks.

Chapter Five

"Who in the world could that be?" Sebastian frowned and started toward the door.

"Wait." Kitty grabbed his arm to stop him. "What time is it?"

"I don't know."

She glanced frantically around the studio. "Don't you have a clock somewhere?" She glanced at the sunlight streaming through the French doors, but she had no idea how to tell the time of the day from the angle of the sun.

"You know how I hate them," Sebastian chided. "Why? What difference does it make?"

"Because if it's past eight-thirty, it could be Harve wondering why I haven't shown up to open the gallery this morning. If it's him, don't let him in, whatever you do." Kitty briefly toyed with the idea of making a dash for the bedroom, but if Harve happened to look in the front window, he would see her.

"Why not? He's found you here before," Sebastian reminded her.

"Not in the morning," Kitty hissed as she backed deeper into the galley kitchen, aware that its area couldn't be seen from the doorway. "And certainly not with me in a robe. You know exactly what he'll surmise from that."

"It would be true, wouldn't it?" Sebastian countered, smiling at her predicament.

"That's none of his business," she whispered angrily as the doorbell chimed again, then repeated its summons insistently. "Go. Get rid of him."

When Sebastian moved to the door, Kitty shrank into a corner, trying to make herself as small as possible. Silently she scolded herself for taking the time to gather up her clothes; she should have left Sebastian's studio the minute she got up.

The snap of the dead bolt was followed by the click of the door latch. But it wasn't Harve's voice that Kitty heard next.

"Monsieur Cole." It was Marcel who spoke, and her heart jumped into her throat and lodged there. "I am concerned for Kitty."

"Kitty?" Sebastian repeated, and she knew he was positively gloating inside.

"Is it possible that you would know whether she arrived safely home last night?" Marcel inquired.

"Had an argument with her, did you?" Sebastian asked instead. "Not over anything important, I hope."

"Mere trifling matters."

Trifling? His outrageous choice of adjective was almost enough to make Kitty charge to the door and confront Marcel. Only the thought that Sebastian would get way too much enjoyment out of such a scene prevented her from doing just that.

"Walked out on you, did she?" Sebastian said, as if he already didn't know that.

"Have you seen Kitty?" There was a note of suspicion in Marcel's question, enough to heighten the sense of panic Kitty felt.

"Isn't she at home?" Sebastian countered.

"She did not answer the door."

"What time is it? Maybe she's already left to open the gallery," Sebastian suggested.

"Not at this hour, surely," Marcel protested. "It is only half past seven o'clock."

"That early? I—"

"What is this?" Marcel demanded suddenly.

To her horror, Kitty saw Sebastian being forced to back up and open the door wider. A clear indication that Marcel had stepped inside. She flattened herself against the corner, her heart pounding like a mad thing.

"This is Kitty's shoe." Marcel's announcement bordered on an accusation, and Kitty realized that Marcel had noticed the pumps Sebastian had set on the catchall table by the door.

"Does she have a pair of heels like these?" Sebastian asked, again deftly avoiding both a confirmation and a bold-faced lie.

That's when Kitty spotted her missing bra. It dangled from the back of the sofa, a strap precariously hooked over the rounded corner of its back. It was clearly within plain sight of the door. Marcel was bound to see it; it was only a matter of when.

For now the open door blocked her from view. But if Marcel stepped past it, she could easily be seen. Kitty glanced frantically around, searching for a better hiding place. Her widely swinging gaze screeched to a stop on the French doors that opened onto the back courtyard.

Did she dare try to reach them? There was only the smallest chance she could escape detection if she remained where she was. But if she could manage to slip outside, unseen, she was home free.

"There is a lady's brassiere hanging off your sofa," Marcel declared in a tone of voice that insisted on explanation.

With fingers figuratively crossed that Marcel would be sufficiently distracted by the sight of the lacy undergarment not to notice her, Kitty tiptoed as quickly and quietly as she could across the Saltillo-tiled floor to the French doors.

"So it is," Sebastian confirmed from the front door area as Kitty fumbled ever so briefly with the dead bolt lock. The latch made the smallest *snicking* sound, but Sebastian's voice covered it. "I had company last night. She must have forgotten to take it with her."

Not a single hinge creaked to give Kitty away. She opened the French door no farther than necessary and slipped outside. Immediately she darted to the left, not bothering to close the door behind her.

Any second she expected to hear a cry of discovery from Marcel. But none came. The minute she reached the security of the exterior adobe wall, Kitty halted to lean against it and drink in a shaky gulp of air.

Now, if she could just make it to the house without being seen.

But she soon realized that was impossible. There was a taxicab sitting in the driveway. Any approach to the house would be seen either by the driver or Marcel.

She debated her next move. She could remain where she was until Marcel left, or— Kitty froze, stricken by the realization that waiting for Marcel to leave wasn't a viable option. Her evening bag was on the coffee table. Sebastian might be able to convince Marcel that two women could have the same pair of shoes. But an evening bag, too? That would be too much of a coincidence.

If Marcel noticed the evening bag, Kitty was certain he would take a closer look. When he did, he would find her driver's license and a credit card inside, along with the usual lipstick, compact, and mascara. Her escape from the studio would have been for nothing.

Kitty knew she had to do something before Marcel discovered she had been in the studio last night. She knew of only one way to accomplish that.

Hastily, she stashed her bundle of clothes under an ancient lilac bush that grew next to the corner of the building. She peeked around its branches to make sure Marcel hadn't stepped back outside. But all was clear. After double-checking the sash's knot, Kitty took a deep, galvanizing breath and dashed from behind the bush toward the studio door, choosing an angle that might convince Marcel she had come from the house.

Marcel stood just inside the doorway. Kitty had a glimpse of Sebastian's bare chest just beyond him, his body positioned in such a way to prevent Marcel from gaining further entrance to the studio.

"Marcel." She didn't have to fake the breathlessness in her cry.

He swung around with a start, a look of utter relief lighting his whole face. "Kitty!"

His arms opened to greet her. She was swept into them just outside the door. Automatically Kitty wrapped her own arms around him while he pressed kisses against her hair and murmured little endearments in French.

A guilty conscience kept her from responding to his embrace—that and the sight of Sebastian leaning a naked shoulder against the doorjamb, an amused smile edging the corners of his mouth.

"Kitty, Kitty, Kitty," Marcel murmured in a mixture of relief and joy as he drew back and framed her face in his hands. "You are all right, *non?*" He ran his gaze over her face in rapid assessment. "I had fear that you came to harm."

"I'm fine," she assured him.

"Where have you been?" The look of worry reentered his aquiline features.

"I . . . I just woke up." Kitty stalled, trying to gain enough time to come up with an explanation that might satisfy him.

With a frown, Marcel glanced past her toward the house, then brought his probing gaze back to hers. "But I rang the bell to your door many, many times, and you did not answer it."

"I should have warned you," Sebastian inserted. "Kitty sleeps very soundly. A bomb would have to go off outside her window before she'd wake up. Even then, I'm not sure she would."

There was some truth in that, but not enough for Kitty to feel comfortable fielding more questions from Marcel. The certainty of that came with his next query.

"Why did you not answer the telephone? I rang you a hundred times after you left the restaurant."

"I wasn't ready to talk to you last night." Which was the truth as far as it went. Attempting to take the offensive Kitty asked, "What are you doing here?"

"When you did not answer the door, I had worry that you suffered a mishap and did not arrive home last night. I came here to speak with Monsieur Cole in the event he was aware of your return."

Sebastian spoke up, "I was just suggesting that he might check with the hospitals or contact the police to see whether you might have been involved in some accident on your way home."

"I see," Kitty murmured hesitantly, then explained, "Actually I was wondering what you were doing here because you had told me that you were flying back to Brussels early this morning."

"Ah." Marcel nodded in new understanding. "I postponed my departure. I could not leave when I was so concerned for your well-being."

"I'm glad you didn't leave today." At least Kitty knew she should be glad. But she felt so much nervous turmoil inside that she had trouble identifying any other emotion.

"We have much that we must discuss," Marcel began.

"Indeed we do," Kitty rushed, and darted a lightning glance at Sebastian, who was unabashedly eavesdropping. "But not here." She tucked a hand under his arm. "Let's go to the house. I'll put some coffee on and we can talk."

Before she could lead Marcel away, Sebastian inquired lazily, "Did you bring your key with you?"

"My key?" She gave him a blank look.

Sebastian nodded toward the house. "I can see from here that the door is closed. It locks automatically when you shut it. Remember?"

That's when it hit her that, as always, she had locked the house when she left with Marcel last night. Without a key, she couldn't get back in. And her key ring was in her evening bag—on Sebastian's coffee table.

Thinking fast, Kitty said, "Do you still have that spare key I left with you?"

"Yes—"

"I'll get it." She pressed a detaining hand on Marcel's arm. "Wait here." She moved quickly toward the door, anxious that he wouldn't follow her inside.

"Do you remember where it is?" Sebastian shifted to the side, giving her room to pass.

"As long as you haven't moved it someplace else."

"I haven't."

"Good."

Kitty slipped inside and hurried straight to the coffee table, resisting the impulse to snatch her bra off the corner of the sofa.

Her evening bag lay exactly where she'd left it. She opened it, took out the ring of keys, and snapped it shut. With her fingers wrapped around the keys to silence their jingle, Kitty rushed back outside, straight to Marcel.

"All set," she declared with false brightness. Her smile faltered when she observed the hint of sternness in his expression. "Is something wrong?" she asked, worried that he had somehow seen through her charade.

"You do not wear slippers." His glance cut to her bare feet.

Kitty almost laughed aloud with relief, but a response such as that would have been inappropriate. "I was in such a hurry I guess I forgot to put any on. Shall we?" As subtly as possible, she urged him toward the house.

Marcel stood his ground a moment longer and nodded to Sebastian. "I regret that I troubled you needlessly."

"Oh, it was no trouble," Sebastian assured him, then let his glance slide pointedly to Kitty. "In fact, it was all pleasure."

Inwardly she did a slow burn over Sebastian's parting shot as she ushered Marcel across the courtyard to her home's rear entrance. When she stepped forward to unlock the door, Marcel took the keys from her.

"Allow me," he said with typical courtesy, then inserted the key and unlocked the door, giving it a slight inward push.

He stepped back, motioning for Kitty to precede him into the house. She had barely set foot inside when he asked, "Why does this artist have a key to your house?"

"Someone had to let the maid in to clean when I vacationed in Cancun this past winter. Since Sebastian lives on the grounds, he was an obvious choice."

Actually that was true; Kitty had left a spare house key with him on that occasion, but she'd also gotten it back when she returned from the trip. But it was another one of those half-truths that pricked her conscience.

"That is another thing I wish to discuss with you," Marcel stated.

At that instant, Kitty knew she was much too tense, and the feeling of dancing around eggshells was much too strong for her to talk to Marcel right now. She needed a respite from it, however brief.

"There is much we need to discuss," she told him. "But it can wait a few more minutes. I'm such a mess." She pushed a smoothing hand over her loose hair in emphasis. "I'd really like to freshen up and slip into some clothes first. I won't be long."

Giving Marcel no opportunity to object, Kitty hurried from the kitchen. The instant she reached the safety of her bedroom, she leaned against the closed door, tipped her head back to stare at the high-beamed ceiling and took a deep, calming breath.

A part of her wished she could stay in the room and never come out, but the rational side knew that was impossible. Pushing away from the door, she headed to the closet. Aware that dallying over a choice of clothes would accomplish little, Kitty quickly selected a pair of hunter green slacks and a cotton sweater in a coordinating apple green.

In five minutes flat, she walked out of the bedroom, fully clothed, a minimum of makeup applied and her long hair pulled back in its usual sleek bun. She decided there was some truth in the old saying that a woman's clothes were her armor. She certainly had more confidence in her ability to handle things.

Marcel had not ventured from the kitchen. He stood by the French doors in the small breakfast nook, staring in the direction of the studio. His hands were buried deep in the pockets of his trousers, his jacket pushed aside, and a heavy frown darkened his expression.

"I told you I wouldn't be long," Kitty said by way of an announcement of her return.

He dragged his gaze away from the view with a trace of reluctance that had little frissons of alarm shooting through Kitty. Had he seen something? For the life of her, she couldn't think what it might be.

Kitty hurried into her carefully rehearsed speech. "Before anything else is said, I want to apologize, Marcel, for walking out on you like that last night. It was—"

He didn't give her a chance to finish it. "It would be best for you to inform Monsieur Cole that he must move somewhere else."

Dumbfounded, Kitty stared. "I beg your pardon."

"I said, it—"

This time she cut him off. "I heard what you said." She simply couldn't believe that he'd actually said it. "But I'm afraid that what you suggest is impossible. According to the terms of our divorce settlement, I got the house and Sebastian received the studio. I can't order him to move out. I have no right."

"Then we must find a different place for you to live until we are married," Marcel stated.

He suspected something about last night. Kitty was certain of it. Some of the inner panic started to return.

"Whatever for?" She forced a smile of confusion. "This arrangement has worked for years. Sebastian lives there and I live here."

"But it is not right that you should live so closely to him."

Worried that she was back on shaky ground, Kitty attempted an amused protest. "Surely you aren't jealous of him, Marcel."

"*Mais non.*" His denial was quick and smooth, completely without question, which in itself was a bit deflating. "I simply do not wish my fiancée to associate so closely with his kind."

"His kind?" Kitty seized on the phrase, then challenged, "Exactly what do you mean by that?"

He gave her a look of mild exasperation. "It is known to all, Kitty, that such people are self-absorbed and self-indulgent, which leads them to loose ways of living."

Outraged by his blanket condemnation of an entire profession, she said furiously, "That is the most ignorant statement I have ever heard. For every artist you can show me who's into drugs and alcohol and wild parties, I can show you fifty who are honest and caring, hardworking people with families to support and a mortgage to pay."

Turning haughty, Marcel declared, "Please do not attempt to convince me that Monsieur Cole is one of these. Last night he entertained a woman in his studio. I saw with my own eyes this morning the articles of her lingerie flung about the room in wild abandon."

That nagging sense of guilt resurfaced to steal some of the heat from her indignation.

"His private life is no concern of mine," Kitty insisted in a show of indifference.

"But your life is a concern of mine, now that we are to be married. And I should think it would be a concern to you. This is what I attempted to explain to you last night, when you objected so strongly to selling your gallery. But you refused to listen to me."

"Try again," Kitty stated, her anger cooling, dropping to an icy level.

"It is quite simple, really," he began with a trace of impatience. "Even you must see that running a gallery of necessity brings you in frequent contact with such people. It would not be acceptable to continue such associations after we are married."

Kitty cocked her head to one side. "Acceptable to whom? You? Your friends? Your family?"

Sensing the hint of disdain in her words, Marcel drew himself up to his full height. "Is it wrong to value the good reputation of the Boulanger name?"

"That is the most supercilious question I have ever heard," Kitty snapped.

But before she could denounce him for being the snob that he was, the doorbell rang. For the first time in as many days, she sincerely hoped it was Sebastian. Right now, nothing would delight her more than to inform Marcel that she was the abandoned woman who had spent the night with Sebastian.

A smile of anticipated pleasure was on her lips when she opened the back door. To her eternal disappointment, the cabdriver stood outside, a heavyset man of Mexican descent.

"Por favor." He swept off his billed cap and held it in front of his barrel-round stomach. "Does the senor still wish for me to wait for him?"

"That won't be necessary. He's ready to go." Leaving the door open wide, Kitty turned back to

Marcel. "It's your taxi driver. I informed him that you'll be leaving now."

His jaw dropped. Kitty found his initial loss for words quite satisfying.

Recovering, Marcel managed to sputter, "But . . . We have still to talk."

"As far as I'm concerned, everything's been said." Kitty walked over to usher him to the door. "And you have a plane to catch. Here"—she paused to tug the diamond off her finger—"take this with you."

When she offered it to him, Marcel simply stared at her in shock. She had to actually open his hand and press the ring into his palm.

Even then he didn't appear to believe her. "You return my ring? I do not understand."

"That doesn't surprise me in the least."

"But—"

Kitty could see him frantically searching for words. "It must be obvious that I wouldn't make a suitable wife for you. And the thought of marrying a bigoted snob like you makes me sick."

In an indignant huff, he opened his mouth to object. Kitty didn't give him a chance to speak as she bodily pushed him out the door.

"Good-bye, Mr. Chocolate. Knowing you has been very enlightening and bittersweet," she added, unable to resist the analogy. "More bitter than sweet, actually, rather like your chocolate."

Marcel reacted instantly to that criticism. "Boulanger chocolate is of the finest quality."

"It's a pity the same can't be said about the family who makes it."

Across the courtyard, Kitty noticed that Sebastian was now standing outside the opened French doors to the kitchen area. As before, he was dressed in his work chinos, a cup of coffee in his hand, still without shirt or shoes.

"As much as I would enjoy trading insults with you, I really need to excuse myself." Her smile was all saccharin. "You see, I left some things at Sebastian's last night that I really need to pick up."

"Last night?" As understanding dawned, Marcel's expression turned thunderous.

"Yes, last night," Kitty repeated happily, then taunted, "I hope you don't expect me to draw you a picture. Sebastian's the artist, not me."

With that, she walked away from him, this time for good and without a single regret.

Chapter Six

The courtyard echoed with the sound of Marcel's hard-striding footsteps as he stalked to the idling taxi trailed by the slower-walking cabdriver. It was a sound that Kitty rather liked, and one that was punctuated by the creak of hinges and the metallic slam of the vehicle door.

Without so much as a backward glance, she walked directly to the gnarled lilac bush that towered by the corner of the studio. She was conscious of Sebastian watching her while she retrieved the bundle of clothes from beneath its lower branches.

"Mr. Chocolate didn't stay long," Sebastian observed when she emerged from behind the bush.

"There was no reason for him to stay." Kitty brushed a leaf off her shoulder.

"I see he took his ring with him." He used the coffee mug to gesture to her bare ring finger.

"I insisted on it," she replied, then added quickly, "But don't start thinking you had anything to do with that decision. Because you didn't. There were simply too many important issues that Marcel and I couldn't agree on." Out in the street, the taxi backfired and rumbled away. Staring after it, Kitty couldn't resist adding a parting shot, one laced with thinly veiled sarcasm. "And I wasn't about to change just to be worthy of being his wife."

"I'm not trying to start another fight by saying this," Sebastian remarked, "but he is the one who wasn't worthy of you."

Everything softened inside her at the unexpected compliment. Kitty flashed him a warm smile. "Thank you."

"For what? It's the truth."

"I know, but it's still nice to hear someone else say it."

"Even me?" Sebastian teased.

"Even you," Kitty replied, then paused thoughtfully. "You know something else? I really didn't like his chocolate all that well, either."

"I can guarantee it couldn't be as good as my hot chocolate."

She eyed him with irritation. "I should have known you wouldn't be able to resist making a reference of some sort to last night. Let's just forget about it, shall we? As far as I'm concerned, it was all a big mistake."

"I think you're a little mixed up. Getting engaged to Mr. Chocolate was the mistake."

"That was a mistake, all right. And I'm not going to compound it by getting baited into a long, fruitless discussion with you. So if you don't mind"— Kitty moved toward the open door—"I'll just get my things and leave."

"Help yourself." With a swing of the cup, Sebastian invited her inside the studio.

As she approached the French doors, she felt a sudden nervous fluttering in her stomach. Kitty hesitated briefly before crossing the threshold. When she stepped into the studio's kitchen area, her heart began to beat a little faster. She felt exactly like a criminal returning to the scene of the crime, as all her senses heightened.

Without looking, Kitty knew the minute Sebastian followed her inside, even though his bare feet made no sound at all on the tiled floor. His presence made the spacious studio seem much smaller and more intimate. Or maybe it was the sight of her silk and lace brassiere still hooked on a back corner of the sofa, combined with her own vivid recollections of last night's events.

"Would you like a cup of coffee?" Sebastian's question was accompanied by the faint sound of the glass coffee carafe scraping across its flat burner, an indication that he was refilling his own cup.

"No, thank you." Kitty snatched the bra off the sofa corner and stuffed it in with her other bundled garments.

"Are you sure? It's—"

"I'm positive." As she circled the sofa to the coffee table, Kitty was careful not to glance in the direction of the kiva and the Navajo-style rug on the floor in front of it.

"Suit yourself," Sebastian said with a shrug in his voice. "Do you know something that amazes me?"

"No, but I'm sure that you're going to tell me." Kitty was deliberately curt, inwardly aware it was a defense mechanism. It bothered her that she felt a need for it.

"It's the way you run straight here every time you break off a relationship with some guy."

"That's ridiculous." She scooped up her evening bag, the last of the items she'd left.

"Is it?" Sebastian countered. "Look at this morning. You barely gave Mr. Chocolate a chance to climb in his cab before you made a beeline over here."

"I'm here to collect my things. There's nothing strange about that," Kitty insisted, and automatically glanced around, double-checking to make certain nothing else of hers was lying about.

"What about all the other times?" he persisted.

"Actually, I've never given it any thought. And there haven't been that many 'other times,' " Kitty retorted.

"But why come here? An ex is usually the last person you would want to tell."

"We are far from being enemies, Sebastian." She threw him a look of mild exasperation.

"But we aren't exactly friends, either," he pointed out. "There's always a subtle tension running between us. Why do you suppose that is?"

"I have no idea." It wasn't something Kitty wanted to discuss, and certainly not now. She moved toward the open French door, eager to leave now that she had retrieved all her things.

Sebastian stood by the kitchen counter, one hip propped against it. "Did you tell Mr. Chocolate you were with me last night?"

"It's really none of your business whether I told him or not."

Kitty wished that she had left by the front door.

It would have been a much shorter route, and one that wouldn't have taken her past Sebastian. But she was committed to her path. If she changed directions now, Sebastian might suspect her reluctance to be anywhere close to him.

"I'm afraid it is my business," he informed her with a hint of a smile. "You know how these Europeans can be. He might decide to challenge me to a duel, and I'd like to know whether or not I should admit you were here."

"He knows. Okay?" she retorted with impatience, quickening her steps to reach the door.

"I'll bet that made him mad." Sebastian didn't move an inch as she swept past him.

"He was furious. Does that make you happy?" She threw the last over her shoulder, then opened the door, safety only two feet away.

"You're a lot more trusting than I thought you would be."

His odd statement brought her up short. On the edge of the threshold, Kitty swung back, curious but wary. "What do you mean by that?"

"I thought for sure you'd check your evening bag and make sure I didn't take anything before you left." He continued to stand there, idly leaning against the counter.

"What would you take? There's nothing in it of any value except a credit card. Why would you want that?" As illogical as it seemed, Kitty knew Sebastian had taken something. Otherwise he wouldn't be drawing her attention to it now.

"I never said I took anything."

But that knowing gleam in his eye advised that she had better look. Kitty stepped over to the small breakfast table, deposited her wadded clothing on top of it, and unhooked the clasp on the slim bag. A quick check of the contents revealed nothing was missing. But there was something sparkling at the very bottom. She reached inside and pulled out a small solitaire ring—at least, it was small compared to the multicarat engagement ring Marcel had given her.

"Find something?" Sebastian wandered over to look.

Dumbfounded, Kitty dragged her gaze from the ring to his face. Staring in confusion, she murmured, "It's . . . It's my old ring. The one you gave me."

"So it is." He nodded in a fake show of confirmation, then met her eyes, a smile tugging at one corner of his mouth. "As I recall, you had a suggestion for what I could do with it when you gave it back to me. But I thought better of it."

"But what's it doing in my bag? Why did you put it there?" That was the part she didn't understand.

"It's very simple, really." He took the ring from her unresisting fingers, then reached for her left hand. "You seem to be determined to have some man's ring on your finger. I decided it might as well be mine."

As he started to slip the ring on her finger, Kitty jerked her hand away, pain slashing through her like a knife, bringing hot tears to her eyes.

"Everything's just one big joke to you," she lashed out angrily. "I'm sure you think this is funny. But it isn't. It's cruel and heartless and mean."

"This isn't a joke," Sebastian replied. "I'm dead serious."

"And pigs fly, too," Kitty retorted, resisting when

he attempted to draw her hand from behind her back.

"I don't know about pigs. I only know about you and me," he continued in that irritatingly reasonable tone. "Since you seem so eager to marry somebody, it might as well be me again."

"That's ridiculous," she said, her voice choking up. She tried to convince herself it was strictly from the depth of her outrage.

"Why is it ridiculous?" Sebastian countered, and pushed the ring onto her finger despite her attempts to stop him. "After all, it's better the devil you know than the Mr. Chocolate you don't."

"Will you stop this, Sebastian! I am not laughing." Kitty tugged at the ring, trying to pull it off. "If this is some twisted attempt to make me feel better about breaking things off with Marcel, it isn't working."

Sebastian trapped her face in his hands and forced her to look him squarely in the eye. "Be quiet for two seconds and listen. I want to marry you again. I don't know how much plainer I can say it."

For the first time Kitty suspected that he really meant it. Suddenly her thoughts were all in a turmoil. "But . . . It wouldn't work." She said it as much to convince herself as him. "We tried it before and—"

"So? We'll try it again." A soft light warmed his eyes and his easy smile was unconcerned.

"You're crazy," Kitty declared, more tempted by the thought than she wanted him to know. "Have you forgotten the way we argued all the time?"

"Not about important things," he replied.

"That isn't true." She was stunned that he could have forgotten their many stormy scenes.

"Think back," Sebastian countered. "Ninety percent of all our arguments were about trivial things—like the proper way a tube of toothpaste should be squeezed. The only time we fought about anything major was when we let our business differences interfere with our marriage."

"Business differences?" Kitty repeated incredulously. "We don't have any business differences."

"Not anymore, now that you've finally stopped trying to promote me and settled for pushing my paintings."

"I never—" But she had. It all came back in a rush. The endless fights over his refusal to attend his own showings or to do any kind of publicity to promote his work. "It used to infuriate me the way you made fun of everything I tried to do to see that you received the recognition you deserved as an artist."

"And you took it personally," Sebastian concluded.

"Yes."

"I'm sorry for that." He pushed back a wayward strand of hair, a loving quality in his touch.

"So am I." Everything smoothed out inside her.

"So what's your answer?"

"My answer?" For a second, Kitty didn't follow him.

"Are you going to marry me or not? After last night, you can't deny the fire's just as hot as it always was."

"I think both of us are crazy," she said instead.

"Why?"

"You for asking and me for accepting."

His mouth moved onto hers even as she rose to meet it. It was a kiss full of promise and passion, a pledge one to the other. For Kitty it was exactly like coming home.

Dear Readers,

Here in Branson, we are busy gearing up for another season. And I have been busy, too, working on another novel. Once in a while a story comes along that grabs you and simply won't let you go. "Story" might not be the right word. In this case, I think I should say "family." Judging from the letters I have received from you, the Calder family has become as special for you as they have for me.

By now, you must have guessed that I have written another Calder novel. This one is called GREEN CALDER GRASS. This time the story centers around Ty and Jessy whose lives become a bit more complicated when Tara returns to Montana. Yup, she's back and causing trouble again. But Tara isn't the only one from previous Calder novels who shows up at the Triple C. I'm not going to tell you who that person is. That's my surprise. As always, GREEN CALDER GRASS is packed with action, romance, danger, and tragedy, too. But the Calder family always survives.

I know you are going to love it. Happy reading,

Janet Dailey

Please turn the page for
a first look at the newest book in the acclaimed
Calder series of contemporary romances
from national best-selling author Janet Dailey

GREEN CALDER GRASS
(A Kensington Books hardcover
available in July 2002)

The grass ocean rippled cold under a strong summer sun. A dirt track cut a straight line through the heart of it. It was a small portion of the mile-upon-mile of private roads that crisscrossed the ranching empire of the Calder Cattle Company, better known in Montana as the Triple C.

It was a land that could be bountiful or brutal, a land that bent to no man's will, a land that weeded out the weak and faint of heart, tolerating only the strong.

No one knew that better than Chase Benteen Calder, the current patriarch of the Triple C and direct descendant of the first Calder, his namesake, who had laid claim to nearly six hundred square miles of this grassland. Its size was never something Chase Calder bragged about; the way he looked at it, when you were the biggest, everybody already knew it, and if they didn't they would soon be told.

And the knowledge would carry more weight wasn't the one doing the telling.

To a few, the enormity of the Triple C was a thing of rancor. The events of recent weeks were proof of that. The freshness of that memory accounted for the hint of grimness in his expression as Chase drove the ranch pickup along the hard-packed road, a rooster tail of dust pluming behind it. But the past wasn't something Chase allowed his mind to dwell on. Running an operation this size required a man's full attention. Even the smallest detail had a way of getting big if ignored. This land and a long life had taught him that, if nothing else.

Which is likely why his sharp eyes spotted the sagging wire caused by a tilting fence post. Chase braked the truck to a stop, but not before the pickup clattered over a metal cattle guard. He shifted into reverse, backed up to the cattle guard, stopped, and switched off the engine.

The full force of the sun's rays beat down on him as Chase stepped out of the truck, older and heavier but still a rugged and powerfully built man.

The sixty-plus years he carried had taken some of the spring from his step, added a heavy dose of gray to his hair, and grooved deeper creases into the sun-leathered skin around his eyes and mouth, giving a crustiness to his face, but it hadn't diminished the mark of authority stamped on his raw-boned features.

Reaching back inside the truck, Chase grabbed a pair of tough leather work gloves off the seat and headed toward the section of the sagging fence six posts away from the road. Never once did it occur to Chase to drive by and send one of the ranch hands back to fix the problem. With distances being what they were on the Triple C, that was the quickest way of turning a fifteen-minute job into a two-hour one.

With each stride he took, the brittle, sun-cured grass crackled underfoot. Its stalks were short and curly, matting close to the ground—native buffalo grass, drought tolerant and highly nutritious, the kind of feed that put weight on cattle and was a mainstay of the Triple C's century of success.

The minute his gloved hands closed around the post in question, it dipped drunkenly under the pressure. The three spaced strands of tightly strung barbed wire were clearly the only thing keeping it upright at all. Chase kicked away the matted grass at the base and saw that the wood had rotted at ground level.

This was one fence repair that wouldn't be a fifteen-minute fix. Chase glanced back toward the pickup parked on the road. There was a time when he would have carried steel fence posts and a roll of wire along with other sundry items piled in the truck bed. But on this occasion, there was only a tool box.

Chase didn't waste time with regret for the lack of a spare post. Instead, he ran an inspecting glance along the rest of the fence, following its steady march over the rolling grassland until it thinned into a single line. In that one, cursory observation, he noticed three more places where the fence curved out of its straight line. If three could be spotted with the naked eye, there were undoubtedly more. It didn't surprise him. Fence-mending was one of those never-ending jobs every rancher faced.

When he turned to retrace his steps to the pickup, he caught the distant drone of another vehicle. Automatically Chase scanned the narrow road in both directions without finding a vehicle in sight. But one was approaching, of that he had no doubt.

It was the huge sweep of sky that gave the illusion of flatness to the land beneath it. In reality the terrain was riven with coulees and shallow hollows, all of them hidden from view with the same ease that an ocean conceals its swales and troughs.

By the time Chase reached his truck, another ranch pickup had roared into view, coming from the west. Chase waited by the cab door, watching as the other vehicle slowed perceptibly then rolled to a stop behind Chase's pickup. The trailing dust cloud swept forward, briefly enveloping both vehicles before settling to a low fog.

Squinting against the sting of dust particles, Chase recognized the short, squatly built man behind the wheel as Stumpy Niles, a contemporary of his and the father of Chase's daughter-in-law. Chase lifted a hand in greeting and headed toward the truck.

Stumpy promptly rolled down the driver's side window and stuck out his head. "What's the problem, Chase?"

"Have you got a spare fence post in your truck? We have a wood one that's rotted through."

"Got it handled." Stumpy scrambled out of the truck and moved toward the tailgate with short, choppy strides. "Can't say I'm surprised. Just about all them old wood posts have started rottin'. It's gonna be one long, endless job replacin' 'em."

And expensive, too, Chase thought to himself, and

pitched in to help the shorter man haul the steel post as well as a posthole jobber out of the truck's rear bed. "I don't see where we have much choice. It's got to be done."

"I know." Already sweating profusely in the hot summer sun, Stumpy paused to drag a hand-kerchief from his pocket and mop the perspiration from his round, red face. "It ain't gonna be an easy job. The ground's as hard as granite. It's been nearly forty years since we've had such a dry spring. I'll bet we didn't get much more than an inch of moisture in all the South Branch section."

"It wasn't much better anywhere else on the ranch." Like Stumpy, Chase was remembering the last prolonged dry spell the ranch had endured.

Stumpy was one of the cadre of ranch hands who, like Chase, had been born on the Triple C. All were descended from cowhands who had trailed that original herd of longhorn cattle north, then stayed on to work for the first Calder. That kind of deep-seated loyalty was a throwback to the old days when a cowboy rode for the brand, right or wrong, through times of plenty and times of lean. To an outsider, this born-and-bred core of riders gave an almost feudal quality to the Triple C.

Chase shortened his stride to walk alongside Stumpy as the pair tracked through the grass to the sagging post. "Headed for The Homestead, were you?" Stumpy guessed, referring to the tower-ing, two-story structure that was the Calder family home, erected on the site of the ranch's original homestead.

Chase nodded in confirmation. "But only long enough to clean up before I head into Blue Moon.

I'm supposed to meet Ty and Jessy for supp[...]
soon as they're through at the clinic.''

"The clinic." Stumpy stopped short. "Jessy's all
right, isn't she?''

"She's fine." Smiling, Chase understood Stumpy's
fatherly concern. "Ty was the one in for a
checkup."

Stumpy shook his head at himself and continued
toward the rotted post. "It's them twins she's fixin'
to have. It's got me as nervous as a long-tailed cat
in a roomful of rockin' chairs. There's no history
of twins bein' born in either side of our family.
Or, at least none that Judy and me know about,"
he said, referring to his wife.

"It's a first for the Calder side, too." Chase
looked on while Stumpy set about digging a hole
with the jobber. "Although I can't speak for the
O'Rourke half."

The comment was an oblique reference to his
late wife Maggie O'Rourke. Even now, so many
years after her death, he rarely mentioned her by
name and only among the family. This belief that
grief was a private thing was one of many codes of
the Old West that continued to hold sway in the
modern West, especially in Triple C country.

"Twins," Stumpy murmured to himself, then
grunted from the impact of the twin blades stab-
bing into the hard, dry ground. He scissored the
handles together to pick up the first scoopful of
soil, then reversed the procedure to dump it to
one side. "Look at that," he complained. "The
top two inches is nothin' but powder. It's dry, I
tell you. Dry." It was a simple observation that
was quickly forgotten as he reverted to his original

topic. "According to that ultrasound thing the doctor did, it's gonna be boys."

That was news to Chase. "I understood the doctor was only positive about one."

"Mark my words, they'll be boys," Stumpy declared with certainty, then chuckled. "If they take after their mother, she's gonna have her hands full. They'll be a pair of hell-raisers, I'll wager—into everything the minute you turn your back. Why, from the first minute Jessy started crawlin', she was out the door and into the horse pens. She dealt her momma fits. If you ask me, it's only right that she gets back some of her own." He glanced at Chase and winked. "It's for sure you won't be complaining anymore about The Homestead bein' too quiet since Cat got married and moved out. By the way, how's the little man doin' since . . . things quieted down."

The thwarted kidnapping of his five-year-old grandson Quint was another topic to be avoided from now on. But Chase knew it had left him three times as wary of those outside the Calder circle. After all, not only had the security of his home been breached, but Calder blood had been spilled as well.

"Kids are pretty resilient. Quint's doing fine."

"Glad to hear it."

"With any luck, Ty will finally be able to throw away that sling today and start using his arm again."

The twin spades of the jobber *whacked* into the hole. Stumpy rotated the handles back and forth to carve out another chunk of hard soil. After it was removed, Stumpy took a look and decreed, "That should be deep enough." He laid the jobber aside and took the steel fence post from Chase. "I thought the doctors originally told him he'd have to have that arm in a sling for six weeks. That bullet he took totally shattered his shoulder. Them surgeons had to rebuild the joint from scratch."

"True, but Ty figures four weeks is long enough. We'll see if he manages to convince the doctor of that."

Stumpy grinned. "He's probably hopin' he'll persuade the doc to split the difference and let him take it off in another week."

"Probably."

"That reminds me." Stumpy paused in his seedling of the post. "I ran into Amy Trumbo at noon. She tells me that O'Rourke's bein' released from the hospital today. Is that true?"

"Yeah, Cat went to get him. She should have him home before dark."

Chase remembered much too vividly that moment when he realized one of the kidnappers had shot his son. He saw again, in his mind, the brilliant red of all that blood, the desperate struggle to stop the bleeding and the gut-tearing mixture of rage and fear he'd felt.

His son Ty hadn't been the only one to suffer at the hands of the kidnapping duo; Culley O'Rourke, his late wife's brother, had also been shot—in his case, multiple times.

Stumpy wagged his head in amazement. "I still don't know how in hell O'Rourke survived."

"He's got more lives than a barn cat." Chase couldn't honestly say whether he was happy about it or not. There had never been any love lost between the two men. At the same time, he knew that O'Rourke lived only for Cat, Chase's daughter and O'Rourke's niece. Maybe it was Cat's uncanny resemblance to Maggie. And maybe it was just plain love. Whatever the case, O'Rourke was devoted to her. And like it or not, Chase had O'Rourke to thank for his part in getting young Quint back, unharmed.

"I guess O'Rourke'll be staying at the Circle Six with Cat and Logan." Stumpy scooped dirt into the hole around the post with his boot and tamped it down.

"That's Cat's plan anyhow. But you know what a lone wolf O'Rourke is," Chase said. "My guess is that it'll only be a matter of days before he's back on the Shamrock."

"Is he strong enough to look after himself?"

"Probably not, but that means Cat will burn up the road, running between Circle Six and Shamrock, making sure he's all right and has plenty of food on hand." Noting that Stumpy had the job well in hand, Chase took his leave. "I'd better get moving before Ty and Jessy wonder what happened to me."

As he took a step away, Stumpy called him back. "Say, I've been meanin' to tell you, Chase. Do you remember that young bull Ty sold to Parker from Wyoming last year? The one he wanted for his kid's 4-H project?"

"What about it?"

"He walked away with the grand championship at the Denver stock show."

"Where'd you hear that?" Chase frowned.

"From Ballard. He hit the southern show circuit this past winter, hirin' out to ride in cuttin' horse competitions and doin' some jackpot ropin' on the side. That's how he happened to be in Denver. He saw a good-lookin' bull with the Triple C tag and started askin' questions." Stumpy's grin widened. "It was grand champion, imagine that. And that bull was one of our culls—a good'n, but not the quality of the ones we kept." With a wave of his hand, he added, "You need to tell Ty about it. As proud as he is of the herd of registered stock we've put together, he'll get a kick out of it."

"I'll tell him," Chase promised.

The high drone of a jet engine whined through the air, invading the stillness of wind and grass. Automatically, Chase lifted his head and scanned the tall sky. Stumpy did the same as Chase and caught the metallic flash of sunlight on a wing.

"Looks like Dyson's private jet." Stumpy almost spat the name. "Coal tonnage must be down, and he's comin' to crack some whips. You notice he's makin' his approach over pristine range and not the carnage of his strip mines."

"I noticed." But Chase carefully didn't comment further.

"That's one family I'm glad we've seen the back of."

Chase couldn't have agreed more, but he didn't say so. Ty's marriage to Dyson's daughter Tara had been relatively brief. Looking back, Chase knew he had never truly approved of that spoiled beauty becoming Ty's wife, although Maggie had. To him, there had always been a cunning quality to her intelligence, a quickness to manipulate and scheme to get what she wanted. Thankfully Tara was part of the past, another subject to be put aside, but not forgotten.

Yet any thought of Tara and that troubled time always aroused a sore point. Chase had yet to obtain title to those ten thousand acres of government land within the Triple C boundaries. The memory of that hardened the set of his jaw, a visible expression of his deepening resolve.

Without another word to Stumpy, Chase walked back to the ranch pickup, climbed in, and took off in the direction of The Homestead.

I KNOW I LOVE
CHOCOLATE

Sandra Steffen

Chapter One

The sea was calm as Sam O'Connor pulled away from the minuscule island he'd named Eagle Isle. Twenty minutes later he was within shouting distance of the mainland. Other than a sailboat a local teenager was doing his best to keep moving, the only boats in the harbor were those belonging to fishermen calling it a day. The woebegone teen waved with his cell phone, the slack orange sail a bright triangle against the dark blue of the Atlantic. Sam lifted a hand in greeting even as he eased out of the path of the noisy old lobster boat coming up close behind him. Seagulls swooped nearby, as accustomed as everybody else to the comings and goings of the people who lived and worked in this small harbor town along the rocky coast of Maine.

"Any luck?" Percival Parnell called, his eyes in a perpetual squint from so many years spent making his living on the sea.

Sam whisked his baseball cap off his head and

slapped it against his thigh. "Slim pickings, Percy. How about you?"

"More of the same, boy." The old lobsterman gestured toward shore. "Looks like you've got company."

Sam nodded, but Percy had already chugged ahead, not wanting or needing, certainly not expecting an explanation regarding the man waiting for Sam on the dock. Here in Midnight Cove, a man's business was a man's business. And that suited Sam to a tee.

A long time ago, he would have at the very least grimaced at the irony of that expression. Today, he simply replaced his cap, and stood, feet apart, his legs automatically adjusting to the rocking motion as his boat rode the wake of Percy's larger vessel.

Maybe old Percy didn't wonder what the man in a hundred-dollar shirt and polished leather shoes was doing here in Midnight Cove, but Sam had a pretty good idea. Not that he could turn tail and run now. No. The time to do that had been years ago, when he'd walked into his assigned dorm room on his first day at Harvard, and a tall lanky kid had stuck out his hand and said, "Grant Isaac Zimmerman the *Thurd.*" Oh, yeah, that would have been the time to run. After all, even a still-wet-behind-the-ears, middle-class kid from Ohio knew that a guy with three names could only be trouble.

Trouble was exactly what Grant had been. A thorn in Sam's side, a pain in the—well, that hadn't changed. The fact that Grant had become Sam's best friend was beside the point.

Sam eased up on the throttle as he neared the dock, then tossed the coiled rope toward his friend.

Grant caught it easily enough. After glancing down to make sure his clothes hadn't gotten dirty, he secured the rope to the piling, then brushed the residue from his hands.

Grant always managed to come out smelling like a rose. He hadn't even gotten dirty that first week at Harvard when some older frat boys had dubbed him Giz, for his initials, and Giz, er, Grant, had taken them on, three against one. At least, that was the score before Sam had entered the fight. It turned out that Grant had a pretty good right hook. Luckily, he also had an extremely influential father, because Grant Isaac Zimmerman *the second* had been the only thing that had stood between them and expulsion their first week at school.

Every now and then Grant reminded Sam how much he owed him, and every now and then Sam told Grant what he could do with his reminder. In truth, Sam owed Grant his life, but that had come later. Today, the two men simply eyed each other, Grant on the dock, Sam in the old lobster boat he'd christened *Birdie* his first summer here.

Grant's smile was begrudging. "A hundred thousand small towns in the world, and you pick one in a rocky cove practically inaccessible to ordinary man."

Sam almost grinned in spite of himself, because in any other circumstance, Grant Zimmerman would have been the first person to insist he was no ordinary man. In his world, he was extraordinary. A renowned psychiatrist, Grant liked to say he also dabbled in parapsychology and other unexplainable phenomena.

And Bill Gates dabbled in computers.

"You look good, Sam, for a bearded recluse."

Now, Sam did grin. Grant looked okay, too. Too well dressed to blend in in Midnight Cove, but okay. "Ever hear of Wal-Mart, Grant?"

"I read an article about it once. You finished feeding your pet lobsters?"

Sam cut his boat's engine. "It's called baiting the traps."

Gesturing with a sweep of a callus-free hand, Grant said, "What *they* do is called baiting the traps." He spoke quietly, so his voice wouldn't carry on the quiet evening air. "Doesn't anybody here notice that you never bring in any lobsters?"

Sam shrugged. It was a barbaric practice. They didn't even kill the poor creatures before they boiled them. "If folks notice, they don't mention it, just like they don't mention that Old Man Potter never actually sells any of the driftwood he keeps hauling in from the ocean, or that his wife wears her clothes inside out. The residents of Midnight Cove don't seem to think it's strange that Pete Jackson hasn't slept in a bed since he came back from his stint in Vietnam, or that you show up here once or twice every year in—" Sam waited to finish until after he vaulted over the side of his boat and landed on the dock a few feet from Grant. "Tell me that isn't a designer imprint on your pocket."

Each took a moment to size up the other. Both were thirty-six, both on the tall side. Sam was tan and lean and rugged. Grant was fair and citified to the bone.

"It's good to see you, Sam."

"You, too." It was true, even though Sam was never thrilled with the reasons for Grant's rare visits because they usually precipitated Sam's temporary departure from this place that asked no questions.

Going elsewhere, even for a good cause, meant risking being discovered. "Let me finish securing the boat. Have you eaten?"

Grant shook his head.

"Do you want to talk at my place? I can throw some steaks on the grill."

"That depends. Have you shoveled your place out lately?"

"It's not that bad, but fine, we'll go on up to Dulcie's for some supper. On the way you can try to talk me into whatever you're going to try to talk me into this time."

"Have you gone into town lately?" Grant asked.

Sam hunkered down, eye level with the knot he was tying. "No, why?"

"Just wondering."

That was Sam's first clue that something wasn't quite as it seemed. Grant never "just wondered" about something. He analyzed things to death, studied, planned, but he didn't "just wonder."

"What's going on, Grant?"

"I want to talk to you about something. An amnesia patient. A woman. Early to mid-thirties. She calls herself Annie Valentine, but she pulled the last name out of thin air. She was brought to my attention by one of my colleagues because her case is atypical."

Grant waited while Sam finished securing his boat. Slowly rising to his feet, Sam brushed his hands on his jeans and finally asked, "What's so unusual about this Annie?"

They walked along the dock. "It isn't her case that's so unusual. It's the woman herself. Somebody hit her on the head with a blunt object before making off with her purse down in Boothbay Harbor nearly a month ago. Witnesses say she probably wouldn't have been harmed if she hadn't fought back. She woke up in the hospital. Instead of being terrified like most amnesia patients, she was spitting mad about the inconvenience."

"You sure her amnesia's legit?"

"We're certain she isn't faking that, yes."

Both men stepped off the dock, the soles of their shoes crunching on the crushed-shell path. "What else does she remember?" Sam was looking for the reason Grant had come to him, and the reason he was being so vague about it.

"She knows tidbits about a lot of things, but not much about herself. Besides her name, she knows she loves chocolate."

Sam stopped walking. "That's it? That's all you've got? She loves chocolate? Hell, what woman doesn't?"

Grant stopped, too, and turned to face his friend. "She has vague memories of a little girl she feels is her daughter."

Now they were getting somewhere. Sam often took cases involving children or people with families they couldn't remember. His last case had involved a dying man with ESP who had some unfinished business with his estranged son. Real uplifting, his work. "I take it she's spoken to the authorities."

"She's gone through every conventional channel as well as a few unconventional means to regain her memory."

Sam was about as unconventional as they came. One day he'd been just an average, everyday world-famous golf pro. The next day a bolt of lightning decided to dance a jig on an iron sculpture a few feet in front of him. Sam didn't remember hitting the ground. When he woke up, doctors said it was a miracle he was alive. At the time, they hadn't known the half of it.

He and Grant started walking again. By the time they reached Harbor Avenue, Sam knew most of the pertinent facts about Annie Valentine, but still wasn't sure what any of it had to do with him. According to Grant, her psychiatrists were fairly certain her amnesia didn't stem from a repressed past. Her neurologist believed it was most likely due to the trauma to her head. It was possible, probable even, that her memory would return in time. Evidently, Annie Valentine wasn't the "wait and see" type.

Sam thought about the drastic measures some people were willing to take in order to regain their lives, and the drastic measures he'd taken to disappear from his. "Did you drive all the way up here to ask me to help her?"

"Not exactly."

The scent of battered shrimp, clam chowder, and strong coffee wafted from Dulcie's Diner before they entered through the screen door. The way Grant glanced around the room at the handful of diners made Sam wonder what he was looking for. "Well?" Sam prodded.

Seemingly satisfied about something, Grant said, "I'll tell you the rest over dinner. Why don't you find us a table. I'll be right back."

While Grant sauntered toward the rest room, Sam removed his hat and ambled on into the square dining room. Grant had once said the place was decorated in early squalor. Sam liked it. Besides, people didn't come here for ambience.

They came to eat. The food was good, the floors and tables clean.

The supper crowd usually thinned out early, and today was no exception. Since the middle-aged waitress was nowhere in sight, Sam chose a table in the elevated portion of the room, away from the others, where he and Grant could talk in private. Staring out the window at the quiet street, Sam wondered about Annie Valentine. If she did indeed have a young daughter, it would explain her willingness to try "anything" to speed up the process in regaining her memory. It didn't explain why the authorities could find no missing person's report on a woman fitting her description.

"Can I start you off with something to drink?"

Instead of Dulcie's sister, Trudy, Sam found himself staring into the face of a waitress he'd never seen before. Close to thirty, she wasn't pretty, exactly. Her eyes were a little too closely set, her lips a little too full, but she was a lot easier on the eyes than Trudy, who was built more like a Mack truck and had a face that looked as if she made a habit of kissing one.

"Sir?"

Oh, yes, this woman was a lot easier on the eyes than good old Trudy. "You must be new here," he said.

This woman was on the curvy side, five-four or five-five. Her dark hair had been secured on top of her head with a simple clasp and was slowly losing the battle to gravity. "This is my second day. It's tougher than it looks."

Her voice was deep and sultry, and stirred up something restless in the pit of his stomach, reminding him of how many days he spent alone and how many nights he spent putting only his boat to bed.

"Do you know what you want?" she asked.

It had been a long time since he'd given much thought to what he wanted. . . .

"Is something wrong?" she asked.

Realizing he was staring, Sam shook his head. She smiled, and that restlessness moved into more dangerous territory.

"Take your time. This is the longest I've stood still in hours. Dulcie hired me yesterday to help with the breakfast and lunch crowd. The regular waitress came down with a migraine so I'm doing a double shift. The cash register hates me and my feet are killing me like you would not believe." She looked surprised, as if she'd told him far more than she'd intended and didn't know why.

Sam knew why. People told the truth around him, whether they wanted to or not.

Out of the corner of his eye, he noticed Grant walking toward the table. "Just bring out two glasses of lemonade for now. We can order later."

"Two lemonades coming right up."

She bustled off in one direction as Grant strolled over from another. "Who was that?" he asked the instant he sat down.

"Beats me, but that's some walk, isn't it?"

"She didn't give you her name?"

If Sam hadn't been so busy watching the new waitress sashay into the kitchen, he might have thought twice about Grant's obtuse question. By the time she emerged, a heavy-looking tray held tightly in her hands, Grant was watching her, too. "You don't know her?"

"She said she's new."

Sam was pretty sure he heard Grant mutter something eloquent, like "Uh-oh."

Holding the tray in front of her, she didn't see the four-inch step elevating this portion of the floor from the other half of the room. She stumbled up it with all the grace of a person tripping on a crack in the sidewalk.

She managed to regain her footing, but there wasn't much she could do about the two desserts that went flying off the tray. One missed Grant by a fraction. The other one headed straight for Sam. He jumped to his feet, but he was too late. The bowl upended on his chest and glided down the front of him, finally clattering to the floor.

"Oh my gosh!" Flustered, she looked all around. "Oh, dear." Her hands were full, her movements jerky as she took a step in one direction, then another. "Here." She shoved the heavy tray into Grant's hands. "Hold this."

Turning to Sam, she grabbed the towel that had been tucked inside the waistband of her apron. "Look at this mess." She began dabbing at the cool, gooey mixture on the front of his shirt. "Why on earth is there a step there? How do waitresses do this?"

Since most of the blood had drained out of Sam's brain, all he could do was stand there and take her ministering like a man, which, among other things meant that his breathing hitched a little more every time her hand inched lower.

Pausing somewhere in the vicinity of his belt, she looked up at him. "Maybe you'd better take it from here." A devilish look came into her eyes, and the imp smiled. "This is a family establishment, after all."

She folded the dirty portion of the towel inside, placed it in Sam's hand, then turned back to Grant. Chatting as if waitresses told Grant Isaac Zimmerman the third to hold their trays every day, she deposited their glasses of lemonade on the table, then relieved him of the tray. Turning to Sam again, she said, "It looks like you've gotten most of it. A pity, too. It was chocolate."

Something nagged the back of Sam's mind.

One of the old fishermen sitting near the front of the diner called, "Bring that pot of coffee this-a-way, would you Annie!"

The nagging moved up, front and center. Annie?

She blew a shock of coffee-colored hair out of her eyes, then bustled away.

Slowly, Sam looked at Grant. "That's Annie?"

Grant studied him in that quiet way that saw too much. "Quite a coincidence, wouldn't you say?"

"The woman with amnesia is right here in Midnight Cove."

"Yes."

Sam looked over his shoulder. Annie was busy splashing coffee into Clem Peterson's cup and saucer. "Why didn't you tell me?"

"I didn't know she'd taken a job here," Grant said. "I was told she was working at a clothing store. Damn. Now she's seen you."

There was something in the tone of Grant's voice that set off an alarm in Sam's head. "You didn't come here to ask me to help her?"

Grant shook his head. "I wouldn't have been too late if you had a phone."

"Too late for what?"

"Perhaps you should sit down."

Sam really did not like the sound of that. He

didn't like the expression on Grant's face, either. Taking the seat he'd vacated when that pudding had gone flying, Sam said, "Don't tell me she's a wanted felon."

"Oh, for heaven's sake," Grant said. "If we knew she was a wanted felon, we would know who she is. They ran her fingerprints. As far as they can tell, she's never committed a crime, at least not a serious one. However, the psychological workups my colleague ran indicated that she . . ." Grant's voice trailed away.

Sam's eyes narrowed a little more with every passing second. "The psychological workups indicated that she what?"

"Those tests are never conclusive, of course, but it does appear as though Annie Valentine shares some strong personality traits with . . ."

Sam waited.

"With reporters, Sam."

A gong went off inside Sam's head.

"It doesn't mean she is a reporter, mind you. It just means she might be."

Sam stared at his untouched lemonade. Given a choice, he would take a wanted felon over a reporter any day. A person knew where he stood with wanted felons. Reporters were a different breed entirely. They pretended. They lied. And either they didn't know that what they did was wrong, or they didn't care. Either way, "reporter" was the dirtiest word in the English language.

Sam's newfound power had scared the living hell out of him. When news of his "abilities" had first leaked out, the press had hunted him. One day, he'd been the number-one golfer in the world. Suddenly, people blurted out the truth when in his presence. Half the world had wanted to prove he was a fake. It was the other half that had finally ruined him. Dirtbag attorneys, wives of cheating husbands, people involved in law suits, statesmen, victims of crimes, and every lowlife with a score to settle wanted to enlist his "services." They were like sharks on a feeding frenzy in a bloody ocean. He was dinner. And every reporter alive wanted the credit for serving him up on a silver platter.

His career in pro golf went down the tubes as people screamed out at him from the sidelines, searched him out wherever he went. He lost his concentration and his edge. Once, the media had been his biggest fans. Reporters had since become his worst enemies. He'd gotten no sleep and less peace. Until six years ago when he'd come here, that is. Here in Midnight Cove, he'd found peace. He had his boat, his house, the island, his anonymity. Quite by accident, he'd found that his newfound power had a quieter side. Not only did guilty people speak the truth when he was near, but an amnesia patient he'd happened to befriend had recalled things, true things, about his past. Although there was always a risk of being discovered, today Sam occasionally helped people remember. But he did so on his own terms, in his own way.

He'd read once that there were four great mysteries in America: *Who really killed JFK? Was Marilyn Monroe's death truly a suicide? Is Elvis dead?* And last but not least . . . *Where is Logan Samuel Oliver Connors?*

Sam felt for his hat and rose to his feet. Without a word, he started toward the door. He was three steps away from freedom when his progress was halted by a hand placed gently on his arm.

"Sir?"

Three measly steps and he would have been gone. How in hell the woman could trip over a step, then effortlessly get between him and the door was beyond him. "What is it?"

She removed her hand from his arm. A lot of people would have taken a giant step backward. Annie cleared her throat, looked up at him, and held her ground. "Um, that is, I was wondering . . . Was something wrong with your lemonade?"

He'd forgotten about the damn lemonade. He reached into his back pocket for his wallet.

"No, no. Don't worry about paying for it. Under the circumstances, it's only fair that I take it out of my wages. At this rate, I'll owe Dulcie money come payday."

Sam knew he was staring. He just couldn't seem to help it.

"I was wondering if you would do me a favor." She blew dark wisps of hair out of her eyes and ignored the people calling for refills and seconds.

A reporter? Sam thought. He didn't know about that, but Annie Valentine sure wasn't going to last long as a waitress.

"I know, I know," she said. "It boggles the mind that I have the nerve to ask after that little accident with the pudding, but I really am sorry about your shirt."

"What favor?" he asked.

She wet her lips and glanced toward the kitchen. "I was hoping you wouldn't mention this unfortunate little incident to Dulcie. I doubt anyone else will. This town isn't much for gossip. I've already tried and failed at three other jobs since becoming stranded up here. This is my last resort. If I lose this one, I'll be forced to apply at the fish processing plant." She gazed up at him beseechingly. "And I don't even like fish."

Something went warm inside him, and he found himself saying, "It was an accident, like you said. Don't worry. Your secret's safe with me."

"Thank you very much." Casting him a smile that made a man rethink the way he measured beauty, she turned on her heel and went back to work.

Sam didn't remember walking outside. It didn't take long for Grant to follow.

"What was that all about?" Grant asked.

Sam took his time putting on his hat and adjusting the bill. "She doesn't like fish."

Grant was quiet as he digested the relevance in that. Finally he said, "Are you considering helping her?"

Sam's first instinct was to say no. Not just no. Hell no. "It's like you said. She's already seen me. Ultimately, the damage could already be done." He rubbed at a knot in the back of his neck.

Grant glanced at his Rolex.

"What's the matter?" Sam asked. "Are you in a hurry to get back to Boston? Do you have a meeting or something?"

"I'm afraid it's more complex than that."

Sam took a closer look at his fair-headed friend. "The only thing more complex than one of your meetings is a woman."

Grant didn't reply, which was extremely telling.

"Don't tell me you're seeing someone."

Suddenly Grant was the one kneading the back of his neck. "She says I'm stuffy."

Sam fought the urge to grin. "Sounds like you're going to need your strength. You might as well grab a burger at Rocky's Tavern before you head back to Boston."

Grant made a sound only a true Boston-born-and-bred blue blood could make. "A burger at an establishment called Rocky's Tavern. How could I refuse?"

Before setting off across the street, Sam said, "You know something, Grant? You are stuffy."

An hour later Grant was digging in his pocket for antacid tablets with one hand and punching in the code to unlock his car door with the other. "What will you do about Annie Valentine?"

Sam shrugged. "I don't know yet."

"Let me know if there's anything I can do to help."

"I will."

"Good luck, Sam."

"Some people don't believe in luck."

"Some people don't believe in a lot of things."

They shared a long look and a brief smile. Sam stood back while Grant got in his Porsche and drove away.

Lost in thought, Sam stared at the street leading out of town.

An amnesia patient was right here in Midnight Cove. For once, he could help her without leaving his quiet haven. He couldn't help but wonder if this little harbor town would still be a quiet haven after Annie Valentine left.

Chapter Two

Annie hiked along an unmarked lane that ran between two side streets named after trees. By the time she came out on Main Street, which ran the entire length of the downtown district of Midnight Cove—all two blocks of it—she'd seen every last street and lane in town.

She'd set out to get lost an hour ago. It wasn't easy to get lost in a village this small. Apparently it wasn't easy to be found, either. At least, no one had found her. It pained her to think that that was because no one was looking for her. Banishing that thought, she continued walking.

It had been a rainy, dismal day. The clouds had finally moved on and the sun was shining, now that it was almost time for it to set. Like all the streets running east and west, Main Street dead-ended at Harbor Avenue. She could smell the ocean from anywhere in town, but from this end of Midnight Cove she could see it, too. Deciding that it was probably inevitable that she would end up there, she crossed the street and headed toward the harbor.

She'd read that the ocean instilled romance in the human heart. Gathering her hair in one hand, she stared out across the water, trying to remember where she'd read that. Had she seen it in a book, a magazine, at a school or college somewhere? She thought. She concentrated. She felt a headache starting. But not a single memory came. It was like cramming for an exam from a notebook full of blank pages.

Her sigh was lost in the incessant breeze, the crashing waves, and the screeching cries of the gulls. Leaving her hair to the mercy of the wind, she hooked her thumbs inside two small pockets at the waist of her long, loose-fitting skirt, and slowly wandered to the edge of a series of docks connected by narrower structures that looked like bridges. Several fishing boats were already parked, if that was what they called it, and a few others were heading in.

One thing she felt all the way to her bones: She'd never lived near the ocean. That left an awful lot of places in between.

The wind blew her hair into her face again, blinding her and making her wish she'd put it up before leaving the one-room apartment where she'd been living these past two weeks. She supposed she could have turned around and gone back to her room. And do what? Sit around feeling sorry for herself? That wasn't her style. At least she didn't think it was.

No. She knew it wasn't. She just didn't know how she knew. But she would. It had only been three and a half weeks. She recalled more every day. The important memories hadn't come back yet, but just two days ago she'd remembered that she didn't like fish. Saying that out loud in a town whose men earned a living off the sea had been a terrible faux pas that could have turned around and bitten her in the butt. Luckily, the fisherman she'd blurted it to hadn't looked offended.

He hadn't looked like a fisherman, either.

Something about his gray eyes had left her feeling strangely unsettled. It wasn't as if she'd never seen gray eyes before. She couldn't actually *remember*, but surely she'd come across other people who had gray eyes. She'd thought about those eyes for two days. In fact, she'd been thinking about them just this morning when she'd been topping off Wilhemina Jones's coffee, which was what had gotten her into her latest predicament.

"Did you come all the way out here to sigh like that?"

First of all, Annie hadn't realized she'd sighed. Secondly, she hadn't known she wasn't alone on the pier or the dock or the wharf. Oh, whatever. The gray-eyed man who'd ended up wearing chocolate pudding on his shirt two nights ago was tinkering with something on his boat. While seagulls screeched in the distance and waves slapped the boats tied nearby, she strolled closer.

He had to have looked up earlier in order to have known she was there, but she reached the edge of the dock before he looked at her again, his eyes in the shadow of the bill of a baseball cap that had seen better days.

"You have the stormiest eyes." Her hand flew to her mouth before she could stop it. "I mean gray. You have the grayest eyes." Stormy gray. She'd convinced herself it had been an optical illusion. He was watching her, his eyes as changeable as the ocean behind him. It hadn't been an illusion at all.

Shrugging as if he didn't much care what color his eyes were, he said, "You're not working the supper crowd tonight?"

She sighed again. "Or the lunch crowd, or the breakfast crowd."

"You've had the day off?"

"Guess you could say I'm between jobs again."

He wiped his hands on a stained cloth with a precision she found mesmerizing. His hair was short, the portion not covered by his hat a sandy brown. His beard and mustache were neatly trimmed, and a shade darker than his hair. His jeans were faded, his T-shirt white, his boots well worn. The man had rugged down to an art form.

"Dulcie let you go?"

"I don't think she wanted to, but Wilhemina Jones was pretty mad, and Dulcie didn't want a law suit. Everybody sues everybody these days. I guess I don't blame Dulcie. She's probably afraid of a lawsuit like that one years ago, when a man sued that fast-food restaurant because he burned himself on a cup of their coffee."

He'd finished wiping the grime from his hands and was watching her closely. Distributing his weight to one foot, he tugged his hat a little lower on his forehead. "You don't seem too upset."

Annie slanted him a smile that was surely brimming with excitement. "I just remembered that old lawsuit. I don't know if you've heard, but I have amnesia."

He continued looking at her in that quiet, thoughtful way he had. "Yeah, I heard. What happened at Dulcie's?"

She rested a hip against a post that had a rope wrapped around it. Holding her hair out of her eyes, she looked out across the water. "I was running back and forth between the kitchen and dining room, being careful, mind you, of that step that gave me trouble the other night. I mean, I may be a little uncoordinated at times, but I learn from my mistakes. Anyway, Wilhemina stopped me and insisted I top off her coffee. I should have told her I'd be back in a second, but she stuck her coffee cup out and I thought I could fill it without dropping the tray."

Annie peered at the islands dotting the horizon. There were more than three thousand islands off the coast of Maine. That was another thing she knew without knowing how she knew. If only she could remember her real last name.

"Did you drop the tray?"

"What? Oh. If only I had. The last I knew, the carafe was half empty, but I guess Dulcie filled it when I wasn't looking, and the coffee came out pretty fast and I ended up spilling some."

"She fired you for spilling coffee?"

"Not exactly. I apologized up and down. The doctor said the burns were only first degree."

"Burns?"

Annie nodded. "Wilhemina doesn't have a high tolerance for pain. Poor Dulcie hated to have to do it, but Wilhemina insisted she wouldn't frequent the diner as long as I worked there. Dulcie offered to give me severance pay. I couldn't accept, of course. I mean, I'd only worked there for three days. That would have felt like charity—or worse, it would have been like those parting gifts they give to people who lose on game shows. Ever notice how the contestants always smile and insist they're thrilled with a board game and some microwave popcorn instead of the twenty grand they almost won? I don't think I could do that, do you?"

"To tell you the truth," he said, looking at her in a manner that drove home the fact that she'd been rambling, "I've never thought about it."

"I guess a person thinks about a lot of things when she doesn't know who she is." Since there weren't a lot of ways to reply to that, she said, "As I was saying, I didn't accept charity from Dulcie. I didn't accept it from Carol Ann, either."

She watched two seabirds raising a ruckus over a dead fish. It made her really glad she wasn't a bird. Or a fish either, for that matter.

"What happened at the dress shop?"

"Pretty much the same thing."

"You spilled coffee on somebody at the dress store, too?"

She turned her head so she could see his expression. He was watching her closely. If she wasn't careful she was going to get lost in his gray eyes. Just to be on the safe side, she wrapped an arm around the post so she wouldn't topple into the ocean. "I didn't *burn* Essie Summers. Well, the truth might have scorched her ears a little, but she asked how she looked in that pantsuit."

"What did you say?"

"I told her the purple polka dots made her look as big as her house."

"Essie lives in the biggest house in Midnight Cove."

Annie nodded forlornly. "She and her husband have a lot of money, and apparently she spends a good deal of it on the clothes Carol Ann stocks, regardless of how she looks in them."

He chuckled, and vaulted off his boat, landing lightly for a man his size. "It'll be dark soon. I'll walk you back to town."

She stared up at him. "I don't know if walking with a man who wears a beard is a good idea."

"I beg your pardon?"

"Beards always make me wonder what a man's hiding."

Sam controlled his gasp, but Annie didn't. She clamped her hand over her mouth and took a backward step. If he hadn't grabbed her, she would have fallen off the dock. She appeared horrified by what she'd just said. Sam had grown accustomed to the way people blurted exactly what was on their minds when in his presence, but he understood how disconcerting it could be.

"I didn't mean that the way it sounded."

"It's all right."

"It's not all right. My mouth is going to be the death of me."

She sounded breathless. Her lips were lush, full, soft looking. She wasn't wearing lipstick. Nasty-tasting stuff, lipstick. He spent far too long wondering what her lips would taste like without it.

"I promise I'll stay in the center of the dock."

"What?"

"You can let me go now. I'll make a conscious effort not to fall in the ocean. Even if I did, I can swim." Her eyes got large again. "That's something else I didn't know I knew." She smiled. "Uh, about letting me go?"

He hadn't realized he was still holding her. At least the realization hadn't made it to his brain. Other areas were all too aware.

She eased backward, leaving him with little choice but to release her. She glanced at the water, and then finally back at him. "If your offer to walk me back to town still stands, I'd like that."

A fishing boat's engine drowned out anything else she might have added. As the boat chugged closer, Sam and Annie made their way toward safer ground. "Tell me about your amnesia."

"There isn't much to tell. I've tried hypnosis. I've been studied, analyzed, prodded. About the only thing they haven't done to me is whack me upside the head with a medium-size club. That's what put me in this situation to begin with."

"Do you remember getting hit on the head?"

"No, but evidently it happened three and a half weeks ago, while I was vacationing at a resort harbor south of here. I woke up in a hospital with a screaming headache, a lump on my head the size of Cleveland, and no memory of how I got it."

He took a moment to sort through the information. "If you'd been vacationing at a resort, why did you come here?"

They stepped off the dock and onto the crushed-shell path that led up the hill toward Harbor Avenue. "I followed my instincts. I know it's not much, but they're all I have. I'm glad I did, too. Since arriving here, I've remembered more every day. Oh, I haven't recalled the important stuff, but when you don't know anything, even the bits and pieces mean the world."

Sam understood how much the little things could mean.

Instead of going directly to the building that housed her room over the dress shop on Main Street, they turned right at Harbor Avenue and then left at Jefferson. She glanced at the street sign and for no apparent reason said, "Thomas Jefferson was born in Virginia in 1743."

"You don't say."

She shook her head and sputtered, "I don't even know where or when I was born and yet I know that."

"You don't know how old you are?"

"I suppose that could have its advantages. I wouldn't be lying if I said I was twenty-five."

"Are you?"

"Am I what? Lying or twenty-five?" Annie peered down the street at the Cape Cod–style houses sitting cozily behind their picket fences. The low drone of a lawn mower was coming from a block away. A handful of kids were tossing basketballs at a dilapidated hoop in a driveway across the street. Bikes were left on kickstands; dogs snoozed in the shade. Two old ladies in orthopedic shoes, their hose rolled down just below their knees stood talking over a low hedge.

"It's an ordinary evening in an ordinary town, or least it might be if I could figure out who I am."

She hadn't meant to say that. She didn't want pity. She glanced at her companion and found him looking at her as if he were unsure exactly how to take her. It occurred to her that a lot of people looked at her that way. Not just here in Midnight Cove, but . . . someplace else. It was as if her memory was right there on the tip of her mind, just waiting to reveal itself to her.

She slanted him another smile. "I know I'm not

a habitual liar. It was my honesty that got me fired from the dress shop, remember? And I don't think I'm twenty-five, either. I feel like I've lived more than that."

She didn't know how on earth her hand ended up on his arm, but she didn't readily remove it. It made her feel connected in a way she hadn't been since she woke up in the hospital with a bump on her head and a huge blank spot between her ears. He felt warm, solid, male. Perhaps he wasn't adverse to her touch, because he made no move to withdraw his arm. Instead, he reached over with his other hand, touching a blunt-tipped finger to one of three charms dangling from the gold bracelet on her wrist.

Again, she found it mesmerizing to watch his hands. "I was wearing this charm bracelet when I woke up in the hospital near Boothbay Harbor. Evidently, my attacker tried to steal this, too. His efforts left a bruise on my wrist. The bracelet was so sturdy the links held. I think that says something about me. Do you know anybody who's going to the fish processing plant?"

He blinked, his only indication that he was having trouble following her jump to unconnected topics. "You said you don't like fish."

Finally, someone who understood her. "I have to do something to earn a living while I wait for my memory to return."

They were back on Main Street. The sun was behind them, their shadows so long and light they glided over the sidewalk like spaceships riding a current of air. Sam slowed near a bench across the street from the building that housed Annie's tiny efficiency apartment. A few steps ahead of him, Annie stopped, too.

"Thank you for the escort, and forget I mentioned the fish processing plant. I'll find someone who's going there and wouldn't mind giving me a ride." Looking both ways, she stepped off the curb.

"Annie, wait."

She glanced over her shoulder, turning first her head and then the rest of her. Sam had noticed that she was wearing a simple green skirt and matching top the first moment he'd seen her walking toward him on the dock half an hour ago. She looked damn good in green.

"Yes?"

If he had to choose one word as his favorite it would have to be "yes," no matter what the language, especially when it was delivered in a voice deep and sultry enough to stir up that pleasing restlessness that was always laying in wait in the pit of a man's stomach. Settling his hands comfortably on his hips, he said, "There must be some other type of work you could do that doesn't involve deboning cod."

She tilted her head as she looked at him. Gesturing toward the handful of stores lining the quiet street, she shrugged. "I've already inquired everywhere I could think of. I even considered asking Wilhemina if she needed a temporary housekeeper, but I'm pretty sure I burned that bridge when I sloshed hot coffee on her sturdy wrist."

"That's not a bad idea."

For once, she was the one who appeared confused. "What's not a bad idea?"

"Working as a housekeeper of sorts."

"Do you know anyone who might hire me?"

He nodded.

She stared at him, as if waiting for him to continue. "Who?" she finally asked.

"Me."

She stayed where she was in the empty street. "You mean it?"

Sam nodded. He'd lost his mind. Any minute now he was going to care. "It isn't brain surgery, but it's honest work."

She crossed her arms, drawing her shirt tight beneath her breasts. "When do you want me to start?"

"Tomorrow morning?" he asked. Since it didn't feel right to be conducting a job interview while she stood in the middle of the street, he joined her on the pavement. With a hand placed gently at her elbow, he escorted her across. "First of all," Sam said upon reaching the other side, "you don't know me from Adam." He hoped. "You should ask for character references."

"Dulcie vouched for you."

The old-fashioned streetlight on the corner flickered as it slowly came on. That easily, it went from day to night. "What did Dulcie say?"

"She said you're not married, for one thing." She looked at him. "Why, are you?"

"No," he answered. "Are you?"

She shook her head. And then she laughed. "I'm not married. I wondered about that."

"What else did Dulcie say about me?"

"Not much. Midnight Cove, Maine, might as well be called Mind-Your-Own-Business, Maine. She did mention that you could put your boots under her bed anytime."

Sam had the uncanny feeling that Annie was

putting his face to memory. "I hate to be the one to break this to you," he said, "but Dulcie says that about every man."

"I guess I'm just going to have to trust my instincts then, won't I? Perhaps we should at least be formally introduced." She held out her hand. "I'm Annie Somebody-or-Other."

He took her hand. "And I'm Sam O'Connor. Would you like to take a look at my house before you commit?"

"It's that bad?"

"A friend of mine refuses to set foot in the place."

"The man in the Gucci shoes?"

"You're very astute."

"I am?" And then, "That's a good thing, right?"

Annie thought that if he had nodded any slower, it couldn't have passed for a nod.

"Is he your attorney?"

"Why do you say that?"

"He has that rich, useless look about him." She clamped her hand over her mouth. "Sorry. Surely I'll wear out that phrase."

"He's a friend from college. And he's not an attorney."

She wound up getting lost in the way he was looking at her. It required effort to drag her gaze away. Other than the handful of cars parked in front of the tavern on the next block, there wasn't another soul on Main Street tonight. "They'll be rolling up the sidewalks soon."

Something about the way he peered up and down the street caused Annie to wonder what he was thinking. For once, she managed to keep from blurting the question out loud. He gave her brief directions to his house. Annie reached into her pocket for her key and strolled toward the lighted alleyway that led to the stairs, only to pause. Looking back at him she said, "Sam?"

He stopped, too. "Yes?"

"What did you study?"

"When?"

"In college. You said you and the Gucci man were friends from college."

She couldn't see his eyes from here, but she could feel the intensity in his gaze as he said, "I majored in English."

"No, kidding? So did I." She knew her mouth was gaping, but she didn't have it in her to care. "I studied English in college. Well, I'll be darned. Good night, Sam O'Connor. I'll see you tomorrow."

Sam's blood pressure was on the rise. He could hear it pounding in his ears. Annie Whatever-Her-Last-Name-Was had a razor sharp mind. Astute and intuitive, she homed in on information with ease. If she wasn't already a reporter, she'd missed her calling. And he'd just invited her to work for him, to poke through his house and his life.

She was strolling away, on up the metal steps to her apartment. He reacted far more strongly than he should have to a woman wearing loose-fitting clothes and plain leather sandals. Which meant that he was reacting to the woman *in* the clothes. He should have been thinking about getting his head examined. Instead, he was thinking about seeing her again. That kind of thinking could be dangerous to a man who was going to have to keep his wits about him. Very dangerous, indeed.

* * *

Annie's efficiency apartment consisted of a square living area that contained a table and one chair, a sofa that doubled as a bed, a little refrigerator, a microwave oven, and a tiny bathroom almost too small to turn around in. Perhaps the apartment's most redeeming quality, other than the price, was the window on the wall facing the ocean. She opened it. Although there wasn't much to see in the dark, the ocean breeze was pleasant, freshening the room in no time.

She visited the tiny bathroom, washed her face, brushed her teeth and hair, and donned a nightgown she'd found on the sale rack when she'd still been working at Carol Ann's. The apartment had come furnished, right down to an old television that picked up one station. She flipped on the TV. The grainy police drama didn't hold her attention, so she turned it off again. Wandering around the one-room apartment killed another three minutes. Yawning, she gave up and went to bed.

Annie loved this time of day when she was totally relaxed and all her cares and worries were tucked away until morning. She lay in the drowsy warmth of sheets scented with an unfamiliar soap and the air scented faintly of the ocean that was slowly becoming familiar. Her body practically floated; her thoughts turned hazy.

The day had started out terribly, but had ended pleasantly. The image of gray eyes filtered across her mind. Turning onto her side, she snuggled deeper into her pillow, thinking that maybe the ocean really did instill romance in the human heart.

She was about a breath away from falling asleep when her stomach rumbled. She tried to remember how long it had been since she'd eaten. Lunch? She wished she had a candy bar. Ah, yes, milk chocolate, maybe with a little caramel and peanuts thrown in for good measure, sure would taste good right now. She tried to think of something else.

She wasn't married. And she had an English degree. She wondered where she'd acquired it. A lot of colleges taught English. Her stomach rumbled again. Mmm, chocolate.

With a groan, she flopped onto her back and stared at the ceiling. Great. Now she'd never be able to get to sleep. As much time as she spent thinking about chocolate, it was a wonder she didn't weigh eight hundred pounds. She swung her feet over the side of the bed and got up, flouncing to the drawer where she kept her emergency stash. She took her time poking through the assortment of chocolate. Breathing in the rich scent, she chose a plain milk-chocolate candy bar and slowly removed the wrapper.

The first bite was heaven, the second almost as good. She strolled to the open window and nibbled on rich chocolate in the dark. She could have been sleeping. Instead, she was eating. Having a chocolate addiction could be a real nuisance. She stared at the lights twinkling faintly from tall poles in the harbor. She sighed as she took the last bite, then returned to the bathroom to brush her teeth. A real nuisance, but such a pleasurable one.

Her craving for chocolate satisfied, she crawled into bed again. This time when she closed her eyes, her stomach didn't rumble. Her mind wandered, her body drifting a little farther toward sleep, her thoughts a jumbled mix that came and went much like the late-night breeze. It had been nice of Sam to offer her a job. Something told her that Sam O'Connor wasn't always nice. That was one of the things that made him so intriguing. That and his stormy gray eyes.

Her breathing grew shallow, and her thoughts slowed.

The directions he'd given her were to a house on the outskirts of town. She wondered how much work it would take to clean it up. Time would tell. And time was one thing she had plenty of.

The curtain billowed gently. She was so relaxed. That walk had been good for her. Hadn't the doctors told her the more she relaxed, the more she would remember?

Her memories were stacking up. She could swim. She was single. She'd gone to college. And she'd studied English. Like Sam.

Ah, Sam, with his stormy gray eyes and the confident stride and rare smiles and a lobster boat named *Birdie*. She wondered if he liked birds. Her last waking thought before drifting off to sleep was *What does a lobster fisherman do with an English degree?*

Chapter Three

Annie tucked the strap of her big plastic purse over her shoulder and started down the metal steps. Sam hadn't told her what time he wanted her to start. She distinctly remembered asking, but all she could recall him saying was something to the effect of "tomorrow morning."

Yesterday, she'd thought he had rugged down to an art form. This morning it had occurred to her that he had vague down to one, too. Since she couldn't call him, she'd decided that eight o'clock was a relatively innocuous yet universal time to start work. She didn't own a clock radio, and she'd slept like a baby. Sam's house was at least half a mile away. She glanced at the clock on the little tower at the head of Main Street. It was a quarter to eight. She didn't have time to mosey.

The only two businesses on Main Street open this early during the week were the diner and the barbershop. Now that she was gainfully employed again, she was a little relieved that she wasn't waiting tables today. Perhaps that was what put the spring in her step. She noticed the old-timers on the bench in front of the one-chair barbershop in the middle of the block. They'd been talking in earnest, but clammed up as she neared. They nodded hellos, though, as did the people driving by. She waved, but mostly she hurried. She was making good time, and had a stitch in her side to prove it.

"Hello, Mr. Potter," she called to the eighty-year-old man who was painting a new sign in front of a huge stack of driftwood. She thought that if the stack got any higher it would hide the house. Mrs. Potter came tottering outside, her house dress inside out. The old lady waved, and Annie thought the people in Midnight Cove sure were friendly. Strange, but definitely friendly.

With the exception of Main Street and Harbor Avenue, all the streets in town were named after trees or presidents. Sam's property was on a dead-end street named after the towering oaks that lined it. Winded, she paused to catch her breath just inside the gate in front of the house bearing the number he'd given her.

Yesterday, she'd thought she'd walked past every house in Midnight. She didn't recall this one. Other than a small area of grass that somebody kept mowed, the place looked . . . Words deserted her. Tangled was the best description she could come up with. The yard wasn't small, but from the looks of things, it had been overtaken a long time ago by overgrown bushes and vines and shrubs. There appeared to be no method to the madness. However, the house looked sound, what she could see of it. The roof didn't sag and the porch wasn't leaning. It had all its shutters, and the windows all contained glass. Like many of the houses in Midnight Cove, it was surrounded by a picket fence. Unlike the others, this one hadn't seen a coat of paint in years. It matched the house. There were no cars sitting on blocks, nor were there rotting benches and discarded items covered with weeds. Sam's yard wasn't messy. It just wasn't noteworthy. Maybe she had been past the house but hadn't given it a second look.

Her knock was answered quickly, as if Sam had been watching for her arrival. "Come in."

Her smile slipped a little at the way his mouth was set in a straight line. She couldn't tell if his eyes were a stormy gray this morning because he turned around before she got a good look.

The door creaked as she entered the front room. It was all she could do to control her gasp. She counted two sofas, several old stands that held lamps, old tins, books, records, radios, and other assorted junk. There was a wide assortment of old chairs, none of which could be used without first finding a place to put the items stacked on them.

Since Sam seemed to be waiting for her to say something, she said the first *nice* thing she could think of. "I wouldn't have pegged you as a man who collected antiques."

"I don't. All this junk came with the house."

Was it her imagination, or did his voice sound clipped? Following him into another room that looked a lot like the first one but had probably once been used as a dining room, she said, "How long have you lived here?"

"Six years."

She could see his face now, and his expression was definitely severe. It occurred to her that he wasn't nearly as friendly as the other people she'd seen this morning.

"Am I late?"

"I don't recall naming a specific time."

Okay. So he wasn't angry about her timing. That didn't explain the reason he clamped his mouth shut tighter than a child refusing to take medicine. All at once, Annie had a vague memory of holding a spoon of bitter-tasting liquid to the closed lips of a very stubborn, brown-haired girl. Her own smile lasted longer than the memory did. She was more certain than ever that there was a very belligerent school-age child out there somewhere, who loved her very much. Strangely, Annie didn't feel that the girl was crying her eyes out without her. Perhaps she was at summer camp and didn't even know Annie was missing. What other explanation could there be? It was all so confusing. At first it had been frustrating to recall only tidbits of memory at a time. Being frustrated only hindered the process. It required conscious effort and surely more patience than she'd been born with, but she was managing to take this slowly, one step at a time.

"Annie?"

She turned her head slowly, only to discover Sam watching her closely.

"Is something wrong?" he asked.

She shook her head. "I just had another vague memory."

Another inexplicable look of withdrawal came over him. Before she could comment, he turned his back on her and left the room. She followed him into an old-fashioned kitchen that wasn't nearly as cluttered as the other rooms had been. "That coffee smells good," she said.

"Help yourself."

Again with the clipped response. This time she knew she hadn't imagined it. Looking at him, she wondered what had changed between last night and today. "Maybe I'll take a coffee break later. Where do you want me to begin?"

"I'll leave that up to you." He headed for the back door.

She hurried after him, stopping on the top cement step, one hand still gripping the doorknob behind her. "Sam, is something wrong?"

His escape thwarted, Sam considered his answer carefully as he turned around. "Nothing's wrong," he said. And then, like an idiot, he added, "Why?"

"Oh," she said, the breeze toying with dark wisps of hair that had escaped the clear plastic clasp high on the back of her head. "I was just wondering about something."

She was staring at him so closely it required a conscious effort on his part to refrain from fidgeting. Mentally, he prepared himself for her to say that he looked vaguely familiar.

"Somebody told me there are less than three hundred people in Midnight Cove."

"Give or take a few, I guess."

"I looked for you in the phone book."

He braced himself. "I don't have a phone."

"That explains why I couldn't find your number."

"Do you need to call someone?"

She pulled a face. "Who on earth would I call?"

"Then what is it?" That had sounded impatient even to him. It didn't stop her from continuing.

"Not only are you not in the phone book, but there are no other O'Connors in the phone directory for Midnight Cove, either. You're not from here?"

Sam believed in telling as few lies as necessary. "I grew up in Ohio."

"Ah. There are probably a lot of O'Connors in Ohio, and O'Malleys and O'Learys." She took her hand off the doorknob and folded her arms in front of her. "O'Leary, now there's a good Irish name. It got a bad rep after the Chicago fire. Did you know that was a farce?"

"The fire?"

"No. The people who claimed it was started by Mrs. O'Leary's cow. I'm not saying there wasn't a Mrs. O'Leary, or that she didn't have a cow. But the Chicago fire wasn't the only fire that started that night in 1871. It wasn't even the most deadly."

Sam didn't remember retracing his footsteps, but suddenly he was standing near the bottom step, looking up at Annie, close enough to reach out and touch her. She drew him. It was that simple. She knew things without knowing how she knew. It was that complex.

She stood in the same patch of morning sunshine that was warming his shoulders. Birds twittered from their hiding places in his overgrown yard. For the first time in a long, long time, Sam didn't want to take his boat to the island. He wanted to stay here and listen to the smooth cadence in Annie's voice. That wasn't all he wanted.

She was still talking about the fire, and she was on a roll. Rather than stop her by asking questions, he simply watched the way her lips moved over the words she spoke with perfect enunciation, and listened to the excited lilt in her voice.

He could picture her in broadcast news. She had the voice for it, and the looks. Attractive without being overly so, she had the kind of face a person could relate to and would undoubtedly remember. Add to that the way she could home in on a topic, asking probing questions, finding a raw nerve with incredible ease, and she was dangerous, all right.

"Other fires broke out in Illinois that night. Some spread all the way to Michigan, but that night on October eighth, the same night as the Chicago fire, Wisconsin was struck by the worst natural disaster in its history. They called it the Great Peshtigo Forest Fire. More than twelve hundred people were killed. Only three hundred died in the Chicago fire."

Sam had never heard this. He hoisted one booted foot onto the first step, the story almost as intriguing as she was.

"Nobody knows how the fires really started. Maybe there was a meteor shower, or maybe it was just so dry that year that all it took was a spark of static electricity and a mild breeze to start a raging inferno."

He considered her theories before asking, "How do you suppose the Mrs. O'Leary's cow story got started?"

She shrugged. "A better question would be why."

"Somebody probably made it up." Probably a reporter. He scowled.

"Do you resent all women, Sam?"

His eyes narrowed.

"Or just me?"

For a long moment, he looked up at her. She was wearing loose-fitting khakis and a sleeveless plum-colored shirt. Her face was free of makeup, her gaze direct. The woman certainly called them like she saw them. Giving his head a self-deprecating shake, he said, "I don't resent all women, or you."

She studied him, as if measuring his sincerity. With a nod, she spun around and opened the door. "I'll get to work now."

"Annie?"

"Yes?" she called over her shoulder.

"Why do you think someone made up that story about Mrs. O'Leary's cow?"

Her brown eyes had a burning, faraway look in them. "Some people want an explanation for everything. Some things just happen. Others just plain are."

He couldn't have said it better himself.

Six years, he'd lived here. Alone. He could count on one hand the times in those six years he'd been lonely. After the fiasco following the lightning strike, he'd never wanted to see another crowd. He'd embraced the solitude of this place. He had four walls and a roof, running water, his boat, and the island. Oh, he'd had to deal with the occasional normal carnal desires. The need thrumming just below the surface of his skin right now was different.

"I know a lot about Wisconsin," she said.

"I noticed." He liked the way she pulled a face, the way she could laugh at herself. He liked the way she smiled and the way she didn't take what life had dished out sitting down.

"I think it's possible I'm from there."

Either that, Sam thought, or she'd done some snooping into the past. Reporters were known for their snooping. She was dangerous, all right, and getting more dangerous all the time. Putting up a stronger guard, he motioned toward his house. "I don't expect you to get everything done in one day, or hell, in one week, but any progress you make will be appreciated. Perhaps you can tackle the bathroom and the kitchen, today. I would appreciate it if you'd stay out of the two bedrooms downstairs." He thought about the door he'd locked at the end of the downstairs hall. "The cleaning products are under the sink in the kitchen. Help yourself to the food in the refrigerator. Work as many or as few hours as you want. Just keep track of them so I can pay you."

He turned then, and quickly left.

Smoothing her hand over her khaki chinos, Annie waited to return to the kitchen until after Sam strode through the gate. She noticed he didn't look back. Sometimes, she swore he seemed attracted to her. And yet he appeared to be fighting it with all the momentum of an apple cart careening down a steep hill. Surely all men didn't go from warm to cool in the blink of an eye.

She thought about that as she ran water in the kitchen sink and squirted in a little dish soap. She washed one plate, one glass, one fork, one pan. She'd met most of the residents of Midnight Cove during her first two days here, and yet she'd only met Sam a few days ago. He lived alone, worked alone, ate alone.

Did he always sleep alone, too? The thought came unbidden. Try as she might, she couldn't dislodge it from her mind. It was like trying to ignore a chocolate craving. Great. Now she wanted chocolate, too.

Once the dishes were washed and dried and the counters wiped off, she made a pass through the first floor, trying to decide what to do next. She swept the kitchen floor, but got very little dirt. Despite the state of the rest of the house, the kitchen had been cleaned recently. She strode to the bathroom next. Other than a few streaks on the mirror and some beard clippings in the sink, the room wasn't terribly dirty, either. Why would Sam clean these rooms while completely ignoring the others?

Something about his house bothered the back of her mind.

She promised herself a candy bar with a cup of coffee when she took her break later. Deciding she might as well mop the floors she'd swept, she started down the hall in search of a closet that might contain a mop. The hall was dark. Of course it was dark. One door was closed tightly and a second was open only a crack.

She took a step toward the second, only to bring herself up short. *He doesn't want you in these bedrooms,* she told herself.

Why not?

It's none of your business.

It required every ounce of willpower she possessed to do an about-face and retrace her footsteps to the kitchen. Fifteen seconds later she was back, one hand flattened against the door that was slightly ajar. It creaked as she pushed it open.

Sunshine spilled across the worn linoleum floor, causing her to blink. So this was where Sam slept. She didn't know what she'd expected, but it wasn't this. The room was comfortably furnished. The bed was big and high and neatly made.

She told herself to retrace her footsteps, close the door, and forget about Sam's bedroom. Quietly, she strolled farther into the room.

The living and dining rooms were cluttered, and that was putting it nicely. This room looked lived in, in a comfortable, masculine, pleasantly disheveled way. It was so like Sam. Something told her he'd brought this furniture with him from wherever he'd lived before. Ohio, he'd said. Two tall chests matched a simple, heavy-looking oak headboard. A television was perched on top of one of the chests of drawers, the usual loose change, gum wrappers, and matchbooks on the other. The table beside the bed held a lamp, an alarm clock, and a hardcover book. Her breath caught as she picked up the book. She hadn't known the latest L.S. Oliver suspense drama was out. She wondered what else she'd missed these past four weeks. Until that moment, she hadn't remembered that he was her favorite author.

Annie smiled. Bit by bit, pieces of her past were coming back to her. Her memories added up to very little, but meant the world to her. Still smiling, she ran a hand along the edge of a small writing desk where a variety of other books were stacked. She noticed a strange-looking battery that was plugged into some sort of charger. She'd seen that kind of rechargeable battery before, but she couldn't recall where she'd been or what it was used for. So far, she'd seen nothing in Sam's house that would require such a battery.

Sam O'Connor was no slob. There were no girlie magazines sticking out from between the mattresses, either. Why had he asked her not to come in here? What was he afraid she would find?

She strode to the open closet next. He had a lot of clothes for a lobsterman—she went down on her haunches—and a lot of shoes.

She didn't invade his privacy to the point of poking through boxes. She was no shrinking violet, and she could have used more tact, especially when she was around Sam. She was relieved to discover that she knew where to draw the line. Sam didn't want her straightening this room. Fine. She looked over her shoulder at the closed door across the hall.

Forget about it, she told herself.

She was across the hall before she'd finished the thought.

"Don't do it," she muttered under her breath even as she reached for the doorknob.

What harm could there be in peeking inside?

She pushed on the door. It didn't open as the first one had. She gripped the antique knob a little tighter and pushed a little harder. Still, the door didn't open. It was stuck. She jiggled the handle. She put her weight into it. It didn't budge. She stood back, bristling. That door wasn't stuck. It was locked.

She did an about-face and returned to the kitchen like she should have in the first place. So he kept a room locked. So what? This was his house. He had every right to lock any door he pleased.

She filled a bucket with hot water and added detergent. She located a mop hanging from a hook in a little nook near the back door, and got busy. All the while she mopped, she wondered why Sam had asked, okay, told her not to go inside that room. And why was that the only door he kept locked?

It was none of her business.

She sure wished she could get a little peek.

She wasn't here to peek. She was here to clean.

What harm could there be in just looking?

The mop slipped out of her hands as an idea washed over her. He'd asked her to stay out of the room. He hadn't said anything about peeking in from the outside. Besides, she had to be patient when it came to regaining her memory, which meant she couldn't learn more about herself. Maybe she could learn more about Sam.

She practically ran to the bathroom and looked out the window, getting her bearings. Next, she went outside and stood peering up at a high window on the back side of the house. That was the room, all right. The curtains were open a few inches. From here, all she could see was a narrow wedge of the ceiling.

Too bad she didn't have a ladder.

There was a shed out back. She had no idea if it contained a ladder. Plus, there were so many overgrown bushes and vines, she would need a machete to clear a path. She didn't have a machete. Even if she knew where one was, she shuddered to think what could happen if she attempted to use one.

She stared up at the window again. Darned high windows anyway. A chair would never be tall enough. *But a table with a chair on top of it might be.*

It took fifteen minutes to clear a path through the junk, er, furniture, in the living room so she could drag a lightweight table and sturdy wooden chair outside. Since she'd proven several times over, this week alone, that she wasn't the most graceful person in the world, she took extra care stacking old textbooks on the uneven portion of the ground under one table leg.

Satisfied that the structure was sound, she climbed on the table. From there, she went carefully up on the chair. It felt pretty solid, but her platform was still a foot too short.

This is a sign, her conscience warned her. *Better heed it. Just put this furniture back inside and forget about that locked room. If you don't, you'll be sorry.*

She'd come too far to listen to the bothersome voice of her conscience now. She made one last trip inside, only to return with a three-legged stool, which she placed on the seat of the chair. She tested it with her hand first. Steady as a rock. Well, almost.

With utmost care, she climbed up. So far so good. The stool teetered the tiniest bit as she put her weight on it, but not enough to keep her from grasping the windowsill for balance. Ever so slowly, she went up on tiptoe and peered through the window. "What the . . ."

She pressed her nose closer to the glass. The room was . . .

That solid-as-a-rock stool rocked slightly beneath her feet. The locked room was . . .

"You just couldn't resist, could you?" Startled, she looked around. Sam was striding toward her.

Uh-oh.

The stool teetered again, and then the whole thing started to crumble. Suddenly, she was airborne.

But not for long.

Chapter Four

Sam had just cleared the back corner of his house when he saw Annie perched on top of a makeshift tower constructed of a stack of books, an old table, a painted chair, and a three-legged stool. Any second now it was all going to come tumbling down, Annie right along with it. Damned fool woman couldn't even navigate the four-inch step at the diner. What on earth was she thinking trying this?

"You just couldn't resist, could you?"

Of course, she turned her head at the sound of his voice. The slight movement caused the stool to teeter and the table to rock. The chair pitched one way, the stool the other, the entire structure toppling like a house of cards.

He saw it happening, but he couldn't get there fast enough to break her fall. Twigs snapped. Cringing at the sound of her body hitting the ground, he dropped to his knees in front of her still form. "Annie, can you hear me?"

She groaned softly.

"Don't move."

Her eyes fluttered open. And of course she moved.

"Damn it, I said hold still." He ran a hand along her face, down her neck, over her shoulders and arms.

"No, you didn't," she whispered. "You said don't move."

Sam swore the woman would argue with the pope, but at least she held still.

"Sam?" she whispered.

He grunted something that meant "what," his attention on the course his hands took as he smoothed them over her, searching for broken bones. This was his fault. He'd put the sharp knives away, but he should have known she wouldn't be able to leave that locked room alone.

She moaned again. This time it sounded different. "Hmm, that feels nice. Um, Sam?" she said, a little louder than before. "Do you think you could help me out of this briar patch before feeling me up again?"

Before feeling her up . . .

He stared at her in complete astonishment. He didn't bother protesting, at least not out loud. He wasn't feeling her up, damn it. And his jeans weren't suddenly a size too small. Finally, he got his composure in check and sputtered, "I'm trying to see if anything's broken."

"Oh." A blush crept slowly up her face, turning her cheeks a vivid scarlet. She moved one leg, then the other, both arms, and her neck. "Nothing's broken." Keeping her gaze averted, she started to get up.

"Easy." He tried to be careful as he helped her. When he was certain she was steady on her feet, he said, "Are you sure you're okay?"

The clasp had come out of her hair and her arms were scratched. She looked a little shaky, but not seriously injured. Nodding, she mumbled, "Am I fired?"

What? He hadn't even thought about firing her. "No."

"You mean it?"

He felt like a heel. "Yes, I mean it. You have my word. You're not fired."

Just like that, her hands went to her hips and her chin came up. If she hadn't taken a backward step, he would have, because there wasn't a man alive who didn't recognize the sight of a woman gearing up to speak her mind.

"It's only ten o'clock. Why did you come back?" Her eyes had narrowed, part suspicion, part accusation. "I think I know. You came back on purpose, didn't you?"

He fumbled for an answer she didn't wait for.

"That room's empty. You locked an empty room."

Sam didn't know what to say. She was right. He had locked that room on purpose, not because he kept anything valuable in there, but because he knew that she would spend her day wondering what was behind that door. And if she was wondering about that, she wouldn't be wondering about him.

"It was a test, wasn't it?" she asked.

He didn't know what she was talking about.

"You *do* resent me. And you don't trust me."

He noticed she failed to mention the fact that

she'd just given him good reason not to trust her. "Look, it might seem as if I . . ."

She shook off his hand. "No, you look. On second thought, go ahead and fire me." She darted around him with an agility that was at odds with a woman who'd just taken a nasty fall and who'd been known to trip over a crack in the sidewalk and that annoying step in the diner. "You know what?" she said. "I have a better idea." She turned and walked away.

He found himself racing after her. "Where are you going?"

"Anywhere but here." She flung the words into the wind. "I think I'd prefer the smell of raw fish to this."

"What do you mean?"

"I mean," she said, turning at the gate, "you can wrap this job up, put it in your Haan loafer, and stick the entire bundle where the sun doesn't shine."

He could tell by her expression that she realized she'd just let another little faux pas slip. There was only one way she could have known he owned that particular brand of shoe. She'd snooped in his closet. If it was possible, it seemed to make her even more angry.

"That's what you can do, Sam O'Connor." She looked at him, brown eyes flashing, daring him to make something of it. "And do you know what else? You don't look Irish!"

She took a shaky breath, raised her chin another notch, and stiffly lifted the latch on the gate. Just then, the little girl with curly red hair who lived next door peddled by on a tricycle. "Anne Elizabeth Hogan come back here! Annie, I mean it!"

her frazzled-looking, freckled older brother called, hurrying after his sister.

The red-haired child didn't even slow down, but the grown woman with scratches on her arms and twigs stuck in her coffee-colored hair went perfectly still.

"Annie?" Sam said quietly.

She turned slowly, her gaze on the child nearing the end of the block. "My name isn't Annie."

She looked at the bracelet on her wrist, fingering the gold block letters, A-N-N-I-E. In a voice so soft Sam had to strain to hear, she said, "Annie is my daughter's name." She slumped against the gate. "I just remembered her face and the sound of her voice. She's twelve. Why isn't anyone looking for me, Sam?"

Sam really hated to bring this up. Keeping his voice low, he said, "Do you think it's possible your daughter is . . . gone?"

"You mean . . . gone to heaven?" She looked at him and slowly shook her head. "I don't think so. I think I would feel it if she were dead." With a sense of conviction that surely had to be part of her character, she said, "I would know."

Annie—make that *What's-Her-Name*—imposed an iron control on her emotions. The child she was slowly starting to remember was very much alive. The certainty was like a rock inside her. Now, who in the hell was *she*? This was getting terribly annoying. Stronger now, she took a calming breath and said, "Maybe nobody's looking for me because nobody likes me."

"That's impossible."

She turned her head and got lost in the heat

in Sam's eyes. "I'm outspoken. I'm clumsy. I'm a snoop."

"You're witty. You're smart. And you're very brave."

She fought to maintain her curtness. "You don't even like me."

"You're wrong about that. I like you." He was moving closer. She knew, because she'd had to grasp the top of the gate to keep from falling when she'd heard the boy call after his little sister. And she could still feel the gate beneath her hand. She hadn't moved. She couldn't.

Sam liked her. She thought about that locked room. He had funny ways of showing it. "Sam?" He was so close now she could see herself in his eyes.

"I'm listening."

"I really don't think kissing me is a very good idea."

"Know what I think?" he asked, his mouth so close she could feel his breath on the tip of her nose. "I think kissing you is the best idea I've had all day."

Her eyes fluttered closed at the first feathery touch of his lips on hers. She'd expected Sam's kiss to take her by storm, and yet this kiss was no more than a brush of air at first, a whisper meeting a sigh on a balmy summer morning. Gradually, it changed. She tilted her head slightly and parted her lips beneath his. Other than his fingers, which he threaded through her hair in order to tilt her head slightly, the only parts of their bodies touching were their mouths. He moved his lips over hers like a man who knew what he wanted, persuading her, lulling her, luring her into the haze of desire that was slowly obliterating everything except the feel of his mouth on hers and what it was doing to the pit of her stomach and the empty space behind her breastbone.

His beard was soft where it brushed her face, adding a sensual dimension that aroused her fantasies. He groaned deep in his throat, letting her know he wanted more but wasn't taking any more than she offered. It was a dreamy notion, which was strange because she wasn't normally given to dreaminess.

It had been a long time since a man had kissed her like this. She couldn't remember other men. She doubted she would ever forget Sam. The idea brought more than a rush of blood and a flutter of her heart. It brought tears to the back of her throat and warmth everywhere else.

"Annie?"

It took a moment for her to realize that the kiss had ended, and another moment for her to open her eyes, which she did, only to find Sam looking at her, his gaze steady, his eyes very, very gray.

He motioned to the sidewalk. The little girl and her brother were watching. The boy blushed; his little sister giggled before putting her feet on the pedals and scooting away toward home, her brother following after her.

What's-Her-Name watched them go. "I guess I should give myself another name."

"It's your decision, of course, but everyone here knows you by Annie Valentine. I see no reason to change it while you're waiting for your memory to return."

He didn't say *if* her memory returned. She appreciated that. "I'll think about it."

"Are you sure you're all right?" he asked.

She thought about that locked room, and how she had fallen for it hook, line, and sinker. "I guess I'm a little hurt."

He reached for her hand. "I'm taking you to Dr. Richardson."

"What? Why? No, I don't mean physically." She touched her chest with three fingertips. "I'm hurt in here."

She shook her head to clear it. What was there about this man that made her blurt out every thought at precisely the moment she had it? Recovering slightly, she put up a stronger guard and said, "I'll be fine."

She opened the gate.

"What are you doing?" he asked.

"I'm going home. I quit, remember?"

"But I thought . . ."

"You thought what? That one little kiss would change everything?" She had his undivided attention now. "I don't even know who I am, yet I speak the truth. Maybe you should try it, because no matter what you said, you don't trust me. You share next to nothing of yourself, how you feel, what you think. It's too bad, too, because I was going to ask you if I could borrow that book by L.S. Oliver I saw on your nightstand."

Oh, for heaven's sake, there she went again, reminding Sam that she'd snooped in his room. She looked at him. For a moment, she felt the way she did when a craving for chocolate came over her. She sighed. "Too bad sex is out of the question."

She heard the sharp breath he took. She struggled with her own sharp breath. Sex with Sam *was* out of the question. She had amnesia. She had a life somewhere. Besides, she'd already shared more of herself with him than he had with her. He'd locked an empty room. As far as symbolism went, it was extremely telling. She'd been open with him while he kept himself locked up tight.

"Good-bye, Sam O'Connor." She walked through the gate. This time she was the one who didn't look back.

Sam watched her go. If she'd had the decency to look, she would have seen that his eyes had darkened like thunderclouds. The woman had a lot of nerve, quitting when she was the one who'd been caught with her nose pressed to the window of a room he'd distinctly told her was off-limits. It sure as hell hadn't been the first time he'd caught somebody snooping through his things. Before he'd disappeared and changed his name, reporters had dogged his every step, camping out in hotels, posing as limousine drivers, pretending to be gardeners. They even went through his trash.

He should have been accustomed to people blurting out whatever they were thinking, and yet Annie's mention that sex was out of the question had rendered him speechless. She was outspoken, clumsy, and a snoop. She'd said so herself. So she'd quit. So what?

Good riddance.

He stomped to the backyard and carted the furniture back inside where it belonged, sputtering under his breath all the while.

He was lucky to be rid of her. Damned lucky, indeed.

No matter what she'd said, that hadn't been just a little kiss, damn it. And what the hell did she mean it was too bad sex was out of the question?

* * *

Annie was getting out of the shower when she heard the knock on her door. She wasn't expecting company. She hadn't made a lot of friends while she'd been in Midnight Cove. Actually, there was only one person she could think of who might pay her a visit this time of the evening, and she wasn't in any hurry to see him.

She took her time drying off, mindful of the sore muscles that ached and the scratches that burned when touched. The knock sounded a second time, louder than before.

She removed her shower cap, shook out her hair. She donned her long robe and took great care hanging up her towel and putting the hairbrush and shower cap away. She wasn't stalling. She was taking her sweet time.

The third knock rattled the door and anything not battened down. Cinching the sash of her robe tight at her waist, she sashayed out of the bathroom and strolled to the door. She looked through the peephole, turned the lock, and opened the door.

Sam's fist wound up knocking on thin air. He let his arm fall to his side. The streetlights were on behind him. The glow gave him a dreamy, superhero-type quality. He'd brought the purse she'd left at his house that morning. In his hand was a hardcover book and one long-stemmed rose. He'd cleaned up, probably in the shower she'd cleaned that very morning. He'd looked darned good in his work clothes. Spit and polished, he was a sight to behold.

"Yes?" she asked, as if he were selling vacuum cleaners door-to-door.

"Did I ever tell you that "yes" is my favorite word in the English language?"

There was a ghost of a smile in his gray eyes. When she failed to reply, the humor evaporated into thin air.

She'd thought about him a lot today. She'd read somewhere that good judgment came from experience, and a lot of that came from bad judgment. She was in no position to make any bad judgments.

"What are you doing here, Sam?"

Sam ran a hand down his short beard, thinking, damned if he knew. She was looking up at him, waiting for him to say something. During the ten years he'd been on the professional golf circuit, he'd made small talk with just about everybody he saw, from fellow golfers to caddies to fans and reporters. And here he was, standing before a woman he wanted to impress, as tongue-tied as a teenager in a new pair of jeans and his father's car, trying to get up the courage to talk to the prettiest girl in school.

"You said I haven't shared any part of myself with you. I came to talk."

She stared at him far longer than was considered polite. And then she stared a little more. He let her look her fill before saying, "What do you think?"

Finally, she tilted her head and said, "I really don't think that purse goes with your outfit."

He did a double take and slowly grinned, taking the fact that she was joking with him as a good sign. He doubted she could have known what the sight of her in a simple, thin yellow dressing gown was doing to his heart rate or his ability to think coherently. Before he lost every last brain cell to fantasy, he handed the bag over to her. "May I come in?"

"Would I still get to read that book if I said no?"

He handed her the book, but kept the rose to the count of ten before holding it out to her, as well.

"You're a scoundrel, do you know that?"

"Would you believe me if I told you I've been called worse?"

"Why wouldn't I believe you? Are you prone to lying?"

He supposed he couldn't blame her for baiting him. "I'm not prone to lying. I've lived alone, been alone, for a long time. I guess I'm not very good at talking anymore. I know, it boggles the mind that I could be bad at anything."

She brought the rose to her nose as she opened the door a little farther. It was all the invitation Sam needed. He stepped over the threshold and quietly walked inside.

The room was small. From the looks of things, it had come furnished. He strolled to one corner of the room; she went to another corner. A lamp was on near an overstuffed chair. As if realizing how intimate the semidark room appeared, she switched on two others. Now that the light was behind her, he could see the outline of her body through her robe.

"Why?" she asked.

He had to clear his throat to say, "Why what?"

"Why have you lived all alone, been all alone for a long, long time?"

He cleared his throat again. "At first, I wanted to be alone. I needed to be alone."

"And now?"

"Now, I find myself wanting to be with you."

Annie's heart tripped in its beat. Being wanted by Sam O'Connor was a heady sensation, but it didn't change her resolve. She couldn't let it. She didn't know why he'd given her a job if he didn't trust her. Obviously, he had issues. She had problems of her own. She examined the bracelet. At least now she understood what the Annie charm stood for. She didn't know what the quill pen symbolized, but she was pretty sure the gold charm that was shaped like a chocolate candy stood for her craving for anything chocolate.

"Are you sore tonight?"

"I ache in places I didn't know I had. I examined every square inch of my body in the shower a little while ago, and I can honestly say that although I have a few bruises and several scratches, the worst damage was to my pride and my tattoo."

"You have a tattoo?"

She dropped her face into her hands, coming dangerously close to poking herself in the eye with the rose. She had little tact and less restraint, and really, few redeeming qualities. No wonder no one was looking for her. She clamped her mouth shut and wasn't going to open it and that was that.

Sam strode toward her with a kind of animal grace and a determined expression that caused her to take a step back. "Where?" he said.

She shook her head.

"Come on, Annie. Where?"

"Never mind where."

"Okay, what is it a tattoo of?"

Her fingers shook slightly as she tucked her hair behind her ear. "My tattoo is none of your business."

Coming to a stop a few paces away, he held her gaze. Slowly, he rolled up the sleeve of his white T-shirt, then presented her with his left arm.

"Birdie," she said, reading the word beneath the bluebird gracing his upper arm. "The same as your boat."

He stood, waiting.

She swallowed tightly. "You think just because you showed me yours I'll show you mine?"

"I like the way you think."

She very nearly got lost in the way he was looking at her, only to come to her senses in the nick of time. "Forget it. I'm not showing you mine."

He rolled his shirtsleeve over his tattoo. "Then describe it to me."

"No."

He stared into her eyes.

And she whispered, "It's a kiss."

Sam heard her moan. He sympathized with anybody who tried to keep something from him, but in this instance he couldn't help using his power to his benefit. "A kiss?" His imagination was in full swing, his gaze trained on her mouth. "Do you mean like lips?"

"Not that kind of kiss. A chocolate kiss. You know. Candy. I love chocolate. Candy bars, brownies, cookies, cheese cake, sundaes. It's amazing I don't weigh half a ton."

She wasn't heavy. She wasn't even overweight. She had curves in all the right places, but he'd assumed it was genetics. Maybe he should be thanking her chocolate addiction. Somewhere on her lush body was a tattoo of a chocolate kiss, somewhere that she wouldn't show him. He pictured a few of those places in his mind. He had a very, very good imagination.

"Did you know that chocolate doesn't really come from cocoa beans?"

He gave his blood a few seconds to make its way back to his brain before attempting to make sense of the question. She was at it again, talking, spouting facts that few people could know.

"Actually, chocolate as we know it today comes from the cacao tree. Because of a mistake in its spelling, which was probably made by English importers a few hundred years ago, the beans became known as cocoa beans."

Sam stared at her, uncertain how to respond. Maybe she wasn't a reporter at all. Then what in the hell was she?

She was beautiful. She was smart. She'd probably known it once. He found himself wanting to be the one who told her, and showed her, until she believed it again.

"There I went again, going on and on about nothing."

Then and there Sam faced the fact that he knew exactly what else she was. She was a woman he wanted a great deal.

"I really hope I don't offend people with my know-it-all attitude."

"Do I look offended, Annie?"

She appeared to consider the question, and then she considered him. "You look rugged and intense and far too appealing for my peace of mind. And that's why you should go." She started toward the door. "Thank you for returning my purse. And for loaning me the book. I look forwarding to reading it." She brought the pale yellow rose to her nose again and breathed in the heady scent. "And thank you for the flower."

That made three thank-yous and one good-bye, which was one good-bye too many. Watching her smooth that rose across her cheek in a movement that was as naturally uncalculated as it was sensual, Sam's imagination took another slow dip into the erotic zone. He didn't know what the hell he was doing. He only knew he didn't want to leave. "You insinuated I was closed off."

"I did?"

"This morning. Before you left." He ran a hand through his hair. He really had lost the ability to carry on a natural, normal conversation.

She looked at him. "Yes?"

There was that word again. "I'm not that closed off."

"Pu-lease. I know nothing about you."

"What do you want to know?"

Annie considered the question. She'd been putting her application in at the marina when Sam had gotten back to the harbor that afternoon. She'd noticed the comings and goings of other fishermen. All of them carted bait and tackle and the days' catch on and off their boats. By comparison, Sam traveled pretty lightly.

"What do you do?" she asked. She held up a hand in a halting gesture. "And don't tell me you're a lobsterman." She pointed to his hands, which were strong and clean. They were rough enough to be masculine, but they weren't weathered and calloused and cracked like the hands of the men whose coffee cups she'd filled during her brief stint as a waitress. "Those aren't the hands of a fisherman."

She sensed a certain tension in his attitude, as if he was drawing away, into himself again. She told herself she hadn't expected him to tell her, therefore there was no reason to feel disappointed.

"You're right."

She swung around so fast the front of her robe opened to the middle of her thigh. Holding the edges together with one hand, she said, "I'm right about what?"

He was still looking at the material bunched in her hand as he said, "You're right about my hands. Know what I think we should do?"

"What, pray tell?"

Sam didn't blame her for being suspicious. He was getting in over his head. He knew it, yet he couldn't seem to do anything about it. He was the one with the powers. She had a few powers of her own, and in this instance hers were stronger.

"Come with me tomorrow and see for yourself."

Her mouth dropped open.

Sam didn't blame her. He was mildly surprised about the suggestion himself. Still, it felt good to be the one who wasn't speechless for a change. "You're not answering. Does that mean you have something better to do?"

She rolled her eyes.

"Or," he said, taking a purposeful step in her direction, "maybe you don't really want to know anything about me. I suppose it's possible that you're secretly afraid to put your money where your mouth is."

That did it. Her shoulders went back and her chin came up. "What time do we leave?"

"Meet me at my house at six tomorrow morning."

"Is the sun even up at six?"

So, she wasn't an early riser. "I guess you're going to find out, aren't you?"

She studied him thoughtfully, then quietly said, "I'll be there."

"I'll be waiting." He reached out, touching her face with two fingertips. Without another word, he walked out the door.

Annie stood perfectly still for a long time after he left, her hand cradling the cheek he'd touched, feeling as if she'd been kissed.

What do you want to know? Sam had asked.

Annie—she hated that she didn't even know her own name—wanted to know how a touch could feel like a kiss. While she was at it, she wouldn't have minded knowing why she was so drawn to him. He was just a man, right? He was an annoying man at that. And he had a beard. Normally, she preferred a man who was clean shaven. Another taste she'd only just recalled.

So what was there about Sam O'Connor?

And why did she have so much trouble keeping her thoughts to herself when she was with him? Perhaps that was the biggest question of all.

Chapter Five

According to the clock radio Annie had borrowed from Dulcie, the sun was up at six the following morning. It just wasn't easy to tell because of the fog.

The lights were on in Sam's house when Annie arrived, but he wasn't waiting by the door as he had been the previous day. Instead, her knock was answered from a few rooms away. "Door's open. Come on in!"

Sam didn't keep his front door locked, and yet he'd locked that empty bedroom. By the time she entered the kitchen, she was mad all over again.

Her withering stare was wasted on his back. If that wasn't bad enough, she rather liked the view. He had broad shoulders, muscular upper arms, a narrow waist. It only got better from there.

She really had no pride. "What are you doing?"

"I'm packing our lunch," he said. "Good morning to you, too."

She yawned. "It's too early to be a good morning."

Finally, he glanced over his shoulder and looked at her. "You didn't get enough sleep?"

Needing some place else to look, she meandered into the dining room. "I was up late reading. You know, Sam, a lot of this junk is probably worth some money."

"I hope you like yogurt and fruit and cheese. Do you know anything about antiques?"

"No. I don't even particularly like them. Huh. What do you know? I mean, I appreciate them, and admire the craftsmen who made them. It isn't as if they had power tools back then, right? The problem is, antiques are old, and they often smell musty. A lot of people pay a pretty penny for old, musty things."

"You think they're worth trying to sell?"

"Sure. I guess."

"Ever had a garage sale?"

She looked around her at the claw-footed chairs, flute-edged tables, trunks, pottery, and pictures. "You'd get more if you called it an antique sale."

"Then do it. We'll split the profits. Are you enjoying the book?"

She could see Sam from her position in the dining room. He was adding cans of soda and bottled water to a large cooler, the epitome of masculine ease in a gray polo shirt and faded jeans.

"I'm enjoying it very much. What kind of split are you talking about?"

"Fifty-fifty. I supply the junk. You do all the work. Even steven. How far did you get?"

She strode toward the kitchen, her mind flooded with ideas and ways to advertise Sam's antiques.

Leaning a shoulder against the trim in the doorway, she yawned again. "I got too far. I should have been sleeping. Have you read a lot of Oliver's work?"

He shrugged those massive shoulders, but said, "Yeah, have you?"

"My mother recommended his books before she died." She stopped suddenly. "My mother died four years ago."

He waited a moment before saying, "That explains why she isn't looking for you."

Her mother had been gone for four years. That was a very good reason not to be looking for her only child.

She was an only child.

"You ready?" Sam turned out the lights, closed the door.

Annie noticed he didn't lock it. Bother the man.

They set off toward the harbor, him in his tattered baseball cap and no jacket, her in turquoise-colored Capri pants and a white windbreaker. "My friend Suzette"—she had a friend named Suzette—"thinks the 'L' in L.S. Oliver stands for Laura or Lisa. I think the edge in his writing could only come from a man. Some people believe he's a priest, like that other writer, Father What's-His-Name. Another friend of mine, Rachel . . . Huh. Well, I'll be darned. Anyway, Rachel thinks he's in prison."

"Why would she think that?"

Annie tried to see Sam's expression, but she was having trouble keeping up with him. She wound up studying his shoulders again, which was not terribly conducive to keeping her wits about her. "No one's ever seen him, for one thing. Personally, I think that anybody who can get into a killer's head the way he does would have to be a little warped."

Sam stopped so quickly she nearly ran into him. He started up again, and she continued. "He probably lives in LA or New York and gets his rocks off by attending all the big parties incognito."

"Why would he do that?" There was definitely an edge in Sam's voice.

"How should I know? I have amnesia, remember? Maybe he likes hearing the praise but doesn't want to own up to criticism."

They'd reached the dock. "That's ridiculous."

A light fog hung over the water, making the air feel cooler and the voices of other fishermen preparing for a day at sea seem louder. Sam untied one rope. Following his lead, Annie untied one, too. "You asked for my opinion." She hopped onto the boat.

"I see you got yourself an apprentice there, aye Sam?" Percy Parnell called, his voice like a foghorn, his eyes in that perpetual squint. "Got enough life preservers with ya?"

Sam nodded and Annie had to force herself to smile nicely. Apparently her reputation had preceded her.

"It isn't what you're thinking," Sam said as he stepped up to the helm and started the engine. "Percy asks everyone if they have the required life preservers on board."

"Oh."

"Don't you want to know why?" he asked.

She shivered as she considered the question. Most people in Midnight Cove didn't offer explanations regarding the whys and wherefores of their daily lives. Even though she reminded herself that

Sam was only offering information about some-body else, and grudgingly at that, she softened a little. "Okay," she said. "Why?"

"One morning sixty years ago, Percy and his brother went out fishing. That night, only Percy came back." He paused for a moment, then said, "Here. You'll need these." She caught the life pre-server and yellow raincoat he tossed at her.

She'd assumed the windbreaker she'd donned before leaving her apartment would be enough protection against the early morning chill. She slid her arms into the sleeves of the storm gear and then donned the life vest, and was instantly warmer. Of course, it could have had something to do with Sam's explanation. It reminded her that everyone had problems, troubles, obstacles, and the occa-sional brick wall to navigate. Somehow that made her feel more understood. And feeling more understood made her feel less desperate for the rest of her memory to return in the next ten min-utes. Maybe brain cells healed slowly. Or maybe things like this just took time. That didn't stop her from feeling impatient at times.

She watched as the harbor grew smaller behind them. One by one, the other boats disappeared through the ribbons of fog. "Your boat is smaller than the others."

"Are you telling me size matters?"

Leave it to a man to get that connotation from a simple statement. "I'm talking about boats." She noticed Sam's beard was hiding a smile. "Where are we going?"

"You'll see."

"Now that you cleared that up . . . "

Sam studied Annie's expression. She was looking

straight ahead, her mouth shut tight. Last night, he'd considered calling Grant to request an emergency head examination. Sam didn't know who Annie Valentine was. Annie Valentine didn't even know who she was. She didn't know who he was, either, and he would just as soon keep it that way.

Then why the hell had he invited her to spend the day with him? His body knew the answer even if his brain was resisting the truth. Part of that truth was tied up in his fantasies about that tattoo she wouldn't show him.

She wanted to know what he did here. That wasn't asking so much. As long as he kept his wits about him, what harm could there be in showing her at least part of what he did and who he was? That was the clincher. This was about more than sex. He couldn't let her discover who he'd been, and yet he wanted her to know who he'd become. The truth was, he wasn't the same man he'd been six years ago, eight years ago, ten. Sam found himself wanting someone to get to know the recluse, perhaps even be glad she knew him. Not just anyone. He wanted this woman who called herself Annie to know the man he was today. And that, in a nutshell, was what made this so dangerous.

"Sam? What brought you here?"

Since she had no way of knowing he'd left his former life, or even that he'd had a former life, she couldn't have been asking about that. She only wanted to know why he'd chosen this particular place to live.

"I like the ocean."

She sank into the seat a few feet from him, seeming to ponder that for a moment. "There are other oceans."

It was disconcerting the way she could home in on the heart of an issue so effortlessly. "I considered living on the West Coast." He spoke into the wind and steered the boat around a sharp outcropping of rock. "Once, I drove through California's wine country and didn't stop until I came to the rocky Oregon coast. I could have made any one of a hundred towns my home."

"But you didn't."

He shook his head. "I spent some time on the Gulf in Florida. The weather would have been easier to live with there."

"Not everyone is looking for a temperate climate. What were you looking for?"

She'd done it again.

Sam shook his head to clear it, uncertain how to proceed. He couldn't tell her he'd been looking for anonymity, so he settled for as much of the truth as he dared reveal. "Although I didn't know it at the time, I was looking for that."

He pointed straight ahead. There in the distance, behind thin wisps of fog that were slowly dissolving beneath the yellow rays of the sun, was an island. His island.

He circled to the far side before dropping anchor. Huge flocks of birds took flight in the distance, eventually landing on the shore once again. When the anchor touched bottom and the boat was secure, Sam removed his yellow storm gear, then hauled a small barrel closer to the boat's edge.

"What's in there?"

He pried open the top. She wrinkled her nose and jumped backward. "What is that horrible stench?"

"Fish heads, mostly."

She was looking a little green around the collar.

"A colony of lobsters live down there." Using a long-handled scoop as a ladle, he began dumping the assorted fish parts over the side of the boat.

"I thought lobstermen put the bait inside traps."

"They do."

She didn't come any closer to the smelly barrel, but her color improved dramatically. "So, I was right. You're not a fisherman."

He shrugged.

"You're a conservationist."

He considered her terminology. "I wouldn't really call myself anything as political as that. I just feed them." Even that hadn't been intentional in the beginning. He'd purchased the bait because he'd been trying to look like a lobster fisherman. He'd dumped it overboard without realizing he was feeding a growing colony. A diver who worked for an agency that counted and tracked the migratory creatures discovered the unusual quantities here. Sam couldn't very well quit now.

"There's a new group emerging that is fighting for a more humane way to kill lobsters," he said, replacing the cover on the barrel. "Somebody's even invented a stun gun that puts them in a trance so they don't feel the pain of being dropped into a pot of boiling water."

Annie said, "I understand the principle, but I've never heard of an eagle being kind to the rabbit in its talons, or a mountain lion being gentle with a gazelle. Maybe since we're humans, we're supposed to be above that kind of cruelty."

She'd done it again. How could she know exactly what was at the heart of any issue he brought up?

"Tell me more about your lobsters."

"Since moving here," he said, "I've heard a lot of talk about conservation and regulation. Ninety-nine percent of the lobster fishermen in Maine know that overfishing would be catastrophic to their livelihoods. In their own way, they believe in preservation. It's become an issue of overfishing versus overregulation."

"You know what they say. With democracy comes dispute." Annie sensed Sam's smile, even if she didn't understand it. She felt a curious, swooping pull at her insides.

The first three weeks she'd had amnesia had been terribly confusing. Sam confused her in a completely different way.

She watched the disgusting fish by-products sink out of sight. "What else do you do besides feed them?"

When he didn't readily reply, she glanced up. He was looking at her, his battered baseball cap in one hand, the breeze ruffling his collar, lifting his sandy-brown hair off his forehead. As usual, his gray eyes held her spellbound.

"Once a month, at low tide," he said, "I try to count them."

"How on earth do you do that?"

He was the one who finally broke eye contact. Striding to the back of the boat, he brought up the anchor, then resumed his place at the wheel. "I would need scuba gear to count these." Pointing to the shallow waters near the island, he said, "I count those. Come on, I'll show you."

Annie felt a lurch of excitement, but remained quiet, content to watch as he steered closer to shore. This island was larger than many of the others they'd passed. The shore was rocky, but the center portion was wooded. Someone had built a dock in a secluded cove. Farther away, nearly out of sight on the jagged shoreline that formed a point, was a small stone cabin and the crumbled remains of a lighthouse that had all but washed into the sea.

High in the sky, flocks of birds glided, circling. "What are those birds doing?" she asked.

"Those are gulls. See there, at the water's edge? Those are herons, mostly. They're waiting for dinner."

"You feed the birds, too?"

"If I didn't, they'd eat the lobsters that nest in the shallow waters."

"Of course they would." All at once, she felt like a breathless girl of eighteen on the brink of discovery. The sensation brought a sudden glimpse of herself at that age. More and more of her memories were coming back to her. Any day now, the rest would return, too. She needed to know who she was, where she lived, what she did. Once she remembered, she would be leaving here to return to her life elsewhere. That brought a sense of urgency, and a yearning she didn't know what to do about.

Sam handed her a small covered bucket. Hoisting a burlap bag to his shoulder, he reached for her hand. She let him help her from the boat, and when he made no move to release her hand, she left it there. "Okay, now tell me how you go about counting lobsters."

"At low tide, when the water is shallow, you just turn rocks over and there they are. You have to have a quick finger, because they're fast. Come on.

Let's feed the birds first and then we'll try to find some young lobsters.''

He walked to a lean-to that housed what appeared to be a small dune buggy. Depositing the birdseed and the bucket in the back, he climbed in. The minute she was seated, he started off across the island, far away from the pools and eddies where the majority of lobsters lived.

She helped him scatter the seeds, but left him to the smellier job of dumping more fish by-products for the gulls and herons. They spent an hour laughing at the birds' antics before he led the way across a series of stepping stones poking above the water.

Although a little wobbly on the rocks, Annie was proud of herself for staying dry.

Reaching a particularly shallow area, he went down to his haunches.

Annie bent at the waist as he lifted a rock. And a dozen tiny lobsters scuttled for cover. "They're adorable.''

"They spend the first several years of their lives growing under these rocks before migrating to deeper waters.''

"Once they do, you feed them.''

He didn't appear comfortable with the wonder in her voice.

"It's a good thing, Sam. What you do, I mean.''

He kept his eyes averted, and she thought, *He's shy.*

She placed a hand on his cheek, his beard tickling her palm. "Why don't you tell people?''

"I don't want the attention.'' He took a sharp breath.

Staring at him, Annie felt on the verge of understanding something important about Sam O'Connor. He wasn't shy, as she'd thought. He was . . . something else, something as elusive as fireflies. There was something about him . . .

Something that seemed . . .

He reached for her before she knew it was happening, his arms going around her, crushing her to him. He pressed his mouth to hers, and all thoughts but one fled her mind.

Him.

Her mouth opened beneath his, his hands gliding over her from shoulders to hip, kneading her backside, drawing her up against the hard ridge of him. Shards of weak sunlight danced through her closed eyelids. Desire uncurled deep in her body, weakening her knees, turning any conscious thoughts into vapors that floated away like the fog.

Sam knew he should be ashamed of himself. A person with amnesia had been on the verge of remembering, and he'd interfered. It had been more a knee-jerk reaction than a conscious decision. Any day now, any hour, perhaps any second, she was going to recognize him. Later, he would take the time to understand his burning need to make love to her before that happened, but Sweet Mother, not now.

Chapter Six

Annie didn't know how long the kiss lasted. She'd lost track of time. No wonder. One second she'd been about to tell Sam something, and the next second she was in his arms. She became aware of the waves washing against rocks in the distance and seabirds screeching and squawking.

"Is it my imagination," she whispered, burying her face against his throat, "or am I floating?"

She felt his reluctance as he slowly lowered her feet to the ground. It wasn't until her eyes were open, the earth firmly beneath her feet, that she remembered where she was and what she'd been doing just before he'd kissed her.

"Why did you do that?"

"Only a woman would ask a question like that."

And only a man would give that kind of answer. She took a moment to straighten her clothes before studying Sam. The front of his shirt had come untucked, and he wasn't wearing his hat. She remembered knocking it askew when she'd threaded her fingers through his hair. It was lying on the ground in a shallow pool.

"Stop looking at me like that," she said.

"Like what?" he asked, all innocence.

Innocent her eye! She'd been on the verge of remembering something. Now, her mind was blank. To make matters worse, he was looking at her the way she often looked at chocolate. With open longing and waning willpower.

The strong ocean breeze fluttered her white cotton shirt, cooling skin she hadn't known was revealed until that moment. Buttoning the top two buttons, she glanced at him again as she tried to recall what it was she'd been about to remember. His brow was furrowed, his mouth set, his jaw clenched. She understood her frustration. What was Sam's problem?

"You're doing it again."

"What am I doing, Annie?"

"You're closing yourself off from me. You said you would be open with me today."

"If that kiss had gone on any longer, right now we would be in the process of being as open as two people can be with each other." His voice was a deep rumble, a slow sweep across her senses.

She didn't trust herself to have this conversation while standing on slippery stepping stones. Feeling shakier than she had getting here, she led the way across the stones to higher, dryer ground. There, she folded her arms and finally said, "I'm not talking about sex."

"I'm all ears."

"No you're not. You're all shoulders and sulk

and mystery. Why do I have the feeling that having sex with you would be a huge mistake?''

"You're the one who keeps mentioning sex."

She couldn't pull off making a face. He was right. She did keep bringing up the subject. She couldn't help it. Her body was too aware of his proximity, her mind too filled with yearnings. "My ex-husband used to say sex is a lot like air. It isn't important unless you aren't getting any." She felt her eyes widen. "I have an ex-husband."

"And I can't seem to get enough air."

This time she knew the kiss was coming. He moved toward her slowly, holding her gaze, giving her time to tell him no.

She didn't have it in her to tell him no. She lifted her face and closed her eyes.

When it was over, he drew away far enough to say, "In case you're wondering, I did that because I wanted to, because I needed to. What are you thinking?"

"Oh, no you don't. A girl has to have some pride."

He looked a little surprised by her answer. It didn't take him long to recover. "Care to know what I'm thinking?"

Warming to the subject, she took a backward step, looked into his eyes, and then slowly at the rest of him. Pride was one thing. Curiosity was another. "All right. What are you thinking?"

"I'm thinking that I'd like a quiet room, a soft bed, a gentle breeze. And you."

That sounded terribly forward and very lovely. "Do you know of such a place on this island?"

His reply was a whispered "yes" as he kissed her jaw, another one as he pressed his lips to the hollow beneath her ear, her neck, the slender ridge of her collarbone.

"Sam?" She reached a hand to his face, his beard surprisingly, sensuously soft. "I think that before the day is through, I'm going to change the way I feel about beards."

"Don't expect me to ask you if you're sure."

The deep rasp of his voice drew her gaze. He made no attempt to hide his desire for her, and yet, no matter what he insinuated, his simple statement was an attempt to do the noble thing.

She said, "You deal with your expectations and I'll deal with mine."

The shock of Annie's wit and wile ran through Sam's body, her rejoinder so spontaneous, so crammed with attitude and spunk, so much like the woman herself, he would have liked to lower her to the ground and take her there and then. He hadn't taken a woman to his bed in years. He didn't know how long it had been for her, but he knew she didn't remember the last time. He wanted to make this something she would never forget, and that required more creature comforts than the ground afforded. Reaching for her hand, he started for the cabin. They'd only taken a few steps when the need to kiss her again forced his steps to slow and his mouth to seek hers.

It was a long time before they reached the cabin.

Sam and Annie stood before the locked door, the air around them as erratic as an electrical storm. Far back in her mind, Annie wondered why Sam bothered locking this door when he didn't lock his front door back in Midnight Cove.

She practically floated inside, where she was vaguely aware of a sparsely furnished front room, wood paneling, and a stone fireplace. "Would you like something to drink?" he asked.

"No, thanks."

"Care to see the rest of the cabin?"

She knew what he was asking, and appreciated the fact that he respected her enough to ask. "I'd like that."

He led her into a narrow hallway, past a room that held a large desk, and into another room that reminded her of his bedroom on the mainland.

"Here's the quiet room you promised me." She closed the door.

"There's the soft bed."

"And the cool ocean breeze?" she asked.

He drew her with him to the window and released her hand long enough to lift the sash. Instantly, a fresh ocean breeze ruffled the heavy curtain.

"Do you sleep here often?"

He shook his head, kicked off his shoes. Annie couldn't think of a single good reason not to toe out of hers. Leaving the sandals where they fell, she strolled to the foot of the bed, where she ran a hand along the heavy wood post. The bed was covered with a simple blue quilt and four oversize pillows. It was a bed designed for comfort, where a person could laze the day away.

She could hear Sam's deeply drawn breath, could feel the heat emanating from his body, but in her mind, she heard the sound of another man's voice. "Come on, Jolie, are you going to sleep all day?"

She closed her eyes for a moment. Keith had always hated those rare occasions when she'd lazed a day away.

"Is something wrong?" Sam asked, his arms gliding around her from behind.

Her head fell back against his chest. Her memory was returning, and she was wrapped in the arms of an incredibly rugged, virile man. "Everything's wonderful. Do that again."

One hand cupped her breast. His other hand made a slow journey down her ribs, across her waist, to her belly.

She sucked in a ragged breath and moaned. Her memory was returning. That meant she would be leaving soon. Time was running out. Before it ran out completely, she turned in Sam's arms, intent upon getting him out of his shirt. He seemed just as intent to get her out of hers.

Their clothes came off tangled and inside out, with no regard for buttons or seams. When Sam had her naked and exactly where he wanted her, he stretched out on his side next to her and covered her breast with one hand. "Now," he said, his voice edged with only the barest control, "where is that tattoo?"

"That's for me to know and you to find out."

The ragged breath Sam took had as much to do with the knowing smile on her lips as it did with the brazen way she encircled him with one hand. Well, almost as much.

He kissed her mouth, her face, her neck, and breasts, checking in several places, some obvious, some not. At times he forgot what he'd been doing. It was amazing he could think at all, considering what she was doing to him with her lush body, her hands, her lips.

Drawing in a ragged breath, he said, "I'm supposed to be looking for your tattoo."

She looked up at him. "Do you want me to stop?"

He never wanted her to stop. But eventually, he resumed his search, and then it was her turn to sigh, to writhe, to need. He'd just about run out of places to look. On a whim, he rolled her over, and there it was, a work of art covering her bottom two vertebrae, a delectable tattoo, an inch and a half by an inch and a half, scratched and slightly bruised. It was a kiss, all right, far sweeter than chocolate.

"Are you going to gawk all day?"

She was one mouthy woman. "I'll show you what I plan to do all day." He rolled her underneath him, taking a moment to appreciate how perfectly they fit, her soft curves molding to the harder contours of his body. She closed her eyes when he joined them, adjusting. She didn't open them until they both returned to earth.

Other than the curtain fluttering at the window and his own deeply drawn breath, the room was quiet. It had taken a long time for Sam to catch his breath and for his heart rate to return to normal. He'd drawn the quilt over them a while ago. His arm was around her shoulder, her cheek resting on his chest.

"Are those kerosene lamps original?"

All he could see of her from this angle was the top of her head and the tip of her nose. "I thought you were sleeping."

"Close."

He knew the feeling. "I imagine the lamps are original. There's no electricity out here. I added the wood-burning stove when I first discovered the island."

"Then this place is yours?" The kiss she placed on his chest felt like a smile.

"Yes. And just so you know? You're the only person I've brought here, Annie."

"Not Annie." She kissed him again. "My name is Jolene. You can call me Jolie if you'd like."

"Jolie. It suits you."

"I know." She tilted her head slightly, and fell asleep smiling.

Sam came awake slowly and with great effort. In fact, it took a pry bar to open his eyes. Why was he sleeping in the middle of the day? And why in the hell was he as naked as a jaybird?

Annie.

He sat up.

No, her name was Jolene. Jolie.

Her side of the bed was empty and her clothes were gone. He threw off the quilt and jumped to his feet. He shoved a leg into his jeans, but had to hop around on one foot because the other pant leg was inside out.

"What's going on in there?"

Sam relaxed instantly. Not that he'd been panicked before.

He finished pulling on his jeans, then strode from the room. He found Annie, er, Jolie sitting at his desk, reading a paper he'd wadded up yesterday. Her feet were bare, her turquoise pants wrinkled, her hair looking soft where it fell over her forehead and across one cheek.

"I thought you'd gone."

She answered without looking up. "Where would I go?"

"Are you saying you're my prisoner?"

Jolene—God Almighty, it was such a joy to know her real name—finally looked at Sam. He stood in the doorway, shirtless and barefoot, his jeans slung low on his hips, the top closure open, the zipper doing little to disguise what he had on his mind.

She rose slowly to her feet, letting the crinkled paper she'd been reading fall to the floor where she'd found it. "Now I understand what you use that rechargeable battery for. I used a similar one in my laptop back home."

"And where is that?"

"I don't know yet. But I will. Soon. My name is Jolene. I was married for four years to a man named Keith. Annie is his daughter, and my step-daughter."

"You've been busy."

She took a step in his direction. "L.S. Oliver isn't a woman." She noticed a vein pulsing in his neck. She took another step. "And he sure isn't a priest." She came to a stop an arm's length away. She ran a hand down his chest, skimming lightly over sparse hair and taut muscles. "He isn't living in Los Angeles or New York."

"You don't say."

"It seems I've discovered the legendary L.S. Oliver."

He went perfectly still. "Are you impressed?"

"In case you haven't noticed, it takes a lot to impress me."

Sam didn't know what he'd expected, but it wasn't that. And yet he'd been waiting six years to hear it. She wasn't a woman who impressed easily, not by status, or bloodlines, degrees, or money, and best of all, not by fame. "What would it take for me to impress you, Jolie?" He held his breath as he waited to see if she knew the rest.

She looked up at him, her eyes wide and round and the darkest brown he'd ever seen. "Say that again."

"What would it take to—"

She shook her head. "Not that."

"Jolie?"

He could feel her melting, and tried to imagine how it must feel to go so long without knowing her name, without hearing it spoken, whispered. "Jolie. You're beautiful, Jolie. Do you know that, Jolie?"

He did away with her buttons. She arched her back. And then his mouth took over. Her clothes ended up on the floor. And they ended up back in the bed in the next room.

It was a long time before they dressed again. It was the need for nourishment that finally propelled them to go back to Sam's boat. They ate cheese and yogurt and pickles and grapes on the dock, their feet dangling over the side. The bottled water was ice-cold and tasted like heaven. It was with great reluctance that Jolie helped Sam stash their wrappers in the boat and prepare to go.

"Do you want me to untie that rope?" she asked.

"Are you in a hurry to get back?"

She looked at the glint in those dark gray eyes, the mouth she'd learned by heart, and the neatly trimmed beard that brought another level of awareness to skin already sensitized by a touch, a kiss, a caress. "If you want me to organize that antique sale before the rest of my memory returns, I'd probably better get started.''

"Jolie?"

"Yes?" She noticed his small smile, and remembered him telling her that "yes" was his favorite word.

"If you want me to take you back to the mainland, perhaps you should take your hand off my fly."

"I have a better idea." She raised her eyes and lowered his zipper.

"Have I told you how much I like your ideas?"

"I believe you have, but you can tell me again."

The dock was fashioned out of wood and extremely hard. It turned out Sam was extremely inventive. Later, they splashed in the surf, laughing like children one minute, kissing like lovers the next. Throughout the course of the idyllic afternoon, more of Jolie's memories returned. Most of the time, she whispered them to Sam. She sensed a tension in him every time, and wondered at its cause.

They finally left the island near seven o'clock. Their water supply had run out, and they'd missed supper. They hadn't gone far when Jolie reached into her pocket and drew out a candy bar. Sam watched the way she unwrapped it, inhaling its scent. "You're definitely a chocoholic."

She nodded. "I know. My mother used to tell me it was a good thing I never developed a craving for vodka."

She laughed, and Sam knew she'd just remembered that particular memory. She regained more by the minute. They hadn't discussed her insight regarding how he earned his living. Maybe she wouldn't tell anyone who he was. Maybe she would never realize who he'd been. Maybe she wasn't a reporter, or maybe she didn't watch sports. Maybe she'd never seen his picture on the cover of every glossy magazine in the free world.

Maybe she'd spent her formative years in a convent.

She took a bite of her candy bar, closing her eyes in rapture. He'd seen her do that several times today. This was the first time it was chocolate she was savoring.

She hadn't learned that in any convent.

She offered him half. He declined.

"You're awfully quiet," she said, scrunching the wrapper and tucking it back in her pocket.

"Woman, I'm damn near spent."

Jolie felt it, warmed by the look in Sam's eyes, flushed with heat, excited by something as simple as his grudging smile. She didn't need the yellow slicker anymore, and somehow she'd lost another hair clasp. Pushing her mussed hair out of her eyes and tucking it behind her ears, she said, "That's too bad, because I feel energized."

She could tell he was warming, even though his voice was gruff as he said, "That's the difference between men and women."

"Sam? I think we just about covered all the differences between men and women today."

They entered the harbor, laughing.

All but one of the other fishing boats were already in when they reached the dock. Normally, Sam beat the others back, but then, normally he didn't spend his day learning the secrets of a woman's lush body.

He'd learned so many other things today. There was a great difference between quietude and loneliness. He'd been lonely. And he hadn't even known. He wondered if it was possible to bank some of this pleasure for all the lonely years that would follow.

"Look!" she said, pointing. "A bat! Did you know bats aren't really blind?"

Jolie's memories had been returning to her like gangbusters all day. Sam had no right to dread the return of the remainder of her memory, and yet a part of him wanted more time with her.

"Betcha didn't know you were so popular, aye Sam?" Percy Parnell called from his big boat as Sam passed.

For once, Sam didn't know what Percy was talking about.

"Isn't that your friend?" Jolie asked, tipping her head toward the man standing at the end of the dock. "It is. It's the man in the Gucci shoes. My, you are popular."

Stepping out of the shadows, Grant Isaac Zimmerman lifted a hand in greeting. Jolie returned the wave. Sam kept both hands on the wheel, a sense of foreboding settling over him like bricks, for a man with three names, especially this man with three names, always spelled trouble.

Chapter Seven

Sam O'Connor was a very changeable man.

If Jolie hadn't known it before, she knew it the instant he saw the man waiting for him on the dock. His entire countenance changed. One minute he'd been relaxed, the epitome of a man who had spent a good share of his day climbing in and out of bed, and not alone. Suddenly, tension was evident in his white-knuckled grip on the steering wheel, in his squared shoulders and set jaw. A thin chill had settled over him, his gray eyes as unreadable as stone.

Jolie reasoned that it must have something to do with the man on the dock. She recognized him from the diner a few nights ago. "He's a friend of yours, right?" she asked.

The question seemed to bring Sam to his senses. He relaxed his jaw and eased up on the steering wheel. "I wasn't expecting him, that's all."

Jolie believed there was more to the sudden

severity in Sam's expression than surprise. But if he wanted her to think that was all it was, so be it.

She was quiet as she leaped to the dock and grabbed a rope as if she'd been doing it all her life. The knot she tied gave her inexperience away. Sam cut the engine, then quietly jumped onto the dock, too. "Grant, this is—"

She beat him to the introduction. "Jolie Something-or-Other."

Grant accepted her handshake. "Grant Zimmerman the Third."

"Is there a fourth?"

"Actually," Grant said with only a hint of an aristocratic lift of his eyebrows, "the woman I'm seeing says she wouldn't do that to a child."

"You're from Boston. I can tell by your accent. I grew up in Pennsylvania."

This was news to Sam. Apparently it was news to her, as well.

Recovering slightly, she said, "It's nice to meet you, Mr. Zimmerman."

"Grant."

She smiled again. "Grant." She looked from him to Sam. "I'll leave you two alone."

Sam took an involuntary step in her direction because, damn it, he hated to see her go.

It was as if she knew. "Don't look so stricken."

Who was she calling stricken?

With a wink that was all sass, she said, "You're the one who said you're spent."

Okay, now he was stricken.

She started down the dock, only to turn suddenly, catching them both watching. "I'll stop by tomorrow and start sorting out your antiques." To Grant, she said, "I know this is none of my business, but perhaps the woman you're seeing was goading you when she said she wouldn't name a child Grant Zimmerman the fourth. I get the feeling it would take a strong woman to goad a man like you."

Her gaze strayed to Sam, as if she was including him in her assessment. Without another word, she continued away from the marina. When her turquoise Capri pants were only a spot in the distance, Grant said, "How long has she known her real name?"

Sam glanced at his watch. "About seven hours."

"What else does she remember?"

Sam had a bad feeling about this. Rather than list all the things Jolie had recalled thus far, he finished tying up the boat. "Why don't you tell me what you're doing here. And when you're finished, you can tell me just how big a mistake I made today."

Grant Isaac Zimmerman the third eyed his friend. "I'd planned to begin by telling you you're screwed. Now that I've seen you, I think it would be best to rephrase that."

Sam glowered, failing to see the humor. "Just tell me what you know."

Grant ran a hand through his hair, across his face, then slowly down his hundred-dollar tie. The fact that Grant hadn't taken the time to change his clothes churned up the acid in the pit of Sam's empty stomach.

"I have some information regarding Jolene's identity."

She'd introduced herself as Jolie, not Jolene. Sam's misgivings increased by the second. "And?"

Casting a careful look around, Grant finally said,

"I left my car at the top of the hill. We can take it to your place."

Grant hated Sam's place. Before the acid in Sam's stomach ate a hole completely through his composure, he turned on his heel and led the way to Grant's car.

Except for the thud of Sam's boots as he paced from one room to the next, his house was quiet. He'd asked Grant all the pertinent questions, and Grant had answered as best he could. The personality tests Jolie's psychiatrist and doctors had run before she left the hospital had been accurate. She was a journalist, and not a two-bit one, either.

Sam stopped pacing when he came to one of the antique tables in the dining room where he'd dropped a grainy photograph and short newspaper article. The article showcased two women who were competing for a prestigious, high-profile job on one of the national morning news shows. One of the candidates had blond hair, flawless skin, straight teeth, and a nose that had surely come straight off an assembly line. The other woman's coffee-colored hair looked slightly mussed, her eyes slightly close set, her smile the sassy variety that made a person look twice and remember forever.

Grant had done a little investigating and discovered that Jolie's ex-husband was Keith Carlton, CEO of Carlton Chocolates. She'd taken back her maiden name but retained forty-nine percent of the shares in the company after the divorce. No wonder she knew so much about chocolate.

She knew a great deal about a lot of things.

According to the article, it was just like Jolie

Sullivan to slip away without telling a soul. Rumor was, she'd gone in search of the story of a lifetime that would put her over the top for the job.

A few days ago Sam had wanted to know what she had been doing in Maine to begin with. It wasn't likely that she'd been following up on an Elvis sighting at some mall.

He raked his fingers through his hair. Hadn't he known she was dangerous? Even he hadn't known just how dangerous. Her memory was returning. Any day now the final pieces would fall into place. She couldn't have planned the amnesia, but it had certainly worked to her advantage. She would take the story of a lifetime and return to New York with bells on. Even if she didn't recognize the bearded man as the legendary former golf pro, Logan Samuel Oliver Connors, she knew where L.S. Oliver, mysterious, reclusive best-selling author had been living these past six years. Knowing her, she would put the two together. Wouldn't that be the icing on the cake? In her case it would be fudge icing on a multilayered chocolate cake.

"Six years." Sam turned to Grant, who was sitting somewhat uncomfortably on an old sofa. "I was celibate for six frigging years. When I finally took a woman to bed, it couldn't have been just any woman. It was the reporter of the century! What the hell was I thinking?"

Grant rose to his feet and struck a pose psychiatrists were notorious for, weight on one foot, arms folded, chin resting on one fist. "You know what you were thinking. Look at her. That hair, those eyes, that body. Why do you think we men name our Johnsons? It's because we don't want a complete stranger making ninety-eight percent of our important decisions."

Sam shook his head. "They teach that at Harvard, Grant?"

"That came straight from the School Of Hard Knocks. What are you going to do, Sam?"

"It's a little late to do anything. Even if Jolie wouldn't have remembered my face before, she will after today."

"That good, were you?"

Sam snorted. She'd been that good. She'd been incredible, warm and pliant and strong and agile as only a woman in the throes of a strong passion could be. Heat stirred anew at the memory alone.

"There are other places to live," Grant said. "Of course, now that she knows my name and face, too, you'll be easier to track. You know I'll help in any way I can."

They were both quiet after that. Grant had said it best earlier. Sam was screwed.

Jolie waited until closer to eight o'clock to walk to Sam's house the following morning. She'd hoped he would stop in last night. He hadn't. He'd made no promises. And he'd said he was spent. She'd hoped anyway. And that really rankled.

Surprisingly, he answered her knock this morning. Her heart fluttered. That rankled even more.

Even though he wasn't wearing the customary baseball cap, she couldn't read his expression. No surprises there. He'd closed himself off from her again. She would really like to understand why. "I said I would organize your antiques today."

He held the door for her as she strode through. And she couldn't help yawning.

"You didn't sleep well, Jolie?"

It wasn't easy to regard him impassively when the sound of her name in his deep baritone weakened her knees. "I finished your book."

Sam noticed effusive praise wasn't forthcoming. He was in no mood to dig for compliments. Her hair was down this morning, long and loose around her shoulders, and still slightly damp, as if she'd recently stepped out of the shower. Her dress was black and inexpensive looking, the fabric lightweight and just loose enough to skim over her curves and delineate the smooth length of her thighs and the narrow ridge of one knee.

"Did your friend go back to Boston?" she asked.

He nodded. She must have realized he wasn't going to add more unless she did some prodding, because she finally said, "You aren't in the witness protection program, are you?"

He almost smiled at that. "No."

"The CIA?"

"Hardly."

"What does your friend do?" She motioned for him to help her move a heavy table.

"Grant is a psychiatrist."

"They must pay you a lot to write those books if you can afford a shrink who makes house calls."

"Grant isn't my shrink." They moved on to another heavy piece of furniture.

"You don't want to talk about Grant, do you, Sam?"

He shook his head.

"You don't want to talk about yourself, either." This time he shrugged.

"A man who doesn't like to talk about himself is a real rarity."

She didn't know the half of it. Any day, she would know the rest. So what the hell was he doing drinking in the sight of her, the soft, clean flowery scent of her?

She picked up an old lamp, examined it, then put it back down. "I had fun yesterday."

She chose that moment to look his way, her gaze meeting his from the other side of the cluttered room. Quickly, she averted her eyes. It was then that he knew he was hurting her. Aw, hell.

"I had fun, too, Jolie." He raked his fingers through his hair. "I've lived alone for years. All of a sudden I've discovered that solitude and loneliness are two very different things."

He clamped his mouth shut. What the hell was happening to him? He was the one with the power, and yet he was telling her how he felt.

She smiled. And he would have said it all over again.

"It's coming back, Sam."

He'd known that. Hearing her say it out loud drove home nearly every misgiving he had. Luckily, she did most of the talking for the next hour. They lined up chairs, straightened trunks and pottery, arranged knickknacks and glass items.

"Last night I pictured my apartment in New York. It's not much bigger than mine here in Midnight. When the rest of my memory returns, I'll be returning to my life."

"Is there a particular man you'll go back to?" Sam asked before he could stop himself.

She made an unladylike sound that drew his smile out of hiding. "I don't think there are too many men out there who would risk life or limb to pull out a chair for me."

He strode to the table and slowly dragged out a chair.

Something nudged Jolie from the inside. She was a hairbreadth away from falling in love. She doubted that was a good thing. The intensity in Sam's eyes reached inside her, spreading to a place beyond her heart, to a place she couldn't name. She had to remind herself that he'd hardly risked life or limb to hold out that chair. He was risking something else. She just didn't know what.

"Do you believe in happy endings, Sam?"

His grim expression spoke volumes.

"That's what I thought. We'd better keep moving if we want to finish. If it's any consolation, my ex-husband cured me of any romantic notions left over from childhood."

"It wasn't a pretty divorce?" he asked.

"It wasn't even a pretty marriage. The best thing about it was loving Annie."

She saw him looking at the bracelet on her wrist. She knew what two of the charms meant. One represented her stepdaughter, the other her love of chocolate. The quill pen was still a mystery. But not as big a mystery as Sam.

Her gaze was drawn to him repeatedly. Over and over, she found him looking at her. She understood what it meant when a man looked at a woman that way. And she understood what could happen when a woman understood what it meant. She rubbed her forehead, and continued to regard him. It was as if she'd seen him somewhere years ago, but couldn't place his face.

Sam knew what Jolie was doing. This time, he

didn't rush her into his arms. What was the use? He'd wandered around his house until all hours after Grant left last night. Even with the television on, the house had been too quiet. He'd thought about having a beer at Rocky's Tavern, but he knew that if he went to Main Street, Rocky's Tavern wasn't the place he would visit.

"I felt restless last night, too, Sam."

He did a double take. Could she read his mind?

She arranged several vases and milk-glass pitchers on a dresser top. "Waiting for my memory to return feels a little like, oh, I don't know. Do you remember how it felt when you were a child waiting for Christmas when you knew you'd been bad a lot that year?"

Sam hadn't planned to laugh. "Bad, as in naughty?"

She rolled her eyes.

He took a step in her direction. "Were you a naughty girl, Jolie?"

"So what if I was?"

"What about now?"

"You know how naughty I can be now."

"Care to refresh my memory?"

She looked up at him. As if propelled by a force greater than either of them, she stepped into his arms. They were in the middle of a long, passionate kiss when the doorbell rang.

"Is it ten o'clock already?" she whispered. "Oh my gosh." She pushed out of his arms. "It's after ten."

"Are you expecting someone?" he asked.

"Yes." She ran to the door.

"Who?" he asked.

A fat woman wearing a flowered dress and half

a bottle of sickeningly sweet perfume bustled in. "Hello. I'm Adaline, of Adaline's Antiques over on the highway just outside of town. Sorry I'm late."

She hurried past them, snapping pictures. "Look at all these treasures. Oh, my goodness. It's you!"

Shards of light flashed in Sam's eyes.

"I don't believe it! It's really and truly you!"

Chapter Eight

"Someone famous, right here in our neck of the woods!" The woman's voice was shrill. "This is so exciting!"

Exciting wasn't the word Sam had in mind.

"Forget the antiques," Adaline exclaimed. "Le'me get a picture of you!"

Ice spread through Sam's veins. He'd dreaded this moment for six years, and yet all he could do was stand there, frozen like a deer trapped in the glare of headlights.

"You know me?" Jolie's voice seemed to come from far away.

Understanding dawned at the exact moment Sam's vision cleared.

"Why, you're Jolie Sullivan." Adaline gushed. "You're that darling reporter up for a position on that morning news program, *Every Day*. If you ask me, somebody could have come up with a better name. Oh, never mind about that. What's in a name anyway, right, dearie?''

Sam's gaze sought Jolie's. Something intense passed between them, for he understood how important Jolie's name was to her.

"Your picture was on the news just last night," Adaline exclaimed. "They showed a picture of you and your contender. This is such a coincidence. What are you doing in Maine?''

Sam stepped in front of Jolie, shielding her from more flashbulbs. "She's recovering from amnesia, which resulted from a blow to her head. Blinding her isn't going to help, damn it.''

Adaline glanced at Sam only long enough to dismiss him as unimportant. After patting her coiffed gray hair, she darted around him and placed a chubby hand on Jolie's arm. "Amnesia? Really? You don't remember who you are?''

"Actually, my memory has been returning a little at a time." Jolie wet her lips. "Sullivan. Of course. That's my last name.''

Adaline clucked like a mother hen. "You need to sit down.''

"I'm fine, really.''

"Young man, bring that chair over here. Quick now.''

Dazedly, Jolie sat in the chair Sam placed directly behind her. Adaline barked more orders to Sam while continuing to hover over Jolie. Aside from her strong perfume, she was gentle and kind and helpful, not to mention talkative.

Unlike Sam.

Adaline barely gave him the time of day. Jolie couldn't keep her eyes off him. Her head was swimming, and yet everything she'd forgotten was right there as if it had been there all along. She could picture her friends, her stepdaughter, her rival, Selina Nelson. Jolie's mother was gone, but her father and stepmother were very much alive and well and retired in Arizona.

"Are you all right, Jolie?" Sam asked quietly.

She'd planned to smile, then changed her mind at the way his gray eyes had narrowed. She couldn't tell if he was generally resentful of Adaline's intrusion, the situation, or something else. "I'm fine, thank you."

Adaline returned with a glass of tap water she'd initially told Sam to fetch. Muttering something about men's uselessness in situations like these, she handed the glass to Jolie and waited expectantly for her to take a drink. Feeling five years old, Jolie took a sip. Adaline bustled away again.

"You're quiet," Sam said.

Something started to click far back in her mind. "Where have I seen you before?"

An inexplicable look of withdrawal came over his features. They were still staring at each other, neither speaking, when the screen door bounced closed. The woman from the antique store was back. Jolie hadn't paid enough attention to know she'd gone outside.

"Aren't cell phones wonderful?" Adaline said, beaming. "I don't know how people ever got along without 'em."

Jolie and Sam both stared at the other woman in confusion.

Adaline started straightening the room as if she owned the place. "I just called a friend of mine who works over in Sedgwick. They're on their way."

"Who's on their way?" Jolie asked.

"Why, the press of course."

"The what?" Sam's voice boomed.

"The press." Adaline's eyes darted from Sam to Jolie.

"They're coming here?" Sam glared at the older woman.

Adaline cast a furtive glance around the room, as if wondering what the fuss was about. "Actually, I told them to meet us at my store." She turned to Jolie. "You don't mind, do you? I could really use the publicity."

Jolie allowed the other woman to pull her to her feet and lead her from the room. That clicking was still going on in the back of her mind. This was what she'd been waiting for. She was thrilled with her memories, and so relieved to know who she was and where she lived and what she did.

Why wasn't Sam saying anything?

She glanced over her shoulder. He was staring back at her across the ringing silence. All at once, her feet froze to the floor. Those storm-gray eyes, that sandy-brown hair, that physique . . .

Adaline tugged on her hand, drawing her out the door.

Jolie noticed that Sam didn't try to stop her. He didn't follow her outside. He didn't even say good-bye.

Sam didn't know how long he stood in the doorway after Adaline helped Jolie into her van and drove away. Ten minutes? Half an hour? Longer? His breath had solidified in his throat and his jaw hurt from clenching his teeth.

He had to get out of there.

He was halfway down the porch steps when he realized it would do him no good to go to the island. He had no place to hide. Jolie had put it all together. He'd seen it in her eyes. She was probably meeting with the press at this very moment.

There was nothing he could do except wait for the wolf to come knocking on his door.

No one came knocking on Sam's door, not a wolf, not the press, not even Jolie. Sam knew, because he'd spent the past eight hours prowling his house like a caged tiger.

Darkness was falling, and Midnight Cove was swarming with reporters, news teams, cameras, and vans with satellites on their roofs. Jolie had been on live television. He'd watched, stretched out on his back on top of the covers, fully dressed right down to his shoes.

The camera crew did a decent job of panning the harbor, Main Street, even the driftwood piled high in the Potters' front yard. Several of the local residents were interviewed. Each and every one of them should have received a standing ovation for the way they answered the reporters' questions without answering at all, only to launch into a lengthy conversation about themselves. It was their five minutes of fame, and they weren't about to squander it. Adaline made a point to mention her many antiques. The woman who owned the dress shop modeled an outfit from her "new" summer collection. Dulcie took the cake when she looked straight into the camera and said, "That's right. Jolie worked for me in the diner. A fine waitress. 'Course, we all knew her as Annie Valentine. Loves chocolate, that gal. In fact, I had her sample some of the desserts in the collection of recipes I'm compiling. I'm calling it Ninety-Eight Ways to Sweeten Your Sex Life."

The reporter's gasp gave Sam a whole new appreciation for live television.

Something pattered the windowpane. Rain? He glanced back at the television where Jolie was being interviewed. She looked good on TV, completely comfortable and pretty. Her memory had returned, and with it the qualities that would endear her to her viewers. She smiled, she laughed, she teared up when she spoke of her stepdaughter. She had the audience eating out of her hand.

She was a pro. Sam rubbed at his sore jaw.

The noise at his window came again. It wasn't rain. It sounded suspiciously like sand or pebbles on glass. He aimed the remote at the TV and hit the mute button before moving the curtain aside and peering out. Jolie stood in the dark far below, wearing the same black dress she was wearing that very second on his television screen.

Sam opened the window. "Amazing how someone can be in two places at once."

She peered around her as if she was afraid she might have been followed. "How long have you known who I am?"

Sam had never heard a more demanding-sounding whisper.

"What difference does it make?" he said, whispering, too. "Your rival doesn't stand a chance after this."

The corner of her mouth twisted in exasperation. Without another word, she darted around the side of his house. Sam met her at the door.

With a thrust of her chin and a toss of her head, she brushed past him. "Did you know before we . . . yesterday . . . you know."

He didn't answer.

"You knew all along, didn't you?"

"Not in the beginning."

"Why should I believe you? After all, people tell the truth around you. That doesn't necessarily work in reverse, now does it?"

There was a long, brittle silence. He didn't know why the hell she was so angry. He was the one about to have his life ruined. "Annie. Jolie. I didn't know when we met, all right?"

He detected a softening around her eyes. "Then our friendship, showing me your lobsters, the island . . ." Her voice trailed away. "That at least was genuine?"

Sam ran a hand through his hair, down his face, across his beard. What difference did any of that make now? "Why are you here alone, Jolie?"

"What?"

He glanced out the window. "Where's the camera crew?"

Jolie stared at Sam longer than was considered polite. She couldn't help it. The past eight hours had been a whirlwind and an eye-opening experience. She knew her full name, her phone number, her seventh grade teacher, her alma mater. She'd spoken on the telephone with her father and stepmother, her boss, her best friend, Rachel. She'd gotten exactly what she'd wanted, what she'd hoped for, prayed for. Her memory was back, all of it.

She hadn't seen Sam in eight hours. And she'd missed him the entire time. Something intense was going on inside her, something she didn't think she'd ever felt in exactly this way. It wasn't just a simple case of her wanting a man. There was nothing simple about any of this. She didn't know what it meant, exactly, or what she was going to do about it. But she knew she didn't want to leave Midnight Cove before she found out if he felt the same way.

A car drove by, its headlights flickering across the living room wall. Sam tensed up even more. Suddenly, Jolie knew what he was afraid of. "You think a camera crew is on its way, is that it?"

"You came to Maine for a story, didn't you?"

"Maybe I did. Maybe I didn't."

She thought his derisive snort was condescending even for him.

"So that's what this is all about. The great, legendary Logan Samuel Oliver Connors doesn't like the press."

"You're a reporter. Reporters exploit. If the truth hurts, I guess you're just going to have to deal with it."

His lack of belief in her not only hurt, but really ticked her off. After everything they'd shared, done, been together. He knew all the secrets of her body. He even knew where her tattoo was, for crying out loud. "You don't trust many people, do you, Sam?"

"Not a lot of people have given me reason to trust them."

"You know, I'm getting a little sick of your attitude."

"My attitude?" His nostrils flared.

"You think I'm going to lead the press to your door?"

"Here's a news flash for you, Jolie. You are the press."

"Yeah?" *Oh, good comeback,* she thought.

They were almost nose-to-nose.

"You know something, Sam? I'm getting sick of your lack of faith in my character. And do you know what else?" She jabbed her finger into his chest. "Just because the rest of the world would be interested in a washed-up, has-been former–golf pro who's completely full of himself, doesn't mean I am!" With a lift of her chin, she spun around. "Deal with that!"

She slammed the door so hard on her way out, the windows rattled. Sam stayed where he was, a hand pressed over the muscle she'd jabbed on his chest. Deeper, he could feel his heart beating. It felt ominous, somehow.

He'd caught glimpses of her temper before, but he'd never seen her this angry. He was an idiot. He should have tried to reason with her. Hell, he should have gotten on his knees and begged her to keep his secret. Instead, he'd insulted her, irritated her, and provoked her.

He might have had a chance before. But she was sure to tell her story now. And there wasn't a single thing Sam could do except wait.

Chapter Nine

Sam leaned back in his chair. The water stain on the ceiling hadn't changed since yesterday. Or the day before. Or the day before that.

It was the end of July. The roof of his cabin had sprung a leak during the last gully washer. He should have been making arrangements to pick up the materials he would need to fix it. He lowered the front legs of his chair to the floor and looked around the room he used as an office on his island but made no move to do anything.

He'd finished his last book and should have been starting another. He came to the island every day. He sat in his chair. More often than not, he ended up staring into space. Consequently, there were no wadded-up papers on the floor.

It was all Jolie's fault.

He told himself he couldn't concentrate because he was waiting for the ax to fall. He'd listened for it on the news, scanned the newspaper headlines, checked out the covers of magazines. He'd waited an entire month. Other than a grainy photograph of the back of a man the reporter claimed was Logan Samuel Oliver Connors, taken in Australia no less, Sam's name hadn't been mentioned.

Just this morning he'd watched Jolie's rival sashay onto the set on her first day on the job. Any fool could see that Jolie was better suited to the position. Why hadn't she used her knowledge to acquire that position? What the hell was she waiting for?

He heard a deep rumble far in the distance. Thunder? He glanced at the laptop, then back up at the ceiling. He really needed to do something about that leak, about his next book, about his life.

The sound drew closer. It wasn't thunder. It was the *whomp whomp whomp* of a helicopter. Sam switched off his computer and slid the battery into his pocket. Might as well call it a day.

By the time he locked the cottage door, the helicopter was in plain view. And it was heading his way. A bead of perspiration broke out on his brow. That tiny bead turned into a river when the helicopter landed in the place he and Jolie had fed the herons and gulls a month ago.

A door opened and Jolie got out. Wearing what appeared to be a green jumpsuit, she crouched low as she ran beyond the perimeter of the whirling blades. Straightening, she strode directly toward him, like a woman on a mission, only to stop twenty-five feet away.

Sam may not have been able to control the fact that she was a sight for sore eyes, but by God he didn't have to let her know it. "I've been wondering what you've been waiting for."

Her eyes widened and her brows rose slightly.

"How did you know I was waiting for you back at your place?" Her eyes narrowed. "That isn't what you meant, is it? You still think it's just a matter of time before I take your little secret public." She folded her arms at her ribs and glared at him. "You know, Sam, you spend too much time alone."

She turned her back to him, and gestured to the man flying the helicopter. With a nod and a wave, the pilot lifted the machine off the ground.

"For your information," she yelled over the loud machine, "Rob didn't forget the big camera. He's a fire jumper, not a reporter." Her ex-husband used to ask her if she wanted cheese with that whine whenever she used that tone. If Sam mentioned it, so help her, she would clobber him.

"He sounds fascinating."

"He's also convinced he's in love with me."

"Then what are you doing here?"

She glared at him. "I guess there's no accounting for taste, is there?"

As the implication soaked through Sam's thick skull, Jolie studied him. His hair looked freshly cut, his beard freshly trimmed. He should have looked fresh. There were dark circles under his eyes, dark emotions in them. Apparently she wasn't the only one who hadn't been sleeping well.

"Why did they give the position to that other woman?" he asked.

"They had to give it to somebody after I turned it down." She held up one hand in a halting gesture. "Hold it right there. From now on, I'll be doing the talking and asking the questions."

She rather liked the way he clamped his mouth shut.

"I'm very mad at you, Sam O'Connor."

He cocked one eyebrow, but he didn't utter a sound.

"Yes, I called you Sam O'Connor. Not Logan. Not L.S Oliver. Sam. I won't tell you what I called you under my breath a thousand times this past month. But I will tell you this." She moved closer so she wouldn't have to yell. "I've been busy."

"What have you been doing, Jolie?"

She pointed her finger at him the way a teacher might at an errant student. Still, soft-touched thoughts shaped her smile. "I visited Annie. I swear she's grown three inches. And I flew to Arizona to see my dad. I sold my shares of the candy company. Oh, and I thought about you."

Jolie was pretty sure Sam hadn't moved. Therefore she must have been the one who'd strolled closer. "I watched a lot of old footage of you before you disappeared. You have a good reason to distrust the press. That doesn't mean I've forgiven you for failing to try to contact me this past month." She held up her hand again when he started to argue. "Grant told me to give you time."

"You've talked to Grant?"

"How does it feel to be kept in the dark? That's what you've done with me from the very beginning. I think I've figured out why. Care to hear what goes on in the deepest recesses of a woman's mind?"

"It'll be dark in three hours."

She stuck her tongue out at him. "Are you seeing someone?"

"Who would I see?"

"I'll interpret that as a 'no.' So I can assume the diamond ring is for me?"

"You snooped in my sock drawer?"

She shrugged. She had to do something to kill

the time waiting for him to return. "It's really a lovely ring. When did you buy it?"

"Two weeks ago."

"What were you planning to do with it?"

"I've considered several scenarios. One involved kidnapping you, another hog-tying you. Why didn't you take the job with the network, Jolie?"

"Because it wouldn't have been ethical for someone in that position to have a husband who has special powers that cause people to blurt out the truth."

Sam's first thought was, an ethical reporter? His second thought staggered him. Husband? "I thought I lost you, Jolie."

"You didn't lose me, you big idiot. You threw me away. Or at least you tried to. But it occurred to me that you didn't ask me to keep your identity a secret. That could have been because you trusted me. Or it could have been because you didn't."

Nothing about the conversation should have been lust arousing, and yet Sam's desire for this woman had never been stronger. "You never intended to tell anybody who I am, did you?"

She shook her head. "I've dropped out of the spotlight. I quit the network. I noticed you got rid of all the antiques. Before you say anything, I already know you worked out a deal with Adaline, who hauled them all off to her store."

So, Sam thought, she'd been in touch with Adaline, too. His house had seemed empty this past month. His house wasn't all.

He watched as she lowered the zipper on her jumpsuit. He wasn't certain what he expected her to do next, but he didn't expect her to reach into her pocket and draw out the little velvet box he'd last seen tucked under his socks. She placed it in his hand, then went back to that zipper.

Stilling her hand with his, he said, "I want to do this right."

Her gaze was on his mouth. Sam had the strangest urge to grin. "Not that. We always get that right."

"What then?"

He felt his Adam's apple wobble suddenly. "It seems I'm in love with a woman who loves chocolate."

She tipped her head an inch to the right. "Chocolate isn't all I love." She eased closer. "Care to hear what else I love?"

"What else do you love, Jolie?"

"Ha! As if I'd tell you."

"All right," he said, his thumb smoothing circles along her wrist. "I'll go first. I love big, round—"

She gave him an arched look.

"—Brown eyes and full, kissable lips and naughty tattoos. I love a woman who gives as good as she gets, often better." He stared into her eyes for interminable seconds. "Everyone tells the truth around me. And yet you don't. Oh, you did in the beginning, but then you stopped. How did you do that?"

She smiled knowingly. "Grant says I probably became immune. He also said you've been a real bear lately. That reminds me. How's the new book going?"

"Not good. Nothing's been good since you left."

"Poor baby."

"I can tell you're all choked up."

She grinned. Birds squawked nearby. "What's

the matter with them? Haven't you been feeding them?"

"They only look like birds. Underneath their feathers, they're hogs. They can wait. Believe me. But I can't wait another minute to do this."

He opened the velvet box. She surprised them both by sniffling. "If you go down on one knee, I'll clobber you."

"Do you want to do this?" he asked huffily.

Something went warm inside Jolie, something far deeper than her jumpsuit and skin. She'd done some investigating into Sam's background. All totaled, she must have watched a hundred hours of old tapes of his golf matches. She learned more from the tapes that came later, when former fans had taunted him, when people had made demands no human could possibly satisfy. The media had dogged his every step, leaving him no room and even less peace. No wonder he didn't trust reporters.

She looked at the ring, and then she looked into his eyes. "I love you, Sam."

"Then you'll marry me?"

She heaved a huge sigh.

"Is that a yes?"

She stepped into his arms. Going up on tiptoe, her mouth an inch from his, she whispered, "Yes. I hope I never have amnesia again. Do you know why, Sam?"

"Why, Jolie?"

"Because I would really hate to forget the next hour."

Birds squawked, waves pounded the rocks, the wind blew, and Sam thought he couldn't have put it better himself.

Dear Readers,

Several months ago, my editor invited me to participate in a novella collection. Other than word count, he gave me only one stipulation. My story had to include chocolate.

A woman? Write about chocolate? I laughed out loud, for surely this would require research I could sink my teeth into.

I'm sure you've already figured out that I love chocolate. I love men, too, which is especially nice since I have a husband and four sons! It so happens that I have a penchant for books, also, especially those about mysterious men and women. That in mind, I let my imagination soar to Maine's rocky coast. There, I discovered a lobsterman with a boatload of secrets and a woman with a bump on her head, a fledgling memory, and a craving for chocolate that rivaled my own. "I Know I Love Chocolate" was born full of mystery and fun and was meant to be enjoyed.

My debut novel with Kensington, THE COTTAGE, is also on the shelves in bookstores everywhere. This full-length novel depicts another woman of mystery, one who is a healer living in the Appalachian Mountains, a runaway boy searching for answers, and the man who followed him there.

I pour my heart and soul into every book I write, but none of them contains more of my soul than DAY BY DAY, a story set on the shores of Lake Michigan in my home state. DAY BY DAY follows the lives of a beautiful family blown apart by a horrible accident. The characters will grip you as they put their family back together, so grab a book off the shelves in July 2002, and hold on.

Indulge yourself, dear readers, with chocolate if you'd like, and with stories I think you'll love.

Sincerely,
Sandra Steffen

P.S. You may write to me via my Web site at www.sandrasteffen.com.

**Please turn the page for
an exciting sneak peek at
Sandra Steffen's newest
contemporary romance**

DAY BY DAY
(coming in July 2002 from Zebra Books!)

Maggie McKenzie hugged her arms close against a sudden chill. She'd been having a relatively innocent, innocuous conversation with Melissa Bradley and Hannah Lewis before Jessica Hendricks and MaryAnn Petigrue had joined them. Within seconds, the conversation had turned into a he-said-she-said gossip session, interspersed with a large dose of male bashing.

"Come on, Maggie!" Jessica declared. "Give us something low-down and dirty on Spence."

Maggie pulled a face. "I hate to disappoint you, but I'm drawing a blank."

"Are you telling me Spence doesn't do anything that annoys the hell out of you?"

Maggie ran a quick check through her mind. The truth was, she didn't have many issues with men. Spence wasn't perfect, but she didn't expect him to be. He'd grown up with three brothers, and the toilet seat had been a problem at first. She'd taken a few midnight splashes early in their marriage, but these days they both knew how to work the lid. He had a serious connection with the remote control, and he loved a clean garage but never seemed to notice when the house was a mess.

For lack of anything more serious, she shrugged and said, "Well, he's late for a lot of things."

"Not Peter," Hannah exclaimed. "He's on time for everything, and when I'm running late, he has this look, not to be confused with *a* look or *that* look. I'm talking about *the* look."

"Uh," Melissa Bradley exclaimed. "I know exactly what you're talking about. Aaron does that, too. Ever notice that when you and your husband are getting along, you like most everything about him?"

"And when you're not," MaryAnn Petigrue interrupted, "you don't even like the way he breathes."

Even Maggie smiled at that one.

The surprise party had been a success in every sense of the word. She, Yvonne, and several members of the Ladies Historical Society had planned it down to the tiniest detail, and yet Gaylord had surprised *them* with his announcement that he was making a six-figure donation to the society. It would be all over the papers tomorrow. Tonight, Maggie just wanted the party to wind down so she could go home, kick her shoes off, slip out of her dress, and unwind with Spence.

She'd been feeling strange all day. She wasn't prone to bad moods, and although she'd read about people who had premonitions, she rarely experienced them herself. Her parents, who were doing missionary work in Africa, would have blamed it on atmospheric pressure and a change in the weather pattern. Neither Joseph nor Adelle Fletcher believed in premonitions. Perhaps premonition was too strong a word. It was more like trepidation. Maggie felt antsy, uneasy. For the life of her, she couldn't say why.

She wondered where Spence was. He said he'd be here tonight, and Spencer McKenzie kept his word. She didn't know many women who'd been married nearly thirteen years and still missed their husbands simply because they hadn't seen each other all day. Sometimes, she worried that she loved him too much. How could she love him too much, when he loved her just as fiercely? She was thirty-four years old, and incredibly, undeniably happy. No one could ever accuse her of being weak. She didn't cling, and she certainly didn't define herself by her husband's success. It was just that she felt more alive when they were together.

The goose bumps that had been skittering up and down her arms trailed away. More relaxed now, she glanced at the guests scattered throughout the courtyard. Her gaze flitted over dozens of people, but it settled on one man.

Spence.

Their eyes met, held. Something unspoken and powerful passed between them. Just over six feet tall, he stood in the shadows with Edgar Millerton, looking more like a shipbuilder of bygone days than a modern-day architect.

No wonder she was no longer cold. He'd been watching her. All these years of marriage hadn't dulled or diminished the passion that had taken on a life all its own the first time they'd met, but time had honed their response to it.

She cast him a small smile, and watched the effect it had on his features. His lips parted, as if he'd suddenly taken a quick, sharp breath. The breeze lifted his dark hair off his forehead and ruffled his tie. She couldn't see the color of his eyes from here, but she knew they were a deep shade of blue, as vivid and changeable as the great lake they'd both come to love.

Spence could have lived anywhere from Alaska to Timbuktu, but Maggie, the daughter of a career army man, had known this was where she'd wanted to grow old the first time she'd visited the area some fifteen years ago. She'd lived in twenty-two towns before she'd graduated from high school, but she'd lived right here in this one small city for the past thirteen. She and Spence belonged here, the way she'd always longed to belong as a child.

Spence nodded his head at the staunch old codger he'd been talking to, but Maggie noticed he didn't take his eyes off her. Almost of its own volition, her hand went to her hair. She twirled a lock around one finger. Nobody watching could have known that the simple mannerism was her way of telling Spence that her thoughts had taken a slow, luxurious stroll to the bedroom. But he knew.

He had an angular face, and, when he chose to use it, a devastatingly attractive smile. Bidding Edgar farewell, he proved it, smiling as he strode closer. He kissed her on the cheek, an old-fashioned, gentlemanly gesture few men bothered with anymore, then said hello to Melissa, Jessica, Hannah, and MaryAnn.

The other four women moved, en masse, to the

buffet table. Maggie shifted slightly closer to Spence, so that her shoulder rested lightly against his arm. "How was the meeting?"

"All things considered, I'd say it went well. I'll tell you about it later. It looks like your party was a success, too, although everyone's more interested in talking about the surprise Gaylord had for all of you."

Maggie nodded. "Even Edgar Millerton?"

Spence ran the tips of three fingers up her arm, as if he'd waited as long as he could to touch her. Goose bumps of a different nature followed the path his fingertips took.

"You know Edgar," he said quietly.

Oh, dear. Maggie knew Edgar, all right. The man moved slowly, and spoke the same way. He took twenty minutes to order a sandwich. For excitement, he watched paint dry. Maggie herself had been known to go on and on about history, but even she had a difficult time staying focused when Edgar launched into conversation about sediment and water seepage. As tightfisted as Gaylord was generous, Edgar's idol was Jay Someone-or-Other, the United States' first Ph.D. to study groundwater. Once, Edgar had invited all the members of the Ladies Historic Society to his home, where he'd shown slides of how water drained through sand, gravel, and rock.

"Fascinating stuff, groundwater," Spence said close to Maggie's ear.

"You don't say."

"Did you know that it travels through pores in rocks one-seventieth of the speed of snails?"

Oh, dear. Maggie loved these social functions. She was perhaps the only person present who knew that they bored Spence silly. He made the best of them for her sake. It was one of the things she loved about him. There were plenty of other things.

"Biological reclamation is going well."

"Spence?"

"Evidently, it works by activating natural bacteria. It seems this natural bacteria eats most pollutants, like degreasers and solvents and septic-tank cleaners we humans have been dumping into the ground since they were invented."

She leaned lightly into him. "He must have had you cornered for a long time."

"It's hard to gage minutes when time is standing still."

She shook her head. "You were bored to death."

"I'm a big boy."

He was a big man.

"I'm surprised to see Jessica Michaels here," he said tersely. "Last I knew, she was living in the Caribbean."

Maggie shrugged. "It's Jessica Hendricks again. She took back her maiden name."

Spence gave a derisive snort. "She took John for everything he had. I'm surprised she didn't want to keep his name, too."

Maggie whispered, "I don't think I could ever do that."

"What? Keep my name?"

"No. Waste so much energy hurting someone I loved."

Sometimes, when Spence looked at her the way he was looking at her right now, she got lost in his eyes.

"I'd be a fool to give you a reason."

She smiled, because Spence was no fool.

With the barest movement of his head, he gestured toward the back steps. That was all it took, one look, and she knew he was asking how much longer she wanted to stay.

Earlier, the courtyards had been busting at the seams. There were still some forty guests milling about on this level, but the party was winding down. "We should be able to make our escape in half an hour or so. What did you have in mind?"

The sound Spence made deep in his throat was half moan, all male. Taking her hand, he led the way to a small dance floor nearby, where two other couples were dancing to music provided by a three-piece orchestra. Fitting her body close to his, he proceeded to give her a detailed outline of what he had in mind.

His words conjured up dreamy images that worked over Maggie like moonlight. Despite the heat emanating from him, she shivered again.

"Cold?" he whispered, close to her hair.

"Hmm. I don't know why, but I've been shivering all night." She closed her eyes, and for a moment, she felt as if she were looking at her life from outside herself, and something precious was about to slip away. A sense of dread washed over her. She kept her eyes wide open after that.

It didn't make sense. Her sister, Jackie, was home with the girls. Jackie loved Grace and Allison almost as much as she and Spence did. Jackie knew their favorite games, favorite foods, their latest secrets and oldest fears. She also knew the Wilsons' phone number by heart. Grace and Allison both knew how to dial 911. There had been no sirens, no weather rumblings or threats of disasters. Even the sky was clear. Why, then, did Maggie have to force herself not to hold on to Spence too tightly?

"About that getaway," she whispered.

"I'm listening."

"Think anybody would notice if we crept away right now?" she asked.

Several guests turned at the sound of the little yelp she made when he followed his smooth turn in one direction with a surprise dip.

"Nice going," she chided once she was back on her feet. "Now everybody will notice."

"I aim to please."

Yes, she thought, he did. She was overtired, that was all. Everything was fine. Perfect. Feeling more like her old self, she finished the dance in Spence's arms. Then, hand-in-hand, they mingled with the other guests, enjoying being together, anticipating being alone.

SEX AND THE SINGLE CHOCOHOLIC

Kylie Adams

All I really need is love, but a little chocolate now and then doesn't hurt.

—Lucy of the "Peanuts" gang

Acknowledgments

This romp is dedicated to the bombshells I admire from afar . . .

Helen Gurley Brown—Is there a smarter woman on the planet? I don't think so.

Madonna—Always full of surprises. And twenty years of great exercise music!

Sharon Stone—She can do no wrong in my book. Fiercely intelligent and knows how to dress for an awards show.

And to the bombshell I know personally . . .

Mary Ann Kirby—She stops traffic in both directions, makes a mint on the job, walks in a room and owns it. Little girls should follow her around at least one day a week to learn how it's done.

Chapter One

New York

"It's better than a multiple orgasm," Tatiana Fox announced.

Candace Rowley smiled. The ultimate rave review. But she held back her excitement. "Are you serious?"

Tatiana leveled a reproachful gaze. "Honey, I never joke about orgasms."

Candace felt the gooseflesh spread, watching expectantly as Tatiana continued to savor her first bite of Passion Truffle with something close to rapture. And then she could hold her patience no longer. Deep breath. "Can you taste the passion fruit?"

Tatiana closed her eyes, concentration total. "Absolutely."

Candace's aerial castles went splat. "It's too strong," she hissed miserably. "I knew it!"

Tatiana opened her eyes, if only to roll them. "Calm down. It's not overpowering." One beat. A raised eyebrow. "Do I taste guava?"

Candace could feel her own eyes shining. "Just a hint."

"Amazing. It makes me want to make out with that intern who escorted us to the green room." And then Tatiana did the unthinkable. Instead of finishing the chocolate, she returned the candy to its pink foil liner.

Candace regarded the act as a personal affront.

"I shoot a nude scene next week," Tatiana explained, skating a hand over her exposed and impossibly flat tummy. "I don't want to look bloated."

"That's *next week!*" Candace implored.

Tatiana shrugged and scarfed down the rest. "Guess I'll double up on pilates classes. By the way, nothing from Godiva could ever make me do that."

Candace beamed.

The green room door swung open. Enter Jackie, the assistant producer for *Coffee in Manhattan,* a girl who looked young enough to be on her way to a fraternity keg party. She stood there with clipboard poised, charmingly disheveled in that Bridget Jones way. "Oh, my God. I'm *so* fired. I can't believe makeup didn't come get you."

"But they did," Candace assured her. "I insisted they not do much. It's not my style."

Jackie displayed no signs of relief. "I'm still *so* fired. Wardrobe could've found you something better to wear."

"They tried, but I prefer this," Candace said. She rose to smooth down the skirt of the conservative black suit she'd snatched up for a steal at a basement sale.

"OK," Jackie said blankly. "Um . . . The woman who's supposed to be on to talk about the vaginal cream is stuck in traffic. A bike messenger got hit by a cab or something. Anyway, we're adding her four-minute segment to yours, so you have seven now."

Candace clapped with girlish excitement. "I can share my story about chocolate in ancient Mayan culture!"

Jackie's brow crinkled. "Uh, this isn't, like, the History Channel."

"Oh, but it's a fascinating tale," Candace insisted. And then she experienced a tremor of guilt. "I hope the bike messenger isn't seriously hurt."

"I heard the taxi was going sixty. He's probably dead. OK, after Didi sings "The Greatest Love of All" we go to a break, and then you're on. I'll be back in a few minutes."

"Seven minutes!" Tatiana exclaimed. "Honey, they should just call this show *Coffee with Candace.*" She reached out to take both of her friend's hands. "A little advice?"

"Of course."

"Don't forget why you're here. It's to get the Decadence Candies name out there and to sell Passion Truffles. Push, push, push. And just when you think that you've whored yourself enough, push some more. I managed to say the title of my last movie eight times in three minutes on *Good Morning, Los Angeles.*"

Candace scanned her memory. *"Lady Cop Undercover II: Massage Parlor?"*

"No, *Lady Cop Undercover III: Escort Service.*"

Candace nodded thoughtfully, even though the straight-to-video R-rated thrillers that Tatiana starred in were difficult to distinguish. "Oh, of course."

On the monitor, the show's cohost, Didi Farrell, was warbling that old Whitney Houston hit like a C-list entertainer with Branson, Missouri, dreams.

I'm on next, Candace thought, experiencing the slightest involuntary shiver. Tatiana was right. She had to push hard. So much was at stake.

On its own merits, Decadence seemed to be performing just fine. The retail shop in New York generated healthy sales, and Internet orders were higher than ever. But the candy industry was brutal, ruled by giants like Mars, Hershey, and Moore. Small companies were quick to shut down or, if lucky enough, to sell out to one of the big three. Insiders had predicted that only one hundred fifty candy companies would be left in the next ten years, down from the peak of six thousand after World War II.

Didi missed a note. *Ouch.* Candace cringed and traded a look with Tatiana.

"Is there any way we can vote her off the island?" her friend asked, inspecting a perfect nail.

Candace's mind shifted into overdrive. *Push, push, push,* she told herself. *Coffee in Manhattan* didn't pack the ratings punch of, say, *The Today Show,* but its numbers were large enough and its viewers responsive enough to jump-start serious buzz on a new product.

I need buzz, Candace reminded herself. *Buzz, buzz, buzz.* She had it all figured out. Promote Passion Truffles as the candy for couples. Her advertising agency already had the campaign pitch: "For a Perfect Night of Romance, Share a Box of Passion Truffles." Granted, it wasn't as clever/revolutionary/shoo-in for a Clio as Nike's "Just Do It," but it worked. Besides, recent surveys suggested that couples who regularly eat chocolate are three times more likely to engage in romantic activity than those who don't. That little nugget, coupled with the proven adage that sex sells, seemed like a recipe for success.

The green room door swung open again. "You're up," Jackie said. "Follow me. We'll get you miked and introduce you to Chip and Didi."

Candace turned to Tatiana.

"Remember, you're a whore," the B-movie queen/ex-*Playboy* centerfold told her. "But instead of your body, you're selling Decadence. Repeat after me. I'm a whore."

Candace tried to force the words past her lips. But for an anthropology major from Wisconsin, it was rough going. "I'm ... I'm ... I'm Britney Spears." That was all she could manage.

"Close enough," Tatiana said.

Candace trailed Jackie through the studio labyrinth and onto the *Coffee in Manhattan* set. A technician dashed over to attach a mike to her collar.

"Say something at normal voice level," he instructed.

"Testing, testing," Candace said, drying sweaty palms on her skirt.

He gave her the thumbs-up sign.

As Chip Hamilton and Didi Farrell appeared to take their places, Jackie made the necessary introductions, then disappeared.

"So you're the vaginal cream lady," Didi said.

"Hey, I feel left out," Chip piped in. "How about some penis cream!".

Chip and Didi broke up into a fit of laughter. Candace stared back, horrified.

"That was hilarious," Didi praised the cohost, who seemed to be wearing more makeup than her. "Say it again for the cameras."

"You got it, doll face." Chip smiled, revealing teeth that were bleached a blinding, almost glow-in-the-dark white.

"Excuse me, I'm here to talk about chocolate," Candace interjected.

"Sweetheart, we have seven minutes," Didi said. "We can talk about lots of stuff." She turned to Chip. "How are my lips?"

He made an obnoxious smooching sound. "Kissable."

Didi cackled, then winked at Candace. "He's such a flirt!"

Candace leaned in to say, "I think there's been some sort of misunder—"

Chip held up a hand to cut her off. "Sorry, love. Time to make magic." And then he fixed a super smile on one of three cameras. "Welcome back!"

"Ditto!" Didi said with a laugh.

"Before we continue with the rest of the show, Didi, I just have to tell you how much your song touched my heart," Chip began earnestly. "I think everyone had a lump in their throat."

Yes, it's called gag reflex, Candace wanted to shout. But she sat quietly instead, praying their little act was just a bad joke.

"Thank you, Chip," Didi said, nodding with humility as thunderous applause broke out. "It's a song with the kind of message that we just don't hear enough of. 'The Greatest Love of All' is, after all, in us, in each and every one of us. Every morning I get up, and I go to the mirror, and I say to myself, 'Didi, I love ya, kid!' I really do!"

More applause.

"Well, guess what?" Chip put in. "I love Didi, too!" He smiled a megawatt smile for the camera. "I think we all do!"

"Enough about me!" Didi erupted, attempting to downplay the praise but clearly loving every nanosecond of it. "We have a show to do." She paused dramatically. "But thank you. I mean that. Our next guest has developed a sexual enhancer that should make every woman in the world very, very happy. Her patented Fantasy Cream is selling like gangbusters, and she's here to tell us more about it. Please give a warm welcome to Candace Rowley."

As the applause rumbled inside her chest, Candace could feel the blood siphon from her face.

Suddenly, and in the kind of lockstep twin movement found only in synchronized swimming, Chip and Didi's faces took on perplexed expressions as their right hands cupped their right ears. "Oops . . . We did it again!" they shouted in unison.

Didi turned to Chip. "What would we do without Toby, the producer?"

"I don't know about you, Didi, but I'd probably be back doing infomercials," Chip said.

"Hey, weren't you that butt firmer guy?" Didi squealed.

"Wanna see?" Chip asked, pretending to get up. The audience howled.

Candace battled hard to mask her annoyance.

"Forgive us, Manhattan," Didi said. "Candace

Rowley is here from Decadence Candies to tell us about their fabulous new Passion Truffles. Sorry, ladies. It's not a sex cream. But it's the next best thing! Good morning, Candace, and welcome to *Coffee in Manhattan*."

"Thank you, Didi. It's great to be here."

"We'll get to your little candies in a minute. Let's talk about this Fantasy Cream. What do you make of this phenomenon?"

Candace blanched. "Frankly, I know very little about it."

"Well, I hear that it increases blood flow to the vaginal area and really ups your orgasm-to-sex ratio," Didi said. "It's about time the ladies got some magic medicine, don't you think? A lot of gals think Viagra is nothing but a nuisance drug. All these men are standing at attention—if you know what I mean—but some women just don't want to be bothered."

"Hey, I feel left out," Chip piped in. "How about some penis cream!"

The audience roared.

Candace tittered politely, her brain searching for a way to get the subject back on point. Precious minutes were fading away with talk of this ridiculous sex cream!

"Isn't he a mess?" Didi asked rhetorically. She shook her finger at Chip. "What am I going to do with you?"

"I don't know. Why don't we meet backstage with a jar of Fantasy Cream and figure it out!" Chip said.

The studio audience lost it again.

Didi slapped Chip's arm. "Oh, you! Behave yourself. We have a guest." She turned back to Candace now, tilting her head in a gesture of seriousness. "Tell us, Candace, what is *your* orgasm-to-sex ratio?"

"I beg your pardon?"

"When you make love with your partner, how often—"

"I know what you mean! I just can't believe you're asking the question!"

Stunned, Didi quickly drew back.

Chip patted his cohost's knee and leaned in toward Candace. "Didi just jumped in there a little too quick. No harm done. Let's start with the more appropriate question. Do you have a sensual lover at the present time?"

"No, I don't," Candace hissed.

Didi made a long face. "Then we're not going to press you for that orgasm-to-sex ratio." Suddenly she brightened. "Let's talk about candy! I don't know about you, but I can't turn down a watermelon Jolly Rancher to save my life!"

Chip raised his hand. "Green apple over here!"

Didi drew in an excited breath. "And what about those Junior Mints?"

Chip rubbed his stomach. "Yummy!"

Candace saw an opening and jumped at the chance to turn things around and finally get *chocolate* into the conversation. Too afraid to let go, she went on about Aztec emperor Montezuma's penchant for consuming fifty cups of chocolate a day, about cocoa beans being exchanged between bride and groom in ancient Mayan culture, and about Columbus encountering the cacao bean on his fourth and final voyage.

"Well," Didi finally cut in, "I'll never look at a Hershey's Kiss the same way again." Then she spun to face the camera. "Stay with us because when we come back, our own Chip Hamilton is going to harmonize with red-hot boy band O-Town!"

Chip mugged for the camera. "You better watch out Justin Timberlake!"

More deafening applause from the studio audience.

From out of nowhere, the technician appeared to snatch off Candace's mike. Just as suddenly, Jackie appeared to escort her back to the green room. "That was . . . interesting. But I thought you were going to talk about the Passion Truffles. We had them right there on the table for Chip and Didi to try."

Candace walked silently behind Jackie, reeling with humiliation. All she could do was play the media event as train wreck over and over again in her mind.

"Sorry about the mix-up. Chip and Didi never read schedule updates. Actually, they never read anything," Jackie said.

Tatiana stood waiting outside the green room.

Candace forced herself to look her in the eye. "Let's get out of here."

Tatiana managed an upbeat smile. "You did great."

"Nice try, but you're more convincing in the *Lady Cop Undercover* movies."

"Oh, my God!" Jackie erupted. "That's where I know you from. A guy I dated in college had one of your movie posters tacked up in his room."

Tatiana grinned knowingly. "Was he in the Greek system?"

Jackie nodded. "Yeah, Sigma Chi."

"Figures. Frat boys love me."

Stepping outside onto the people-packed Manhattan street, Candace wanted to scream.

Tatiana pulled her in for a quick side hug. "You need champagne. I believe it can solve almost anything."

Candace did a double take. "It's not even ten o'clock yet."

"We'll throw in a splash of orange juice and call it a mimosa."

They ducked into the Plaza Hotel, found a cozy spot in the lounge, and ordered up the day's medicine.

"Have you ever seen anything more pathetic?" Candace grumbled.

"Than your interview?"

Candace nodded.

"That's hard to say. I missed Chip harmonizing with O-Town. But Didi's version of 'The Greatest Love of All' was definitely worse."

Candace relaxed and laughed a little. "Let's talk about something else. How's your husband?"

"Kerr? He never wants to have sex and all he does is make noises about wanting children. That would make him my *wife,* right?"

Candace felt her eyes widen. "Kids?"

"Not this body," Tatiana shot back. *"Lady Cop Undercover V: Maternity Ward* is not in my future." She sighed. "He's looking into adoption."

Candace downed the rest of her mimosa in one greedy gulp. "I blew it."

Tatiana signaled for another round. "That you did, honey."

"I've invested so much in the development of Passion Truffles, and if the product doesn't take off, I don't stand a chance in Hollywood."

"What do you mean?"

"There's a movie called *Chocolate on Her Pillow* that's about to go into production—"

"Greg Tapper's starring in that!" Tatiana broke in.

"I know. He's also the executive producer."

"You know, we used to be in the same acting class." Tatiana moaned. "If you could ever imagine Brando from *The Wild One* and James Dean from *Rebel Without a Cause* having a baby, then it would've been Greg Tapper. He was *so* sexy." She savored the image a moment, then gave Candace a curious look. "I don't get it. What does this movie have to do with Passion Truffles?"

"Product placement," Candace said, pausing to start in on the second mimosa that had just arrived. "The chocolate that's placed on the leading lady's pillow plays a pivotal role in the movie. And this project is big budget. Most of it's being shot on location in Capri. Anyway, if Passion Truffles were to show up in the film, it could put Decadence on the map in a major way."

"Phone home," Tatiana said in a froglike voice.

Candace just stared.

"Phone home!" Tatiana repeated impatiently, thankfully in her own voice this time. "From the movie *E.T.!*"

"Oh!" Candace yelped, finally getting it. The Reece's Pieces product placement. Battle stories behind the lovable alien visitor loving Reese's Pieces instead of M&M's were legendary. Before the movie came out, Reese's Pieces sales were in serious trouble. But within two weeks of *E.T.*'s release, distributors had reordered the candy as often as ten times. In some circles it was still considered the biggest marketing coup in history.

"You know Greg Tapper," Candace said, thinking out loud. "And you've got connections in Hollywood."

"Honey, you're not looking at a girl with connections. I mean, I just signed up for *Lady Cop Undercover IV: Red Light District.* As for Greg, I knew him briefly about ten years ago. I couldn't even get my hands on a script for *Chocolate on Her Pillow.* I was begging my agent to get me a walk-on part just for the free trip to Capri."

Candace sighed, all hope fading. She needed an inside edge. All she had was an early draft of the script thanks to a winning e-Bay bid. As if the bottom of mimosa number two held the magic answer, she turned up the champagne flute.

Tatiana reached for an abandoned *New York Post* at the next table and turned directly to the gossip section. She scanned the columns for several seconds before announcing, "Speak of the devil. He's here in the city."

"Who?"

"Greg Tapper." Tatiana peered closer at the tabloid. "It says here that last night he was seen club hopping with Strider Moore. Never heard of him. But he's gorgeous." She turned the paper around for Candace's benefit.

Strider Moore! She peeked at the photo. As much as she hated to admit it, he was gorgeous. And filthy rich. And the playboy prince of the Moore Candies fortune. And obviously trying to schmooze the company's Private Selections brand into a product placement deal. Damn him! Her blood began to simmer. At this point, a third mimosa wouldn't hurt. She raised her empty glass to the waiter.

"Strider Moore is the competition," Candace said. "He's obviously vying for product placement, too."

"Maybe you'll have to pull a Julia Roberts and sleep with the enemy." Tatiana gave the candid newspaper photo a serious assessment. "I could imagine worse scenarios."

"Please," Candace scoffed. "I've heard stories about this guy. He only goes for Victoria's Secret catalog clones. And his idea of a long-term relationship is having breakfast with a girl the morning after."

Tatiana laughed. "Sounds like every actor, agent, and producer I know in Los Angeles." She studied Candace for a moment. "Think about it, though. You could play the chocolate Mata Hari. Seduce him, draw out his secrets, and then use them to your own advantage."

Round three arrived. Candace drank up immediately. The mimosas tasted so good, and she felt deliciously light-headed now. Even so, Tatiana's idea was insane! Play spy and sleep with Strider Moore? "Shut up!" Candace said, a bit too loudly.

A trio of uptight ladies turned to sneer at them.

Candace giggled. "Sorry." She started to speak in a loud whisper, "How can you sit there and suggest that I sleep with him? Look at me. Do I even remotely resemble a Wonderbra model?"

The laughter in Tatiana's eyes dimmed a little. "You could be a real stunner, Candace, only you hide behind your work and your books and your cheap clothes and your refusal to wear makeup."

Inside Candace's fuzzy mind, the accusation bounced around.

"I know girls in LA who go broke paying a colorist to get the exact shade of honey blond to their hair that you have *naturally*. And those same girls struggle with color contacts every morning for the cobalt blue eyes you were *born* with. When's the last time you exercised?"

Candace shrugged, her head buzzing. "I did a walkathon for breast cancer last summer."

"See! Girls in LA starve themselves and go through torture with personal trainers for that slender and fit look you don't have to work for." Tatiana curled her lips into a faux snarl. "Bitch. You're beautiful, and you don't even try."

Candace had not consumed *that* much champagne. She was not beautiful. Not even close. "That's the alcohol talking."

Tatiana leveled a ray-gun gaze. "Get your mother's voice out of your head, Candace. Listen to my voice. Listen to your own."

The giddy feeling faded fast. Suddenly her mother's constant refrains boomeranged in her mind. *Your eyes are too close together, Candace. It's a shame that you have your father's nose. You're going to have to develop some amazing makeup skills to do something about that mouth.*

A familiar bitterness crept up on her. For so long, Candace had considered it a personal victory to ignore all that, to not even try, to embrace the ugly duckling her mother had so often criticized. But it was really a hollow win. And Tatiana knew that. As college roommates, their friendship had been instantly sealed in the crucibles of freshmen fear,

Madonna's *True Blue* album, Ramen Noodles, and strained mother-daughter relationships.

"Did you think your mother was beautiful?" Tatiana asked.

"Of course," Candace answered matter-of-factly.

"I used to believe the same thing about my mother, but Dr. G helped me see it a different way."

Candace braced herself for the psychobabble. Tatiana spent an hour of every week in therapy.

"I never would've known how beautiful *she* was if she hadn't always been pointing out how unbeautiful *I* was."

Candace merely stared for a moment. This point really hit a nerve. It was so simple, yet so . . . *true*.

Tatiana splayed out her manicured hands. "Is this the girl you met at the University of Wisconsin in ninteen eighty-six? No way, honey. That was Mildred Walker. I changed my name, I changed my hair color, and I changed my attitude. But Dr. G says I'm still that insecure girl. That's why I jumped at the chance to do the *Playboy* layout. Plus, I wanted a house. Do you know how much money I threw away on rent? Anyway, it's also why I'm game for these movies that require me to take off my clothes. It's just one more way to shut out those things my mother told me and to prove to myself that I'm beautiful. I mean, nobody wants a homely girl to get naked. Well, maybe a homely boy. But she won't get paid for it. And they're paying *me.*"

Candace felt a ripple of self-awareness, the tug of an emotional undercurrent.

"How badly do you want the product placement deal in this movie?"

Candace didn't need to contemplate her answer. *"Very."*

Tatiana nodded. "Then we need to transform you, honey. Hollywood is all about artifice. It's only big enough for one brainy chick, and Jodie Foster's got that covered."

Candace could feel the dread spread across her abdomen. For just a moment, she closed her eyes. When she opened them, Tatiana was grinning devilishly. "What?"

Tatiana mulled an obviously amusing thought. "Every covert strategy needs a code name. We're going to call this one Operation Bombshell."

Chapter Two

To take off the underwear or not to take it off? That was the question.

"Come on!" A girl at the corner booth egged him on. "Don't tease! Show us the package!"

Strider Moore looked down at her from his king of the mountain position on top of the table. "Who are you?" he shouted over a pulsating Jennifer Lopez remix.

"I'm Ashley!"

Something about her was tickling his memory. Somewhere in this dark mahogany-limestone lounge were his shirt, pants, and shoes. Somehow getting up here for this impromptu striptease had seemed like a good idea.

"We hooked up in the Hamptons last summer!"

He remembered now. The pool party at Puff Daddy's mansion. There were no shootings (a major plus), but Strider had worn his bullet-proof Speedo just in case. Ashley had introduced herself as a model, and since she was a gorgeous heavy smoker who stayed away from the food and laughed a lot, he had no choice but to believe her. Quite naturally, they'd ended up on a chaise in a heavy make-out session, that is until a buddy tapped his shoulder to tell him that the only *modeling* Ashley had done was school picture day at Spence. She was seventeen going on twenty-five and the daughter of some billionaire media titan.

"I'm eighteen now!" Ashley screamed.

Strider's fingers were splayed out, his thumbs hooked under the waistband of his Calvins. He glanced down at his entourage, which included Greg Tapper and assorted hangers-on, Ashley among them.

The movie star laughed at him. "Get down from there," Greg said. "You don't have the balls to—"

Off went the underwear. In fact, Strider sailed it past the actor's head before he could finish the sentence.

Greg stared up in openmouthed amazement. *Size insecurity?*

Ashley blushed. *Not so worldly after all, are we?*

A gay waiter slapped twenty dollars and a phone number in his hand. *Are the Prada shoes I just threw off too queeny?*

His main point proven (never dare a well-endowed exhibitionist who works out regularly to get naked), Strider jumped down and proceeded to hunt for his clothes, fielding high fives and whistles from the cadre of party people vacuum-packed into Lotus, a three-level bar/lounge/club/restaurant/place to be seen in the meatpacking district.

He easily tracked down everything but his shirt, an orange sherbet-colored Oxford. Then he caught sight of it—angrily gripped in a woman's hand. Seeing the Cartier panther watch curled around her wrist triggered a feeling of dread. *Please, God, no.* His gaze traveled upward for confirmation. There stood Tiko, a one-night stand in Tokyo who'd metamorphosed into an international stalking incident. *Thanks for nothing, God.*

"You lied to me!" Tiko shrieked. She took in Lotus with a circular gaze. "These people don't look hungry." She focused in on a pack of models. "Well, maybe they do. But you told me that you were helping starving children!"

Strider's brain computer went to work. Open file name OUTRAGED FORMER LOVER. Scan for LIES SHE MIGHT BUY. Search complete. "Every time I had a chance to call you in Africa it was after midnight in Japan. Then I got an urgent call from my father to take the lead on a business deal here in the States." He rubbed his temples. "It's been crazy. I don't even know what day it is. How did you know where to find me anyway?"

In Tiko's other hand was a crumpled *New York Post*. She thrust it at his bare chest. "I can read!"

Good. Then you should have no trouble understanding the restraining order. That's what he wanted to say. But all he gave voice to was, "Can I have my shirt back?"

Tiko stared daggers. *"The Full Monty* is playing on Forty-ninth Street. Why are you stripping here?"

Strider tried to take the shirt but Tiko held fast. He shrugged. "It was a dare."

"Then I dare you to marry me."

"This was a guy thing," Strider said quickly. "You had to be there."

As if against her better judgment, Tiko handed

over the shirt. "I finished new tracks in the studio today. Tonight we will make love and listen to my music."

Suddenly the waiter's offer didn't seem half bad. Tiko fancied herself a singer/songwriter, pretty easy to do if your father happens to be CEO of a worldwide recording label. With three albums and maybe twelve singles to her credit, she'd managed to churn out one minor hit, "I'm Gonna Get Your Love." The song went something like this: *I'm gonna get your love, boy/I'm gonna get your love/Don't try to run and hide, boy/Cause I'm gonna get your love.* Repeat chorus about a million times and there you have it. Obviously, she believed in her life imitating her art.

Normally, Strider wouldn't complain. After all, Tiko was an incredible Asian beauty. So much so that if Lucy Liu were her sister, the *Charlie's Angels* star would be the ugly one. And the sex was amazing. But her music. Oh, man, it was bad. Really bad. Imagine being trapped in an alternate universe where all they played was Debbie Gibson. Well, compared to listening to Tiko, that's a good place to be. But to get the Tiko sex you had to endure the Tiko music. At the end of the day, the two canceled each other out.

Slipping his shirt back on, Strider tried to think of an escape.

Suddenly Greg Tapper swaggered up beside him, hooking an elbow around his neck and pulling him in for some conspiratorial macho talk. "You're a crazy man, Strider. Can't believe you took it all off like that. Not a bad show. I've got at least a half an inch on you, though." He laughed, punctuating his delivery with a soft sucker punch to the ribs.

"What do you say we take a few of these lovely ladies back to the hotel." Greg cast a lascivious gaze on Ashley. "I've got dibs on the brunette."

Strider felt a surge of protectiveness. "She's a schoolgirl, man. Just turned eighteen."

This didn't faze Greg. "You know what they say. If she's old enough to vote, she's old enough to—"

"Could you excuse me for just a minute?" Strider cut in. He gestured to Tiko. "I've got a little situation here."

Greg nodded his understanding and headed back to the booth.

Strider locked his best come-on-baby-do-me-a-favor gaze on Tiko. "I've got to close this deal tonight." He kissed an index finger and touched the tip of her nose. "Rain check. Promise."

Tiko pouted. It was her default expression.

Strider reached into his pocket and flicked a few hundred dollar bills off his money clip. "See that young brunette over there? Her name's Ashley. She's eighteen and in over her head." He pressed the cash into Tiko's hand. "Take this and treat her to a dessert in the restaurant. Make sure she gets home safely, too."

"What about my songs?" Tiko whined.

Not a priority. It was almost past Strider's lips, but what prevailed was, "Tomorrow night."

Tiko looked suspicious. "What kind of *deal* are you working on?"

Strider pulled Tiko in close to whisper confidentially, "Greg's producer and star of a movie called *Chocolate on Her Pillow.* I'm under a lot of pressure to secure product placement for my family's Private Selections brand."

"But I want you to listen to my new song, 'Love, Love, Love.' "

No, no, no. "Listen to me. Both my father and grandfather think I'm a screwup, and if I don't make this deal happen, then my ass is going to be kicked out of the family business."

Tiko huffed a little.

Strider massaged her shoulders. "Take care of Ashley for me. I'll call you tomorrow."

"Tell me I'm beautiful."

"You're beautiful."

"Kiss me."

Not the worst job in the world. He planted one on her—deep, sensual, passionate, tongues at war. Over the steady hum of nightclub conversation and a thumping Madonna number, Strider heard the click of a paparazzo's camera. He could just imagine the headline: HOT-BLOODED HEIR TO CHOCOLATE FORTUNE GETS PHYSICAL WITH ASIAN POP TART. Dad and Grandpop will be so proud.

"Rule number one: Never pay for anything," Tatiana said. "The only cash you need is thirty-five cents for a phone call."

Candace gave her a quizzical look.

Tatiana put a hand to curvy hip. "I haven't paid for a drink since my sophomore year in college."

Candace scribbled down the instruction and underlined the word never.

"Rule number two: Always be late. But for a good reason. I mean, don't be Diana Ross. Maybe you come across a stray kitten. Or your cousin calls because her husband's fooling around, and she's trying to decide about getting breast implants. Advise against it, by the way.''

Candace scratched furiously on her yellow legal pad.

"Tantrums are generally acceptable," Tatiana went on. "So is light criminal activity."

A pang of panic. This bombshell act was serious business. "I need examples."

Tatiana paused a moment. "Throwing drinks in people's faces is always a good way to show the room that you're angry. As for crime . . . light stuff like never returning jewelry to boyfriends you dump or forgetting to take back designer clothes you borrow for big events."

"I get free clothes?" Candace asked.

Tatiana nodded. "I haven't paid retail for a formal dress since my senior prom." She gave Candace a studied glance. "We need to do something about your name, too."

"What's wrong with my name?" *Candace Rowley*. She'd always kind of liked it.

"A bombshell needs a name that pops. In my case, Mildred Walker became Tatiana Fox. Did you know that Veronica Lake was once Constance Francis Ockleman?" Her eyes brightened. "I've got it. Candi Rowe. With an i. Write it down. That's your new name."

"Candi Rowe?" Candace threw back the moniker like a wrong fast-food order. "You're supposed to turn me into a bombshell not a porn star." She considered the situation. "How about Lana Rowley? My middle name *is* Lindsay. That's not too far off."

Tatiana shook her head. "Lana will always be off-limits because Lana Turner was arguably the best bombshell of all time. Besides, only drag queens steal names. Actually, though, Rowley isn't that bad. OK, you can keep the last name, but you have to drop Candace for Candi. It'll look better when you sign letters and postcards. You can do something fun like dot the i with a little heart."

It seemed reasonable, so she nodded her agreement.

Tatiana grabbed Candace's arm and sniffed the pulse point of her wrist. "What perfume is this?"

"Eternity."

Tatiana pulled a face. "Not anymore. Throw it out. Pick up Spring Flower by Creed. You'll love it."

Candace shot a glance to the top of her lingerie chest, where a brand-new bottle of Eternity perched peacefully. She grimaced.

Tatiana was in her closet now.

This will definitely be a bloodbath.

"Not as bad as I imagined," Tatiana said.

Candace perked up. "Really?"

"The shoes are a disaster, of course. We'll need three new pairs to start. That's at least a thousand dollars."

"For shoes?" Candace's stomach did a flip. "I've never paid more than—"

Tatiana raised a hand to stop her. "Don't say it out loud. The physical evidence speaks for itself."

"But—"

"The wrong shoes can be deadlier than napalm." Tatiana scanned the room. At the sight of Candace's leather purse on the bed, she raised a disapproving eyebrow. "Ditto the handbag. We hit Chanel and Gucci after we deal with shoes. Count on another thousand."

"I can't afford all this!" Candace wailed.

Tatiana didn't so much as blink. "Right," she scoffed. "Says the girl who's saved fifteen percent of every dollar earned since setting up a Kool-Aid stand at age seven."

"This is why Americans are saddled with so much debt! They think savings is there to be dipped into! It should be off-limits!"

"New rule: A bombshell should never sound like an anal-retentive accountant." Tatiana shook her head, unzipped the offensive purse, and dumped the contents onto the bed.

Candace watched her daily necessities bounce and clang into a messy pile.

"Ridiculous," Tatiana sniped. "Lose the Palm Pilot."

"My whole *life* is on that!"

"Is there a guy listed who takes you on exotic trips?"

"No."

"Is the man who gave you the best sex of your life downloaded?"

"No." Quietly this time.

"Then it's useless." Tatiana shoved the gadget aside. "Lose this, too," she added, tossing aside the cellular phone.

Candace could hardly believe it. "What am I supposed—"

"Borrow one when you need to make a call. A bombshell should be hard to reach."

A terrible sense of futility came over her. "Come on, Tatiana. Let's get serious. You can't just hide my Palm Pilot, buy me a new pair of shoes, and expect me to be some kind of sex goddess." Candace slumped down onto the bed. "This is never going to work."

"Before you give up, read this story." Tatiana fished a *New York Post* out of her shoulder bag (not sure of the brand, but it looked expensive), turned to the gossip pages (what else?), and pushed forward a photograph of Strider Moore (still gorgeous) kissing an Asian woman (also gorgeous).

HOT HEIR TO CANDY FORTUNE SEXES UP NIGHTCLUB

Strider Moore, heir apparent of Moore Candies, engaged in some naked play at Lotus last night. Sharing a corner booth with **Greg Tapper, Ashley Beckham,** and a cluster of mere mortals, he jumped on the table for a Chippendales-inspired routine that proved this much: It's true what they say about a man with big feet—and Strider wears a size thirteen shoe! The prince of chocolate celebrated the act in a steamy lip lock with Asian pop star *Tiko.* Heading out in the wee hours, Moore and Tapper looked chummier than two summer-camp kids after a panty raid. Is there a business deal in the works, or is this just two rowdy boys having a good time?

Candace stewed in the sinister possibilities. Those damn Moores! They were going after the product placement deal with a vengeance. She thought back a few months to that unannounced visit from A.J. Moore, Strider's cousin and reportedly the family's more serious young business mind. He'd made an offer (a pretty good one, actually) to buy Decadence lock, stock, and hazelnut. Of course, she'd said no. The very idea of selling out to one of the big three that routinely gobbled up any small company that posed even the slightest threat made her sick.

Just then an ominous feeling came over her. Why *did* Moore Candies want Decadence? How could a single-shop candy company with a growing-by-the-inch Internet business be on their radar? And suddenly it hit her. *Passion Truffles!* The offer had stunned her so much that the obvious signs had escaped her. A.J. paid a visit just after Passion Truffles had been written up in *Confectioner* magazine.

"Oh, no!" Candace gasped.

"I thought the same thing," Tatiana said. "Tiko's not a pop *star*. She's had one hit, and it didn't even go top ten."

Candace slung the newspaper across the room.

Tatiana merely stared. "You're taking it worse than I did."

"It's not that. I don't care about Seiko."

"Tiko."

"Whatever. You don't understand. This is just like what happened to Victoria Mancini. She developed a new candy called Chocolate Obsession. Oh, God, it was heaven—milk chocolate, dark chocolate, white chocolate. Anyway, A.J. Moore—"

"I thought his name was Strider," Tatiana interrupted.

"A.J.'s his cousin."

"Cuter cousin?"

"Less cute cousin."

"Oh." The look on Tatiana's face conveyed considerably less interest now.

Candace's stomach tightened with anxiousness. "Please let me finish. A.J. offered to buy Victoria's company. When she refused to sell, Moore put out an almost identical candy called Chocolate Maniac. Her company's still around, but basically limping along. I heard she's willing to sell it now. There's no other choice."

"Why didn't she sue? You know, Tom Cruise's lawyers can win almost any case."

Candace shook her head. "The candy business is quirky. First, there are just so many ingredients— chocolate, caramel, nuts, peanut butter."

"You're making me hungry."

"We'll order take-out from a great little Korean place in a minute. Anyway, beyond the limited ingredients, there's the limited range of customer tastes. This is how my industry works. Companies borrow a successful product, alter it only slightly, and then resell it as their own."

Tatiana returned a knowing nod. "Honey, that's business as usual in LA. We call it Hollywood."

"I know Moore is planning to do the same thing to me. They must have a copycat to Passion Truffles in mind for *Chocolate on Her Pillow.*" Candace clenched her fists. "I *have* to get this product placement deal. I *have* to get Hollywood to notice me." For a long second, she stared lasers at Tatiana. "Show me how to dress. Tell me what to say. Make me a bombshell!"

Tatiana smiled. "Rule number three: Never sound desperate."

Chapter Three

Oh, God, Candace half thought, half prayed as she woke up. Too much champagne. But this hangover went far beyond that late-night bottle of Perrier-Jouet.

Too much Korean food. She rested a hand on an uncertain stomach. Do Hwa around the corner had delivered cold japchae glass noodles, mandu gook soup with fiery dumplings, and the bi bim bop hot pot.

Too much Shania Twain. She raised fingertips to her throbbing temples. How many times had they listened to "Man! I Feel Like a Woman" at deafening volume? At least fifty.

Too much Jayne Mansfield. She rubbed her weary eyes. It had taken hours to watch *Will Success Spoil Rock Hunter?* and *Too Hot to Handle* because Tatiana stopped the tape every five minutes to point out particular bombshell moves. Pause. *See how Jayne lingers in the entryway, breasts jutted out like torpedoes ready to fire.* Rewind. View again. Pause. *See how Jayne blows kisses with both hands.* And so on. By the end of it, Candace felt about as sexy as a fisherman's wife after cleaning the day's catch.

Going to Blockbuster had been a hoot, though. The guy checking them out (barely nineteen, still fighting acne) was over the moon to meet Tatiana in person and insisted that she autograph all the *Lady Cop Undercover* movies as well as his arm.

Too much coffee. That's what Candace needed now. She gently rose.

Heading into the tiny kitchen of her cramped West Village apartment, Candace found Tatiana slumped on the couch. On the pillow near her cheek lay a cucumber. After the last round of bubbly and before passing out, Tatiana had started to demonstrate bombshell rule number . . . one hundred thirty-seven: Be highly skilled at fellatio.

Tatiana stirred with a start. "Shit! I fell asleep with my makeup on. Where's the phone? I need to call Elizabeth Arden and see if I can get in for a deep-pore cleansing."

Candace motioned to the cordless.

Tatiana bulldozed her way in to a ten o'clock appointment, refusing to buy the booked to capacity line. The poor receptionist never had a chance.

"Coffee?"

Returning the phone to its base, Tatiana shook her head. "Bad for the skin. Drink lots of bottled water in the morning. And throughout the day, too. Hydration is key to a bombshell's luminous complexion."

Candace pushed the Colombian grounds to the far reaches of the counter. OK, maybe she had the hang of this now. If she just started doing the *oppo-*

site of what she might normally do, then chances are she would be acting the part of a bombshell.

Tatiana opened the fridge.

"You'll have to settle for tap," Candace said.

"Tap?" When it came to expressing disapproval, the B-movie queen could emote better than Meryl Streep. "Why don't you just ask me to drink out of the toilet?"

Candace shrugged. "I'm so bad. I hardly ever drink water." She paused. "But coffee's made with water. So is tea. And Tang. Maybe—"

"Stop before you start counting the cocoa bean as a vegetable." Tatiana raked her fingers through her tangled red mane, then opened the freezer and began to poke around. "Do you still keep your credit cards in a block of . . . Yes, of course you do."

"Leave—"

But before she could protest, Tatiana dumped the Visa/American Express/Discover Card ice in the sink and proceeded to run hot water over it.

Candace watched it thaw. *Fast.* She snatched the Visa. "I'm only using one of these, so you have to make me a bombshell on a budget."

"What's your credit limit?"

"Three thousand."

Tatiana considered the challenge. "Expect to reach it."

A wave of doubt crashed over Candace. "I just thought of something. Do we even have a plan? I mean, I have no idea where Strider Moore is going to show up next. Do you?"

Tatiana bit down on her lower lip. "No, but I can find out." Her tone was one of total absoluteness.

Candace shut her eyes, still mourning the loss

of coffee. "I was afraid you might say something like that."

"Let's call Enrique, my personal assistant. He's a party boy just like Strider. Men of that breed think alike. Enrique's a bit younger—early twenties—but Strider's probably still fourteen in his head, so it all balances out." She dashed for the cordless again. "Does this work on speaker?"

"Look for the blue button."

Tatiana pressed it, a dull dial tone hit the air, and she punched in a number.

"Hello?"

"Hi, it's me."

"Are you back?" The male voice—deep, melodious, instantly sexy—carried a hint of alarm.

Tatiana grinned. "I'm in a cab five minutes from the house."

There was a loud thud, followed by a girl yelling, "Ow! You pushed me off the bed. Asshole!"

Candace covered her mouth, not wanting to laugh but unable to resist.

"Why didn't you call earlier? I would've picked you up at the airport." Enrique again. Officially frantic.

"Gotcha!" Tatiana squealed in good humor. "Actually, I'm still in New York."

"Wait! Carrie! It's OK now," Enrique yelled.

"Fuck you! I should've known this wasn't your house!" Carrie this time. Officially pissed off.

Enrique groaned.

Tatiana giggled. "Wash the sheets—including the comforter—and replace the liquor. How did you get away with this? Where's Kerr?"

"He said something about a business trip."

Tatiana grimaced. "What kind of business? He's an unpublished poetry writer."

"I didn't ask. I'm your assistant, not his. What do you want?"

"Snappish, are we?"

"I really liked Carrie."

"Never lie to impress a girl. You should've learned that much from reruns of *My Three Sons.*"

"Telling a girl like Carrie that I share an apartment with two waiters and work for twelve dollars an hour as a personal assistant is not the strongest opening line at a club."

"Oh, that reminds me. Did you pick up that sunblock I like? I'm almost out."

"Done."

"OK, here's the deal, Romeo. Greg Tapper's in New York doing the town with Strider Moore. Last night they hit Lotus, and the night before that they were holed up in the Hudson Hotel bar. Any idea where they might show up tonight?"

Enrique didn't pause so much as a beat. "If I were in Manhattan tonight, I'd be at the Cutting Room. There's a private party for the release of Ben Estes's new CD."

"The disco Sinatra guy?"

"Yeah. Have you heard his new version of 'My Way'? His cool factor is off the charts. Every A-lister will be there."

"Thanks. Listen, I get in at one o'clock tomorrow. Pick me up at LAX. And no more sex romps at my house!" She clicked off the speaker phone. "We have a plan now."

"Crash a private party? I don't even know Ben Estes."

"Not a problem," Tatiana said. "Chris Noth—

he plays Mr. Big on *Sex and the City*—is part owner of the club. I played a stripper in one of his TV movies once. We had a thing on the set. This was before Kerr, of course.''

"I should call Lily," Candace murmured. "It doesn't look like I'll make it into the shop today."

Tatiana stretched. "Everything's in motion. Today we shop. Tonight we vamp. Tomorrow you conquer Hollywood."

Strider was chatting up a WB actress (he couldn't remember her name or the show she starred in) when he caught sight of arguably the sexiest woman in the world. He didn't bother with a surreptitious glance. This matter required a stare of the laser-focus variety. Katie Michelle Whatever would just have to be patient.

"Surprise!"

Not the pleasant kind, Strider thought miserably as Tiko pounced into his line of vision.

"Tiko wants a kiss."

Strider tried to smile, but it died on his lips. He hated to hear people refer to themselves in the third person.

The WB girl left in a huff.

Tiko just stood there, posing expectantly.

Strider ignored them, unable to take his eyes off this mystery woman for any length of time. To simply call her amazing was the understatement of the millennium. Everywhere around him women were either trying too hard (some designer said circus-girl-on-crack was the in look this season) or not trying at all (the see-how-cool-I-am-not-to-care look of jeans, boots, and one-hundred-fifty-dollar

Helmut Lang T-shirt). Both sides of the equator bored him.

But this woman walked through the Cutting Room door and became the bar's centerpiece in a heartbeat. She wore a snug, robin's egg-blue V-neck cashmere sweater that showed enough cleavage to get a man's attention but not so much to incur the hostility of every other girl in the room. Instead of a short skirt (the predictable approach), she wore a pair of black hot pants. Her long shapely legs seemed to go on forever until they reached the impossibly sexy, gravity-defying black sling backs. The only jewelry adorning her body was a silver necklace from which dangled a modest pearl pendant. In her right hand she held a small zebra-print clutch, a smoke signal to the world that this lady had a wild side.

Pop! Strider reeled from the slap. Stunned, he stared back at Tiko.

She glared with triumph. "Now that I've got your attention . . ." And then she yanked his head down with both hands and kissed him as if the fate of civilization depended on it. He responded (he was distracted, not comatose), tried to steal a glance at this heavenly creature (Tiko closed her eyes when she canoodled), then gave in fully to the make-out assault, determined to find the girl later on, after he figured out a way to get rid of this bad pop singer/stalker.

"That was a great move to linger in the doorway for so long," Tatiana praised.

"Believe me, it was unintentional," Candace said under her breath. "Walking in these heels is murder." She stared at Strider Moore and Tiko. "Do you know where we can find a jaws of life this time of night? Otherwise I don't stand a chance of getting a word in."

"Honey, you have more than a chance. He *definitely* noticed you. Stay here and look sexy. I'm going to find Chris and thank him for putting our names on the list. Remember: Let the men come to you."

Candace watched Tatiana disappear into the smoky crowd. She tried to appear cool, but a sudden panic played over her. What if a man did approach her? She couldn't be herself. *Candace* was overly cautious, interested in school/career background first, and passed out work number only until at least the third date. *Candi* had to be confident, glamorous, thrilled by anything a man decided to talk about, clever, and always amusing.

She looked up to see Greg Tapper smiling at her. *Greg Tapper the movie star.* The one who earns twenty million a picture to run in and out of exploding buildings between love scenes with an actress at least ten years younger. Now he was approaching!

The moment of truth. Candace wanted to flee. But Candi had to stay put. She felt a bead of sweat form on her brow. Bombshell rule number forty-six: Never sweat unless you're on the treadmill or in bed with a guy. Deep breath. Desperate prayer.

"You know, I think I've met every beautiful woman in the world. How is it that I've never come across you?"

Wave of nausea. This was his opening line? Even a bombshell in training deserved better. "Maybe you have attention deficit disorder."

Greg leaned in closer. "Maybe I'm cured now."

And then he gave her the benefit of his heat-stoked gaze.

Candace was struck by the oddness of being face-to-face with a man she'd only seen on screen. He was shorter than she'd imagined and no way near as dazzling as he appeared in the movies. Makeup and lighting were good friends to this guy.

"I'm Greg Tapper," he said finally. "You might know me from my films, or maybe *People* magazine. They voted me 'Sexiest Man Alive' last year."

"Are you and Brad Pitt still on speaking terms?"

He laughed a little. "You're funny. What's your name?"

"Call me Candi."

He winked. "Sweet enough to eat, I hope."

Candace wanted to deck this creep. But Candi giggled, knowing that having the star and executive producer of *Chocolate on Her Pillow* in her corner could only help close the deal.

"If you play your cards right, Candi, tomorrow you could be on the phone bragging to your friends about how you went to bed with a movie star."

Coolly, she shifted positions to gaze at the room, not looking at him when she said, "You've got two things wrong. First, I *never* kiss and tell. Second, if we did sleep together, *you* would be the one using speed dial." And then she concentrated really hard on walking away in those damn heels without toppling over.

Tatiana appeared to intercept, grabbing on to both hands to stave off a Humpty Dumpty incident. "You just gave Greg Tapper the brush-off!" She practically jumped up and down.

Candace pulled a face. "I considered it a moral duty. He's disgusting."

Tatiana returned a knowing nod. "You could probably get better pick-up lines from a bald Amway salesman in a Holiday Inn bar. But remember, women never say no to Greg. He hasn't had to do more than crook a finger for years."

Candace couldn't stop smiling. "That felt good," she admitted.

Tatiana giggled. "Now he's not going to rest until he gets you into bed."

Candace experienced a moment's pure fear. "I'm not sleeping with him!"

"Oh, stop. Look around you. There's not a single woman in this bar—except for the rather butch girl arguing with that bartender—who wouldn't go for a tumble with Greg Tapper. It's a good story for the steam room at the gym."

"I never go into the steam room."

"Sauna?"

Candace shook her head.

"Well, talk really loud when you're on the treadmill then. A bombshell's attitude toward sex is that it's no big deal. I mean, when you think about it, why all the fuss? A man's got to do most of the work and worry about whether you've seen a bigger one or not. We can just lie there, moan a little, and if he's really successful like Greg, maybe a nice piece of jewelry shows up in a week or so."

"What's the difference between that and a prostitute?"

"Better shoes, patience, and more flexible hours."

Candace's mouth dropped open.

"I'm kidding. About everything but the shoes."

Candace pursed her lips.

"Honey, there's a big difference between being

celibate and being celibate for too long. When's the last time you hit the sheets with a guy?"

Candace didn't want to do the math. Too depressing. All she knew was this: Around the time of her last sexual experience (which clocked in at under three minutes, thank you Ronald Sykes) *Seinfeld* was still on the air in original episodes. Oh, God! If you went that long without it, were you technically a virgin again?

"I assume it wasn't in this century," Tatiana said.

"It's only 2002," Candace whined.

Suddenly Tatiana was distracted. "There's Ben Estes, the guest of honor. I want to meet him." She splayed out her fingers. "His wife owns a cosmetics company. I'm wearing her nail polish now, Jacqueline Feels Radical in Red. Sounds like an ice breaker to me." And off she went.

Candace stood there a moment and decided she wanted a drink. Something sweet with a kick. Maybe a green-apple martini. Did bombshells get their own? Wasn't a man just supposed to show up with one?

"I took a chance that you're a Midori sour kind of girl."

She spun to find Strider Moore holding out a cocktail for her benefit. "I am now." Accepting it, she took a generous sip to buy time, to build up her nerve.

Up close, he was amazing. Brown haired, brown eyed, six-foot-two, handsome to the point of distraction, athletic. His smile—dimpled, devastating—revealed a hint of rich-boy mischief, a bolt of laid-back charm. "That was quite an entrance you made," Strider said.

"You noticed?"

"Every man in the room did, including the gay ones."

"Where do you fall?"

"In the straight column. Didn't you see my floor show?"

"I've never been a fan of the circus."

He grinned.

She sipped on her drink and grinned back.

"I don't like that woman you saw me with," he said earnestly. "Really."

"Not even a little bit? You did have your tongue down her throat."

He laughed. "You're not going to make this easy, are you?"

"What?"

"Me hitting on you."

"I figure a man like you should work hard at *something*."

"Oh, believe me, I can put the effort in." He winked.

Candace could feel a blushing heat stain her cheeks. "So where did the other half of your act go?"

"I had a friend call her cell phone to say her hotel room was on fire."

Candace nearly collapsed from laughter. It was so outrageous. She could hardly believe it. "You're not serious."

Strider bobbed his head up and down.

"What a horrible thing to do!"

"It sounds worse than it is. This woman is stalking me. I should be in court right now filing a temporary restraining order."

"So you don't want to see her anymore?"

"No."

"You could be sending her mixed signals with this habit of kissing passionately in public."

"You think?"

And then a dance beat dropped, cocooning the room in an urgent rhythm, the base throbbing, seductive, infectious. The volume went up, the lights went down, and the crowd responded. It was why they were here. To celebrate Ben Estes's disco reworking of "My Way." To be seen. To dance.

Without warning, Strider took Candace's drink, placed it along with his own on a nearby table, and pulled her toward the center of the bar, where several party people were already working up a sweat.

He was a fantastic dancer—fluid, not too showy, interactive. She'd boogied with guys who zoned out and forgot she existed, but Strider's gaze never left her. By the first chorus she forgot about the heels. Her legs felt strong and steady, her body free and limber. For the first time tonight, the clothes and shoes weren't wearing *her*. She was wearing *them!*

With both hands in the air she swayed her hips to the urgent beat, tilting her head back, closing her eyes for a spell, then opening them again to take in the scene. The sensation was glorious. Greg Tapper wanted her. The chocolate prince wanted her. Other men were checking her out. The realization became alternately frightening and arousing. Because she knew the man twirling her around would be the first in a long time. Instinctively, she knew that getting into bed with Strider Moore was inevitable. There were just a few details to negotiate. When and where.

A third point lingered ominously. How would

she deal with the fact that this monumental move for her was just another conquest for him? Unlike Tiko, she didn't have a powerful father, a pseudo career in entertainment, or anything else to get her name in boldface when the gossip columns pointed out Strider's flavor of the week. At the end of the day, she was just a plain girl. But tonight she was a bombshell, and life was a movie, and she was the name above the title. *Candi Rowley.*

So she kept on dancing.

Chapter Four

They were lost in the music, grooving to the instrumental break of tribal drum beats, when all hell broke loose. Tiko was back and looking furious enough to upgrade from stalker to killer as she pushed through a cluster of dancers to wedge herself between Candace and Strider.

"Somebody played a mean trick on Tiko!" she screamed. Then she turned on Candace accusingly. "Did you call my cell phone?"

"No."

Tiko narrowed her angry eyes to mere slits. "Why should I believe you?"

"Because I've never met you, don't know your number, and have no reason to call you." She looked at Strider, a question in her gaze. Would he fess up and put an end to this nonsense?

"It was probably just a prank," Strider told Tiko. His voice was soothing. "I heard the same thing happened to Christina Aguilera last week."

"Really?" The possibility sunk in and Tiko appeared mollified. After all, if it happened to Christina . . .

The floor was getting crowded on multiple levels. Candace hated to admit it, but she was experiencing a twinge of jealousy. One dance and she wanted Strider Moore all to herself. Not the best turn of events. A bombshell was supposed to make people jealous, not *be* jealous. Hmm. She was even thinking like one now. Tatiana would be proud. Feigning indifference, she turned to go.

"Candace Rowley. I almost didn't recognize you." It was A.J. Moore, Strider's cousin, the man who had tried to convince her to sell Decadence to their company's Private Selections division.

"I . . . I . . . I go by Candi now."

A.J. raked her up and down, his gaze settling on her chest. "You've changed more than your name, I see. Implants? Good work. Who's your doctor? My wife is thinking about—"

"It's a Wonderbra!"

Strider stepped in, pulsing with hostility. "What are you doing here, A.J.? I thought your idea of fun was swimming in shark tanks."

"Hello, *Lansing.* Actually, I do that for relaxation." He was a few inches shorter than Strider and looked up at him smugly. "Your father has been trying to get in touch. If I see you, I'm supposed to pass along this message: *Focus on the deal.* As usual, though, I see you're focusing on everything else." He gave Tiko a once-over. "I'll be sure and report back." Turning back to Candace, A.J. said, "If you change your mind about selling, please call me to discuss the particulars. Lansing here is a bit fuzzy in that area."

Strider took a menacing step forward. "You know her?"

"She owns Decadance," A.J. informed him. "The Passion Truffle is her baby."

Strider turned his gaze on Candace now. He looked dumbfounded.

A.J. relished the moment. "You should try to learn more about a girl than her room number, Lansing."

Strider's face flushed. His fists clenched. "Stop calling me that." It was so angry-little-boy-on-the-school-yard. Really cute.

A.J. clearly enjoyed the reaction. "Why? That's your real name. It's good enough for your father. It's good enough for his father. Of course, with your track record, I can understand why it's not good enough for you."

"Tiko's bored!" After this enlightening announcement, the pop star (a very minor one according to Tatiana) stomped away, turning back once to glare at Strider, daring him *not* to follow her.

Strider, cool and confident, metamorphosed into Strider, tense and uncertain. This cousin really knew how to push his buttons. "Did they send you here to check up on me?"

A.J. returned a small, triumphant smile. "Can't keep anything from you." And then he turned to Candace, gently taking her arm. "Why don't you let me give you a lift home, dear? I have a car and driver out front. Any minute now you're likely to have an attack of vertigo in those heels."

Strider's lips parted in amazement. His number-one worst-case scenario was painted all over his face: Losing a girl to A.J. He managed to steal a glance at Tiko, but he would've chosen Candace tonight. She saw the decision in his eyes. That's why she left with A.J. To drive Strider crazy. To keep him on his toes. Tatiana had taught her well.

A.J. traveled in high style. In the dark she couldn't tell whether the Mercedes was black or blue. Like a true gentleman, he opened the door and ushered her into the rear cabin. The first thing she did once she sank into the rich leather was take off her shoes. Manolo Blahniks or not, her feet were killing her. A.J. dashed around to enter the car from the other side, then called out Candace's West Village address to the driver.

She gave him a sharp look.

"Relax. Whenever we're interested in acquiring a company, we run a thorough background check."

"Pop quiz. Where did I attend college?"

"The University of Wisconsin. Majored in anthropology. Graduated with a four point."

Suddenly she felt at ease and lay back in the seat. Inside her head she could still hear the music. "My Way." The campy vocal. The insistent beat. Had Strider left with Tiko? It worried her how badly she wanted to know.

"You're a clever girl, *Candi,* but you don't need to go to all this trouble." A.J. gave her a little smirk and turned away to gaze out the window as the car cruised down Twenty-Fourth Street.

She wondered what he meant by that. She wondered if he could only speak in condescending tones. And, once more, she wondered if Strider had left with Tiko. Just then her zebra-print clutch started to ring. Snapping it open, she fished out her cell phone. Right away she knew it would be Tatiana.

"Honey, you left with the wrong man! I didn't put you through bombshell boot camp for you to go home with the creepy cousin! You could've mastered that skill in a mail-order course!"

Candace sighed. She was still curious about A.J.'s statement, *You don't need to go to all this trouble.* "I have to go. I'll meet you back at the apartment."

"Maybe," Tatiana threatened. "I'm being hit on left and right, and my husband hasn't touched me in months."

"Don't do anything you'll regret. Come home. We'll order a pizza and gossip about everyone we saw tonight."

Tatiana squealed with delight. "Just like we used to do in college! Oh, I miss being twenty. I'm looking at all these girls here with their whole lives ahead of them. It makes me feel old. I mean, I'm twenty-nine—"

"Five years ago you were twenty-nine."

"Shit, you're right! I'm starting to actually believe my Hollywood age. That's what Los Angeles will do to you. But don't tell."

"Your secret is safe with me." Candace clicked off her friend and laughed a little. She shifted in her seat to address A.J. "Sorry about that. A girlfriend in crisis. She's an actress, too, which makes everything exponentially serious."

"This would be Tatiana Fox, right?" A.J. asked.

Candace nodded.

"I'd hardly call her an actress. She's more like a nude model who does occasional line readings."

His rudeness continued to stun her. It just hit

without warning, like sniper fire. "You're one of the meanest assholes I've ever met."

A.J. arched a single brow. "Promise?"

Candace fumed in her seat. Suddenly she lurched forward to address the driver. "Stop the car. I prefer to walk from here."

A.J. laughed. "In those shoes? You couldn't manage a single block before twisting an ankle."

She turned on him angrily. "Then I'll catch a cab."

"In that outfit you might catch a vice cop."

"Screw you!" Candace covered her mouth as fast as the words hit the air. She never talked like that. But this man brought out the absolute worst in people. He was pure evil.

A.J. sat there unfazed, as if she'd just offered up a nice-to-meet-you have-a-nice-day.

They rode in silence for long seconds. Finally, she cleared her throat and calmly asked, "You said something earlier about me not needing to go to all this trouble. What did you mean by that?"

A.J. opened up a beautiful Hermes attache and pulled out a thick packet of paper fastened with three brass butterfly clips. It was the script for *Chocolate on Her Pillow*.

Candace fought hard to show no reaction.

"I suppose you think your Passion Truffles are the ideal product placement for this film."

Candace stared out the window impassively. They were minutes from her building. She really could get out and walk now. Barefoot if she had to.

"Moore Candies happens to believe that our Love Truffle—that would be a new chocolate launching soon from our Private Selections line— is a more suitable choice."

The rage came so fast and furious that it sucked away her breath. The injustice smoked inside her head. She immediately thought of Victoria Mancini and her brief success with Chocolate Obsession until Moore hit the market with Chocolate Maniac and practically drove her out of business. Big, bad Moore Candies. Taking on the little companies and squashing them like bugs. Forget Bill Gates and Microsoft. The Justice Department's time would be better spent looking into these bastards!

She turned to say something, but the words stalled on her lips. There was a satisfied expression on his face. What a snake. He was enjoying this, and the offer for a lift home was just a chance to gloat. A hot, angry tear formed in the corner of her right eye. Decadence couldn't take on Goliath. It was over. "I stand corrected, Mr. Moore. You are *the* meanest asshole I've ever met. Hands down." Defiantly, she wiped the tear from her cheek.

A.J. regarded her curiously. "Do you ever take a moment and count to five, Ms. Rowley?"

She just stared at him. No wonder he was so cruel. Here he sat, short, thinning hair, a nose too large for his face, small eyes, acne scars, a double chin. And then there was Strider. The golden-boy cousin, better looks, a winning personality. In short, all the sex appeal.

"You've made a number of dangerous assumptions during this brief ride," A.J. went on.

The Mercedes slowed to a stop in front of Candace's building. She slipped back on her shoes and said, "Thank God for brevity," as she opened the door and swung one impossible heel onto the pavement.

"I want to help Decadence secure product placement in this film."

Candace froze. She eased her leg back inside, shut the door, and turned to him. "You've got forty-five seconds to tell me why."

A.J. launched in immediately. "My father was the less successful Moore brother. He drank too much, and he gambled constantly. Finally, they gave him a lump sum of cash to get lost. Dad burned through it in less than a year and was dead broke for the first time in his life. That's when he found Jesus. He runs a church in Florida now. Sometimes they run his sermons on Christian cable. I've got an M.B.A. from Harvard, and I know Moore Candies better than anyone in the company, but I'm still just the son of the black sheep brother. Strider doesn't work hard. He never has. Whatever the minimum is to get by—that's all you'll wrangle out of him. But his father and grandfather are losing patience. They've given him an ultimatum, in fact. If he doesn't land this deal with the movie, he's out. And I'm in. *That's* why I'm going to help Decadence get the placement."

Candace studied him for a moment. "That was sixty seconds. You could've skipped the bit about your dad discovering the Lord."

A.J. shrugged.

"You would deliberately sabotage your own company's chances?"

"To push Strider out of the heir-apparent seat? Definitely. Besides, *Chocolate on Her Pillow* is a love story for adults. The real product placement money is in films for children. No huge loss there."

She tried to process this odd turn of events. It seemed too good to be true. And it seemed so sinister. When people said life in the business world could get down and dirty, this is what they meant. Hardball. Cutthroat competition. A blood thirst to move in for the kill.

A.J. opened the attache again. This time he took out a large manila envelope and slid it across the seat. "A marketing proposal for Love Truffles in conjunction with the release of the movie. You should find it worthwhile."

She simply stared, as if it were forbidden reading, like the Judy Blume novel *Wifey* that she used to sneak into the closet and devour by flashlight back in middle school.

A.J. shook his head patronizingly. "A man would never hesitate."

Candace glared at him.

"Don't let a schoolgirl crush stand in the way of a lucrative business opportunity."

"How do I know I can trust you?"

A.J. gestured to the envelope. "The proof is right there."

"Those plans could be fake. I need hard evidence."

He considered this, then gave her a shrewd smile. "I underestimated you, Candace."

"It's Candi."

"So I see. I'll have the car pick you up in the morning. Say nine o'clock. We'll fly by private plane to the Love Truffles factory in Virginia. Will that be proof enough that I'm serious about helping you?"

"Yes, it will." She got out of the car, leaving the envelope on the seat.

"Aren't you forgetting something?"

"When I want to read fiction, A.J., I pick up an

Anita Loos novel. Bring the real marketing plans with you tomorrow."

He laughed, his eyes wide with genuine surprise. "How did you know?"

"Just because a girl dresses a certain way doesn't mean she's easy." And then Candace slammed the door and raced up to her apartment, first stopping at the bottom of the stairwell to take off her shoes.

Once inside, she rummaged through every closet until she found the foot spa, a gift from Aunt Janet she'd been intending to recycle. She opened it up, filled the basin with water, poured in the special salts, and let the bubbles and vibrating power work their magic. Should she order the pizza now or wait for Tatiana to get here? Hmm. The decision felt like *Sophie's Choice*. She stretched for the phone and called Professor Bombshell.

"Hey."

"Where are you?"

"In a stinky cab. I think the last passenger peed in here. How do people live in New York without their own car?"

"Try finding a parking space in the city. You'd grow to love those smelly taxis. How far away are you?"

"Hold on."

Candace heard Tatiana struggling to communicate with the driver.

"This guy doesn't speak a word of English. But he offered me a cigarette. That was nice. I've been riding for at least ten minutes. It shouldn't be much longer."

"Was Strider still at the bar when you left?"

"I didn't notice. The DJ put on Tiko's record, and I got out of there as fast as I could."

"I'm hanging up to order the pizza. See you soon." She called Patsy's Pizza on Third Avenue. They made the best thin-crust brick oven pie in the city. Her place was outside the delivery area, so she had to make a second call to a courier service to fetch the order and bring it to her door. But the extra expense was always worth it.

When Tatiana arrived, Candace filled her in on everything that happened with A.J. The retelling made her feel ashamed, larcenous, and guilty. So much for the glory of victory.

"This cousin is something else," Tatiana said. "Remind me never to marry into this family."

Candace barely cracked a smile.

"At least he's on your side."

"That's a good thing? He's a slimeball."

"You're getting the product placement. That's what you want, isn't it?"

Candace shook her head. "Not this way."

"You can't always write the script, honey. This is business. Even worse, it's Hollywood business. What I'm hearing is that A.J.'s determined to ruin Strider. If that's true, another company is going to have their candy in *Chocolate on Her Pillow*. Why shouldn't it be yours?"

"Because I'm afraid that I might not have the stomach for this."

"You're not selling Girl Scout Cookies anymore," Tatiana said. She got cozy on the couch Candace had bought secondhand, tucking her feet under her legs and stretching sideways. "This is the big leagues—money, media, ego." She made a small fist and placed it over her heart. "You've got to want this more than anything else in the world. I've been in LA for over ten years, and I've wanted to quit at least a million times." She shook her head. "What I've seen that town do to girls who want the same thing I do . . . It makes me sick, but I just keep going and try to focus on my own goals."

Candace sighed. She never imagined that something as sweet as candy could become so bitter. Tatiana was right, though. Deep down she knew that she had to take this opportunity and move on. Playing the righteous one would get her nowhere. But A.J.'s smug face continued to flash in her mind. Damn him. He was the last person on earth she wanted to align herself with.

"Of course, you realize that A.J. will come after you next, so be prepared."

Candace looked at her blankly.

"You're useful to him now, but once Strider gets the boot, you'll be a threat. He didn't mention anything about Moore Candies *not* marketing the Love Truffle, did he?"

She shook her head, getting the picture, feeling sick.

"Well, when this is over, watch out."

Candace buried her face in her hands. There were two choices. Roll over and watch Passion Truffles die. Or play ball with A.J. and pray like hell that the attention of *Chocolate on Her Pillow* strengthened her market position enough to withstand his attack later on. This was like some kind of war game! Where's General Schwarzkopf when you need him?

The pizza arrived. Candace tipped the delivery man five dollars, and they sat down to eat on the

Pier One table she'd had since college. Suddenly her appetite was pathetic. She nibbled on a single slice and barely finished half of it. Tatiana proved worse, moaning about a love scene she had to shoot next week and how the camera adds ten pounds. Any other girl would've pushed this woman into a ravine, but Candace forgave her friend's actress/ model/object-of-desire neuroses and simply lobbed encouragement of this sort across the table: You look great, you're so skinny, Ashley Judd is fat, etc. It managed to impart the desired effect. They shoved the pizza in the fridge and consumed a pint of Godiva white chocolate raspberry ice cream.

After helping Tatiana pack, Candace washed her face, slathered on some expensive night cream essential to a bombshell, and crawled into bed. Tomorrow A.J. would fly her to Moore Candies' Love Truffles factory. That should've occupied her mind until sleep came. But all she could think about was Strider and whether or not he'd left the Cutting Room alone or with Tiko.

Strider played the nightclub hero and escorted a drunk Tiko back to her hotel. Now she lay asleep in her bed while he added up regret on the terrace of her suite at the Mark, a sixteen-story luxury hotel and unofficial hideaway to music-industry types.

The wind whipped and chilled Strider to the bone. He hated the way A.J. possessed this uncanny power to play voodoo with his moods. Everything had been going great tonight. Talking with the blonde, dancing with the blonde.

He couldn't believe she'd turned out to be Candace Rowley, the same girl he'd seen profiled in *Confectioner* magazine, the same girl who'd put him to sleep on whatever show those dingbats Chip and Didi hosted. She'd undergone some kind of transformation. A total Sandy from *Grease*, only without the cigarettes, home perm, and penchant for breaking into song.

From inside the room his cell phone jingled. Shit! Strider scrambled for it in record time, desperate in his attempt *not* to awaken Tiko. He didn't want her waking up and getting amorous. "Strider," he whispered, rushing back to the terrace.

"You disappeared on me." It was Greg Tapper. Strider could barely hear him over the Sugar Ray song and female laughter in the background.

"Sounds like you found your way."

"I sure did. Reeled in too many. I could use some help over here."

"I'm kind of tied up."

"With that knockout blonde I saw you dancing with?"

"Not her."

"Good. Because I'd be jealous. Then I'd do something petty like pull the plug on that deal we're trying to cut." He laughed, as if to say it was all a joke.

But Strider knew he was dead serious. "Relax," he assured him.

"She shot me down. Can you believe that? I'm Greg Fucking Tapper! Who is this woman?"

Strider hesitated. "I don't know, man. Madame X, I guess. Never caught her name."

"It's Candi something. See if you can find out her last name. You know everybody. Shouldn't be hard."

"I'll work on it," Strider promised. But he wasn't going anywhere near that, not when he was so close to wrapping up this product placement for Greg's new movie.

"You should come to the location in Capri," Greg suggested. "Meet the producer and director. That way our party won't have to stop. I keep a yacht there."

"So do I."

"How big is yours? Mine's one hundred forty feet."

Strider shook his head. This guy never stopped reminding you who he was. "It's not the size of the boat that matters. It's how you handle the water."

Greg Tapper cackled. "Whatever helps you sleep, man." And then he hung up.

Strider's mind zeroed in on the issue that was really driving him crazy tonight. The sight of Candace leaving with A.J. He really hoped she would turn down A.J.'s offer to buy Decadence. Strider hated the way his family went after these small companies. They didn't pose any real threat. Hell, there seemed to be enough chocoholics out there in the world for everyone to get a piece of the business. It was not like the Moore ledger needed another million posted to get through a day.

And then the contradiction hit him. He didn't want Candace to sell, but he didn't want her to soar, either. After all, he'd just lied to Greg to keep her as far away from this movie deal as possible. Part of him felt like a heel. The rest of him knew that he'd done it out of self-preservation.

He splashed cold water on his face and quietly slipped out. Tomorrow he left for Capri. Maybe he'd forget about Candace Rowley. Maybe Tiko would forget about him. If somebody dared him to put money on it, though, he'd bet no on both.

Chapter Five

Richmond, Virginia

To travel by private plane was heaven. Larger seats, more leg room, no doofus causing passenger gridlock as he tried to squeeze luggage that was too big into the overhead bin, etc.

As the Cessna Citation X touched down, Candace decided to add wealth beyond measure to her list of husband-material must haves. It joined the Brad Pitt gene pool requirement and other impossibilities that would likely keep her single forever.

She ignored A.J. for most of the flight. The *real* marketing plans for Love Truffles were waiting for her in her seat, so she studied them to avoid conversation. The documents were printed on special paper that couldn't be Xeroxed. This trick of Moore's was legendary. Material of this type was also routinely shredded after presentation.

Getting the inside track triggered conflicting

feelings. On one level it was exhilarating. She probably knew Strider's pitch better than he did. But on another level, what she learned was disheartening. How could she compete with Moore Candies in terms of razzle-dazzle, shelf space, and advertising muscle? They were offering the moon; Decadence could only hold out a moon rock.

In the midst of this psychic meltdown, Candace had to endure A.J.'s spirited attempts to impress her. He blathered on about his vintage car collection, how this Cessna was the world's fastest business aircraft, and other matters of no interest to her.

A white Lincoln Town Car was waiting on the tarmac to take them to the factory. That she would soon see firsthand how Moore Candies were made was all the proof Candace needed. A.J. had every intention of seeing this scheme through. Destroying marketing plans was just one of the company's 007-like tricks to ensure secrecy. They even blindfolded repair technicians when equipment went down, ushering them to the exact problem to be fixed and then out again once the work was done.

The factory looked like an old warehouse you might find anywhere in the country. A modest Moore Candies logo decorated the entrance. A.J. scanned a card and entered a secret code to gain entry.

Once inside, Candace realized that all the stories were true. The factory gleamed. *A surgeon could perform an operation here,* she thought. *It's that sterile.* Workers went about their tasks in starched white uniforms, looking more like scientists than candy makers. She watched a woman swab her area with a cloth.

"We measure work areas for bacteria several times per shift," A.J. explained. "One could argue that our floor is more sanitary than the china in any five-star restaurant."

Candace believed him. Not a single drop of chocolate scandalized the floor. It positively sparkled. Everything did, the steel all slick and polished, the entire facility dust free.

She watched warm, thick, liquid chocolate being piped from one end of the plant to the next. In another area, a latex-gloved production-line worker used calipers to measure the width of Love Truffles as machines squirted in fruit purees. The whole process seemed to take about five minutes. By the end of it a high-tech, self-loading wrapping machine had four candies packaged and ready for retail.

A.J. gave her a superior smile. "It's not too late, you know. The offer still stands. In fact, I have the papers in the car."

This bastard never stopped. He'd lured her here not just to earn her trust but to intimidate her into selling Decadence. She just stared at him.

"The price is now contingent on you winning the deal, of course, so this doesn't change the arrangement we have regarding Strider."

"Why do you hate him so much?"

"You would too if you'd grown up in this family." A.J.'s face darkened a bit, revealing the angry little boy inside. "He just skates along, doing as little as possible, yet everybody regards him with such awe. You should see how other executives stumble over themselves to win his approval. They'd probably sacrifice a limb to go out drinking with Strider. The women are worse. One conversation with him and they're blushing for a week. At least my uncle and grandfather have run out of patience. But they still take *me* for granted. I've busted my ass for years with little to no acknowledgment. Yet Strider can charm a grocery chain CEO into giving us six inches of additional shelf space, and it's cause for a parade. I'm sick of it. That's why I want him out. Maybe with him gone they'll notice what I'm doing for the company."

Candace said nothing. In a way she understood A.J.'s envy. As a child, she'd been jealous of almost everyone. The girl next door whose mother offered I love you's instead of why don't you's. The girl across the street whose father stuck around. The girl down the block who never felt alone because she had a brother and sister to play with.

A.J. reached for a Love Truffle just off the assembly line and presented it to Candace. "Care to sample the product that will ultimately eclipse your Passion Truffle?"

Any empathy she felt for this son of a bitch evaporated. "You're mean, condescending, and arrogant. What makes you believe that with Strider out of the picture, people are going to be falling at your feet? Your problems have nothing to do with him and everything to do with your terrible personality."

"How insightful," A.J. snarled.

Candace tasted the Love Truffle. Hmm. They really should call it the Like Truffle. Granted, it was good. But her Passion Truffle was better. Fantastic by comparison. Suddenly a brilliant thought struck her. She knew how to close this deal! For every bombastic marketing promise Moore Candies made, Decadence could make a subtle one.

She gobbled up the rest of the Love Truffle in one bite. Still no reaction, the taste experience hardly one to savor. The whole issue was analogous to the difference between Chanel eye cream and any cheaper variety you could find at the drugstore. Some would argue that eye cream is eye cream. But it's not. The key divider is the *purity* of ingredients. Just like her Passion Truffle. Where Moore mass-produced the Love Truffle with barnyard chocolate and standard flavorings, Candace lavished her Passion Truffle with tender loving care, using fine imported chocolate and passion fruit and guava nectar of the highest quality.

"You seem to be at a loss for words," A.J. said.

"Not exactly. 'Mediocre' comes to mind."

"No need to bring up your educational background."

Candace glowered. A.J. Moore was the worst kind of Harvard man—he never missed an opportunity to point out that he graduated from there. But she felt equally smart right now. Because she had a plan.

The script for *Chocolate on Her Pillow* was sophisticated, a sweeping love story, something like *The English Patient* only with a happier ending. Nothing got blown up. Nobody got killed. There was no deafening hard-rock soundtrack. This was a movie for adults, and in the area of product placement, it called for a grown-up chocolate. Yes! Strider Moore didn't stand a chance.

"I've seen enough," Candace suddenly announced.

A.J. ushered her out of the factory and back to the car. His body language talked upper hand, but this fool had no idea. The moment he slid into the rear cabin of the Town Car, his cell phone rang. The caller did most of the talking. When A.J. hung up, he turned to Candace. "My cousin is on his way to Capri to join Greg Tapper on the movie set."

Candace experienced a flush of nervous heat. She didn't know if it was the new development or just the mere mention of Strider. "That was him?"

"No, that was a private investigator I've retained to keep an eye on him. As incompetent as my cousin is, he could very well schmooze his way into this deal if we don't act quickly." A.J. ran his index finger across his thin lips, concentrating hard. Then he rudely sized up Candace. "Bikini or one piece?"

"What?"

"Your preference in bathing suits."

"Bikini. Why?"

"I suggest you pack one and get to Capri as soon as possible."

Instantly she thought of Tatiana, who was on her way back to Los Angeles to begin shooting *Lady Cop Undercover IV: Red Light District*, which meant Candace had no choice but to handle this mission alone. A rookie bombshell on exotic foreign soil, mixing it up with Hollywood types and playboy heirs. *Oy*. The butterflies took flight.

"Care to share your thoughts, Ms. Rowley?"

She shot A.J. a polar glare. "Yes. It's pronounced CAH-pree, not CahPREE."

Capri

Strider always stayed at the Capri Palace Hotel and Spa. It was Moroccan inspired and built high on Anacapri, the island's tallest peak at almost two thousand feet. He never worried about reservations because he partied often with the owner, Tonino Cacace.

He saw Sergio right away, a front desk clerk who knew him by name.

"Mr. Moore," Sergio said. "Welcome back. It's been too long, sir."

Strider laughed a little. "Too long? I was just here four weeks ago."

"A few days is too long. You should move to Capri. You're one of us."

Strider grinned. "Maybe I will."

"Your companion has already arrived. She's resting in your room."

Strider tilted his head as if questioning his own hearing. "Companion? I'm here alone."

Sergio looked confused. "But Tiko . . ."

Strider stood there, shocked and frozen. How in the hell did she find out where he was going *and* manage to get here first? Jesus Christ! Even Glenn Close had never been that good.

"Is there a problem, Mr. Moore?"

"Yes, Sergio, there is. But I'll handle it." He paused a moment. "On second thought, give me another room. Under the name . . . Charlie Townsend."

Sergio returned a secret smile. He obviously knew the seventies' TV show about the three beautiful female detectives.

"And please instruct the rest of the staff to keep this information from Tiko . . . my . . . ahem . . . *companion.*"

"Of course, sir."

Somewhere in the Sky

Candace had spent a full day getting ready for the trip to Capri. At times she felt like a psychotically driven efficiency expert, checking status on this, investigating that, always armed with her Palm Pilot. Thank God for Lily. She managed the Decadence shop to perfection and always volunteered to take on additional responsibilities. That helped Candace feel secure enough to steal away.

The flight seemed to go on forever. An urgent restlessness had her on edge. She made several fitful attempts to sleep but stayed wide-awake. She tried reading an Olivia Goldsmith novel but gave up after a few pages. She gave the Passion Truffle marketing proposal a go but abandoned that, too.

And then the airfone beckoned. She knew the call would cost her a fortune. She had no idea what time it was in LA. No matter, she swiped her credit card, followed the international calling instructions, and punched in Tatiana's mobile number.

"Hello?" Her friend sounded bored.

"You'll never guess where I am."

"In bed with Strider Moore?"

"No!"

"Greg Tapper?"

"No!"

Tatiana gasped in quiet horror. "Not the creepy cousin!"

"Stop!" Candace pleaded. "I'm in a plane headed for Naples."

"You're going to Capri. You bitch!"

Candace giggled. "Everything happened so fast."

"That's the life of a bombshell. You have to be

ready for travel at a moment's notice. Only grand-
mothers take two weeks to get ready for a trip.''

Candace gave Tatiana the lowdown on her jaunt
to Virginia and her strategy to land the *Chocolate
on Her Pillow* product placement.

"You are *so* smart," Tatiana said. "The Mercedes
syndrome will never die. Americans are ruled by
status. Take me. I'm a total snob about everything—shoes, handbags, beauty products. And
chocolate, too. You'll never catch me with something by Hershey or Moore. I'm a serious actress.
I don't want chocolate that's thrown in every trick-
or-treat bag from here to Delaware. Give me Godiva! Give me Decadence!" Suddenly her voice went
down an octave. "Honey, give me an extra-strength
Altoid. My costar had something with garlic and
onions for lunch, and we're shooting a love scene."

"Yuck!" Candace couldn't imagine.

"I think he did it on purpose."

"Why?"

"We've been rolling around this bed for hours,
and he's been soft as a Beanie Baby the whole time.
I know with the lights and the camera and the
extras and the choreographed directions it's hardly
the most romantic thing in the world, but with
most actors I usually feel a poke now and then. If
this guy isn't gay, then I'm on the short list for the
Best Actress Oscar this year."

"But why show up with bad breath for an intimate
scene?"

"To torture me. Some gay men hate women. Dr.
G explained it to me once, but I can't remember
the fine points. I think it goes back to their mothers
or something. Or is that the oedipal thing? Who
cares? The point is I've got a soft man at home

and a soft man at work. I should hang up and dial nine-one-one. This girl needs Russell Crowe on the double.''

Candace took a deep breath.

"Honey, are you OK?''

"I'm nervous. What if I can't pull this off?''

"Oh, shut up. This deal is yours. And so is Strider Moore, if you want him.''

Candace stole a glance to the passenger on her right, then inched closer to the window and cupped her hand over the phone to whisper, "Just in case, I bought some really sexy lingerie.''

Tatiana let loose a long, sweet sigh. "Honey, men don't care about lingerie. They just want to get it off you. Jot that down in your little notebook. It's an important point to remember.''

One of the flight attendants made an announcement about returning tray tables to their upright positions and turning off electronic devices.

"I have to go," Candace said. "Any parting words of wisdom?''

"Yes. Capri is famous for unusual romances. Don't be surprised if you leave there with a husband.''

Candace steadied herself. For a moment she thought the plane had suddenly dropped altitude. But then she realized that it was just her stomach.

Chapter Six

Capri

If ever one could conjure up a true definition of breathtaking beauty, then it would be the sight of Capri when traveling by boat on the Bay of Naples. The island rises majestically out of the Mediterranean, the kind of gorgeous accident that only God can make.

Candace tried to just enjoy the view, to simply marvel at the mass of rugged limestone that made up the looming paradise. But loneliness got the best of her. This wasn't something to *ooh* and *ah* over all by yourself.

There should be a special guy here, she thought. For once, she ditched her list of must haves. He didn't need to be established and successful in his career or look like Benicio Del Toro or possess a startling intelligence and lightning-fast sense of humor. Right now, just a decent man would do. Say, for argument's sake, that Prince Charming missed his flight but Prince Doesn't Have a Criminal Record and Bathes Regularly made it. Yeah, she could go for that, as long as this guy held her hand, embraced her, and kissed like a champ.

Candace's nose tingled. She felt like she might cry at any moment. How pathetic was this? Instead of enjoying the incredible scenery, here she stood playing pity party over her single status. In defiance of her own emotions, she decided to draw up a mental ledger of the positive outcomes a girl could garner while living without love.

Hmm ... OK, there was the focus on one's career. Yes! Where would Decadence be today if she'd been distracted by a serious relationship? Probably in bankruptcy. Ooh! And then there was the ability to keep everything under strict control. Falling in love could make a girl do very stupid things. She knew someone who knew someone whose best friend followed her boyfriend's ex-girl-friend for weeks on end just to make sure he wasn't seeing her on the side. Turns out he wasn't. But then he later learned of the stalking, freaked out, and dumped her. So much for earning peace of mind.

Candace felt a little better now, but the specter of loneliness lingered. On impulse, she snatched out the cell phone she wasn't supposed to be car-rying (a bombshell no-no) and called Tatiana.

"Hello?" Once again, her friend sounded bored.

"It's me. Are you still filming that love scene?"

"Honey, these things can go on for three days. They're relighting it now." Tatiana yawned. "I hope this guy I'm working with isn't a biter. I've got a tiny scar near my left areola from a scene I did with Michael Nouri once.''

"The guy from *Flashdance*?"

"Yes. And FYI—he's not gay. That man was into it, if you know what I mean. Anyway, I'm glad you called. I never eat lunch on nude days, and I didn't know what to do with myself over the meal break, so I tracked down Greg Tapper. He couldn't talk long. Or so he says. Prick. I remember him when he was working at a car wash and doing bad James Dean channeling in acting class. Well, I wanted to get the dirt for you on the *real* producer of that movie. Greg's got the executive title, but that's just an ego credit. It doesn't mean shit when it comes down to the actual work. According to him, though, Leigh Crawford is tough as nails and a major budget Nazi. That's code for a very driven, stressed-out man. A bombshell is the perfect girl to relax that kind of guy. Just laugh at everything he says and tell him you think power's an aphrodisiac.''

"I think I can do that," Candace said, her voice more somber than she intended.

Tatiana allowed a few seconds of silence to pass. "Honey, you sound sad."

Candace sighed. "I was just thinking."

"About what?"

"Do you realize that I've never even moved in with anyone?"

"So? That's for college kids. A bombshell insists on marriage. Don't worry. If you do this the right way, you'll probably have five husbands before you turn fifty.''

"I'm not talking about being a bombshell," Candace snapped. "I'm talking about *me.*"

Tatiana gasped. "Oh, honey, I should've seen

this coming. My radar's off because I'm trying to act passionate with a gay man who doesn't brush his teeth often enough."

"Huh?"

"You're in Capri! Paradise! A place for lovers! Of course you're going to get all melancholy about being single. Listen, just go to the piazzetta. It's Capri's main square and most popular hangout. Plenty of men will hit on you there. In five minutes you'll feel like Zsa Zsa Gabor, the early years."

"I miss Jason," Candace said wistfully, naming her most significant ex.

"Oh, please," Tatiana scoffed. "You don't miss him any more than I miss wearing a retainer at night."

"But I do," she argued weakly. "I loved him."

"Honey, he criticized you just like your mother does. That wasn't love. It was only something familiar."

Now she started to laugh and cry a little at the same time. "God, why am I getting so emotional all of a sudden? It's not like I didn't get my period two weeks ago."

"Blame it on Capri, honey. It's the turquoise water, the sun, the villas. You see all that and want Steve McQueen by your side."

"Steve McQueen?"

"I know, he was manic depressive, but still sexy as hell. I would've fed him Zoloft like candy and lived happily ever after."

Candace found herself smiling. "I guess there's a point in there somewhere."

"You know, I just remembered something that Dr. G told me once. We should really be pissed at those feminists."

"What?"

"They ruined a whole generation of women. Subconsciously, we inherited all their rage. It's no wonder we're so fucked up. I married a man who refuses to have sex with me. You've come nowhere near an engagement."

"Thanks for the reminder."

"But it's true. The women's movement is so five minutes ago. I earn more than my husband. You have your own business. Face it, men are useless. Ask Jodie Foster. She's winning Oscars, having babies. She doesn't need a guy. You know, Dr. G always tells me that you have to recognize unhealthy behavior in order to change it."

Candace had never been so lost. This was a hard spiel to follow, even for Tatiana. "I'm almost afraid to ask this, but what exactly are you suggesting?"

"Honey, you need sex. Promise me you'll do it with the first hot guy you see."

"Promise me you won't hold me to that promise. I'll call you later."

Even before the boat reached port, Candace felt herself drawn in by the perfumed air of jasmine and pine. It made her spirit dance. Everywhere she looked there were people who seemed to have all the time in the world, men and women with tans as deep as their bone marrow, wearing loose-fitting cotton separates and shoes without laces or hard soles.

When she reached the Palace, the hotel's extreme splendor and high speed glamour didn't rattle her. Yes, A.J. had suggested that she stay here, if only because it was Strider's home away from home in Capri. No, she couldn't afford the three-day reservation. At these prices she should only be booked for, like, a half hour, forty-five minutes tops. Regardless, she presented her credit card to the charming man whose badge announced him as Sergio.

As he handed over her room key, Candace couldn't help but laugh to herself, Tatiana's voice echoing in her mind: *Promise me you'll do it with the first hot guy you see.* And then she turned around and came face-to-face with Strider Moore.

The man momentarily robbed her of breath. That's how handsome he was. He wore a sea island cotton shirt laundered a brilliant white, sleeves folded up to his elbows, the front unbuttoned down to his midsection, the tail hanging loose over calf-length khakis. His bare feet were dressed in pristine Gucci sneakers. He gave off strong Capri native vibrations—tall, healthy, glowing.

Strider pointed at her. "Hey, you're the girl who's dating my cousin."

Candace gave him a dumb look. "Your cousin's married."

"I know. Shame on you. We probably shouldn't dance and flirt anymore. I don't want to come between you two."

"I'm not dating him."

"Really? Sorry that didn't work out."

"I never was."

"I guess that means we can dance and flirt again."

She looked around. "So where's your stalker?"

"Upstairs in my room, I think." He paused a beat. "It's a long story. Don't worry, though. I'm working on a plan to send her back to the States."

"Maybe you should just stop sleeping with her.

I think that's called giving your stalker too much encouragement."

He leaned in closer and perked up his eyebrows. "If *you* want to start stalking me, I promise to encourage you, too."

She couldn't help but smile.

Strider smiled back. "You didn't have to come all this way to congratulate me. A nice card would've been fine."

"Congratulate you?"

"On getting the product placement deal in *Chocolate on Her Pillow.*"

"Don't alert the media quite yet," Candace said. "I came all this way to take that away from you." She brushed past him, carrying two pieces of small luggage. One good thing about being a bombshell was this: You didn't wear a lot of clothing and therefore had no choice but to pack lightly.

Strider moved to follow. "Let me get this straight. *You're* going to take it away from *me?*"

Candace continued walking. "Yes. And you can bet your trust fund on that, playboy."

He stepped in her path, grinning as if pleased with himself (more than usual, apparently), obviously loving the game, the thrill of the chase. "I've got an edge. Greg Tapper's a good friend of mine."

"That's nice. I've got a stronger edge—he wants to sleep with me."

"That's not exactly an in. Greg wants to sleep with everyone. Back in New York he hit on my cleaning lady. By the way, do you do windows?"

She maneuvered around him. "I've been known to push men out of them on occasion."

His brown eyes got big. "Remind me to move to the first floor."

She smiled, preparing to play her trump card. "Actually, I don't have time for Greg Tapper. I prefer to deal directly with the real decision makers." To build the drama, she just stared at him a moment. "That's why a no-nonsense man like Leigh Crawford is so appealing."

Strider's eyes twinkled. She thought he was about to laugh, but in the end he kept a straight face. "Is that so? Because Leigh's one of the toughest producers in the business."

"That's what I hear. My guess is that he and I share a low tolerance level for bullshit." She gave him a pointed look, then stepped into the elevator and delivered this Parthian parting shot: "Maybe we'll find *other* things in common as well."

Just as the doors closed, Strider blurted out, "More than you know!"

She took the ride up to the tenth floor, feeling a little uncertain now. Strider seemed to know something that she didn't. What had he meant by that last statement? Hmm. Candace dismissed the thought. He was merely trying to keep her off balance. A bluff game. She was sure of it.

After a quick shower and sea-salt scrub, she sat down to apply makeup using the tricks Tatiana had taught her. *Honey, I learned these from the hand of the master—Kevyn Aucoin—so consider yourself a supermodel.* Then she sifted through her clothes and decided on a baby doll cropped T-shirt with the name CANDI boldly made out in glitter and rhinestones. She squeezed into some metallic gold hot pants so daring that a little ass cheek was on display. Even Mariah Carey would blush. But when she slipped on the Dolce & Gabbana sling backs (so towering that she felt a little dizzy, but it passed), Candace knew the look was a winner.

Getting around on heels had become much easier. At least she didn't have to break out into a synchronized dance routine like the girls of Destiny's Child. All she had to do was stay erect. She gave herself a final once-over in the mirror. "OK, bombshell. It's time to detonate."

Capri was just four square miles, so it took no time to pinpoint where the movie people had set up camp. They were filming interior scenes in a famous villa on the Via Tragara. Candace made it there only to learn from a stray crew member that production had wrapped for the day.

"Head for the piazzetta," she was told. "That's where everyone goes to unwind." He turned around to display the *Chocolate on Her Pillow* title emblazoned across the back of his beige crewneck polo shirt. "We're easy to find."

Determined to get her man, Candace headed over there, stopping for a bottled water at Gelateria Scialapopolo just off the piazzetta. That's when she spotted a trio of beige polo guys clustered around a small table. She approached to ask about Leigh Crawford and rolled sevens. They pointed to the back of a pear-shaped figure about one hundred feet away.

She tottered over with no idea in her head of what she might say. But Tatiana had made clear that in an outfit like this, all a bombshell really had to do was just stand there and let things happen naturally.

When Candace got closer, she stopped, suddenly transfixed by Leigh Crawford. It was the strangest thing. The producer stood about five-foot-six, wore crudely styled ultrashort hair ... and had *breasts* ... literally. Candace was struck by the hands, too. Short fingers, square-cut nails, yet something dainty about them.

"Do you have a problem?" It was Leigh Crawford talking, in a voice very much like all the rest, of indeterminate gender.

"Uh ... No ... I was just ..." Candace stammered, stalling for time, trying to make sense of this. Tatiana had definitely said that Leigh was a man. And Strider hadn't corrected her when she referred to Leigh as one.

Yet here she was, directly in front of Leigh, and the doubts were piling up. There was no hiding the fact that the man had breasts. But some men did, Candace reasoned. Unfortunate but true. She once heard about a guy in Connecticut who was a C cup after a major weight loss.

"You were just what?" Leigh demanded.

"I was just hoping to meet the legendary Leigh Crawford," Candace gushed, then giggled, tilting forward a little to give the producer the full benefit of her cleavage.

Leigh's annoyed expression turned suspicious. "All the speaking parts are taken. If you're interested in extra work, show up tomorrow morning at five."

"Oh, I'm not an actress."

"Hooker, huh? I was trying to give you the benefit of the doubt."

"I'm not a hooker either!" Candace practically jumped up and down to drive the point home.

Leigh gave her a look and started to walk away. "Hey, that's between you and your wardrobe stylist."

The producer proceeded to lope down the cobbled street with an ambiguous gait that offered no clue to the million-dollar question. Candace felt as if she'd just stepped inside the "It's Pat!" skit from *Saturday Night Live*. Still game—and more curious than ever—she went tippy-tip after Leigh. "Wait!"

The producer stopped, spun, and sighed. "I'm not into lipstick lesbians. I prefer earthy women."

Candace got it now. Suddenly an Indigo Girls song started playing in her head. How had Tatiana missed this point? Of course, Strider had known all along. That sneaky bastard.

"I just wanted to introduce myself," Candace said, hoping to turn things around. "I'm not into lipstick lesbians, either. Well, any lesbians, if you must know. But I support the lifestyle. I saw k.d. lang in concert once. And I even practiced kissing with a girl at summer camp."

Leigh's eyes lit up with amusement. "Is that so?"

Candace nodded.

Leigh held up her right hand, thumb and index finger about an inch apart. "You're this close to being family."

"I'm Candi Rowley."

Leigh threw an obvious look to the glitter and rhinestones spelling that first name out across Candace's chest. "Apparently."

She reached into her bag and presented Leigh with a Passion Truffle.

"I've read the script for *Chocolate on Her Pillow*. This is the candy that Sam should leave on Grace's pillow."

Leigh studied her for a moment. "That script is top secret. How did you get your hands on it?"

"E-bay," Candace said. "I was the high bidder with thirty dollars."

Leigh made a face. "I knew I recognized your name. I should've set a higher reserve price."

"You're TomBoy35?"

Leigh returned a guilty nod. "Don't rat me out. I swiped one of Greg Tapper's undershirts, and it went for two hundred bucks."

"Yuck. Wasn't it dirty?"

"Of course. A famous person's sweat and grime is like gold. If I could just get his underwear. Or a jockstrap. That's where the real money is." Then Leigh unwrapped the Passion Truffle and stuffed it into her mouth in one greedy gulp. "The nougat tastes weird."

Candace was horrified. She would've rathered Leigh Crawford just spit out the candy and call it elephant dung than call it "nougat." *Nougat.* As if! Decadence wasn't jockeying for space in the Whitman's sampler. Candace made her candy with a special Valrhona chocolate imported from France. She used only the purest guava and passion fruit nectars, and most noteworthy, she didn't add a single granule of sugar. Any chocolate that required extra sweetening to please the palate was inferior. Of course, all that would be lost on this woman (what a relief to finally know!) who didn't know a truffle from a Snow Cap. But Candace had to give it a go.

Leigh made a terrible sucking noise with her teeth. "Not bad. Do you have a few more of those?"

Candace offered her a handful. "I was hoping to talk with you about product placement. I have some thoughts that might—"

"Save your breath, cutie pie," Leigh cut in. "I've

got a lead actress who thinks *walking* qualifies as a stunt. She wants a double to do it, so she can stay in her villa zoned out on pills. I just had to fire an actor in one of the supporting roles. He's an Oscar winner, yeah, but he's also a drunk and can't remember his lines. Oh, and Greg Tapper took off on his yacht with some bimbo a few hours ago, so we lost half a day's shooting. And he calls himself an executive producer. Now, these are the issues I'm currently facing. Do you really think I have time to worry about what kind of candy we use in the movie?"

"But—"

Leigh held up a hand and started to leave. "Talk to Greg. I've left that monumental decision in his hands. But thanks for the chocolate."

Candace watched her walk away. "My pleasure," she murmured softly, but Leigh was out of earshot. Oh, God, what now? Swim the Mediterranean until she happened upon Greg's yacht?

"Well, you were right about one thing. You both have a low tolerance level for bullshit."

Candace turned to see Strider Moore sipping red wine nearby. In the center of his quaint table was an open bottle of expensive vintage. An empty glass sat beside it.

He gestured to the chair opposite him. "Join me."

She didn't move an inch. "What about my low tolerance level?"

"I'll check my bullshit at the door. Promise."

Candace smiled. She started toward him, feeling lucky. Those were the exact words that every single woman wanted to hear from a guy.

Chapter Seven

Strider poured as Candace sat down. "That went well. For a minute there I thought she was going to ask you back to her villa."

"Why didn't you tell me?"

"And miss the show?"

She took a generous sip and embraced the sun beaming down on her. "I deserve that, I guess. Maybe I was a little cocky back at the hotel."

Strider raised his eyebrows. "Maybe? A little? You had bigger *cajones* than a gladiator. In fact, I heard them clang when you walked."

"I was that bad?"

He winked and drank some more wine. "Not really. I like to torment."

"So . . . Greg Tapper is the last word on the product placement."

"Right you are." He refilled his glass. "Speaking of Greg, I don't know whether I should be celebrating or drowning my sorrows."

"What do you mean?"

"He left on his yacht."

"I know. Leigh's in an uproar because he didn't finish today's scenes."

"Tiko is with him."

This pleased Candace to no end. "Well, I thought you wanted her to go away."

"I did." He raised his wine in salute. "That's the part I'm celebrating. But I didn't want Greg to go away. I need him here to make a decision."

Candace shrugged. "He has to be back on the set tomorrow."

"Greg's a name above the title star, and he never lets anyone forget that. The truth is, he doesn't *have* to do anything. Besides, Tiko has a way of . . . *distracting* men. I wouldn't be surprised if they stayed gone for a few days."

"A few days?" It came out as a shriek.

Strider gave her a worried look. "Calm down. Tiko's *my* stalker. If I'm handling the absence OK . . ."

"It's not that. I can't afford to stay here much longer."

"Corporate espionage on a budget, huh? I take it you don't have any cool gadgets."

A reluctant smile pushed past Candace's lips. "Don't make fun."

"You know, I've been known to yell out anything during sex—Jesus, Buddha, first and last names of the Backstreet Boys, the secret ingredient of our Love Truffle. There's no telling. Sleeping with me won't cost you anything, but who knows, you might get lucky and learn something that'll help."

She gave him a warning look. "You promised to check your bullshit at the door."

Strider held up both hands, as if coming clean. "Everything I said is true."

She decided to test him. "OK, who's the youngest Backstreet Boy?"

He didn't pause so much as a beat. "Nick Carter."

"I can only assume you know what you're talking about because I don't know the answer."

"I'm a man who knows his teen pop."

Now came Candace's turn to give the worried look.

"I keep MTV on as background noise," Strider explained.

She laughed a little.

"But I must admit . . . I really do love 'I Want It That Way.'"

"I can't stand the Backstreet Boys, so the idea of you yelling out their names during—"

"Not so fast," Strider cut in. "That's not my whole act. Sometimes I name the Beatles, the Rolling Stones, even the Pointer Sisters once."

"That's a great trick for VH1's *Rock and Roll Jeopardy,* but it doesn't say much for your skills as a lover."

He put the wineglass to his lips, then stopped, placed it back down, and smiled. "I've got references. Testimonials from every partner except one. That would be a girl I met in Cancun on a college spring break trip. I was drunk and passed out on top of her during the act. Not my finest six and a half minutes."

Candace sat there, charmed by him, attracted to him . . . but ultimately cautious of him. She knew about Strider Moore's stripe of worm. A woman would warn you about this kind of man in the bathroom of a hot nightclub. But that same woman would end up going home with him. He was the guy who kept mental lists of how many girls he'd been with and all the weird places he'd had sex with them, the guy who made you laugh, the guy who made you come more than once. But the most important thing to remember was this: He was the guy who wouldn't call you again.

A bombshell like Tatiana could handle the Striders of the world while running a 10K and moderating a world peace summit—at the same time. But Candace, with only the emergency course, a few vampy encounters at the Cutting Room, and a disastrous interlude with a lesbian behind her, considered herself bombshell *lite*. Tangling with a man like Strider could only mean a world of hurt.

"Penny for your thoughts," Strider said.

She came back from her reverie. "It'll cost you much more than that."

He glanced down, reached for her foot, and slipped off her obscenely expensive sling back in one single, fluid movement. "Didn't your mother teach you about sensible shoes?"

"Don't get me started on my mother."

"Ah, parent issues," Strider said, grinning knowingly as he proceeded to massage her inner leg, working from her ankle to just beyond her calf. He used his thumbs first, then his palms, making firm circles, leaving no doubt that he knew how to handle a woman's body.

It felt too damn good to protest. Everything started to intoxicate her at once—the buzz of the wine, the proximity to this sexy beast, the arousal of the energy line that began at her big toe and steadily traveled up her leg to her groin. *Ooh.* She felt something where it counted. For a moment she closed her eyes.

"I have a boat here, too," Strider announced softly. "It's not as big as Greg's, but it will get us to the nearby island of Ischia. What do you say?"

Candace slipped off her shoe and kicked up her other leg. "I say you're not done yet."

He laughed and took her ankle in a firm yet sensual grip. "My real specialty's the lower back. It comes free with the boat trip. Pretty good deal."

The sensations started all over again. She thought she might moan out loud but fought hard against it. With a deep breath through her nose, she steadied herself. *Promise me you'll do it with the first hot guy you see.* Tatiana's words played inside her head.

"There is one condition, though," Strider said. "We have to call a truce before we board the *Candy Girl.*"

She smiled at the name of the boat. "That's cute."

"It was a college graduation present from my parents."

"How nice. I got a toaster oven."

He grinned. "Don't hate me because I'm rich. That's my great grandfather's fault."

It struck Candace how remarkably different the two cousins were. She couldn't detect that Strider was capable of anything but kindness. A bit caddish, yes, but harmlessly so. She imagined that all of his ex-girlfriends remembered him fondly. He probably never forgot their birthdays and always sent them a Christmas card.

"I really should get back to the hotel," Candace

heard herself say, but the words hit the Capri air with no conviction.

"Just a quick jaunt," Strider pressed. "There're still a few hours of sun left. You'll love it. Trust me." Something in his eyes smacked of a child imploring an indifferent friend to come out and play.

Candace gave in. And she imagined that it wouldn't be the first time, either.

He emptied the bottle of wine into her glass. Just an inch or so remained. "Drink up, mate." Strider's gaze zeroed in on the glitter and rhinestones spelling out her new name. "Where did this Candi business come from?"

She touched the heart symbol that dotted the i just above her breast. "A friend of mine suggested it."

"You need a new friend."

She turned up her glass and slipped her shoes back on.

"Candace is a beautiful name."

She rose quickly. Compliments unsettled her. She'd never learned how to accept them gracefully. "That's nice of you to say."

"It's not just nice. It's the truth. You're too smart to walk around with a name like Candi. By the way, that's one of the reasons I'm being so persistent here. It's refreshing to meet a girl with a sharp mind."

"Lots of us are out there. We're just not models or pop stars."

He nodded guiltily. "I know. The gossip columns have given me a certain reputation, and smart girls actually read the columns, so they never give me the time of day. Models and pop stars just scan them for their photographs or their names in bold type. If you take the time to think about it, I'm really a victim."

"Maybe Tiko will do a benefit concert for the relief fund."

He took her arm, and they started to walk. "You're not going to give me a break, are you?"

"The odds are slim."

Strider's hand moved down to thread his fingers through hers.

Candace let it happen, heart banging inside her chest, stomach feeling like a vacuum, but once the initial surprise subsided, it seemed the most natural and comforting thing in the world.

They made it down to the Marina Grande, Capri's main harbor, where they navigated through the maze of boats big and small until they reached the *Candy Girl*, an all-white, sleek vessel with a flat sundeck that stretched for at least eight feet.

Strider started the engine. It gunned to life on the first try. Candace slipped off her shoes and held fast to the guardrails as he negotiated the busy harbor, then revved it once the *Candy Girl* had an opening. The water was smooth, a spectacular infinite blue. Suddenly the other ships in the harbor, the villas, all the details of Capri, began falling like ninepins. The island's rugged twin peaks were more pronounced now. Beneath the soles of her feet she could feel the throb of the motor.

Suddenly she forgot the whole bombshell bit and just started being herself. Breathlessly, she pointed out the icicle-shaped mineral deposits in the distance, the ones hanging from the roofs of caves. They chugged past the Blue Grotto, the famous cavernous wonder that was every serious diver's dream. She marveled at the other grottoes in the distance. It was right there that the Sirens had tempted the mythological hero Odysseus, tempting him with their sweet but treacherous song.

Candace told him about Book Twelve of Homer's *The Odyssey,* getting caught up in the story, prattling on with the whole tale. About Odysseus cutting up a wheel of wax with his sword, kneading it under the sun until it became soft, and stuffing it into the ears of all his men. How only that way could they avoid the sinister seduction. She made clear that the Sirens enchanted all men, that those who got too close met a quick death. And then she went on about how his men sailed past, oblivious to the murderous music as only Odysseus listened, having first ordered his crew to tie him up to the mast of the ship. With great enthusiasm, she relayed her favorite part of this tale, how the song tempted the hero, how he forgot his will and wanted to row toward the Sirens. But his men would not hear of it, so they tightened the ropes that bound him and drifted past the island.

Suddenly Candace stopped and covered her mouth. Oh, God. This was just like that dreadful *Coffee in Manhattan* segment with Chip and Didi. This was just like any other time that she got carried away with a favorite subject. She looked at him sheepishly.

He stared back in amusement.

"I'm sorry. You probably want to push me overboard."

"No, I enjoyed your story. In prep school I read the Cliff Notes and missed all that rich detail."

Candace studied him for a moment, gauging his

sincerity. He seemed earnest enough. She shrugged. "I love mythology."

"I can tell that you love a lot of things. You have a sense of joy about you. That's rare. It's refreshing, too."

"What do you love?"

He took off his shirt, started for the platform, and sat down. "I love the sun this time of day." His chest was flawless—smooth, sculpted, and golden, all the way down to the chiseled abs that looked as firm as a sheet of steel. "You know, it's not uncommon for women in Capri to sunbathe topless. You should try it."

Candace knew that Strider expected her to either laugh it off as a joke or to get flustered and flat-out refuse. That's why she decided to do something wild. On impulse, she peeled off her shirt and tossed it onto the deck.

His jaw dropped, the surprise on his face total.

She joined him and tilted her head back to bask in the bronzing heat of the hottest burning star. It seemed to feed a hungry part of her. In a strange way she felt a sudden awakening. Everything shined—the quiet in the aftermath of the killed engine, the turquoise water of the Mediterranean, the sexual energy between them. The sum of it all made her feel emboldened. "Your turn."

Strider began to unfasten his pants.

She giggled and pulled his hand away from the zipper. "No! I mean your turn to tell a story."

"From *The Odyssey?*"

"It doesn't have to be."

"There's actually a long-lost tale that Homer left out. You see, there was a goddess whose incredible breasts could make slaves of men. All she had to do was take off her shirt, and men would sign over their fortunes and agree to do anything she asked.''

"This goddess must have traveled with a good lawyer.''

"Oh, the best. He was the Marvin Mitchelson of his day.''

Candace shielded her eyes from the glare to ask, "Are you *ever* serious?''

"Why ruin a good time?''

"Or make it meaningful?''

His gaze lingered on her breasts. "You have no idea how much this means to me.''

"Models and pop stars might not notice when a man is glib twenty-four hours a day, but I do. Every time the conversation starts to get real, you make a joke.''

"At least they're good jokes.''

Candace started to see him in a different light. What if she scratched the surface and nothing was there? Men like that were legendary, especially in New York. They were rich and successful and dated a series of pretty models, actresses, and glamour job holders. This went on for years and years. Obviously, growing up was hard to do. Candace *knew* men like this. One owned the advertising firm that did creative for Decadence. Every conversation with him was the same. Maybe four strokes back and forth and then nothing left to say.

Strider seemed to wince under her silent scrutiny. "Do you really want serious, Candace? Because serious is this: If I don't make this product placement happen, I'm out of the family business.'' He leaned back, making a pillow for his head with both hands, and let go of a heavy sigh. "Maybe that's not such a bad thing, though. Even if I'm lucky enough to pull this deal off, there's going to be another do-or-die test down the line. My cousin will make sure of it. He wants me gone.''

Candace watched as Strider's face took on an inscrutable sadness. It was the polar opposite of the malignant envy that A.J. had revealed in Virginia. "Moore Candies is a huge company with interests all over the world. Why can't the two of you coexist?''

Strider looked genuinely perplexed. "I don't know. I've tried to stay out of his way, but it's not enough. It really didn't hit me how much A.J. hates me until I was thirteen. Before that, we were inseparable." He grinned at the memory. "Thick as thieves. And whenever we got into a scrape, I took the fall. A.J.'s mom was a mess, and his dad had been branded the family loser. He seemed to live for the approval of my father, and I didn't care much whether I had it or not, so I didn't mind playing the screwup. But then we were both at Brambletye. That's an English boarding school about thirty miles outside of London. A.J. pulled a prank that went way too far. He vandalized the dressing room of the headmaster's wife and threw all her undergarments into the pool. They found a button on the floor with the Moore family crest on it, so they knew it was one of us. A.J. begged me to cover for him. He was a year younger, and I was graduating in a few months, so . . .''

Candace couldn't believe where the story was going. "You didn't.''

"I did. At the time I had no idea about the vandalism. I just thought it was a few bras and girdles in the pool. After I fessed up, I found out how serious the charges were. My father came over, they expelled me, and I lost my slot at Eton. That's the senior school Prince William attended. When we came out of the headmaster's office, my father got in my face and said, 'I'm ashamed to call you my son. You disgust me.' A.J. was in the hall. I saw him crack a smile. That's when I knew. He hated me. And I actually had thought of him like a brother."

"How could you accept so much punishment for something you didn't do?"

Strider sighed again. Deeper this time. The kind of sigh that revealed years of baggage being lugged around. "I don't know. I've asked myself that question a million times. Part of me was in shock. Another part of me wanted to believe that as the shit got deeper and deeper, A.J. would stand up and do the right thing. No one really expected much from me after that. It kind of became a self-fulfilling prophecy. I didn't expect much from myself either. You know what's funny? I've been partying my ass off for twenty years, and it's been a blast. Hedonism all the way. But I'm still pissed about what happened when I was thirteen." He turned away from her, faced the sun, and blinked back a tear.

"My friend Tatiana's been in therapy for years," Candace said softly. "Her doctor once told her that we spend more years getting over our childhood than we do getting through it."

"I've never told this to anyone before. Must be the boobs."

She laughed. "Oh, God, he's *back*."

"I do have a reputation to uphold." He rolled over and stopped mere centimeters from her mouth, his hand sweeping over to cradle her waist.

Candace took in a sharp breath.

"What's the going rate for psychotherapists these days?"

"I'm not sure. Maybe one hundred fifty dollars an hour."

"Then I better kiss you. That'll mean conflict of interest. You won't be able to send me a bill."

Candace's lips trembled on the brink of his. "You can afford it."

"I might be unemployed soon." Strider's face was so close. His appeal haunted her. It was the stuff of ancient evenings. He hovered there for the longest time, looking into her eyes, *really* looking into them.

She wondered if he could see the pools of guilt there, as she lay under him, heart hammering, telling herself a lie she didn't believe, that there was nothing to be ashamed of, that everything about this was honest. Just then an internal panic began to set in.

That's when Strider jumped off the cliff of intimacy and claimed her mouth without warning. Her lips were dry from the sun. He used his tongue to coat them with moisture and thundered on.

Candace could feel the blood speeding through her. It pulsed in her veins and pounded in her heart as the old world closed and a new world opened. A soft moan escaped her.

Strider responded, drawing her closer with his tanned and muscled arms, pushing his tongue into her mouth in a feverish attack of longing. One hand skated across her breasts, which were slick with dampness brought on from the heat.

Candace tried to push him away, her mind and body at war, but when he pressed his body against her, advertising how eager he was, how much he desired her, the mind lost ground and all thought went away. She arched her neck. His mouth eased down, to her nape, over her breasts, onto the throbbing nipples, feasting there, distending them to the point of overflowing lust.

Bit by bit, her body uncoiled. It had been too long, but even before, it had never been like this. Every part of her felt like a wet fire, slippery but scorching hot. The cool slab of the platform lay under her. The gorgeous chocolate prince lay on top of her. The need for more sent her reeling with astonishment. In one sweet second of flicking change, she became an animal, a shuddering creature desperate to satisfy the craving that mattered more than her next breath.

And so with trembling fingers, she reached for his zipper. . . .

Chapter Eight

Candace wanted to call Tatiana and tell her that she'd just had sex with a man who made her come three times. But she could barely move, so she just lay there, wiping tears of sweat from her eyes.

Strider kissed his index finger, then touched her nose. "You're insatiable."

You would be too if Clinton had been in office the last time you got your freak on. That's what went through her mind. But she just smiled and released a cute sigh that spelled out SATISFACTION in all caps.

Suddenly something occurred to her. "Who is George Lazenby?" When he climaxed, Strider had yelled out the names of all the actors who played James Bond.

He grinned, obviously pleased with himself, looking like a grade-schooler who'd just won a statewide spelling bee. "Sean Connery, Roger Moore, Timothy Dalton, Pierce Brosnan—those are the easy ones to remember. It takes a true 007 fan to know

George Lazenby, *On Her Majesty's Secret Service*, 1969, featuring Diana Rigg as a Spanish contessa. Thank you. I'll be here all week.''

She sighed again. "Give it a rest, Shecky."

Strider rose on one elbow. "Shecky?"

"Aren't there any number of bad comics in Las Vegas named Shecky?"

"I'm not sure, but I think I should be offended."

Candace crinkled her eyes. "Go with your instincts."

He glanced down at his crotch. "Give me about a half hour. I know how to entertain you."

She laughed—amused, delighted. This was, without a sliver of doubt, the most positive sexual experience that Candace had ever known. Almost every time before had left her wondering. Was she pleasing him? Why couldn't he please her? Even Jason, the man she thought she might marry, had been a bore in the bedroom.

With Strider, sex was so much more than a clumsy interaction between two naked people. It was a carnal roller-coaster ride—fun, thrilling, full of surprising dips, turns, and upside-down moves that triggered occasional screams. There was something more, though . . . something . . . spiritual.

His hand skated onto her stomach and started drawing imaginary circles around her belly button. "Did you see *Grease*?"

"Of course. Who hasn't?"

"Some people hate musicals."

"But everybody loves *Grease*."She started to hum "You're the One That I Want."

"My cousin walked out after the 'Summer Nights' number."

"A.J.?"

Strider nodded.

"He's not of this earth," Candace said.

"You remind me of that movie."

She lifted her head to look him directly in the eyes. "How?"

"In the movie there's the goody-two-shoes Sandy and the tight-leather-pants Sandy."

Candace nodded.

"That's how you are. There's the good Candace who was profiled in *Confectioner* and appeared on *Coffee in Manhattan,* and then there's the bad girl Candace who showed up at the Cutting Room and here in Capri."

"And which one got your attention?"

"Both, actually. When I saw you on TV, I liked your story about Montezuma's big appetite for chocolate, but I must confess that I fell asleep when you started in about Christopher Columbus."

She covered her face and giggled nervously. "That was *so* embarrassing. They'll never have me on again."

"I thought you were cute. Really. Embarrassing was Didi's version of 'My Heart Will Go On.' "

"You mean 'The Greatest Love of All,' " Candace corrected.

"Oh, that's right. I must be thinking of another show because I know I've heard her butcher that song, too. Back to my point, though. Why the transformation?"

"Good girl Candace didn't stand a chance with the Hollywood brigade."

"But Greg Tapper is MIA with Tiko, and you struck out with Leigh Crawford."

Candace thought about it. He definitely had her there. "Well, *you* responded to the bad girl."

"Initially . . . Yes, that's true. But you really hooked me with your mind, especially that story from *The Odyssey*. That's when you let your guard down and were so real. I think I even fell in love a little bit. You don't know anything from *The Iliad*, do you?"

Candace smiled at the joke, but it didn't register. Her mind was stuck on one phrase: *I think I even fell in love a little bit.* She felt her heart lurch. Wow. What would Tatiana say about this? Probably something along the lines of, "Honey, men like Strider fall in love all the time. It's like a viral love. Usually it lasts twenty-four hours. Vegas is the best place for these illnesses because it's so easy to get married there."

Strider picked up on her inner turmoil. "Are you freaking out because I actually know about *The Iliad*?"

"Not exactly," she managed, "although that is a bit of a shock."

"See? I'm full of surprises." He stretched out flat and pulled her toward him, resting her head on his chest and stroking her hair. "If I don't get the product placement, will you hire me? I know a thing or two about chocolate."

The sun blazed—a bright orange ball bathing them in steam heat. Candace wanted the moment to stretch on forever. There was something so familiar about this, as if she were hanging out with a buddy. It felt meant to be. That's why an unstoppable urge to come clean rained down on her. "I have to tell you something."

"Oh, don't tell me you faked it. Those three orgasms are some of my best work."

"No." She laughed. "I didn't fake it." Her hand

moved down his navel, stopping just at the point where his hairs gathered thickness. "I don't want to fake anything with you."

"That's good. We can be two people who keep the Truth Channel on all the time. I'll start. First sexual fantasy. Mine was Angie Dickinson. I loved *Police Woman*. I wanted her to handcuff me. Pretty kinky for an eight-year-old. What about you?"

"Captain Kirk from *Star Trek*. I wanted to be one of the alien women that he kissed."

He pulled her closer. "That's just weird enough. *We* are made for each other."

"I have to share another truth. An ugly one." She pressed her fingers to his lips. "Don't make a joke. Please. Let me get this out. A.J. showed me the marketing plans for the Love Truffle. He also took me to the factory in Virginia and told me that you were here in Capri and where you were staying."

Strider's body tensed. "Asshole. He told Tiko I was coming here, too."

"He's hired a private investigator to keep tabs on you."

Strider's face darkened, his temples pulsed, and he shook his head incredulously.

"I didn't ask A.J. to do any of this," Candace went on. "He just offered it on the spot. At the time, I wanted this deal so bad that I couldn't resist. But now it doesn't mean anything, not if getting it means that you'll be hurt."

Strider just stared at her.

Candace had no idea how he might react. But a tremor of fear ran through her, a fear that whatever they were to each other could be over as soon as it had begun. "Go find Greg. Close the deal. I'll go back to New York."

"You deserve it more than I do. What have I done besides party with a movie star? You've actually created something."

"I don't want it this way," Candace argued.

"Neither do I. If A.J.'s willing to go through all this to get me out, then fine. I'll just leave. Maybe it's time that I struck out on my own anyway."

"Don't let him make that decision for you. That's giving him too much power." She watched him, still beautiful even in all his misery, weighing his options, considering his future, the guy with all the one-liners a million miles away. There was a depth to Strider, a capability for thought and feeling that he rarely accessed. It was at this realization that she knew, from the bottom of her uncertain heart, she knew.

Candace brushed a tendril of hair from his eyes. "I think we're both in a similar place right now. I understand the ambivalence and anger you feel toward your father. I've got the same thing with my mother. It's like we both carry around this feeling in ourselves . . . this sense that we're not good enough or that whatever we do doesn't quite measure up. We've both got fears and doubts and mistrust. Maybe we can heal each other."

Strider said nothing. He just kissed her fiercely, his lips bruising, his tongue aggressive, his hands all over. When he rolled on top of her, the intensity of his need was overwhelming. He locked his eyes onto hers and entered her quickly, making love with a passion so naked, so alternately vulnerable and ferocious, that her own pleasure seemed irrelevant. And at the moment of climax, he didn't shout out anything silly. Instead he kissed her deeply and breathed a soft moan of pleasure into her mouth. Lying there, with him still inside her, she felt complete and at peace. It was poetry.

"Pull up the anchor," Candace whispered. "Let's float away."

They were just off the coast of Ischia.

Strider sighed his longing to do exactly that. "This is a famous spot, you know. Elizabeth Taylor and Richard Burton were photographed here in a compromising position."

Candace giggled. "I'd say we look pretty compromised, too. I wonder if someone will take our picture."

Someone did take their picture. It had been wired to New York, downloaded in a nanosecond, and then splashed across the gossip columns for society gawkers to gulp down with their morning latte. Sergio delivered the faxed pages in a discreet brown envelope.

"Oh, shit." There were no better words that came to mind as Strider read the cover letter from his father. It was an angry missive that talked of irresponsibility and disappointment, ending with the news that both father and grandfather were on their way to Capri from one of the overseas plants. He was to meet them in the library of *The Chocolate Bar*, the Moore family yacht, a vessel that made the *Candy Girl* look like a toy boat for the bathtub.

Strider zeroed in on the media damage.

CHOCOLATE RIVALS MAKE LOVE, NOT WAR

Filthy rich candy hunk **Strider Moore** is playing musical beds in Capri, that Mediterranean paradise known for naughty goings-on. Moore played sensual music with international chanteuse **Tiko,** then took up with **Candace Rowley,** the Passion Truffle queen who made even Chip and Didi seem interesting during a recent (snore, snore) appearance on *Coffee in Manhattan*. But don't cry for Tiko, Japan. She sailed away with **Greg Tapper** on his yacht. In case readers are wondering, we've seen both boats, and Greg's is definitely bigger than Strider's. Wink.

The accompanying photo was carefully cropped for publication. Strider's back blocked Candace's breasts, and they were locked in a passionate kiss. He worried if racier shots would turn up elsewhere. Maybe some cheap magazine or a tacky Internet site. It infuriated him how nothing was sacred in the information age. It angered him more that this column had ridiculed Candace. He was tempted to call up Page Six's Richard Johnson and bitch him out, then decided that such a move would only aggravate matters. Tomorrow another scandal would hit, and everyone would forget about this. Everyone but his family, of course.

He tried calling Candace's room, wanting to warn her of the ambush. She'd gone there to pack, but the phone just rang and rang, finally going to voice mail. Strider dressed quickly and left his suite to go find her.

* * *

"Nasty girl!" Tatiana squealed. "Your love scene looks much hotter than the one I'm *still* filming."

Candace was genuinely perplexed. Her cellular had rung, she'd picked up on the second ring, and Tatiana had started in without preamble. "What are you talking about?"

"I'm talking about you and Strider Moore going at it like teenagers after the prom in this morning's Page Six. It looks like you're on a boat or something."

Candace froze in the middle of the piazzetta. She dropped the bag that contained the jewelry she'd just purchased from the little shop that had framed pictures of Aristotle and Jackie Onassis everywhere. She almost dropped the phone. She came close to throwing up.

"Please tell. These days Kerr falls asleep as soon as we get into bed. I haven't had real sex in weeks. Let me live vicariously."

"Tatiana, I'm in shock. I haven't seen this."

"Don't be upset. You look great, and there's a single, straight, and gorgeous guy with a trust fund all over you. Any woman who criticizes is simply jealous that it's not *her* in the picture."

Candace collected her bearings and bent down to pick up her jewelry. "What does it say?"

"Oh, something about you being boring on Chip and Didi's show, but that's old news. Besides, people will just read the headline, look at the picture, and move on to their horoscope."

Candace braced herself. "So what *is* the headline?"

"Chocolate Rivals Make Love, Not War."

Candace groaned. It was worse than she'd imagined.

"Greg Tapper must be furious," Tatiana continued with thinly veiled delight. "There's mention of him hooking up with Tiko but no photo, so Strider gets all the stud points. OK, tell me, on a scale of one to ten . . ."

"Tatiana, I need you to stop for a second and think about something. I don't live in Hollywood. I'm not an actress. Having my half-naked body splattered across a tabloid page is not good for my image profile. It's just *humiliating*."

"I disagree on the last point," Tatiana argued. "A picture of you getting busy with the creepy cousin—*that* would be humiliating. But honey, Strider Moore is *hot*. He could make a girl push Brad Pitt out of the way. FYI, it looks like you're all the way naked, not half naked."

Sitting at a cafe table up ahead, a familiar figure captured Candace's attention. He was deep in conversation with another man, unrecognizable from this distance, but tugging at her memory just the same. She moved closer, falling into step with a small crowd to escape notice. *No, it couldn't be.*

It was A.J. Moore! Damn him. And why was he huddled with Eric O'Donnell, one of the top marketing executives at Hershey?

"Honey, are you still there?" Tatiana said.

"Yes, but I have to go."

"Don't you dare hang up this phone until you—"

"Oh, all right," Candace hissed. "It was out of this world. I came three times."

Tatiana gasped.

"I'll call you later."

"Wait! Does he have a brother?"

"No."

"How old is his father? Never mind. It doesn't matter. There's always Viagra!"

Candace hung up, shoved the cell into her purse, adjusted the brim of her Burberry hat, moved stealthily ahead of A.J. and Eric, and crisscrossed to a vacant table within earshot.

And then she listened, fury rising with every syllable she could make out.

Sergio knew nothing of Candace's whereabouts. Strider considered heading for the piazzetta, then checked his watch and decided against it. The meeting from hell was less than an hour away.

"Is there any way I can help, sir?" Sergio inquired.

"Yeah. Get me a pen and paper."

Dutifully, Sergio produced a Mont Blanc and fine stationary embossed with the Palace logo.

Strider scribbled down a note to Candace and implored Sergio to get it to her as soon as possible. Leaving the hotel, he ran into Greg Tapper and Tiko. "Back so soon? You didn't give us a chance to put your faces on a milk carton."

Tiko glared.

Greg managed a tight smile. "Strider. Just the son of a bitch I'm looking for." He turned to the one-hit wonder. "Give us a minute. I'll meet you inside."

Tiko pouted. "Tiko wants an ice-cream sundae!"

Greg placed a proprietary hand on Tiko's ass.

"Have I denied you anything since we've been together, baby? Now run along."

Tiko gave Strider a triumphant look and darted into the lobby.

"My publicist faxed me today's Page Six," Greg said coldly. "All I asked you to do was find out her last name."

"I didn't see the point, Greg. Candace deserves better than you."

Greg took a menacing step forward. "Since when is a spoiled rich kid better than a self-made man?" His nostrils flared. This fool was ready to rumble.

"Easy, action star. Are you sure you want to fight? Everybody knows you don't do your own stunts."

Greg's lips curled into a smug, superior smile. "Want some good advice, Strider? Never upstage a movie star. Hershey got the product placement deal. They made us an offer we couldn't refuse. I'll make sure you get the press release." He started to go. "Hope you and the chocolate slut live happily ever after."

Before Strider knew what was happening, his anger bomb went *tick, tick, boom!* He clobbered Greg Tapper, sending him down with one punch that landed squarely on the shit heel's cheek. It would swell, turn purple and black, hurt like hell, and delay shooting. Mission accomplished.

Strider stood over the silver-screen tough guy. "Don't bother trying to sue me, Greg. I can afford just as many lawyers as you can. And I don't think you want it widely publicized that everybody's favorite action hero got his ass kicked by a trust-fund baby."

And then Strider took off for the Marina Grande to meet his fate, massaging his aching right hand all the way. When he arrived, his father, Lansing Jr., and grandfather, Lansing Sr., were smoking cigars.

The greetings proceeded awkwardly—a few disapproving looks this way and that, stiff handshakes all around, the tension so thick in the air that it was almost hard to breathe.

His father spoke first. "I assume you've heard the news that Hershey landed the deal."

Strider nodded.

His grandfather fixed a piercing stare on him. "Maybe things would've turned out differently if you'd had your eyes on the prize and not your hands all over the girl."

Strider shrugged. "What can I say? There were forces working against me."

"Only one that I can see," his father said. "It's called immaturity."

Strider knew what was coming. But he didn't care. He wanted out. So why fight it? In the end, A.J. would get his. Life had a way of balancing out all the wrongs.

"Our position was clear as to the outcome of this matter, Strider," Lansing Sr. put in. "Your cousin A.J. is dedicated to the company in a way that you never have been."

"More than you know," Strider said.

The two Lansings exchanged annoyed looks.

His father stood up. "This isn't easy, son."

"Mr. Moore, wait, you don't have the whole story."

Three generations of Moores rubbernecked looks to the doorway.

Candace stood there, slightly out of breath, yet still beautiful. "Excuse me for interrupting. I'm—"

"Candace Rowley," his father cut in. "With clothes on, I see."

"How observant of you, sir. Your nickname should be Columbo."

Lansing Jr.'s face registered the hit.

Lansing Sr. chuckled.

Strider wanted to high-five her. *That's my girl.*

"Put out the cigars, boys. Smoke is murder on a bombshell's skin. Now someone get me a drink, and I'll tell you a little story about cousin A.J."

The three men scrambled for the bar in unison. Strider got there first. Reaching for the tongs in the ice bucket, he smiled. Nothing like a woman who knew how to work a room.

Epilogue

New York,
Six Months Later

Didi Farrell was singing "The Morning After," the love theme from *The Poseidon Adventure,* as Strider and Candace watched from the green room.

"Isn't someone supposed to have gonged her by now?" Strider asked.

Candace laughed. "I take it you don't want her new CD, *Didi's Turn.*"

"Think I'll pass."

"Well, too bad. It's in the gift basket we get for appearing on the show. There's also a copy of Chip Hamilton's new book, *Smile When You Get Up in the Morning and Other Things My Mother Taught Me.*"

"Remind me why we're torturing ourselves again."

"It's called publicity, darling. You're a boring husband now. It's harder to get media attention."

"Oh, that's right. I could cheat on you with a hot young model. That'd get some press."

"But then I'd kill you, and your death would get *too* much press. It's better this way. Trust me."

Enter Jackie, the assistant producer for *Coffee in Manhattan.* "The arrival gates are backed up at JFK. Our next guest is on a plane that's still circling the airport. He's the guy who invented the penis gel that supposedly adds an inch after fourteen days of application."

"Really?" Strider interjected. "I hope there's a sample in the gift basket."

Jackie grinned. "There isn't. Sorry."

"But Didi's singing makes my penis shrink. I need it to stay even steven."

"Here's the short of it," Jackie went on, "no pun intended—your segment is now seven minutes." She gave Candace a curious look. "Hey, didn't this happen to you last time?"

"Yes, only it was vaginal cream."

"Weird coincidence." She glanced at her clipboard. "As soon as Didi finishes her number, we'll take you to the set and get you miked up. I'll be right back."

Strider embraced Candace from behind, nuzzling her neck. "What do you suppose we'll talk about for *seven* minutes? That's almost a Barbara Walters interview."

"Don't be surprised if they ask you how big your penis is."

"You know, I've actually never measured. Don't know how. Chip might have the answer. Maybe that's one of the things his mother taught him."

Candace slapped Strider's thigh. "Please act normal. There are millions watching."

"My dad left me a voice mail. He's got a meeting, but mom's taping it, and they're going to watch it tonight before dinner."

Candace reached out to stroke his freshly shaven cheek. "That's nice."

Strider grinned sweetly. "It is nice." He paused a beat. "And I owe it all to you."

She started to protest.

"Accept the credit. If you hadn't stormed onto that yacht—"

"I didn't *storm* in. Ask the captain. I boarded the craft gracefully."

"You did something that I was just too stubborn to do, and that's tell my father the truth about A.J. I don't know. I could never get past how angry I was about the whole thing. But all my anger was directed at the wrong person."

"None of that matters now. You've got your father back. He's got his son back. Life is perfect."

"Almost perfect."

Candace stared at him.

"What about your mom?"

"One family miracle at a time please."

"It's just that—"

"I called her," Candace confessed. "We had a pleasant talk."

He looked hurt. "You didn't tell me."

"Because you would insist right away that she visit for two weeks. I'm not ready for that. Let me fix this at my own pace."

Strider pulled her in for a half embrace. "Can I take back what I said about *me* being stubborn?"

"No, that's in the official record."

"Oh." He shrugged.

"Do you think your cousin will be watching?"

"Probably not. He's too busy banging away on the organ at his father's church in Florida."

Didi warbled to a big finish with a note far beyond the range she didn't have anyway. Tone-deaf as always, the studio audience erupted with enthusiastic support. Overwhelmed, Didi pumped a fist in the air. "There *is* a morning after!" she roared.

"Not if you heard that song," Strider said.

Just then Jackie returned, and they ran the gauntlet through the studio and onto the set. Two technicians dropped in to attach microphones, then asked them to count to ten to check volume levels.

Moments later, Chip and Didi took their places, said a quick hello, and began scanning some notes.

"How did Chip manage to get on more makeup than Didi?" Strider whispered.

Candace giggled. "Hush."

Didi looked up. "So you're the chocolate lady, and you're the man with the penis."

Candace shut her eyes. *Not again.*

"I think you mean penis *gel*," Strider said. "That's a different guest. His plane—and his enlarged penis, I presume, is circling JFK, as I understand. But for the record, I am a man with a penis."

Now Chip joined in. "If you applied the gel for a month, could you expand your penis by two inches?"

"You don't understand," Candace said. "That guest—"

Chip held up a hand to cut her off. "Time for that later, love." He fixed a blinding smile on the camera. "Welcome back!"

"Hey, no fair! I wanted to say that!" Didi screamed.

They both laughed uproariously.

"Didi," Chip started, placing a hand on her knee for emphasis, "that number from your new CD, *Didi's Turn,* was fantastic! It was so real. For a minute there I thought I was Ernest Borgnine from *The Poseidon Adventure.*" He gestured to the audience. "Am I right, people?"

They thundered their agreement with hearty applause.

"Thank you, Chip. That song is so special to me, and it really has a powerful message, because no matter what obstacles you're facing, there *is* a morning after."

"Say it, sister!" Chip said.

"It's just like in your new book, *Smile When You Get Up in the Morning and Other Things My Mother Taught Me.* I think it's chapter two where you talk about not letting life get you down."

"Mother always said, 'If you fall off your bicycle, get right back on!'"

Didi beamed. "Which is exactly what our next guest did. He had a really small penis, and one day he just said, 'Heck, I think I'll invent a gel to make it bigger!' Please welcome Strider Moore and his lovely wife Candace."

Chip leaned forward to gently ask, "Strider, how small was your penis before this miracle invention did its handiwork?"

Suddenly, Chip and Didi's brows crinkled as their right hands cupped their right ears.

"Oh, my," Didi remarked. "We goofed."

"Hey," Chip chirped. "Just like my mother says—smile when it hurts."

"As it happens, our penis gel inventor is stuck at the airport," Didi said. "Strider and Candace are here with us today from Decadence Chocolates, the upscale division of Moore Candies. Welcome to *Coffee in Manhattan*."

"Good to be here," Strider said. "I'd like to start out by saying that I have a large penis. Any number of women in New York can attest to that. This is before I got married, of course. All the sex, I mean."

Candace jabbed him with her elbow.

"But we have sex," Strider said quickly. He put his arm around his wife. "Often. And it's great. Tell everyone how big my penis is, honey."

"Your parents are taping this, darling."

Strider blanched.

"Ooh, tell us more," Didi cooed.

"My husband's penis is fine," Candace said flatly.

"Fine?" Chip pressed. "Or fine and *dandy*?"

"That would be fine and dandy, Chip. Thank you for clarifying," Candace said.

"Now there's a funny story about how the two of you met," Didi began. "I love hearing a couple's history. Strider, why don't you tell us about that? And enough about that big penis of yours. Stick to the romance, mister!"

Strider hesitated a moment. "We met at a club here in New York. The Cutting Room to be exact."

Chip and Didi howled with laughter.

"Oh, that is hilarious!" Didi squealed.

"Only in New York!" Chip put in.

"Actually, the funny part of the story is what happened later," Candace said. And then she launched into the whole tale, blathering on about the competition for the product placement, the scandalous photo from Capri, how A.J., in his obsession to oust Strider, played double agent with Hershey to get that company the deal. But then *Chocolate on Her Pillow* went through a major rewrite and title change, became *Love on a Rooftop*, and ultimately featured *no* candy in the final cut. And how could she leave out the details concerning Strider's examination of the Private Selection division's books, his discovery of its low profit margins, and the manner in which he brilliantly proposed that Moore shut it down and buy Decadence under the provision that Candace run the line autonomously. That way Moore had a leaner investment *plus* a stake in the lucrative high-priced chocolate market. By the end of her story, Candace was exhausted. No question is simple when you really take the time to think about it.

"Well," Didi finally cut in, "thank you for sharing, but I believe we're coming up close on a commercial break."

"One more question before we wrap up," Chip said. "Husband wears the big, bad corporate hat, and you're the division head. Does that put any stress on the marriage?"

Strider slipped his hand into hers.

Candace beamed.

"Not really," he said. "At the end of the day, we're just two chocoholics madly in love."

Darling!

I hope you had fun with "Sex and the Single Chocoholic." It was a hoot to write, but all the talk about chocolate triggered fierce cravings that I had no choice but to satisfy. Well, thank you Godiva, M&Ms, Dove Bars, etc., for the extra five pounds! Grrr.

I'm counting on the fact that you had a blast with Tatiana Fox. Why? Because her story is coming next! I never knew what was going to come out of this character's mouth. She surprised me so many times. Can you imagine her as the mother of twins? Well, get ready! Look for Tatiana to take center stage in my upcoming book, BABY, BABY, set for release this August. In that story you'll also see more of her personal assistant, Enrique, and the egomaniacal movie star Greg Tapper. But her love match turns out to be Jack Thorpe—a hero I know you'll go banana cake over. Here's my recipe for this hunk: take one Russell Crowe, add a Pierce Brosnan, then stir until you get the best of both!

If this novella was your virgin voyage on the Kylie Adams Express, check out my first novel, FLY ME TO THE MOON. It tells the full story of Ben Estes, who was mentioned briefly here as the cool crooner who puts a disco spin on Frank Sinatra tunes.

Until the summer . . .

Air kisses,

Kylie

P.S. If you're on-line, go to my Web site at *www.kylieadams.com*. That's where the real Kylie secrets are spilled. Plus, if you join my VIP section, you'll get my monthly e-newsletter, *"Kylie Says,"* which is chockablock full of beauty tips, what's hot/what's not lists, Kylie Kontest news, and more!

Get in touch with Kylie . . . c/o Zebra Books, 850 Third Avenue, New York, NY 10022 or e-mail *www.kylieadams.com*.

Please turn the page for
an exciting sneak peek at
Kylie Adams's newest
contemporary romance

BABY, BABY
(coming from Zebra Books
in August 2002!)

"I want a man who can make love all night long, and if you're not that man, then just do me a favor and drop dead." Tatiana delivered the line with such deadly insouciance that she stunned the room.

David Walsh stared back as if she were Charlton Heston in *The Ten Commandments* and had just parted the sea.

Kip Quick looked equally mystified. He flipped his Dave Matthews Band hat to the back and regarded her strangely.

She gestured to the battered script on Kip's lap. "It's your line, unless I'm auditioning for the male lead, too."

"Oh, right," Kip blurted. He searched for his place on the page. "Is it true about your last two husbands granting you that favor?"

Tatiana stretched and spoke in a breathy voice enriched with dirty promise. "It's true that they were lousy in bed. It's true that I buried them. The rest is just gossip.''

Kip lost his train of thought again, gazing at her in awestruck wonder.

She couldn't believe that he would actually be the movie's director. After all, he looked like he needed a note from his mother to be here. In fact, he still lived with his parents. Probably had a *Penthouse* stashed under his mattress, too. Yet here he sat, after only a few videos on MTV and one Pepsi commercial, playing with the grown-ups on a big-budget film for a major studio. Only in Hollywood.

Tatiana cleared her throat.

"Does nudity make you uncomfortable?" Kip asked.

She glanced down at her pages. *Not* part of the *Sin by Sin* screenplay.

This man/child had obviously missed her series of *Lady Cop Undercover* movies. Chances are he hadn't peeked at her pictorial in the April 1998 *Playboy,* either. If he had, it would've been while under the covers with a flashlight.

"My comfort level depends on the situation," she announced matter-of-factly. "A relatively closed set is no problem. Shooting on Sunset at high noon is another matter entirely. I mean, I'm not Madonna.''

David smiled at Kip as if to say, "See, I told you so.''

And then a horrifying thought struck Tatiana. It hit like a clap of thunder. She went from confident actress auditioning for the big part to manic mother wanting to put child-safety locks on, well, *everything*. Shame rained down, *soaking* her. She was officially the *worst* parent in the world. By comparison, Joan Crawford was Carol Brady. "I can't do this right now." She started to shake. She needed a cigarette. She didn't even smoke.

David's smile faded faster than Cindy Crawford's hope of a movie career after the release of *Fair Game*.

"I just realized that I left my children with a complete stranger," Tatiana said breathlessly. "I mean, he could be a serial killer, or one of the Kennedy boys that Jackie O didn't raise, or Paula Poundstone in disguise." She placed a hand over her heart and shut her eyes for a moment. "Promise you won't tell social services. This is all new to me."

"I didn't realize you had kids," David said.

"Don't you read the tabloids? My ex-husband insisted on adopting twins and then left me. Anyway, today my nanny quit without notice, I couldn't reach my personal assistant, and the only other person available was September Moore. She's a friend and all, but I wouldn't let her watch my purse. Would you? Let her watch your wallet, I mean. Or your man purse. I hear those are big in Europe. OK, so I packed up the kids and here I am. By the way, if you smell something sour it's because Ethan threw up on me in the car." Tatiana took a deep breath. "Is this too much information?"

David and Kip stared back in slack-jawed amazement.

"This is *my* part. I *am* Nikki Alexander. But now I have to go. Don't worry. I'll work out child-care issues before shooting starts. You know what would be great? On-set day care." She paused a beat. "I'm

kidding. I don't want the kids to see me running
around with a knife or shooting people or having
simulated sex with different men. That could be
traumatic for them. And that's instinct. I didn't
have to read Dr. Spock to come up with that. Pretty
good, huh? I think I'm getting the hang of this
mommy business. OK, are we done here? Do you
need to see my boobs or anything before I leave?"

There was a long second of telepathy between
David and Kip, after which they traded a discreet
nod.

"We'll set up a screen test with Greg Tapper,"
David said.

This meant she was on the short list. Under nor-
mal circumstances she would be so excited that
cartwheels in rush-hour traffic might be in order.
But she was worried sick about Ethan and Everson.
"That sounds great," she said, somewhat absently.
"I'll wait for your call."

Unable to stand it one more second, Tatiana
dashed back to the reception area. The twins were
perched on either side of the man's hips like Anne
Geddes bookends, listening in peaceful rapture as
he read a story from the sports section of the *Los
Angeles Times.*

"Sammy Sosa hit three homers in the first round
to barely squeak into the semifinals but made the
finals by outhomering Luis Gonzalez," he was saying softly in his heavily accented voice. Could be
English, could be Australian. Tough to call. But
she wanted him to read the Yellow Pages. He
sounded *that* scrumptious.

Ethan and Everson peered up at him, little
mouths agape, as if he were Barney or something.

Tatiana was instantly suspicious. They *never* sat still like this for her. "Did you give them drugs?"

He stopped reading and just stared at her.

"I've never seen them stay in one place unless they're sleeping. Or eating. Well, Ethan does hold his position behind the sofa when he's pooping. But the rest of the time it's an insane level of activity. I can't keep up."

"I think these kids are perfect."

No, honey, you're perfect. The words were almost on her lips. She zeroed in on his firm forearms, mesmerized by the muscles flexing under his skin as he folded up the newspaper and tossed it aside. He looked sharp and mod—three-day beard, dirty-blond bed-head hair, lean body coiled into well-worn jeans and a 1999 World Cup T-shirt ripped at the left sleeve, skin basted a honey bronze.

Los Angeles was chockablock full of great-looking guys. They worked on it just as hard as the women, if not harder, slaving at the gym, sticking to the Zone diet, checking the mirror twenty times a day to ask, "Am I handsome enough?" Hot men were in such supply that Tatiana could fill a tour bus with just the ones she'd seen this week. So it said something about the one front and center that he could not only make her take a second look, but hold it—steady. Simultaneously, he gave off grit and luminosity. An unbeatable combination.

"How did your audition go?" he asked.

"They want me to do a screen test."

"Congratulations. You should ring your mum. I always ring my mum when there's good news."

She was instantly put off by this and decided to openly mock him. "Well, I'm not speaking to my *mum* at the moment. What about your audition?"

"It was horrible."

Now she felt bad. There was a slow, vague sweetness about him. "Which part were you reading for?"

"Greg Tapper's partner."

"But he dies in the opening scene after just one line."

"I tried, 'See you tomorrow, Josh' several different ways, but they just weren't feeling it."

Tatiana giggled and moved in to scoop up Everson, who started to cry immediately.

He stood up, hoisting bulky Ethan onto his hip with Mr. Strong ease, then smoothed Everson's unruly hair with his free hand, a gesture that instantly mollified her. If thirteen-month-old girls could fall in love, then Everson Janey Fox, positively swooning now, was head over heels. Tramp.

"Who are you? I should know your name since my kids think you're better than Big Bird."

"Jack Thorpe, god-awful actor, smashingly good baby-sitter."

She smiled in a way that she hadn't smiled since running into George Clooney in an elevator at the Beverly Center. "I'm Tatiana Fox."

"I know. I subscribe to *Playboy*. You were the girl who posed naked climbing on the side of a building."

"*Half* naked. I *was* wearing a thong. So how long have you been a bad actor?"

He checked his Patek Philippe watch. "About fifteen minutes. I don't think I'll stick with it. I'm actually a footballer." He pointed to his knee. "Or was. An injury put an end to my career."

"Which team?"

"Manchester United."

Tatiana's memory registered nothing. *Manchester United?* It sounded like a bank, not a football team. "Is that one of the new leagues?"

He smiled at her, revealing immaculate porcelain teeth. "I forget that you call it soccer here in the States." A sudden look of inscrutable sadness came over him, weighing down his features like old age. "I miss my mates."

Tatiana wanted to know where he came from, why he was here. This unnerved her. She usually only cared about her own problems. Meanwhile, Ethan clung to him like a koala bear. It was really adorable.

Everson started to squirm and stretch out her arms. She wanted Jack Thorpe again. The deafening cry that came next could've been picked up as far as Malibu.

Reluctantly, he stepped forward to take her.

The very second Everson's tiny hands touched him was the very second she stopped fussing.

Tatiana's humiliation was only ameliorated by the sight of him standing there, shrugging with pride, the twins climbing all over his hard body. It *defined* sexy. Any woman who melted whenever Tom Selleck showed up on cable in *Three Men and a Baby* needed to take a memo. That was then; Jack Thorpe was now.